THE VACATION

John Marrs is an author and former journalist based in Northamptonshire. After spending his career interviewing celebrities from the worlds of television, film and music for numerous national newspapers and magazines, he is now a full-time author. He is the bestselling author of: *The One*, *The Passengers*, *The Minders*, *When You Disappeared*, *The Good Samaritan*, *Her Last Move* and *What Lies Between Us*.

Follow him at www.johnmarrsauthor.co.uk, on Twitter @johnmarrs1, on Instagram @johnmarrs.author and on Facebook @johnmarrsauthor.

Also by John Marrs:

The One

The Passengers

The Minders

When You Disappeared
(previously published as *The Wrongred Sons*)

The Good Samaritan

Her Last Move

What Lies Between Us

PRAISE FOR JOHN MARRS:

'One of the most exciting, original thriller writers'

Simon Kernick

'Marrs is brilliant at twists . . . for the addicts of adrenaline-fuelled twisty rides'

Peter James

'Another savagely clever near-future thriller. Provocative, terrifying and compulsive. If you loved *The One*, you'll love this!'

Cara Hunter

'A tense, thrilling read – I found it impossible to put down. It's dark and twisted, and I loved it'

Alex Michaelides, bestselling author of *The Silent Patient*

'Dark, twisted, and full of surprises'

Mark Edwards, bestselling author of *Here to Stay* and *The Retreat*

'Gripping from the start and full of surprises, this kept us up long after lights out'

Isabelle Broom, *Heat*

'Wonderful concept, ridiculously entertaining . . . an absolute pleasure, the malevolence and impishness of a young Roald Dahl'

T. A. Cotterell, author of *What Alice Knew*

'Fantastic . . . I can't remember the last time I was simultaneously this entertained and this disturbed. *The One* is a clever story with great pacing but it's the characters that make this a standout thriller'

Hollie Overton, *Sunday Times* bestselling author of *Baby Doll*

'This will have you gripped'

Woman's Own

'Brilliantly inventive thriller, *The One* is a must-read for anyone who's ever braved the dating pool'

Good Housekeeping

'Engaging concept, craftily executed'

Adrian J. Walker, bestselling author of *The End of the World Running Club*

'This psychological thriller is a real page-turner'

Fabulous (Sun)

'[Marrs'] most sinister novel to date'

Daily Express

'An excellent psychological thriller. Twisty, moving, and chilling'

Sarah Pinborough, bestselling author of *Behind Her Eyes*

'Great premise and masterful use of twists'

Claire McGowan, bestselling author of *What You Did*

'Totally absorbing, creepy, intense and utterly compelling. I loved it'

Mel Sherratt, bestselling author of the DS Grace Allendale series and *The Girls Next Door*

'I loved it although I'm not sure I've read anything as dark, ever . . .'

Susi Holliday, author of *Violet* and *The Lingering*

'It's a pitch-perfect psychological thriller, with a captivating power play at its heart. I don't recall reading a novel that so expertly toyed with my sympathies. Great stuff!'

Simon Lelic, bestselling author of *The House* and *The Liar's Room*

'Packed full of darkness and suspense, John Marrs once again proves himself as a voice to be reckoned with . . .'

Phoebe Morgan, author of *The Doll House* and *The Girl Next Door*

'Magnificent. Extremely dark and twisted and tension filled and incredibly well written. First class'

Claire Allan, author of *Her Name Was Rose*

THE VACATION

JOHN MARRS

PAN BOOKS

First published in 2015 as *Welcome to Wherever You Are*

First published as *The Vacation* 2021 by Pan Books
This paperback edition first published 2022 by Pan Books
an imprint of Pan Macmillan
The Smithson, 6 Briset Street, London EC1M 5NR
EU representative: Macmillan Publishers Ireland Ltd,
1st Floor, The Liffey Trust Centre, 117–126 Sheriff Street Upper,
Dublin 1, D01 YC43
Associated companies throughout the world
www.panmacmillan.com

ISBN: 978-1-5290-8086-5

1 3 5 7 9 8 6 4 2

A CIP catalogue record for this book is available from the British Library.

Typeset in Celeste OT by Jouve (UK), Milton Keynes
Printed and bound by CPI Group (UK) Ltd, Croydon, CR0 4YY

‘Our goal is to discover that we have always been where we ought to be. Unhappily we make the task exceedingly difficult for ourselves’

ALDOUS HUXLEY

PROLOGUE

Venice Beach, Los Angeles

'That's her,' the driver yelled to the three men waiting in the rear of the transit van.

He pointed a gloved finger in the direction of a slender woman walking along the sidewalk up ahead.

'You sure?' a gruff voice asked. 'It's pretty dark out there.'

The driver was very sure. He'd watched carefully as his target walked with purpose in her high heels. He recalled her appearance an hour earlier as she made her way up a stainless-steel pole before slowly, seductively descending.

'Yeah, man,' he replied. 'You don't forget a pretty little ass like that in a hurry, even from this distance.'

He was confident their mark was completely oblivious to her impending fate. She stopped suddenly, searching for something that was seemingly wedged in her clutch bag; the street lamps and neon shop signs illuminated the glitter in her hair. The driver lifted his foot slightly from the accelerator and dipped the headlights as he continued to stalk his prey. Meanwhile, his colleagues slipped black balaclavas over their heads and adjusted their bodies into position – one knelt with his hand gripping the door lever, ready to open it on command; another held plastic restraints, and the third clasped a hunting knife with a serrated blade.

'Ready?' the driver asked. They grunted in unison.

The van speeded up, but not so fast as to throw the hunters from the positions they'd rehearsed earlier that day. Then, as it pulled up alongside the woman, the door flew open and the first of her assailants sprang out.

The man with the restraints was the first to reel backwards into the vehicle as a bullet from her revolver tore its way through his shoulder blade, taking fragments of collarbone with it.

For a split second, the flash from the gun's muzzle illuminated the van's interior as she pinpointed two more would-be assailants poised to drag her inside. Twice more she pulled the trigger; twice more she heard the men screaming. The driver remained rooted to his seat, baffled by how off-kilter their mission had suddenly gone. They had been so confident of its success that there was no Plan B.

'Go, man, go!' yelled a desperate voice as another bullet found its target.

Tyres squealed as the van lurched forward, veering across the central reservation and then criss-crossing back towards the sidewalk.

A combination of adrenaline and fury propelled the woman to kick off her heels and run after it, firing twice more and shattering its rear windscreen. The vehicle clipped an *LA Times* newsstand, hurling newspapers into the air; they fell like large chunks of confetti.

She fired one last time, but the van had already corrected itself and sped off out of range. Then she watched in horror as that final shot sent a stranger up ahead, carrying a backpack, sprawling face forward onto the pavement.

Time froze as the consequences of her last reckless bullet resonated.

She had just killed an innocent tourist.

PART ONE: THE ARRIVALS

1

Day One: Two Months Later
Venice Beach International Hostel, Los Angeles

Empty bottles of Budweiser and paper plates stained with remnants of spaghetti Bolognese littered the corridors as Tommy made his way from his dormitory room towards the hostel reception desk.

He passed three young men lying in a crumpled, unconscious heap by the stairs, wearing only brightly coloured underwear. Their drunken state had been taken advantage of and their faces and chests used as canvases for felt-tip pen graffiti. The expletives, slurs and crude images of penises and breasts appealed to the childish side of Tommy's sense of humour.

At this ungodly hour most of the guests at Venice Beach International Hostel were fast asleep, scattered throughout the building's twenty-five rooms of varying sizes. Some contained up to eight bunk beds, others were private and housed just two people. But it was a rare day if the hostel reached its 120-person capacity. Those drowsily slumped across lounge sofas were surrounded by rucksacks, awaiting shuttle buses to transport them to LAX airport or the Amtrak railway and coach stations.

Tommy knew it didn't require a genius to do his job, checking people in and out of the hostel. There wasn't even a computerized system to master – just a tatty, leather-bound ledger with a date written in biro on each page and the names of who was allocated to which room. Payment was cash only, no contactless credit cards, bank transfers or even traveller's cheques. But it was a role he enjoyed, despite the long hours. Secretly he got a kick from being responsible for choosing which rooms the backpackers looking for no-frills accommodation were placed in. Those who barely spoke English – and so were less likely to complain – were squirrelled out of the way towards the back of the building, and those with whom Tommy hoped to build up a rapport were placed in the dormitories that surrounded his. But the bunk adjacent to his own was kept free for when his friend Louis arrived. If he ever arrived.

Tommy reached the end of the corridor, walked down a small flight of steps and arrived at the reception desk where he would spend the next couple of hours. He turned on a portable television and scanned the ledger to see who'd checked in or out.

Once up to speed, he gazed around the room as the darkness outside began to lift and the orange morning light crept through the thin film of dirt covering the large windows. A yucca plant had outgrown its pot and its roots spilled from cracks in the side; a water cooler missing a plug housed a half-full plastic bottle, with the water surface supporting a delicate skin of green algae. The brown carpet tiles that covered patches of the floor were frayed and mismatched. A rack of pamphlets was mostly empty with the exception of a few outdated excursion opportunities to Disneyland, Six Flags Magic Mountain and Universal Studios. There was no getting away from it: the hostel was a dump. But it was a dump Tommy affectionately called home.

He glanced at the photographs pinned to the wall, containing familiar faces he'd met during his last two months in Los Angeles. Most, like him, were in their early twenties, and while he couldn't always recall their names, he never forgot a face and they never failed to conjure up a smile. Examining an image of himself, he realized his irregular eating patterns meant he'd lost weight since the picture had been taken some eight weeks earlier. He could easily feel his ribs under his t-shirt now and even his many friendship bands hung loosely from his wrist. His dark brown stubble disguised the gauntness in his face. He made a vow to himself to eat at least two proper meals a day.

'Morning, Ron,' Tommy chirped as the hostel's owner appeared from a small office behind the reception desk.

Ron's glasses hung from a silver chain around his neck, broken links held together by sticky tape. His grey comb-over lifted from his thinning scalp with each step he took and his posture reminded Tommy of a question mark.

'Find me some roach traps for the kitchen,' Ron muttered, making his way up the stairs and out of sight.

'I'm fine, thanks for asking,' mumbled Tommy.

'I didn't,' Ron called from the distance.

A poster peeling from the wall drew Tommy's attention, like it always did – '*Welcome to Wherever You Are*', read a large font placed over an image of a white sandy beach and the bluest of blue oceans. When Tommy had asked what it meant on the night he arrived, Ron had replied: 'It means it doesn't matter where you are, just as long as you're somewhere.'

The hostel was Tommy's somewhere, and it was a million miles from the nowhere in England he'd run from.

2

Beads of sweat gathered across Eric's hairline, the breeze wafting through the vehicle's open windows failing to cool him down.

He pinched the corners of his eyes, pushed his Ray-Ban aviators up to the bridge of his nose and continued to drive slowly along Pacific Avenue. Hunched over the steering wheel, he peered through the windscreen, searching for building numbers. A night spent behind the wheel of their 1970s pick-up truck, with no air conditioning or power steering, had left him grouchy, achy and feeling more than his thirty-two years. The wonky visor couldn't keep the rising sun from touching his head and he was glad he'd decided to clipper his thick auburn hair short before he left England.

'We've been driving in circles for hours,' he moaned.

'It would help if at least some of these buildings were numbered,' replied Nicole, his passenger and closest friend. 'Maybe buildings in LA think they're too cool for that.'

Her thighs were stuck to the leather seats and made the sound of breaking wind each time she fidgeted. Eleven hours ago it had amused them both; now it was just another thing that irritated them. Nicole swept her damp cinnamon-brown hair behind her ears and brought the map closer to her eyes so she could read the small print. A gust of warm wind rustled the empty potato chip and candy wrappers strewn across the rear seats.

'So just for the record, remind me again why I gave up a good job in London to join you on this magical mystery tour?' Eric asked.

'Because you hated your "good job" just as much as I hated mine. And once we find what we're looking for, we might not need to work again for a very long time.'

'Providing this thing gets us there.'

'I hope so; I paid enough to ship it over. Besides, it's a classic American pick-up.'

Eric raised his eyebrows. 'And who are you now, Jeremy Clarkson? We could've rented a new SUV over here with that money, or a convertible. Or at least something with air-con, satnav, TuneIn access and electric seats.'

He reached into the door pocket, but the bottle of water he was hoping to find wasn't there. He glanced down to see where it had fallen.

'Eric!' Nicole yelled.

Alarmed, he looked up to see a dishevelled young man in dark skater shorts and a backward-facing baseball cap and shirt, shuffling across the road. Eric jammed on his brakes and swerved; the truck's tyres hit the kerb with a jolt and a bang. Unharmed, the man continued ambling onwards in his own little world, oblivious to his close call, disappearing into a nearby building.

'Bloody idiot!' yelled Eric, craning his neck out the window while Nicole took deep, calming breaths. He clambered out to examine the damage and then kicked the hubcap in frustration.

'Brilliant,' he said. 'I bet it's already started deflating.'

'I know the feeling. But if it helps, I think we're here.' Nicole pointed to a rectangular building in front of them. Eric tilted his head towards a faded sign reading *2323* and *Venice Beach International Hostel.*

Even from this distance they could see that its once white-washed walls were greying; plaster had flaked and fallen from the façade, leaving parts of the brickwork exposed. Trainers and towels had been hung out to air from the open windows on all three floors. From the side of the flat roof, poles and tatty flags from around the world drooped, including some from countries Nicole was sure no longer existed.

She offered a half-hearted smile, but Eric was too busy rolling his eyes to notice.

3

'You nearly got yourself killed there, mate!' Tommy warned Joe as he stumbled up the stairs towards his room, only stopping to rotate his baseball cap into the correct position.

Tommy wondered why Joe always waited until he entered the building before sliding his cap around, as if the hostel had a straight headwear dress code. Then he realized that trying to second-guess a crystal meth addict was as pointless as giving a dog a Rubik's cube. He hoped that one day, Joe might have a lightbulb moment, like those Tommy had read about in the self-help books travellers often left in the hostel library. They'd helped get him through many a boring night shift, and Tommy briefly considered anonymously leaving one about addiction on Joe's bed. But he knew that unless Joe actually wanted to alter his life, he'd be stuck in his ever-decreasing circle until an inevitably premature end. And as long as Joe paid for his bed, Ron didn't care what his guests' extracurricular activities involved.

Outside, Eric and Nicole unstrapped their suitcases from the flatbed truck and faced the hostel's mucky glass doors, which were propped open by two buckets of sand littered with cigarette butts. Eric removed his sunglasses and Nicole just about heard him mumble something about jumping out of a frying pan and into the flaming bowels of hell.

'If I'm going to have the American experience Mrs Baker wanted me to have, then I'd like to meet people in the same boat as us – not a bunch of cheerleaders on spring break,' she retorted.

'So you were serious when you said we were staying in a hostel and not a hotel? I hoped you were kidding.'

'My travel guide says it's a rite of passage to stay in Venice Beach,' she replied defensively. 'John Steinbeck, Jack Kerouac and Truman Capote are supposed to have slept under this very roof back in its heyday.'

'Oh, did they? And who are Steinbeck, Kerouac and Capote, just out of interest?'

'Um,' Nicole paused and thought back to the Wikipedia entry she'd skimmed. 'That's not the point.'

Eric shook his head at her ignorance and let out an exaggerated sigh.

'Besides,' she continued, 'the only difference between a hostel and a hotel is the letter "s".'

'Yeah, and in this case the "s" stands for "smells like a shit pit".'

Nicole was aware she was fighting a losing battle. For the most part, Eric was her kindred spirit; he could make her laugh like nobody else, and he'd been there for her in her darkest days when she'd needed him most. He'd put his career on hold to spend the last six weeks with her in America on the hunt for something that might not even exist, so she was willing to forgive his occasional moodiness.

'Are you looking for a room?' said Tommy, ignoring Eric's presence and focusing entirely on Nicole. He was instantly attracted to her warm grin, her fresh face and her casual attire of cut-off shorts and white vest. Such attention didn't go unnoticed by Eric. She, meanwhile, was surprised by Tommy's British accent, considering his golden California tan and surfer-dude appearance – albeit a skinny, undernourished surfer dude who likely didn't know one end of a board from the other.

'I emailed a few days ago to reserve a private room for three nights,' Nicole replied.

'The internet connection's a bit iffy and nobody checks the emails,' replied Tommy apologetically. 'We don't have any private rooms left, I'm afraid. But we've got beds in dorms, if that helps?'

'We're expected to share with other people?' interrupted Eric.

'That's the hostelling experience,' said Tommy.

'No, that's the homeless shelter experience.'

'It's forty-five dollars a night each, plus a five-dollar key deposit. Cash up front, I'm afraid. You'll be in room fourteen; your beds have clean sheets on them already, blankets are an extra two dollars, as are towels. The pool's out back and open 24/7, and the beach is on your doorstep. There's free food served every night in the kitchen, although the chef's not Gordon Ramsay, so I hope you don't have high standards. Oh, and there's free beer on Wednesday and Saturday nights at the party in the lounge. I'm Tommy – if you need anything, just come and find me.'

Nicole and Tommy shared a glance. As she paid him in cash, a cockroach scuttled across the counter.

'Are those complimentary?' asked Eric, wryly.

'Only if you buy them dinner first,' replied Tommy.

While Nicole smirked at the lame joke, Eric frowned at Tommy and picked up the pair's luggage, heading towards the staircase. A thin man in baggy clothes and a patchy beard attempted to slip in behind them, unnoticed.

'Oi, there's no reason for you to be in here, Wayne,' said Tommy firmly, and shook his head as the man left without argument.

'Don't think I didn't see you giving him a look,' Eric said as he and Nicole made their way along the hostel corridor, examining their new surroundings.

'What look?' she replied in mock innocence, willing herself not to break into a schoolgirl blush.

'A look that'll have you tagged and on the sex offenders' register for ten years.'

'He's not that young.'

'You're thirty-two, hun. He's old enough to be your son.'

'Yeah, if I'd had him when I was about twelve,' sighed Nicole, stepping over a discarded trash bag. 'Okay, so the rubbish doesn't make it the Chateau Marmont, but it has charm.'

'Hey, here's an idea – why don't we just climb into a couple of cardboard boxes and sleep under a bridge tonight?'

'Anyway, *Grazia* says it's flattering to be thought of as a cougar by a younger man.'

'A cougar? You're more like one of those mangy old alley cats on their last legs, with no teeth and half an ear missing.'

Nicole was opening her mouth to respond when the door to the room beside theirs burst open and four young men in shorts ran past them, carrying beach towels and chatting in a language neither she nor Eric understood.

'Of course, hostelling isn't *all* bad,' conceded Eric, turning his head to watch as they disappeared down the corridor.

4

The cardboard sign Ron had stuck above the six-foot by three-foot cubbyhole with the words 'Internet Suite & Cafe' was wishful thinking, Tommy decided.

One desk with two back-to-back green iMac G3s and an ancient modem that required six minutes before a connection was made did not constitute a suite. Likewise, a vending machine that reluctantly dispensed lukewarm coffee failed to make it a cafe. But with poor cell phone reception and no wi-fi in the hostel, it was the quickest way to get online without having to leave the building.

Tommy inserted his quarter into the vending machine, pressed number nine, counted five seconds like always and kicked the base, before it angrily spat brown powder and water into a plastic cup.

He sat down, logged into his iCloud account and scanned his emails. The only new ones were spam offering bargain bitcoins, his online credit card bill – which he deleted without opening – mail-outs from clothing retailers and discount codes.

He scanned his Facebook timeline updates and clicked on an image in his Friends section so a profile slowly loaded. He checked when it had last been updated; some nine weeks earlier, when they were still together. Irked, he addressed a new email to BackpackingLouis@gmail.com and put three question marks in the subject line. '*Where the hell are you?*' he wrote, and then jabbed the send button.

As he leaned back in his chair, his wallet fell from the pocket of his shorts. The corner of a small photograph poked out. Tommy picked it up, opened it and stared at the picture of his parents.

Two Years Earlier: Northampton, England

From his seat at the kitchen table, Tommy watched his mother through the window as she stood alone on the decking in the rear garden.

She stared blankly across the lawn, through the wire fencing and into the recently ploughed fields, only moving to take long drags from a cigarette.

Tommy had observed her rapid decline from a vibrant, enthusiastic mother of three to an empty shell in the space of hours. He recalled how, when he was a boy, he had nagged her to quit her 'stinky sticks' as he loathed the smell, and for well over a decade, she'd gone without. But since *that* day, everything had changed. She had gone from zero to two packs a day in less than a week.

She remained with her back to the house Tommy had grown up in, a place he now avoided whenever possible. What had once been a home crammed with love and comfort was now just a shell.

Tommy turned his eyes towards the goldfish swimming in circles around the glass bowl on the worktop. The bowl contained no ornamental garnishes, only sandy-coloured pebbles where one lonely fish swam day in, day out, round and round, going nowhere. The symbolism wasn't lost on him.

Suddenly the door to the hallway opened and his father entered. Once a tall, imposing figure, he too had noticeably withered, Tommy thought. Then, on spotting Tommy, he stopped in his tracks. Father and son made eye contact, neither saying a word, before he turned to leave.

'Dad,' began Tommy, and he rose from the table and grabbed the crutches propped up against it. His father paused, but without looking back, exited the kitchen and quietly closed the door.

'It wasn't my fault,' Tommy called after him, as the fish swam another aimless lap.

5

Today

'Pretty comfy,' nodded Nicole as she tested the bottom mattress of the dormitory bunk bed nearest the window.

'That'll be the extra layers of skin shed by everyone who's ever slept on it,' replied Eric, choosing the one above her.

Nicole could hold her tongue no longer. 'For God's sake, Eric, you've spent all day bitching and moaning. Believe me, I'm as frustrated as you are that we haven't found anything yet, but at least I'm trying to make the best of it. Please, can you just stop complaining for five minutes and meet me halfway?'

Eric dropped from the bed to the floor below and looked at his friend sheepishly. 'Sorry, Nic. I'm just hot and knackered, and this place isn't exactly what I was expecting.'

'I know. I think the website's pictures had the Instagram treatment. But we're here now, so let's have a look around, take some time out to rethink and make the best of it before we continue.'

Eric nodded as Nicole looked around the room. Each dormitory had four curtainless double-length windows, and with no air conditioning, they were the only way to let out the stuffy air of eight bunk beds and sixteen sweaty bodies. Above them, damp clothes were pegged to makeshift washing lines running the length of the room. In the corner was the door to the shared bathroom, next to a small area housing grey lockers.

But while the rooms were shabby, it seemed reasonably clean, and Nicole liked that the walls were plastered with photographs of past guests framing a world map mural. Coloured cotton threads linked faces to countries and, despite Eric's vocal reservations, there was an aura about the hostel that Nicole admired. She recognized the face of the sleeping man on his bed in the corner of the room. He was the one they'd almost hit with their truck earlier that afternoon.

There was one other person in the room: a woman sitting in a chair with her legs outstretched, apparently placing newspaper cuttings into a scrapbook. Her skin was pale, her frame dumpy, and Nicole noted that despite the heat she wore jogging bottoms and a long-sleeved t-shirt. Nicole smiled at her and the woman smiled shyly back.

'Shall we see if our stowaway has made it here intact?' asked Eric, pointing to a cardboard box in the centre of Nicole's suitcase.

Before Nicole could reply, there came a thumping sound and the sudden appearance of a pair of skinny legs breaking through a ceiling tile. The legs were quickly followed by a man falling to the floor in a heap of tangled limbs and dust. An astonished Nicole and Eric hurried towards him, urging him not to move, then to wriggle his hands and feet one at a time. Small fragments of plasterboard were caught in his wiry hair; under the dust, his face was freckled. A roll-up cigarette remained between his lips despite his plunge.

'I'm fine, guys, I'm fine,' he reassured them in an Anglo-Dutch accent, adding 'I'm Peyk,' as the door burst open and Tommy appeared.

'What the . . .' he began, his eyes darting from Peyk to the hole in the ceiling.

'It's all good, Tommy-boy, it's all good,' grinned Peyk, before picking up an electrical cable from the floor and leaving. Nicole and Eric looked at each other and then at Tommy, awaiting an explanation.

'Uh, he's our handyman. Probably best not to ask,' said Tommy. Like God, Peyk moved in mysterious ways. 'I was coming to find you guys anyway. I'm heading out for my break and wondered if you wanted a quick tour of Venice? I'll tell Peyk to fix the ceiling while we're gone.'

'We've got some unpacking to do,' Eric replied dismissively, and returned to his bunk.

'Well, do you mind if I go?' asked Nicole.

'Do what you like,' said Eric, his attitude resembling that of a sulky teenager.

Glancing over his shoulder as Nicole and Tommy made their way out of the door, he vowed to nip Nicole's burgeoning friendship in the bud. There was too much at stake for him to stand idly by.

6

'Your boyfriend doesn't like slumming it, does he?' began Tommy as he and Nicole headed along the corridors towards reception.

'Oh, Eric's not my boyfriend,' she replied. 'You're more his type than I am. Just ignore him when he moans, because if he's not complaining about something, he's not being Eric. Once he gets used to the place he'll be fine.'

As they made their way out of the building, Tommy waved when he spotted a familiar face approaching them. Savannah slurped on a thick milkshake through a straw. She pushed her black Jackie O-style glasses up into her platinum blonde bob and grinned.

'Hey, you,' said Tommy.

'Hi, honey, where are you guys off to?'

'Nicole's just checked in, so I'm showing her the local sights and sounds.'

'And you're hitting on her already?' teased Savannah. 'You could at least give the girl time to unpack.'

'That's what I thought,' said Nicole, playing along as Tommy's face reddened.

'Nice to meet you,' continued Savannah as the women introduced themselves and shook hands. 'I'm only messing, Tommy's a sweetheart.'

'Are you working tonight?' asked Tommy.

'Yeah, I'm picking up a few shifts later but I need to get some sleep first. Have a good day, guys.'

'That's the first American accent I've heard since we checked in,' Nicole remarked, as Savannah left and she and Tommy headed for the beach.

'Yeah, we're more geared towards Europeans than Americans. Euros are quite happy to stay in a hovel if it's in a foreign country, and the Americans are more up for experiencing this type of place when they're abroad rather than on their own doorstep.'

'Does Savannah live at the hostel?'

'Pretty much. She's mates with Peyk. She gets a room to herself and I only ever put people in there if we're really busy.'

'And what does Peyk get in return for his generosity?'

'Nah, I don't think it's like that. He's an odd guy but he's harmless, and Savannah doesn't put up with crap from anyone.'

'What's her story, then?'

Tommy shrugged. 'Not sure. She keeps her cards close to her chest.'

That's the best way to play it, Nicole thought to herself, and wondered if she'd ever meet anyone she could trust as much as Eric.

7

Savannah closed her bedroom door behind her and locked it, pulling down the handle to reassure herself it was secure.

She slid her imitation Hermès handbag off her shoulder and placed it on the single unoccupied bed opposite her own. Opening it, she took out a tightly wound roll of $20 bills, then moved towards two lockers and pushed one aside to reveal a jagged hole in the brickwork. She placed the money in the hole next to seven more bundles of notes before moving the locker back into its place.

Then she put her fingertips under her hairline, removed her blonde wig and dropped it on a stool. She ruffled her mousey brown hair before removing a revolver from her bag and placing it under her pillow.

Two Months Earlier: Venice Beach

Savannah clasped her hand over her mouth and ran towards the motionless young man lying on the sidewalk, just as Ron appeared from the entrance of the hostel.

'What the hell?' he began, as they both reached the body at the same time.

'I didn't see him there, Ron,' she cried. 'They were trying to kidnap me. He knows where I am!'

Ron glanced up and down the street, checking whether anyone had witnessed the chaos, before grabbing the boy under his arms and struggling to hoist him to his feet.

'Savannah, help me,' he snapped.

She involuntarily trembled as they dragged the boy, rucksack and all, through an open doorway and into the brightly lit reception area, laying him on the floor. Ron turned the lock on the door and pulled down a roller blind.

The first words to come from the boy's bloodied lips were followed by a desperate intake of breath, taking Ron and Savannah by surprise. 'Am I dead?' he gasped.

'No, thank Christ,' whispered Ron as he rolled him onto his chest. He removed the large canvas rucksack strapped to the boy's back. Light from a fluorescent bulb above bounced off an object inside a small hole in the lining.

Ron sat the boy up and steadied him, watching as he struggled to focus his eyes. The last thing the boy remembered with clarity was listening to The Weeknd through his headphones before something propelled him forward. It had happened so swiftly that his forehead smashed against the pavement before he'd had time to stretch his arms out and minimize the impact.

Ron fished out the contents from the front pouch of the backpack, including a book he'd vaguely heard of from the 1990s called *The Beach.* Wedged into its spine was the bullet Savannah had fired moments earlier. The boy was still too dazed to question why a stranger he couldn't see properly was hoisting his t-shirt up to his shoulders and rubbing cold, thin fingers across his back.

'Lucky bastard,' muttered Ron, and sat him down on a plastic chair.

The boy touched his forehead and felt a swelling. There was a graze to his cheek and grit embedded in his bottom lip. He rolled his tongue around his mouth to check his teeth were still in place. He looked at Ron standing before him, but everything was clouded by a shadow. He only realized there was a third person present in the room when the man spoke again.

'Stay in your room while I clean him up, and hide that thing. Peyk didn't give it to you so you could fire at random strangers.'

Savannah didn't question Ron's orders. She sprinted up the stairs and out of sight before the boy had a chance to remember her. His blurred vision was slowly dissipating and he scanned his new surroundings, unsure if it was the place he had been searching for when fate threw him a curveball.

'What's your name, kid?' Ron asked.

'Tommy,' he replied. His accent was British. He pointed to a poster that was peeling away from the wall opposite him. 'What does "*Welcome to Wherever You Are*" mean?'

'It means it doesn't matter where you are, just as long as you're somewhere.'

Today

Savannah rested her hands on her hips and looked critically at her reflection in the full-length mirror attached to the bathroom wall.

She was disappointed to see the dark circles under her eyes were still showing through her carefully applied make-up, and her cheeks were red and blotchy. She'd felt under the weather for much of the day and hoped the soya-and-fruit milkshake might give her the sugar rush she needed to wake her up. Yawning, she headed back into her bedroom and set the alarm on her phone for four hours' time, when her working day would begin again.

As she fell asleep, she was being watched. Behind the two-way mirror in her room, a hand slowly traced the outline of her body with one finger.

8

From behind the blue metal fence, Nicole stared at a dozen or so men and a few women, bulging veins close to bursting point, as they went about their daily workout routines in the weightlifting area known as Muscle Beach.

She'd read about the fitness fanatics' mecca in her guidebook but was a little disappointed to find it was no more than a large concrete cage crammed with human gorillas, vying for the validation of strangers to further boost egos as swollen as biceps.

As she and Tommy made their way along Venice Beach's boardwalk, it was obvious to Nicole that the creative and artistic beatnik generation who founded the area back in the 1950s and 1960s had long since departed. They'd been replaced by a hotchpotch of tacky tourist retail units interspersed with independent boutiques running parallel to the sandy beach. The other side of the boardwalk contained an assortment of craftsmen and chancers sheltered under a canopy of 40-foot-high palm trees. Tarot card readers predicted the fates of tourists, self-proclaimed experts in Chinese medicine offered acupuncture and neck massages, and fold-up tables were stacked with pamphlets promoting everything from political causes to the health benefits of hemp.

Tommy pointed out the handball and paddle tennis courts,

the skate dancing plaza, the numerous beach volleyball courts and a bike trail that went past lavish beachfront properties on Ocean Front Walk, where the wealthy and a sprinkling of celebrities had their homes.

To describe Venice Beach as diverse was an understatement, Nicole realized. Clearly, one afternoon wouldn't be long enough to explore all the nooks and crannies that piqued her interest. Muscle Beach aside, she felt the area's appeal.

After an hour of sightseeing in the eighty-degree heat with Tommy as her eager guide, they took a break and sat on benches under the shady arches of a cafe, eating generous portions of pistachio ice cream from plastic tubs. Not for the first time that afternoon, a group of young tourists waved at Tommy as they passed by.

'Is there anyone here who doesn't know you?' Nicole asked.

'It's a combination of my movie-star looks and masculine physique,' he deadpanned. 'Or it's that they're guests at the hostel and I'm the first face people see when they check in, so they remember me.'

'I'd say the latter is more likely.'

'Harsh. So is this your first time staying in a hostel?'

'Yep. I'm more of a book it on lastminute.com, two-star hotel in Ibiza kind of girl. This is my first road trip and I'm finding that challenging enough. To be honest, I'm not even sure what life as a backpacker entails.'

'The general consensus is you live out of what you can carry, you travel at your own pace and you sleep where you can.'

'Like tortoises.'

'That makes you "Me Shell".'

'Oh, you're funny,' Nicole groaned, despite being quietly amused by Tommy's banter. 'And what do people *do* at hostels?'

'Meet other travellers, sleep with other travellers, smoke a lot of dope, drink a lot of beer, tell strangers their life stories, and then continue travelling knowing they'll probably never see them again.'

'That sounds fun . . . but kind of sad at the same time.'

'I'm not going to lie, it can be both. I've been hanging around with some of the most incredible people one day, and the next I've been at my loneliest. But I wouldn't change the last seven months for anything, as it's been the best thing I've ever done. I'm sure I've discovered parts of America most Americans haven't even seen, and the hostel – well, it's not the Sunset Marquis, but it's become a rite of passage for backpackers.'

'That's what I told Eric, but I don't think he believed me.'

'How did you and your non-boyfriend end up on a road trip?'

'That's a conversation for another time,' Nicole replied, looking at her watch. 'I should be heading back.'

They took their ice creams with them and retraced their steps along the boardwalk back towards the hostel. She found it endearing how he tried to mask his nervousness around her with over-confidence.

'Are you coming to the party?' he asked hopefully.

'Is that tonight?'

'Uh-huh, and the beer's free.'

'You really know the way to a girl's heart, don't you?' Nicole winked and patted his leg. She was actually beginning to sound like a cougar, she realized.

9

Savannah struggled to find a comfortable sleeping position, so she abandoned her power nap after an hour and relocated to the kitchen to read about Kim Kardashian's exploits in an old *In Touch* magazine another hosteller had left on top of a bin bag.

As she turned the page, she spotted a headline about handsome young actor Zak Stanley that should have been followed by a story and pictures. Instead they'd been ripped out, and she wondered what was so interesting that it had to be taken. She'd almost finished her take-out bowl of yesterday's vegetable soup when a grinning Tommy appeared.

'Hey stud, how was your date?' Savannah asked.

'It wasn't a date, we just went out for a walk and some ice cream,' he replied, and poured hot water into the dirty crockery-filled sink.

'Where did you go, back in time to the 1960s?'

'It was nice.'

'Well, it sounds like a date to me. You like her, don't you?'

'She's cool,' Tommy admitted.

Actually, he did like Nicole a lot. In the course of his American adventure he'd kissed a handful of girls but had only become intimate with two – which, judging by his conversations with other backpackers bragging about their globe-trotting antics, was way below the norm.

But Nicole was different from the other girls he'd met, and he enjoyed her company. She gave as good as she got, she had a sense of humour he appreciated and, of course, he was physically attracted to her. He estimated she was at least a decade his senior, and that only added to her appeal. The most important lesson he'd learned from sharing time, space and philosophies with total strangers was that he was attracted to a personality, above all else.

However, Tommy wasn't naive, and he identified two issues that could stand in the way of something blossoming between them. The first went by the name of Eric: even in their brief encounters, he had made it clear that Tommy's presence was unwelcome. And the second was that Nicole was only on an extended vacation, not a gap year. She was planning to stay in LA for just a few days.

It dawned on Tommy that Nicole hadn't actually revealed much about herself during their afternoon together. He didn't know where she was from, what she did to pay her bills, what she had given up to go travelling, or even why.

He was distracted from his thoughts by the appearance of Peyk, who began wandering around the kitchen and looking up towards the ceiling tiles.

'What are you up to?' Tommy asked.

'Looking for wires,' Peyk replied without making eye contact.

'For fun?'

'For Ron.'

'For what purpose?'

'For it's none of your business.'

Peyk frowned, squinted at something and then nodded. He pulled a joint from behind his ear and lit it on the oven's electric hob. He took a long drag and then offered it to Tommy and Savannah, who both shook their heads. Then, with a wide grin spread across his face, he blew a smoke ring and left.

Out of sight, he took out his basic, text-and-call-only mobile phone, typed in the words '*We're back in business*', and hit send.

10

As soon as he heard the bedroom door creaking open, Eric closed his eyes and pretended to be asleep.

He'd been lying on his bed, quietly brooding over Nicole's decision to spend time with a boy she didn't know rather than with him, planning the next chapter of their vacation. Even though neither was sure where they were supposed to be heading with the vague instructions they'd been left, he was keen to escape the squalor currently suffocating him.

Nicole sat down on her bunk, making the bed frame bend and squeak. Eric opened his eyes and sat up.

'What time is it?' he asked, continuing the charade by rubbing invisible sleep from his eyes.

'It's just gone three. Sorry, did I wake you?'

'Yeah. Where've you been?'

'Tommy was showing me Venice Beach, remember? You'll love it down there, Eric. It's got this fantastic vibe to it; there are so many places we can explore.'

'I'm sure there are, but we're only here for a couple of days, aren't we.' It wasn't a question.

There was a pause before she replied. 'Well, there's no reason why we can't stay a bit longer, is there? It's not like we're on a tight schedule or anything, and we've got enough money to tide us over for at least a couple more months.

We've been on the road going from one motel to another on this wild goose chase. Perhaps we need to take time and start enjoying ourselves more.'

Eric bit his tongue, quietly cursing Tommy for opening Nicole's eyes. He was also sore at himself for not protesting when she'd asked if he minded her going out.

'If that's what you want,' he replied, using a tone that made it clear he was irked, but not irked enough to warrant a confrontation. 'But remember why we're here and what we're trying to find. And I know this place is a pigsty, but is there any chance you can tidy your stuff away? You're the messiest person I know. I don't want anyone rifling through our stuff when we're not here like it's a car boot sale.'

'Sure,' said Nicole, giving him a peck on the forehead. 'Oh, and Tommy says there's a party downstairs tonight if we fancy it?'

Eric grunted, which Nicole took to mean 'yes', and moved towards the bathroom, only to spot the woman in the jogging bottoms and long-sleeved t-shirt. She was still sitting in the same place she'd been hours earlier.

'Hello,' said Nicole.

'Hi,' replied the woman, closing her scrapbook. She clutched it to her chest before Nicole could work out whose face was stuck on the cover.

'My name's Nicole.'

'I'm Ruth,' she said in an Australian accent, before lowering her head, rising to her feet and scuttling from the room. She headed towards the empty kitchen and, once she was confident she was alone, carefully placed her book on the table, her face brightening at the magazine cutting of Zak Stanley stuck to the cover.

Five Weeks Earlier: Victoria, Australia

'Chips for breakfast? For Christ's sake, girl, you've just got out of bed!'

The disgruntled tone of her mother, Denise, failed to move Ruth to push her unconventional breakfast to one side or turn her tablet off. Instead, she remained sprawled across the white faux-leather sofa, her head propped up by a cushion and a bowl of corn-based snacks balanced on her stomach.

'Hey, I'm talking to you,' Denise continued to jibe, pointing at her daughter with a French-tipped fingernail. 'Get your arse up, turn that thing off and go out and do some exercise.'

Ruth ignored her mother's obvious frustration and remained transfixed by the figure on the screen. No matter what weight-related insult Denise or Ruth's younger brother, Kevin, threw at her, her indifference to dieting, make-up and fashion persisted.

In Ruth's universe, the only person whose opinion mattered was Zak Stanley. He was someone who had never picked on her, criticized her, mocked her appearance or made her feel any less of a woman in spite of her 5-foot-8-inch, 15-stone frame. Zak made Ruth feel like a real princess – and not Princess Fiona, the *Shrek* character Kevin often compared her to.

And if Zak were ever to leave his Hollywood home and cast aside his A-list movie career for a relationship with a stranger who could offer him more love than all of his thousands of fans put together, Ruth would be waiting for him with open arms.

When Ruth heard Denise's stiletto heels tap their way across the lounge's laminate flooring and into the kitchen, she turned up the tablet's volume. Although she'd watched the YouTube clip many times over the last two years, Ruth still scowled at the blonde-haired, clearly fake-breasted presenter proudly standing on the red carpet in London's Leicester Square. Ruth didn't care for the way she flirted with Zak but conceded that anyone in the presence of such talent and masculine beauty would find it impossible not to try their luck.

'So what made you take the role, Zak? It's quite a departure,' asked the presenter, whose name Ruth had no interest in remembering.

'Well,' began Zak, struggling to hear through the screaming teenage girls penned in behind metal barricades. He brushed his hand though his dark, floppy fringe. 'I've always been a big supporter of animal rights, and if my movie helps bring the illegal trade in elephant ivory to the forefront of people's minds, well, that makes it all worthwhile.'

I bet he loves dogs like I do, too, thought Ruth. Along with pizza, sunsets, *Friends* re-runs and cuddles, animals were yet another thing she could add to their list of common interests.

'And what about love – have you found a potential Mrs Stanley yet?'

He grinned bashfully. 'No, I'm still looking for her.'

'And what qualities does a girl need to have?'

'I'm a simple kinda guy. All I want is an ordinary girl who inspires me to be a better man, and who I can wake up loving a little bit more each day.'

'And you think she's out there somewhere?' The interviewer fluttered her eyelashes and no longer tried to disguise her desire to be auditioned as Mrs Stanley.

'Oh, I'm sure of it. Who knows? She could be right here

tonight or she could live on the other side of the world, but I believe in destiny, and I'll know who she is the moment we meet.'

The butterflies that always materialized in Ruth's stomach when she thought of Zak were now fluttering so briskly, they made her feel light-headed. 'You mean me,' she mouthed silently, and then smiled.

Once Zak moved on to greet a British boyband she'd never heard of, Ruth played the interview twice more before her mother appeared again.

'You're never going to find a boyfriend if you're stuck in this bloody house every day,' Denise barked. 'Your iPad won't love you back.' She picked up her jacket, folded it over her arm and swung her bag over her shoulder. 'Look at the state of you. It's no wonder your father left.'

Ruth waited till she was gone, then began to eat a partially melted chocolate bar she'd kept hidden under a cushion and away from her mother's sight.

11

Today

By 8.15 p.m., the first of the week's two hostel parties was in full swing.

Five beer kegs placed on the floor by the window overlooking the street below were quickly being drained as guests queued to fill their red plastic cups and glasses with free booze.

Others took turns in selecting their own carefully composed playlists from smartphones plugged into a speaker dock. All styles of music, from hip hop to EDM, from drill to pop, played as residents danced, chatted, flirted and quaffed beer or cheap bottles of wine they'd purchased from the liquor store across the road. Some travellers played pool on a table with torn felt, using cues with worn-down tips. Others regularly left the room to smoke cannabis out of sight on the building's two second-floor balconies.

Tommy scanned the room and spotted Eric and Nicole talking in the corner. He waited for Nicole to approach the kegs and refill their glasses before he approached Eric. If he could get Eric on side, he reasoned, then he might be able to persuade Nicole to stay in LA a little longer.

'How are you settling in?' Tommy began with a rehearsed smile.

'Oh, this place is just delightful,' replied Eric, making no attempt to disguise his disdain. 'A shared bedroom that reeks of stale feet, people falling through ceilings, and German techno music deafening me. What more could I ask for?'

'Well, there's something I wouldn't mind asking you – is Nicole seeing anyone?'

Eric glared at Tommy, making him instantly uncomfortable, before Nicole reappeared.

'Hi, Tommy,' she smiled.

'How are you enjoying the party?'

'Yeah, it's good fun. Oh, and we've decided to stay in California a bit longer.'

'Really?' Tommy tried to contain a grin.

'Have we?' interrupted Eric.

'Okay, *I* have decided we'd like to stay in Venice a bit longer.'

'You don't seem so keen, Eric.'

'Do you blame me?'

'I've stayed in worse places. This hostel is more about the people than the decoration. There's a good crowd here if you just give them a chance. Some are passing through like you guys and the rest of us have been here for a while. I'm sure you'll make connections if you keep an open mind.'

Just as Eric was formulating a suitably sarcastic response about how he wasn't going to be lectured by someone barely out of high school, a plastic tap burst from the side of a keg and a fountain of beer sprayed his face and chest, drenching him.

'For fuck's sake!' he yelled, wiping alcohol from his stinging eyes and dropping his glass to the floor. 'I'm soaked!'

'Go back to the room and dry yourself off, it's not the end of the world,' suggested Nicole.

'It's the end of this All Saints t-shirt,' Eric shot back, and turned towards the door, mopping his face with a paper napkin. Before he left, he turned to Nicole and whispered in her ear: 'Don't tell him anything.'

With Eric gone, Tommy could no longer suppress his laughter.

'Stop it!' Nicole smirked.

'All Saints? He's such a tourist.'

'Why?'

'The difference between backpackers and tourists is that backpackers don't wear fifty-pound t-shirts. In fact, fifty pounds is probably the total value of my wardrobe.'

As Nicole nodded, she fiddled with the Calvin Klein label at the bottom of her vest, ensuring it wasn't visible.

Tommy bent down to pick up Eric's glass, failing to notice a hairline crack down its side. As he reached for the rim, it shattered and tore into the palm of his hand.

'Shit,' he yelped, and pulled a shard from his wound. Nicole instinctively reached for his hand and inspected it, before pressing a handful of paper napkins against it to stop the flow of blood.

'Where's the first aid kit?' she asked.

'In the kitchen.'

Tommy clasped his throbbing hand and led Nicole upstairs to the kitchen, where she rinsed his hand under the cold-water tap.

'It's not deep enough to need stitches, but it might be worth going to an emergency department.'

'You're assuming I have medical insurance,' replied Tommy. He watched as Nicole carefully cleaned his wound with iodine, her movements practised and confident. 'You've done this before.'

She wrapped a bandage around his hand, securing it with two safety pins and some gaffer tape.

'I may have, once or twice,' she replied. 'I'm a nurse.'

Twelve Weeks Earlier: London

'So much for being bloody waterproof,' muttered Nicole to herself as the torrential rain lashed against her Mackintosh and seeped into her collar, dripping down her back.

The rain that had begun as harmless drizzle was now torrential and soaking her to the skin. Nicole regretted her decision to cycle the six miles to work instead of catching the bus, and reminded herself of her late mother's words, 'a bit of rain never hurt anyone'.

Suddenly, with the hospital in sight, the hem of her coat became caught in the back wheel's spokes and yanked her body to the right. Trying but failing to regain her balance, she toppled off the saddle and landed cheek first on the pavement.

'Bollocks,' she cursed, picking herself up and then her bike, before kicking it and walking with it the rest of way.

Hospital rules stated that a person could only run through a ward in an emergency.

But having fallen foul of the charge nurse's displeasure over poor time-keeping three times already that fortnight, Nicole decided that to avoid being any later than she was, it was indeed an emergency. Quickly she squeezed sanitizer from a wall-mounted dispenser into her palms and rubbed her hands as she dashed past the beds on the geriatric ward, before reaching the room behind the nursing station where

Eric sat in uniform. He was reading *GQ* next to a half-full, tepid pot of coffee.

He mimed looking at his watch, tapping it and then raising his eyes towards Nicole.

'Don't start,' she snapped, in no mood for a lecture. 'What are you doing up here?'

'Quiet day on Orthopaedics. Thought I'd come up and meet you for breakfast before your shift.'

She swept her sopping wet hair from her face and glanced into the mirror at the graze on her cheek. 'Do we have any antiseptic?'

'Nic, we're a hospital. We bleed antiseptic.'

Nicole was searching a desk drawer for the first aid kit when a surly charge nurse entered in.

'Late again, Nurse Grainger?' she asked rhetorically, then regarded Nicole's injury. 'I hope you'll be covering that up. Your patients don't want to see the results of your drunken nights out.'

Before Nicole could protest, the charge nurse had exited the room to make someone else's life miserable.

'I need to see how Mrs Baker is,' Nicole said, powdering her cheek with foundation. 'Drinks after work?'

'Sure,' Eric replied. He made his way out of the ward while Nicole moved into the nurses' station. She shuffled clipboards around on the desk until she found Mrs Baker's charts, then headed towards a private room.

By the time the cancer had reached Grace Baker's bones, she knew it was unlikely she would see her seventieth birthday.

In the space of eight months she had shrunk from a sturdy, strong-willed woman with a passion for foreign travel to a thin, frail, grey-skinned pensioner waiting to take one last journey. Mrs Baker could easily have afforded to end her days in a private hospital, but she knew from her late husband's experience just how quiet and soulless such places could be. And without a family to visit her, the hustle and bustle of an NHS hospital made her feel less alone.

After a night where sleep was disrupted by pain and her loss of bladder control, Mrs Baker struggled to keep her eyes open and drifted off to sleep moments before Nicole entered her room. Nicole pulled up a seat and sat by her side, holding her hand.

'Bridget?' mumbled Mrs Baker, vaguely aware she had company.

'No, Mrs Baker, it's me. How are you feeling today?'

'I can't really feel much because of the morphine. I've asked, but they won't tell me what will happen next.'

'I don't think they can, I'm afraid. It's now just a case of managing the pain rather than trying to find the cause of it.'

Mrs Baker nodded and slowly opened her bloodshot eyes. 'Do you have time for my usual?' she asked.

Nicole turned her head towards the door for any sign of the charge nurse, then reached into the bedside table drawer and pulled out a lipstick before applying it to Mrs Baker's lips.

'That's better,' beamed Mrs Baker. 'A girl's got to look her best even when she's feeling her worst. Did Bridget come while I was asleep?'

'Um, I'm not sure; I've just started my shift . . .'

'You can tell me the truth.'

Nicole hesitated before answering. 'I really don't know. But you've told me how busy she is.'

'Yes, it must be hard juggling Pilates classes along with

nannies for grandchildren I never see. I've done well, haven't I? A daughter who married for money and social standing and a son I haven't seen in a decade since his father died, and he tried to put me in a home and take control of my finances. Don't get me wrong, I know I have made many mistakes of my own, and some of them are hard to come back from. But I'm not a bad person, am I?'

'No, not at all.'

Without warning, a stern voice behind Nicole startled her.

'Nurse Grainger, may I have a word, please?'

Mrs Baker squeezed Nicole's hand in anticipation of what was to come and Nicole followed the charge nurse into an office. During working hours, she discouraged fraternization between staff and patients. Her old-school approach bore little relationship to modern nursing methods.

'May I remind you – once again – that there are more patients in this ward than Mrs bloody Baker,' the charge nurse snapped. 'Just because her husband was on the trust board so she gets her own room does not mean she can expect preferential treatment over everyone else. Do I make myself clear?'

'Yes.'

'Now start your rounds and visit this woman in your own time, or you'll be on report – again.'

Nicole followed her out of the office. If the charge nurse had turned, she'd have seen Nicole giving her the finger behind her back.

Today

'A nurse, eh?' said Tommy, his eyes lighting up. He'd not eaten much yet and the beer was going to his head, allowing him extra bravado. 'Does that mean you wear one of those sexy uniforms?'

'Yes, that's right,' sighed Nicole. 'We all skip around in high heels, fishnet tights and miniskirts with our shirts buttoned so you can see our bras, and every now and again we'll pull a stethoscope out from between our boobs.'

Tommy felt his face flush.

'How long are you in LA for?' Nicole asked, changing the subject.

'As long as it takes to figure out what I want to do with my life.'

'And what do you want to do? You know, in an ideal world.'

'I know what I want to do right now,' he replied. His expression wasn't hard to read.

'I know what I want do, too,' whispered Nicole, drawing his head closer to hers and then her mouth towards his ear. She placed her hand on his chest and his heart felt as if it was about to beat its way out of his chest.

'And what . . . what's that?' he stuttered.

'I . . . want . . . another beer. Now be a good boy and go get me one.'

In the ten minutes Nicole and Tommy had spent in the kitchen, they'd failed to realize they were not alone. Now a gentle snoring caught their attention. They turned together to see Joe, sitting on a stool in the corner of the room and slumped fast asleep across a work surface next to two large steaming pots. Tommy examined the pots' contents – one contained an almost solid, rust-coloured mass of sauce, and the other was crammed with charred spaghetti and no water.

'Joe, wake up!' yelled Tommy.

Joe's eyelids sprang open. He was clearly unsure of his surroundings.

'Mate, you've incinerated the pasta. There's a room full of hungry people waiting for this.'

'Sorry, just . . . busy . . . forgot.'

Tommy helped Joe back to his dormitory, removed his baseball cap and put him to bed. As he left, he was startled by Ruth's presence; she was sitting on the top of a bunk bed and viewing something on her iPad. One headphone was plugged into her ear and the other dangled by her shoulder.

'Hello,' Tommy began, and Ruth gave an awkward, tight-lipped smile. 'It's Ruth, right? I checked you in.'

Ruth continued smiling but didn't reply.

'Aren't you coming downstairs to the party? There's free beer.'

Ruth shook her head.

'Not much of a drinker?'

Ruth shook her head again.

'Or talker?'

By the time Ruth plucked the teeth-whitening trays from her mouth, Tommy had given up on the conversation and left her with only the sounds of the party a floor below and a snoring Joe to keep her company.

12

Madonna's breathy vocals floated over the trip-hop drum loop and heavy bass as 'Justify My Love' boomed from the speakers.

The punters watched in silence as the dancer began her slow, sensual descent down the pole towards the rubber-matted floor. She held on with a baseball-style grip, swung her outside leg into a hook and picked up her inside leg, which followed suit. She threw her head and shoulders back to accentuate her breasts and pouted. Despite the track being older than her, she knew every word and every beat off by heart as she'd danced to it twice per shift for the last four months.

Before Savannah had stumbled into a career as an exotic dancer, she'd had a preconceived notion that strip clubs were sleazy dives patronized by paunchy, middle-aged men, like she'd seen on TV shows like *The Sopranos.* But both the décor and the clientele of Santa Monica's Pink Pussycat Club changed her mind.

Open twenty-four hours a day and only a ten-minute cab ride from Venice Beach, the spacious lounge area housed two runway stages with poles at the end of each. While it was hardly what you might call homely, wipe-clean leather armchairs and Chesterfield-style sofas surrounded the stages, and there were lamps with purple shades balanced on dark wooden tables. The Club also had smaller corner booths roped off and reserved for VIP guests or parties who spent their dollars freely.

Savannah had no desire to work in *any* strip club. But compared to the first place she'd danced at, days after arriving in the City of Angels, this one was like a palace and offered her the security she needed. She could also bank up to $500 on a busy night – more than Dunkin' Donuts or Wendy's paid in a week.

In order to do the job, Savannah had imposed upon herself a moral code. She would do runway and pole dances fully nude, along with peep show performances, which involved customers in private booths watching her from behind a two-way mirror. But private backstage lap dances and dating the clientele were all strict no-nos. They were sure-fire ways of doubling her daily income, but while she didn't judge the other girls who took that route, she feared losing even more of herself than she had already.

As 'Justify My Love' gradually faded out, she scooped up her tips and made her way back towards the changing room, where she stared into an illuminated mirror. Glad her shift was over for the night, she wiped the perspiration from her forehead and underarms, then reached into her handbag for her mascara and found an embossed business card Tommy had given her two days earlier.

'Some bloke came in here looking for you,' he'd informed her. 'He didn't give me a name, but he was an intimidating bastard. Had two big guys with him. He gave me his card but I didn't tell him you were a guest.'

Savannah had forced herself to sound calm as she took the

card, then raced up the stairs and into her room. Inside, she'd shut and locked the door, made for the bathroom and vomited into the toilet bowl.

But she'd kept the card. All it contained was a number that she didn't recognize, but that was enough to worry her. She knew being afraid of the unknown was worse than being afraid of the expected, so she took her phone from her handbag, changed the settings so her number remained anonymous, and nervously dialled.

Seven Months Earlier: Montgomery, Alabama

'Be gone, devil! With the spirit of Jesus in me, I am ordering you to leave this child's body and make her clean again!'

The audience was transfixed by Reverend Devereaux in anticipation of the miracle they had queued much of the morning to witness. With the exception of scattered 'amens' yelled by pockets of onlookers, the only voices to be heard through the arena speakers were those belonging to the Reverend and his male assistants, muttering their approval of what was to come.

The Reverend allowed the tension to build gradually before he cupped the chin of the young girl who stood trembling before him. He placed the palm of his other hand on her forehead, clasping it so tightly that it left the impression of his gold sovereign ring on her ochre skin.

'Speak, child . . . speak!' he yelled. The temperature from the bulbs in the lighting rig above made sweat trickle down his forehead and drip from the microphone fastened from cheek to ear.

'Speak to me! Speak to your people! Speak to us all!'

The girl's head continued to quiver as he gripped her face.

'Tell everyone how Jesus has saved you!' he bellowed.

'Je . . . Je . . . Je . . .' she began. She looked into the Reverend's narrowed eyes and then finally parted her lips.

'Jesus has saved me,' she blurted out.

'Louder!' he repeated, specks of saliva landing on her cheek. 'Say it louder!'

'Jesus has saved me,' she repeated, her voice rising to a more confident yell. 'Jesus has saved me!'

The audience rose to its feet, applauding and roaring its approval as the fifteen-strong brass band on the lowest tier of the stage launched into 'When the Saints Go Marching In'.

Reverend Devereaux had already left the girl to his assistant's devices. The assistant hurried her from the stage and into the wings, away from the audience, before her stammer returned. They'd learned from mistakes made years earlier about how quickly 'miracles' wore off once adrenaline levels subsided.

The Reverend took to the centre of his stage, outstretched his arms like he was attached to an invisible crucifix and nodded to the audience. Indoor fireworks exploded behind him as the encouraging noises continued, before he waited patiently for the crowd to quieten. The television cameras focused close enough to capture the broken capillary veins snaking their way across his cheeks and nose, beaming his image across the amphitheatre on a huge screen.

'Today,' he began in hushed tones, 'Jesus made a crippled woman walk again; He aided a boy born without eardrums to hear for the first time in his life; and He removed cataracts from the eyes of a blind grandmother. He gave voice to this dumb girl. This is what happens when – not *if* – you allow the power of Jesus into your life. And for the benefit of our friends at home, just think what you could accomplish if you let Him into your life too. You can do that, right now, by picking up your telephone and calling the number on your screen. It doesn't matter how much you donate, but the more you can afford, the more people we can help. Galatians 6:10 said, "Let us do good to everyone, and especially to those who are of the household of faith." Thank you, my friends, and may God's love be with you.'

Reverend Devereaux bowed to his audience as they hollered, whistled and applauded. In return, he clapped them and his stage helpers before leaving the podium.

There was only one person in the arena who failed to rise and show her appreciation of the miracles that afternoon had witnessed, and Reverend Devereaux was fully aware of this. Instead of hanging onto his every word, she was more interested in whatever was filling the screen of her phone.

He would have stern words with Savannah Devereaux later, but she had no intention of obeying her father.

Today

Savannah's hand trembled as she held the phone to her ear.

After three rings, the call was answered, but nobody spoke. The stalemate lasted for several seconds before the door behind Savannah opened and Roxy walked in.

'Hey Savannah, I thought you'd gone,' she called cheerfully before Savannah could hang up. Breathing quickly, she wondered if her call had just opened Pandora's box.

13

The pan of water was too large and too heavy for one person to lift alone, especially with a wounded hand, but Tommy attempted it anyway.

When it was clear his bravado was bordering on embarrassing, Nicole stepped in to help in case he accidentally poured the contents across the floor.

'Thanks,' Tommy mumbled.

'It's my first night in Los Angeles and you've got me chained to the kitchen sink. This doesn't bode well for our relationship.'

'Well, I can make pasta for one, but not for sixty, and definitely not on my own.'

'And you assume that just because I'm a woman, I know how to cook. I thought your generation was supposed to be more "woke" than that?'

'My generation? You make it sound like there's decades between us.'

'I'm only teasing,' Nicole replied, scraping burned pasta from Joe's pan with a wooden spoon. 'So how did you end up here?'

'You were with me – Joe was cremating the dinner.'

'Oh, lord,' sighed Nicole. 'I meant how did you end up in LA?'

'Oh right, sorry. Well, I could tell you, but it's not exactly a barrel of laughs.'

Two Years Earlier: Northampton, England

'Do you ever turn that damn thing off?'

Adam glared at Tommy's reflection in the rear-view mirror as he drove. Tommy chose to ignore him and continued to pan the lens of his digital camcorder around the Mini.

'What are you even filming?'

'Nothing much, just you two and whatever we go past that looks interesting,' replied Tommy as the trees outside began to thin and make way for a succession of residential houses and shops. 'I need a backdrop for an idea I'm working on.'

'Being around you is like living in a shitty reality show and having a camera following you around, recording everything you say and do.'

'Only at least there's some eye candy to look at in *Love Island*,' added their brother Daniel. 'And sun. And a luxury villa. And booze.'

'Did you click on that link I sent you to the new Drake mixtape yet?' asked Tommy, ignoring them. Both shook their heads. He removed his iPhone from the back pocket of his joggers and scrolled through his playlists while his video camera continued to record. 'You should try surfing the Russian websites; there's so much illegal pre-release stuff online if you know where to look.'

'Yeah, I've heard some of the Russian websites you surf when you think everyone else is in bed asleep,' Adam smirked.

'Oh yes,' teased Daniel. 'Even Mum admitted she's heard your bed squeaking to the sounds of online Russian girls groaning in your bedroom for seventy roubles a pop.'

'You are such a liar!' Tommy snapped as his face reddened. Daniel and Adam made a sport out of embarrassing their younger sibling. But despite the two-and-a-half-year gap separating the twins from Tommy, and the fact that Daniel and Adam had both signed up to the Marines after leaving school, they had remained a close family.

Lee slowed down as they approached the traffic lights and Tommy continued to hunt through his extensive collection of downloaded music.

'When you're done with your friends, can you pick me up from Louis's house?' he asked.

'You can catch the bus back – we're going out of our way as it is to give you a ride there,' replied Adam dismissively.

'That's not fair, Mum and Dad bought you a car while I still have to cycle everywhere like a loser.'

'And they'll probably buy you one too if you get into uni. You're the one who took a gap year and then did sod all with it,' said Adam. 'You need to get your arse into gear, start looking at courses and get your applications in.'

'Well, some of us need a bit longer before we commit,' Tommy replied. He was quietly bored of being lectured by his parents and his brothers.

'Don't tell Dad that, or before you know it he'll have you signed up with the rest of the new recruits at commando training centre,' added Daniel.

'I get seasick. I couldn't be a Marine like you two even if I wanted to be.'

'That doesn't rule out the army, though. But if it's film school you really want to get into then he might come round eventually. Just make a decision and go with it instead of wasting time.'

'Okay, okay, enough of the pep talk!' Tommy knew full well that at nineteen, he needed to get his act together. Louis aside, most of his friends were finishing their first year at university; meanwhile, he'd floundered, working part-time on the Tesco bakery counter. Unlike his brothers, he had no interest in the family tradition of joining the armed forces. Instead, he preferred to be holed up in his darkened bedroom making mini-movies and editing them on his laptop.

His focus was typically landscapes – inner city, coastal and countryside – and exploring new ways of filming them. He had saved up and bought a reconditioned camcorder and barely went anywhere without it. Tommy constantly uploaded clips to YouTube in the faint hope a famous director would see his potential and invite him to work as a trainee cinematographer on the set of a movie. But David Fincher had yet to call.

'Plug this in and open the music app,' Tommy said, handing Daniel his phone. The car was too old to have a Bluetooth option.

As the green traffic light turned red and the Mini accelerated across a junction, Daniel lost his grip of the phone and it bounced off Adam's thigh and into the driver's footwell.

'Be careful, you dick,' barked Adam, unclipping his seat belt to fumble around for the phone.

For a split second, Tommy noticed a dark shadow through the lens of his camcorder, but it moved too quickly for his eyes to process what it was. Then the brothers' world became deafeningly loud and faded to black as the shadow ploughed into the side of their car, forcing it to roll over twice before it settled on its side.

Today

'I've been looking for you,' glared Eric, interrupting Tommy's recounting of his past and Nicole's gradual understanding of the vulnerability of the young man standing before her in the hostel kitchen.

'Sorry, it's my fault, I asked for Nicole's help,' replied Tommy.

'Could I have a word, Nic?' Eric asked.

'Um, sure.'

'In private?'

Nicole followed Eric from the kitchen and along a corridor before he came to a halt. The smell of beer remained on his skin.

'I've been standing downstairs like an idiot waiting for you, but surprise, surprise, you're up here with him,' he began heatedly.

'What's your problem with Tommy?' Nicole replied, startled by his outburst.

'I don't have a problem with Tommy. What I do have a problem with is being left alone while you make a fool of yourself.'

'Jesus, Eric. I'm getting sick of your mood swings today.'

'I don't trust him. He's probably tried it on with every girl here.'

'He's not like that, and what business would it be of yours if he had? I can look after myself.'

'Yeah, you did a great job with Pete, didn't you?'

Nicole scowled at Eric, angry that he would bring up such a

painful memory to use against her. 'That's not fair,' she replied quietly, and Eric softened his tone accordingly.

'No, okay, it's not. I'm sorry. But I'm your best friend, Nic, and if it weren't for me, you wouldn't have even known Pete was screwing around on you. I'm a good judge of character, so trust me on this, Tommy's no good. I'm a bloke, we know this kind of thing.'

Nicole said nothing, eyes on the floor.

'Look, we're here for a reason,' he continued. 'Maybe thousands of pounds' worth of reasons. All I'm saying is, don't let some kid you hardly know get in the way of that. Now come here.'

Eric put his arms around Nicole and kissed her on the cheek. She always felt safe when she was with Eric even when he was thoughtless, but she was reluctant to believe Tommy had any agenda. He was right when he told her about travellers wanting to share their lives with others in short spaces of time. But it wasn't something she could reciprocate.

'Let me help him out with dinner, and I promise I'll be down soon,' Nicole conceded.

Eric nodded his approval and Nicole headed back into the kitchen.

'Everything okay?' asked Tommy chirpily.

'Yes, it's fine,' replied Nicole, and said very little else during the rest of the time it took to remake the meal.

14

Day Two

Matty and Declan left the cooling ocean water in just their underwear and made for the towels they'd left spread across Venice's sandy beach.

'You might wanna cover that li'l thing up,' began Matty, pointing to Declan's boxers, the water having made them transparent.

'Less of the "li'l",' Declan replied, rubbing his face with his towel. 'It was fecking cold in there.'

Their walk from Santa Monica via Venice Beach Boulevard in the blistering heat had been exhausting, especially with two bulging rucksacks strapped to their backs. So their brief respite in the ocean had been a welcome diversion.

Declan hadn't stepped inside a gym for the best part of a year, so he was grateful for the genetic good luck that meant his chest and arms retained their naturally muscular shape. He'd used the last squirt of sunblock earlier that morning and with each passing hour he felt his milky Irish skin reddening further.

'I'll kill you if they're fully booked after days of travelling on that stinking thing,' warned Matty, and he took a swig of water.

'It was your idea to save money and go freight-train hopping.'

'You're supposed to be the sensible one and talk me out of stupid ideas like that! Besides, we could've managed a Holiday Inn if you hadn't spunked our money in Reno trying to be Billy Big Bollocks to impress showgirls.'

'Where else am I going to find a bird with firm breasts and feathers stuck to her arse?'

'A henhouse?'

Their arrival in Los Angeles early that morning was the culmination of a five-day expedition riding the railways from Seattle to Idaho, then the length of Nevada, cross-country to Utah before finally reaching LA. Although strictly illegal, freight-train hopping was the cheapest way to travel long distances and witness parts of America that couldn't be negotiated by car or bus.

An article in a *Reader's Digest* magazine Matty found in a hospital waiting room in Florida had given him the inspiration to trek by boxcar. The written recollections of former rail-riders got him wondering what it must have been like to travel the country in search of new careers and new beginnings during America's Great Depression. In reality, his romanticized plan had proved an arduous ordeal.

The first hurdle was finding freight yards where trains and their boxcars passed through or were parked up. Then, once a slowed-down train was in sight, they had to run to keep up with it, promptly pick a carriage with an open door, then hurl themselves and their luggage into it. Twice they'd failed and had been forced to wait ten hours for the next train to pass.

Once inside, the final hurdle was to find somewhere safe to settle, avoiding badly packed loose goods that might fall on them or over-spacious cars that would see them being hurled around like wrestlers in a ring. The sound of the grinding wheels on the steel tracks was often so deafening that they'd insert their in-ear headphones to nullify the noise.

The nights were cold and the carriages often stank of the products being transported. For two of their six journeys they'd picked the wrong boxcars and slept on bags of fertilizer and boxes of bottled bleach. Another had been spent in an open carriage, zipped up head to toe in sleeping bags to protect them from the 60 mph winds. Only their last journey was more pleasant, tucked up amongst crate after crate of televisions and games consoles.

Matty and Declan learned to avoid other freight-train hoppers. Often they were nomadic souls unwilling to have their space invaded, or were suffering addictions to narcotics or alcohol and wanted to rob you at knifepoint. Matty noted the magazine story had failed to mention such perils.

Only once, during a routine check at a station in Utah, had an armed security guard discovered them. But experience had taught them they could get away with a lot by exaggerating their accents and asking Americans whether they had any Irish in their heritage. Invariably the answer would be yes followed by a claim to be one-eighth Gaelic, to which Matty and Declan would respond that they'd sensed it immediately. A little flattery, a moment to reminisce about the homeland, and with luck they'd be left alone to go about their business. But as uncomfortable and anxious as they'd often felt, it had been the journey of a lifetime and they'd seen more of America than they'd ever thought possible.

Once they finally reached LA, reeking of train grease and

body odour, they made their way to the coast and charged straight into the ocean to clean up.

As they walked along the beachfront, they soon dried off from the impromptu swim. Declan unclipped his water bottle and took a long swig, offering it to his friend. Matty's damp shirt clung to his skinny body and he felt one of the blisters on his heels burst and weep inside his once white, now filthy Converse trainers. The straps of his rucksack dug into his bony shoulders and chafed his skin.

'Hold up, this is the place,' said Matty suddenly, pointing to the dilapidated building ahead of them.

'Here we go,' Declan replied, staring at the faded sign reading *Venice Beach International Hostel.* 'Another shithole we can't afford.'

'But we always find a way, don't we?' replied Matty, patting his rucksack and grinning. 'And this time we have a secret weapon.'

15

In the 217 days since Tommy and Louis's plane had taxied towards its stand at New York's JFK airport, much of the £8,000 Tommy had carefully scrimped and saved from his supermarket job had been spent on travel, accommodation, food and alcohol.

Now, with a depleted bank balance and mounting credit card bill, he was a beggar who couldn't afford to choose from the jobs Ron the hostel manager threw at him. So he worked eight-hour days across a variety of tasks, from cleaning rooms to cash-and-carry food collection, all to pay for his bed and board.

For the rest of the morning until Gabby took over, Tommy was on rota to cover the reception desk. Bored, he resisted the temptation to peek under his bandage to see how his cut hand was healing; instead, he grabbed a pile of magazines and stacked them on a shelf, colour-coordinating their spines. He picked out a couple of roll-up cigarette butts from the always-close-to-death-but-never-quite-there yucca plant and inhaled sharply, recognizing their familiar cannabis scent before flicking them in the bin. While smoking dope was commonplace in dorms and on the roof, it was an activity he was wary of.

He thought back to the conversation he'd begun the previous night with Nicole, the only person on his vacation he'd told about the car accident that had changed the course of his life. Even then, he hadn't explained to her the complete story. So in retrospect he was glad Eric had interrupted them even if Nicole's mood had shifted somewhat on her return.

'Tommy!' yelled Gabby's voice from upstairs in the lounge. He recognized her distinctive, overbearing New York twang immediately and wondered why, even though he was her equal on the reception desk, she appeared convinced he was her employee. 'Get your ass up here.'

'What's up?' he replied, narrowing his eyes.

'Now!'

Tommy took the stairs two at a time, and when he reached the lounge above reception, he frowned in puzzlement before breaking into peals of laughter.

16

'I'm not sure I really get it,' began Eric, removing his shades and turning 180 degrees to gain a better view of Venice Beach boardwalk and its colourful residents.

'What's not to get?' asked Nicole.

'I just don't get the appeal or why the guidebooks say it's so special. It reminds me of Blackpool but with a better beach – and weather.'

Confused by his indifference, Nicole's patience was wearing thin. She placed her hands on her hips. 'You have got to be kidding me.'

Eric shrugged. 'Just saying.'

She and Eric followed the route Tommy had taken her the previous day, before kicking off their flip-flops and making their way across the warm, sparkling sand. The beach was quiet, apart from a few families eating picnics close to the ocean's waves. In the distance they could almost make out Santa Monica pier as the sun hid behind clouds of smog. But a hundred metres out to sea, brightly coloured sails bobbed up and down as windsurfing boards glided across the water's surface.

Eric removed his everyday rucksack, took out two plastic bottles of Sprite and placed them on either end of a weathered road map to stop the light breeze from carrying it away. Nicole flicked through the dog-eared pages of an atlas, skipping past pages of towns leading off Route 66 they'd circled in red.

'So we went where we thought we were supposed to go,' began Nicole, 'and that was following Route 66 from where it starts in Illinois to where it ends in Santa Monica.'

'I was there, hun, I do remember this.'

'I know, I'm just saying it out loud to get it clear in my head. And somewhere en route, we missed what we were looking for. So our options are this: reread her letter, take a closer look at each town on the internet, or completely retrace our steps and do it again.'

'Are you kidding me? It's a miracle that truck has made it three thousand miles – there's no way in hell it will manage another three thousand. And neither will I, sweating my arse off inside it.'

'I don't think we'll need to. I have a feeling we're in the right neck of the woods, give or take a few hundred miles.'

'You have *a feeling*.'

'Yep.'

'You want us to go back on the road based on *a feeling*. And do your spidey senses offer any indication of what we might find when we reach this hallowed, promised land?'

Nicole shook her head. 'Not a bloody clue.'

Eleven Weeks Earlier: London

Nicole fanned herself with her hand as the digital clock on the TV above Mrs Baker's bed reached nine p.m.

'It's a little warm in here, isn't it?' she commented, and went back to painting Mrs Baker's fingernails. Her shift had ended an hour earlier, but Nicole wanted to cheer up her patient and friend. Mrs Baker's nails were grey like her skin, so Nicole was painting them a deep red.

Mrs Baker was sitting upright for the first time in days, albeit awkwardly and with pillows supporting her aching spine and neck. 'Back in 1971, before Joseph took over his father's jewellery business, we spent the first year and a half of our married life travelling around the world,' she recalled. 'I hadn't even got used to wearing a ring on my finger or no longer calling myself Grace Collins when we found ourselves honeymooning in an Indian ashram before exploring the rest of Asia, then South Africa, Australia and America. It was quite a wild, dangerous thing to do back then. Everyone else our age was settling down and having babies.'

'That sounds incredible,' said Nicole. 'What was your favourite part?'

'Probably when we travelled Route 66. We bought a brand-new pick-up truck in New York, started from the road's origins in Chicago and drove all the way over to California, visiting everywhere from big cities to ghost towns. You can get the most pleasure from the simplest of things. The happiest night of my life was when we stumbled across a beautiful silvery lake in the middle of nowhere and we spent the night in the truck just staring at the view. I can picture it so clearly; the light of moon made the waves shimmer. The wind was so cold, but we pushed the seats down, snuggled up and just lay there listening to a cassette over and over again, looking up at the stars. They were like diamonds . . .'

Nicole caught herself smiling as the old lady began to hum a strangely familiar melody.

'That was our song,' Mrs Baker explained. '"American Pie".'

'That's lovely. I've never really had the time or the money

to travel,' said Nicole. 'I've only ever been able to afford cheap package holidays.'

'I'm sure that will change one day. But enough about me. Do you mind me asking what made you become a nurse?'

'Well, I was thirteen when my mum was diagnosed with breast cancer. For years she was in and out of hospitals having tests and treatments and operations, and I'd see how hard the nurses worked to make her feel comfortable. And when she lost her battle four years later, I thought it might keep a bit of her alive if I could help other people.'

'And did it work? Because – and tell me if I'm speaking out of place – but you don't seem too happy with your lot.'

Nicole sighed. Eric had once called her 'Clingfilm Face' because she was so transparent and, try as she might, she found it near-impossible to disguise whatever it was she was feeling at that moment.

'It's harder than I thought,' she admitted. 'I don't get along with my charge nurse, I never have any money, and I have more bags than a Prada catalogue under my eyes. It's not the life I thought it'd be.'

Mrs Baker clasped Nicole's hand. 'I hope you don't mind me saying, but I'm sure your mother would've been very proud of you. I know I would be, if you were my daughter.'

Nicole blushed. It had been fourteen years since her mother passed away, and although her father had appeared intermittently throughout her life, it had been five or six years since their paths last crossed. She'd grown to understand that she didn't need a relationship with a name on a birth certificate.

'Is there a young man in your life?' continued Mrs Baker. 'Someone to go home to, who cooks you dinner or massages your tired feet?'

'No, not since my fiancé Pete,' Nicole replied, and for the first time that week, his face appeared from the smoke in her memory. Pete had claimed the drunken girl had thrown herself at him. But Nicole had believed her best friend when he'd told her he'd seen them together at least twice before in the bar. Eventually Eric had been able to take an incriminating photo and WhatsApped it to her.

Pete had begged his childhood sweetheart to stay with him – he claimed the picture was taken from a deceptive angle – and for a while, Nicole had remained. But try as she might to convince herself it was just a bump in their well-travelled road, she knew she could never trust him again. She'd always think the worst if he was 'working overtime' at the estate agent's or out late with the boys – or if he received after-hours texts. So, with Eric's help, she had packed her clothes and moved out of their terraced house into a one-bedroom flat, leaving behind everything that Pete had tainted with his infidelity. He'd gone on to buy her out, but she hadn't made much from the sale.

At first, Nicole had missed him terribly. Then, gradually, it was only their future she'd missed rather than the man himself. A small piece of her crumbled each time she saw a happy couple walking arm in arm in the street or on TV. She'd even changed her route to work so that she no longer passed a bridal shop. And where possible, she avoided the hospital's maternity unit so that she didn't have to witness new parents tenderly cradling their babies, knowing she and Pete would never be like them.

She did still want to be a mother and considered going it alone, but she had never imagined being a single parent like her own mum. She'd once broached the subject of co-parenting a child with Eric in a roundabout, joking kind of way, but he seemed dismissive of the idea of being either a hands-on or hands-off father.

So Nicole vowed that if she hadn't found Mr Right by thirty-five, she would go it alone and explore artificial insemination. While Eric wasn't willing to supply his sperm, he did supply her with company, nights out and a shoulder to cry on.

'I thought maybe you were courting that young man I hear you with sometimes outside,' Mrs Baker continued. 'My ears can't hear speaking voices very well from a distance any more, but I often hear you two giggling together.'

'No, he's my best friend, but we're not each other's type.'

'You're a pretty, intelligent girl with an enormous heart. Any man would be mad not to snap you up.'

A deliberate cough from the doorway interrupted their heart-to-heart. Both turned their heads to see an immaculately dressed woman with a pashmina draped over the shoulders of a cream Burberry patterned top.

'Hello, Mother,' said the woman coldly as she stepped into the room. 'That will be all, nurse,' she added without making eye contact. 'Close the door behind you.'

'Did you take a wrong turn getting here, Bridget?' asked Mrs Baker.

'No, why?'

'Because I've been here almost a fortnight and this is your first appearance. I presumed you'd got lost in the car park.'

Nicole felt uncomfortable as the atmosphere iced over and Bridget glared at her. She gathered her things and stood up, backing awkwardly towards the door. 'I'll see you tomorrow, Mrs Baker,' she waved, then closed the door behind her.

17

Today

Tommy couldn't stop laughing at the sight of Peyk's head hanging upside down from a jagged hole in the ceiling tile. No sooner had he repaired the last one he'd damaged, he had fallen through a second.

'Right, now's the time to tell me what you're doing or I'm leaving you hanging,' he threatened.

'Like I said before – I'm doing something for Ron.'

'So Ron's asked you to fall through every ceiling in his building, has he?'

'Are you going to help me down or not?' Peyk replied crossly as two joints fell from his shirt pocket to the floor below.

'Well, if you stop smoking that crap, you might keep your balance.'

'And if you start smoking this crap, you might chill out and get laid.'

Tommy shook his head and waved goodbye to Peyk and Gabby. He headed back to reception with the sound of Peyk's Dutch obscenities following him down the corridor. They could still be heard when he reached the top of the stairs and spotted Joe's unkempt pal Wayne entering the building, with a mangy dog wearing a rope for a collar.

'How many times do we have to go through this?' asked Tommy.

Without protest, Wayne turned around and shuffled away sheepishly. However, his dog had its own agenda and suddenly bolted past them both and into the hostel. 'Oscar!' he shouted.

Tommy chased after him up into the kitchen, where he found the dog hovering by Ruth's feet, its head bowed, eagerly licking her ankles. A delighted Ruth scratched behind his ear, enjoying the attention from the four-legged stranger.

Five Weeks Earlier – Dog Sanctuary, Victoria, Australia

'Uh-oh, you-know-who is on his way over here,' warned Colleen, straightening her back as she took a break from sweeping the floor.

'Who?' asked Ruth, placing her dirty mop in the plastic bucket. She wiped the sweat from her brow with her shirt sleeve.

'As if you have to ask,' chuckled Colleen, 'Your bloody shadow, who else? Whenever you're here, you know he's never going to be that far behind. We work with enough dogs to know when one's on heat.'

Ruth felt her face redden as a smiling Mickey strolled towards her. Dogs leapt as high as their hind legs would allow in their gated pounds, and poked their snouts through the metal bars when he passed.

Mickey was five foot five with unremarkable features, but

what he lacked in stature and looks he made up for with persistence and optimism. The three eager strays at the end of the leads he was holding strained as they approached Colleen and Ruth. Ruth paid them more attention than their walker.

'And what can we do you for?' asked Colleen.

'I've come to see this beaut,' Mickey began, his big, beaming smile revealing a less-than-proportionate tooth to gum ratio.

'Well, there's a surprise. Don't distract her for too long, we've got the rest of these pounds to scrub before clocking-off time.'

'So how's about it, then?' Mickey directed this at Ruth.

'How's about what?' she replied shyly.

'The same "it" Mickey asks you about every time,' interrupted Colleen.

'Oh, that.'

'Every week I ask you out and every week you tell me you're busy. C'mon, Ruthy, do I have to get down on my hands and knees like a dog and beg?'

At twenty-four, Ruth had yet to accept a date invitation from Mickey – or from any man, for that matter. When she'd relayed to her mother Mickey's interest some months earlier, Denise had trawled through his Facebook profile and offhandedly advised her daughter, 'Neither of you are in a position to be picky.'

Ruth was sure Mickey would make some girl very, very happy, at least at the beginning. Because eventually, he would leave that girl and break her heart, as that's what all men were programmed to do to women. Her mother had reminded her of that enough times over the years.

Even her brother Kevin took pride in showing Ruth the begging texts he'd received from girls he'd duped, slept with and then dumped. And she'd watched enough movies and soap operas to know that relationships rarely worked out like they were supposed to. Men would say all the things you wanted to hear, but in the end they'd grow tired of you and replace you. Ruth wouldn't allow Mickey to do that to her.

There was only one man she was certain would love her as much as she loved him. Zak Stanley's lips would be the first – and only – pair to press against hers.

'Thanks, but I can't,' Ruth told Mickey assertively, then paused. 'I'm seeing someone.'

Mickey and Colleen looked at each other, then at Ruth.

'You don't know him,' she added, then picked up her bucket and walked towards a drain to empty the dirty water.

'Maybe if I had four legs and licked my own balls she'd be interested,' mumbled Mickey before wandering off, while Colleen pondered who on earth Ruth could have fallen for so quietly.

18

Today

On those lazy mornings when his parents had been out and Tommy had promised them he'd spend his time job-hunting, he had instead spent many an hour lying on the sofa flicking through hundreds of Sky channels.

Overtly charming presenters desperately flogging ostentatious must-have watches and clothes that went up to size XXXXL amused him the most, but he'd never lingered on the religious channels until he arrived in LA. Now he'd become fascinated by their broadcasts on the reception desk television. He puzzled at how people could be so gullible as to readily hand their money over to preachers who claimed to be carrying out God's work, when they were blatantly serving their own financial agendas.

Today's focus of attention was an evangelist by the name of Reverend Devereaux; a peculiar-looking man who could rant for twenty minutes without seeming to take a breath. Tommy leaned back on his chair, flicking peanut butter M&Ms into the air and trying to catch them in his mouth. Most bounced off his lips or nose before he finally succeeded.

'Quiet afternoon?' asked Savannah, watching him from the

doorway. Surprised, Tommy fell from his seat and quickly scrambled back to his feet, to her amusement.

'It's dead. Everyone's sodded off to the beach or the pool except yours truly. I'm here until dinner. How's your day been?'

'Dull, apart from a few Bunker Hill financiers putting their lunch money between my breasts instead of in their kids' college fund. Am I still sleeping alone?'

'Yep, the room's all yours.'

Savannah approached Tommy, leaned over the counter and gave him a peck on the cheek. She felt comfortable and unthreatened by him; they'd talk with ease about how they'd just spent their day, but they never went into detail about their pasts. Sometimes when Savannah returned from work in the early hours and Tommy was working a shift, they'd keep each other company watching old black-and-white films before she'd invariably fall asleep. Neither enjoyed spending time alone, and neither told the other why.

On several occasions, Savannah had considered confessing that on the night of his arrival she had been the one who came within two book chapters of blowing a hole through Tommy's spine. But then she would have felt obliged to reveal why she possessed a weapon and what she was really hiding from in Los Angeles, and those were secrets she'd only shared with one other person under that roof. So she decided against unburdening herself, as it would likely damage their friendship and serve no purpose to either of them.

'Where's your girlfriend today?'

'Nicole's not my girlfriend,' he replied, absent-mindedly tugging at the bandage on his hand. 'And I haven't seen her yet.'

'Well, there's always tonight . . .' Savannah's voice trailed off as she recognized a familiar voice coming from the television, preaching about sinners and Satan. A shiver ran through her and she collected herself before she spoke. 'Why are you watching this?' she asked.

'There's something quite . . . hypnotic about this guy. Have you seen him before?'

Savannah's eyes narrowed. He's not hypnotic, she thought, he's a dangerous, sadistic sonofabitch.

Seven Months Earlier: Montgomery, Alabama

'Get me a towel and a change of clothes,' Reverend Devereaux snapped at a teenage boy.

The terrified lad grabbed two white cotton face towels from the table in the Reverend's dressing room and began to dab at his employer's clothes. Meanwhile the Reverend took a handful of wet wipes from a packet and rubbed his jowls and hands.

'Why do you allow them on stage if you don't like touching them?' asked Pastor Jackson, flicking through his employer's emails on a cell phone.

'Because the blacks are where the money's at,' the Reverend replied with disdain. 'All those Ella Mae Joneses sitting in front of their televisions in the projects are praying for their criminal sons to see the error of their ways. And to ease their consciences about parental failure, they donate money to my ministry. Over the years all those dollars add up. So if I have to touch them to convince them their cash is worth my prayers, then I'm willing to make that sacrifice. But I don't have to like it and I ain't gonna have their smell on me a second longer than I need to.'

'I think you're very brave,' the Reverend's wife said, and kissed his forehead. A strand of curly dark hair fell from his shoulder and landed on the hem of her Diane von Furstenberg skirt. She brushed it to the carpet with the tip of her fingernail, then cleansed her hands using a pocket-sized bottle of antibacterial gel.

Reverend Devereaux took a swig from a bottle of chilled sparkling water, his eyes darting towards Savannah and her younger sister Roseanna, sitting quietly side by side on a sofa.

'And next week I expect to get a little more support from my kin,' he added.

'I'm here, aren't I?' Savannah replied, making little effort to disguise that she'd rather be anywhere else.

'When one of the dozen television cameras pans across the audience to focus on my "beloved" family, I expect my viewers to see them caught up in the joy I'm bringing,' he continued, 'not sitting there hooked to their phones or screwing up their faces as if skunks have crawled up their asses. Do you understand me?'

Savannah and Roseanna nodded.

'Good. Now bring me good news from the world of ticket receipts, Pastor Jackson. Tell me how blessed we have been this evening.'

His head of finances and right-hand man clicked on the latest email to reach his phone. 'Preliminary numbers suggest around the $75,000 mark so far from the folks at home, and they're still counting donations from the collection plates. But with twelve thousand seats sold the arena was full to capacity, so that's going to be a lot of donations for the church.'

'Good, good,' said the Reverend. 'You may all leave now. I need to decompress.'

He closed the door after his team left and turned to his wife. 'The Lord was smiling on us tonight, wasn't he?' she said.

'He sure was,' the Reverend replied. 'And if he keeps smiling, it looks as if we'll buy that estate by the lake just in time for summer.'

'I hate him, I absolutely hate him,' Savannah whispered.

The heat from the Starbucks coffee mug began to burn her hands as she clasped it tightly, but she kept them in place. Physical pain helped to block out the self-loathing and frustration she felt each time she failed to stand up to her father and his racism.

After each Sunday morning and Wednesday evening wasted at his weekly telecasts, Savannah spent the rest of the day begrudging the genes she shared with a man who so eagerly misled the vulnerable. She felt a permanent unease about people who could barely afford to eat regularly, yet saved up their cash and spent twenty-five dollars a ticket to witness one of his sermons in person.

That afternoon, Savannah kept recalling the shy little black girl with the stammer and the terror that had spread across her face as the fat white man shouted at her and tried to withdraw imaginary demons from her young body. There was nothing demonic inside her; she was made of love and trust, raised by parents who believed in their hearts that they were doing what was best for her. The Reverend was not God's vessel on Earth like he claimed; he was a charlatan who profited from blind faith.

Savannah wondered if she was the only audience member to have noticed the child wetting herself when Reverend

Devereaux gripped her face. She was convinced the Reverend had seen it too and got a kick out of it. Then Savannah remembered later, backstage, passing the crippled woman who'd taken baby steps in front of the audience earlier that day. Moments later and out of view, she was back in her wheelchair, praying for the pain in her knees to subside.

Savannah often chastised herself for remaining under the Reverend's roof and accepting his soiled dollars. As a beneficiary, she felt complicit, and it sickened her.

'Baby, you just have to hold on for another year and then we'll be able to get somewhere of our own,' reassured Michael from his seat opposite her. He placed his hands upon hers. 'Let him pay for your college fees, and once you graduate I'll put in for a transfer and we can move to New York like we planned.'

'It's not my dad who's paying for all this, is it though?' she reasoned. 'It's his congregation, it's the collection plate he drains so we can live in a twenty-room mansion, so I can drive a Mercedes, go to dance classes, buy clothes, shoot guns at the rifle range and have the best education other people's money can buy.'

'But you'll make it up to those folks once you leave college,' Michael continued. 'Do some volunteer work, work full time for a charity . . . whatever you need to earn yourself some good karma. And you're doing this for us, not just for yourself.'

Savannah knew what Michael said made sense. If she were to storm out of the family home on principle to go it alone, he too would suffer from the loss of her generous allowance, which also helped her to pay for his college tuition. Michael abhorred his inability to pay his own way, but he knew he was benefiting for the greater good.

'I can't afford to put myself through med school on my own or I'd be paying off loans until I retired,' he reminded her. 'But once I'm qualified, I'm going to work in the public sector. I'm going to help you give back what your daddy has taken away.'

All Savannah had to do was offer an occasional half-smile in front of her parents and the cameras for a little while longer, and then she'd be free to start living her life as she should, with Michael. And she couldn't wait. Keeping a boyfriend secret from her family for almost three years had been difficult.

She was also ashamed that for a long time, she had shared her parents' abhorrent views. It was only upon meeting fellow students with diverse ethnic backgrounds during her first college semester that she'd quickly come to understand how wrong her family was. Savannah had no choice but to learn to lie to her parents in order to spend time with Michael. She would tell them she was seeing friends, attending non-existent college parties, social mixers and extracurricular college classes, when she was actually with him. But as their studies approached the final furlong, there was a light at the end of the tunnel. Soon she would be free to live her most authentic life, the one she so often dreamed of.

'Okay, I know, you're right,' she admitted. 'It's just tough sometimes.'

Michael clasped her hands gently. 'I know, baby, I know. But you're doing real good. And once you leave that house forever, think of the look on that racist's face when he realizes his daughter's boyfriend is a black guy.'

Savannah grinned and leaned over the table to plant a kiss on his lips. Neither of them noticed that her father's most trusted employee, Pastor Jackson, had stopped in his tracks outside the coffee shop and was staring in at them, wondering whether his eyes were deceiving him.

19

Today

'Hey, buddy, how's it going?'

Tommy looked up from the TV set to find two men standing before him – one tanned, one the colour of a boiling lobster, and both unshaven and sweating. Tommy wasn't sure if they were drunk, or friends of narcotics enthusiast Joe.

'Can I help you?' he asked curtly.

'Actually, we're here to help you,' replied Matty, and flashed him a big, crooked grin.

Tommy raised an unconvinced eyebrow. By sight alone, he knew their type, because every hostel he'd ever stayed in had had them. They were the loudest; the most opinionated; the funniest; the effortlessly confident; the biggest boasters; the ones who were first to laugh at themselves; who'd travelled further and longer than you and experienced more than you. And they were always the most popular. They were everything in a traveller that Tommy disliked because they were everything he didn't have the confidence to be. And he didn't want them under his roof.

'By special delivery from Ireland, we've brought to you the life and soul your hostel needs, in two rather handsome packages, if I might be so bold. I'm Matty, and my friend here is Declan.'

Tommy remained deadpan. Already, their presumption that the hostel could not function without their presence was making his hackles rise.

'My esteemed pal and I need shelter from the elements,' Declan persevered.

'It's thirty degrees outside,' Tommy replied.

'Precisely,' added Matty. 'We need a roof over our heads to cool down.'

'The trouble is, we have a wee cash flow problem,' added Declan. 'We're waiting for some euros to be transferred from home, but we can settle up with you at the end of the week if you can offer us a couple of beds?'

'Does it say "homeless shelter" outside?' asked Tommy. 'We're not a charity, so you'll have to sleep on the beach till you sort out your *cash flow*.'

'Ah, but that's illegal,' replied Declan, still smiling.

'That's not my problem.'

'That's not very Christian of you,' added Declan, tilting his head towards Reverend Devereaux's television broadcast, 'and I can see you're a man of faith.'

'The telly only gets three stations.'

'Okay, what if we made a donation in the form of these?' asked Matty. He and Declan unclipped their backpacks and removed a PS5 and an Xbox they'd taken as souvenirs from a boxcar. They smiled hopefully at Tommy.

'So let me get this right. You have no money, but you want to pay for a bed with stolen electronics? I don't think so.'

'Come on, man, have you got no heart for a neighbouring countryman? You look as if you might have some Irish in you.

Am I right?' pleaded Matty. They were used to talking people around to their way of thinking.

'No. Now it was nice to meet you, but goodbye,' replied Tommy, smiling to himself.

'Why are you being such a fecking bellend?' snapped Declan, banging his fist on the counter just as Ron appeared from his office.

'Is there a problem, Timmy?' he asked gruffly.

'It's Tommy, and no, there's no problem – these gentlemen are trying to pay for a room with stolen goods.'

Ron scanned the boxed-up gaming consoles on the desk, before eyeing Matty and Declan up and down.

'Put them in room four,' he said.

'But these consoles have obviously been nicked.'

Ron scooped both boxes into his arms and retreated to his back-room office. 'Can you boys cook?' he asked.

'We certainly can, sir,' replied Matty.

'Then you can organize the evening meals,' Ron added before closing the door behind him, leaving Tommy and his new guests alone.

'We'll have two keys, please, Timmy,' added Declan with a mischievous grin. 'And bring our bags to our room, there's a good lad.'

20

34.02419N was the first line of numbers the needle began to etch into his skin in black ink.

Once the tattoo artist finished, he dabbed blood and excess colour from between the seventh and eighth of Jake's ribs with a tissue. Then he continued with the next row – 118.4814W. Jake had chosen a simple Arial font, the same as the other twenty-two rows of numbers that preceded it and that stretched from just under his armpit and down towards his hip bone.

The tattooist cleaned Jake up and passed him a mirror. Jake appeared satisfied as he examined the latest numbers in his collection. Once a thin plastic sheet had been taped to his side to protect his body art, Jake paid his forty-five dollars for the work, then swept his long, chestnut-brown hair into a ponytail, threw his battered rucksack over his back and continued his journey along the Venice Beach boardwalk.

'Remember who you are, not who you were,' he repeated over and over in his head as he walked.

21

As the morning progressed, Tommy's light began to dim to a darkness that would often reach his world without warning or fanfare.

Matty and Declan's appearance hadn't helped his mood, but they weren't the root cause of it. He didn't know what had encouraged the clouds to blow in late that day; all he knew was that each time they appeared, he'd get the sudden urge to break from the norm of surrounding himself with others and ensconce himself in silent contemplation.

He made no effort to placate a grouchy Gabby when she arrived for her shift and took him to task for not helping her to rescue Peyk from the ceiling the previous day. Instead, he made his way towards his empty dormitory and curled up on his bunk bed. After a few moments he reached into the rucksack under the frame and removed a small leather pouch, from which he poured four memory cards into his bandaged hand. Three of them he'd sometimes slot into his digital camcorder to watch and remind himself of how far he'd come with his new life as a backpacker.

But the other he could still not bring himself to play. He kept it in the centre of his palm and stared at it, surprised that something so small could frighten him so much.

Two Years Earlier: Northampton, England

Tommy wasn't sure how long he'd remained unconscious in the back of his brothers' car before he came to.

His eyelids flickered as he struggled to acquaint himself with his whereabouts, before becoming distracted by an abstract blurry figure peering through a window at him then disappearing out of view.

As his vision slowly returned, Tommy's forehead throbbed like the time Daniel had accidentally smacked him full-force with a cricket ball. And as he turned his head in the direction of a sudden noise, a shooting pain ripped through his left shoulder and up into his neck.

Tommy knew his world was askew but through his fog, he couldn't fathom out how or why it had become this way. Now, through a cracked window, he could see an unfamiliar woman and a second man, and he didn't know why he was watching them from a peculiar angle. He felt strangely calm, as if he were caught in that cosy period just before falling asleep, when he'd already started to dream.

Suddenly the gentle thumping on the window became a louder, more urgent banging and he thought he heard someone say something like: 'One in the back . . . moving.'

Then, like the sudden force of the impact of the shadow that had ripped into their car, Tommy remembered exactly what had happened. Fear and panic rose in tandem as he twisted his aching head from side to side, absorbing the carnage Adam and Daniel's car had become.

He couldn't understand why he was alone. From where he sat, the driver's seat was empty, with a twisted gear stick protruding at a right angle. The door had been struck so hard that it jutted inwards, towards the passenger seat. Tommy accepted the shadow he'd seen through his camcorder must have been the other vehicle that had collided with them and pushed their car onto its side. And judging by the state of the internal and external fittings, it had been a serious smash. But where were his brothers? Why would they have left him there without trying to help him escape?

'Adam!' he cried. 'Dan?'

'Don't move,' came Adam's voice from outside.

Thank God, he's all right, Tommy thought, and for a moment his alarm began to subside. He patted down his arms and legs; only his foot looked wrongly placed. It was pointing at an awkward angle, but it didn't hurt as much as his neck. He reached for the seat belt buckle and clicked the release button; only after several attempts did it come loose. He grabbed at the other seat belt, hoping to use it as leverage and haul himself towards the window. However, a bar of metal wedged across the glass prevented his release.

His eyes darted around the car, desperately trying to find another route to freedom. He noticed the windscreen had shattered but the roof had been pushed down, leaving a gap only a child could squeeze through.

It was at that moment he caught a glimpse of the front passenger seat. At first, his brain couldn't deconstruct what lay twisted on it – heaps of clothes, stained by a red liquid and what resembled sinew and bones jutting out in strange positions. Then, with a similar impact to the crash itself, the realization struck him hard and suddenly.

His brothers' bodies shared the seat, melded together with torn flesh and metal like Siamese twins. Tommy stared at them in horror, unable to work out who was who. One of their heads was now concave, while the other's was only held in place by a visible sliver of bone. Tommy couldn't make sense of it; he would have sworn on a stack of Bibles he'd just heard Adam's voice outside. But here lay Adam with Daniel, tangled together with no pulse between them. He remembered Adam had unclipped his seat belt to reach for Tommy's phone seconds before the moment of impact. Now he and Daniel had left the world as they had entered it: together.

Sheer terror flooded Tommy. He had to get out of the car and he had to get out *right now*. He began screaming at the people outside for help, but no sound came from his throat. He kicked and pulled at the back seats to smash the rear window, but it just made the bones in his foot snap.

'Help me,' he said quietly, his voice gradually returning. 'Help me, please help me.'

'There's an ambulance and a fire engine on its way, son,' came a voice, and Tommy saw that a small crowd had gathered. He felt like a terrified circus animal surrounded by baying crowds and swore he could see a camera flash. Tommy gradually became more and more numb until he curled himself up into a tight ball, where he remained for the longest hour of his life.

Today

Tommy continued staring at the memory card in his hand – the final footage he'd taken of his brothers.

He was afraid that watching it would bring back more of the day than the fragments he remembered and that he had run so many miles to escape. He was afraid to see Adam and

Daniel's faces again; to be reminded of that awful sound of pounding metal against metal; metal against tarmac; shattering glass and the helpless feeling of being trapped inside that tomb.

Tommy knew that if he could gather the courage to insert the card and press play, then maybe, just maybe, he could come to terms with what had happened that day. But the risk that it would make him feel even lousier than he already did was one he wasn't ready to take.

The police officer who came to the family house and handed back his camcorder had explained that it had stopped filming seconds after the impact, but offered investigators little more information than the broken traffic cameras mounted above the junction. They had their suspicions as to the identity of the driver of the stolen car that had collided with them, but it was hard to prove.

Now Tommy was becoming increasingly overwhelmed by the need to find a distraction from his dark place. He remembered it was his turn to pick up supplies for the hostel kitchen from the cash and carry, and he needed to borrow Ron's car to do so. So he climbed out of bed, changed into his joggers and made his way to Ron's office behind reception.

On his approach he heard Ron's voice coming loudly from the office. Tommy stopped in his tracks to eavesdrop. Ron was arguing about something but it was too muffled to decipher precisely what. Tommy realized the longest conversation they'd shared had been on the first night he'd appeared on the hostel's doorstep. His memories were still a little fuzzy, but he recalled hearing a loud crack and then feeling something shove him forward before his head smashed against the sidewalk. Later, Ron had told him he'd been shot, but fortunately the bullet had stopped short of his flesh. Instead of being upset about his second brush with death, Tommy had felt strangely accepting of the news. He wondered how many more times he'd need to stare death in the face before it took him once and for all.

Ron had offered him a bed and work at the hostel in the hope that Tommy wouldn't report the incident to the police. The last thing Ron needed was for anyone to bring unnecessary attention to a hostel that walked a fine legal line when it came to building code regulations, underage drinking, drugs and a whole host of other dubious activities. Tommy had agreed, and the only question he'd asked was about the identity of the woman's voice he'd heard as he came to. He couldn't remember anything else about her, even her accent or what she'd said. Only her presence. Ron acknowledged someone had helped to pull Tommy inside, but said it was a passing stranger. However, Tommy was left with the impression Ron wasn't being entirely honest with him.

He was returned to the present by Ron raising his voice further. 'If I had it, I'd give it to you!' This time his voice was clear, as was the hurling of an object against a wall.

Tommy didn't hang around to check on Ron's welfare, and he was sure now wouldn't be the time to ask to use his car. Instead, he made his way to the lounge. His mood finally lifted when the first face he saw was a familiar and friendly one.

22

Nicole turned left at the traffic lights off Ventura Boulevard before pulling her truck into the car park of a collection of medium-sized retail outlets.

'Thanks for helping me out,' began Tommy as they grabbed a shopping cart and walked through the open sliding doors and into the cash and carry. 'Where did you tell Eric you were going?'

'I said we were going to get the tyre checked out as it looked a little flat after we hit the kerb when we arrived.'

Tommy liked that she'd lied for him. 'I don't think he likes me very much, does he?'

'He's just a little overprotective. I don't have the greatest record with men and he doesn't want me to get hurt.'

'And he thinks I'll hurt you?'

'You're presuming I'd allow you close enough for that to happen! But no, he thinks any man has the potential to hurt me.'

'Apart from him, right?'

'Probably.'

'You know there's a fine line between a best mate who has your back and someone who's trying to control you.'

Nicole felt her hackles rise. 'Yes, I'm aware of that, but I'm a big girl, Tommy. I can look after myself.'

But quietly, she had wondered if Eric was doing just as Tommy suggested. During their great American adventure, she'd come to notice he had a way of coming between her and any fellow traveller who paid her even the slightest bit of attention. She also knew that if it continued, she might need to have a quiet, awkward word with him.

Earlier that afternoon, when she and Eric had returned to the hostel from the beach with still no idea of where they should travel to next, she had bumped into Tommy in the lounge while Eric was showering in their dorm. He'd asked her to drive him to get hostel food supplies, but as Nicole didn't have a licence, she'd explained the pick-up truck was insured for any driver and offered to accompany him if he got behind the wheel. Nicole knew from the previous night's warning that Eric wouldn't have approved of her and Tommy spending time together without him. But he wouldn't have wanted to tag along either, and while she hated dishonesty, it seemed like holding back the truth was the only real choice.

There was something about Tommy that she was drawn to, even after such a short time. He possessed an innocence and naivety that she appreciated, and the older she became, the less often she found such qualities in men her own age.

On their way to buy supplies, she'd asked him to continue the story he'd begun the night before. As he quietly told her more about the car accident that had killed his brothers, she instinctively felt closer to him.

His honesty made her want to reciprocate and explain why she was in America, but she felt that by revealing that, she would be going against Eric's wishes. And she wasn't prepared to do that.

23

Matty and Declan aborted an attempt to convince two women in the McDonald's queue to treat them to lunch.

As visually appealing as the girls were, they were mainly just a means to an end – their marks could afford food, and the boys were broke and hungry. But when it became clear the women couldn't understand their Irish accents, Tommy and Declan admitted defeat and continued their walk along the boulevard. That morning they'd already filled themselves up on other hostellers' boxes of cereal in the kitchen, but their stomachs were rumbling again.

'How much cash have we got left?' asked Matty.

Declan opened his wallet and pulled out some low-denomination bills and scraps of paper.

'We have the grand total of eleven dollars, plus five euros, and coupons for ninety cents off a Wendy's salad or a free bag of potato chips if we spend more than ten dollars at Subway.'

'Feck.'

As Matty replaced the money in his wallet, a newspaper cutting fell to the floor. Declan picked it up.

'What are you doing keeping this? You need to throw it away,' snapped Declan.

'It's a reminder.'

'It's a fifteen-year stretch behind bars if anyone recognizes us.'

24

Tommy parked Nicole's truck in the multi-storey opposite the hostel.

He'd already dropped her and the industrial-sized bags of food in the alley behind the building, away from Eric's beady eye. And as she helped him carry them up the stairs and into the kitchen, she rehearsed a story about why she had been away for so long, blaming rush-hour traffic.

'Thanks again,' said Tommy, unpacking the shopping and placing it onto shelves in cupboards with missing doors and handles.

'You're welcome.'

'So I'll see you later, then, I guess?'

'I guess.'

They stood face to face like nervous teenagers at a school dance, unsure of what to do next. Tommy took a silent breath, slowly tilted his head and moved his mouth towards Nicole's. But just as she closed her eyes, they were interrupted by a resounding bang from the corridor. They hurried towards the source of the commotion and found a trembling Peyk. By his side lay electrical wires leading out of a smoking plug socket. He smelled like burning cannabis and toast, Nicole thought.

She checked there was no danger of electrocution before placing him in the recovery position and assessing the damage.

Once it was clear he wasn't seriously hurt, she beckoned Tommy over to help him to his feet.

'Let's get you back to your room,' she said. 'Between you and Tommy, I should get paid for being the hostel's care worker.'

Although concerned for his friend, Tommy cursed Peyk's appalling timing.

25

Ruth removed an orange dress from her suitcase and laid it neatly across the dormitory floor.

She began to press out the creases with her travel iron, but to little effect. Frustrated, she pressed harder – and then the door behind her opened, knocking her off balance.

'Oh crap – sorry,' apologized Nicole, holding out a hand to help Ruth back up.

'No worries,' replied Ruth.

'Ooh, Zak Stanley, you are gorgeous,' continued Nicole as she picked up a magazine cutting stuck to the hem of the dress and handed it back to an embarrassed Ruth.

'You think so?'

'Of course! Did you see him in that film *Baby Baby*?'

'About fifteen times!'

'That bit when he says, *I know this is the first time we've met . . .*'

'*. . . But I don't ever want to lose sight of you again!*' finished Ruth. 'It makes me cry every time.'

'I know what you mean. And about five minutes before he's run over by that car in *Forever Us,* I always turn Netflix off so that in my head, that's where the film ends and he and Margot Robbie live happily ever after.'

One minute spent talking to Nicole was the longest

conversation Ruth had had with anyone during her six days in America. She opened her mouth to continue, but closed it again when she recalled her mother's reaction on hearing why she was going to LA. Ruth didn't want to hear the same words from somebody else. But Nicole seemed nice, she thought. Maybe she could trust her?

'Are you busy?' Ruth asked with a whisper, even though there was nobody else in the room.

'Not really, what's up?'

'Can you keep a secret?'

I'm an expert in them, thought Nicole. 'Sure.'

Ruth rifled around in her suitcase until she found an envelope with a piece of white A4 paper inside and handed it to Nicole. Nicole unfolded it and began to read. Halfway through, she gasped. Her eyes opened wide as she looked up at Ruth.

'Oh. My. God. Is this for real?'

Three Weeks Earlier: Victoria, Australia

Bare-breasted, rake-thin women with long blonde hair extensions tumbling down their backs posed in sexy positions on the posters behind Ruth.

For a long time she'd avoided going into her brother's bedroom, as it felt like a dozen pairs of beautiful strangers' eyes were laughing at her sturdy frame. But since Zak Stanley had come into her life, everything was different. There was only one opinion that mattered, and it belonged to Zak. He could see beyond a plastic façade; he'd told that interviewer on YouTube he was looking for an ordinary girl. And Ruth was nothing if not ordinary, as her mother and brother frequently reminded her.

She'd waited for Kevin to leave the house for the second of his twice-daily gym pilgrimages before she crept into his room. He was fiercely protective of his iPad. But after she'd spilled a milkshake over her own a fortnight earlier, rendering it useless, she had also used up the data allowance on her mobile phone for the rest of the month. Therefore, if she wanted to get her fix of Zak, she would have to improvise. And as long as Ruth deleted the browsing history after each session, Kevin wouldn't be any the wiser.

Ruth sifted through her emails. She hadn't been online for almost a week, and four new messages were waiting in her inbox – three more than she usually received. One was from Facebook, informing her she had a new friend request. Out of curiosity, she clicked on it and realized it was from someone writing in a foreign language she didn't understand, but she accepted it anyway, taking her total number into double figures. The other emails were newsletters from online forums she'd joined like 'Zak Stanley Web Ring', 'Circle of Zak' and 'Zak's World'. She scanned them and then added the most recent photos to her Pinterest board.

Satisfied with her latest harvest, she was about to log off when she noticed a message hidden in the junk folder. She clicked on it to read the subject heading: 'Official Zak Stanley Fan Club – You're A Winner.'

Curious, she clicked on a link, and an audio file began to play as a computerized voice spoke. *'Congratulations, Ruth Donovan, you have been chosen by the Official Zak Stanley Fan Club as this month's winner of our Meet Zak competition. On June 4, you will accompany Zak for a private lunch for two in Los Angeles. Please reply to this email to confirm your attendance and we will furnish you with an address and further details.'*

Then a GIF of Zak's smiling face appeared on the screen. Ruth replayed the message five times until the news sank in – she'd won the online competition she'd entered last week. Her heart began to beat so fast that it made her body tremble.

'Mum!' she screamed. 'Mum! *Mum!*'

'What?' her mother snapped from another room.

'Come here!'

Denise tutted and reluctantly made her way towards her daughter's excited voice. 'What are you doing in here? Kevin's going to—'

'Read this!'

Denise removed her glasses from her tracksuit pocket and squinted at the computer screen.

'I'm going to meet Zak!' squealed Ruth. 'I'm going to meet him!'

Her mother removed her glasses, raised her eyebrows and let out a long breath. 'Are you sure it's not a fake?' she asked.

'No, look, it's got the logo and address of his management copy in the signature. And I did enter that competition.'

'Well, I guess you didn't have to send a photo to win,' Denise mumbled rhetorically, and left her daughter to celebrate alone.

Today

'I'm so jealous,' admitted Nicole. 'You're a lucky girl!'

'I can't believe it,' said Ruth. 'I'm going to take my scrapbooks to show him what a big fan I am.'

'Maybe that's not the best idea? You don't want him to think you're an obsessive fan.'

'Oh, right,' replied Ruth, who hadn't considered that. 'How about this, then?'

She went back into the suitcase and pulled out a half-completed jumper she'd been knitting, which hung by the needles. 'It's not finished yet, but see? It's Zak's face.'

Nicole was unsure how to react to the crude likeness – Zak's eyes were looking in slightly different directions, and he had an unnaturally wide mouth that made him look a bit like The Joker. But she didn't want to hurt Ruth's feelings.

'I'm sure he'll love it,' she said, and a huge grin spread across Ruth's face.

26

Day Three

Tommy examined the crusts framing two slices of white bread and used his knife to chip away circles of blue mould.

He reached for a variety pack of store-brand cornflakes, pulled open the plastic packing and poured them between the slices to make a sandwich. It tasted just as he guessed it might: like two things that can sit together comfortably on the same table but shouldn't be combined into one dish. But one cooked meal a night courtesy of the hostel didn't provide him with enough fuel to keep going throughout the day. He wondered how supermodels managed it.

'Living the high life, eh, Tommy-boy?' began Peyk, as he wandered in with Savannah and slouched across the table. There were bandages wrapped around his wrists, covering the burned skin where he'd electrocuted himself.

'Prisoners eat better than I do,' Tommy replied, taking another mouthful of his arid snack. 'I need to find a job. My work here only covers bed and board. If I don't make money soon, I'll be going home before the summer's out.'

'Don't say that, sweetie,' said Savannah. 'I can lend you a few bucks if you need it?'

'Thanks, Sav, but I need some regular work.'

'I know someone who might be able to help you,' offered Peyk.

Tommy eyed him suspiciously. 'This isn't going to be something dodgy that'll get me arrested, is it?'

'Trust your Uncle Peyk, Tommy-boy. This job has your name written all over it.'

27

As a rule, Ruth and mirrors were not a compatible match.

It wasn't that she deceived herself into believing she was movie-star beautiful and only became disillusioned by the truth once she saw her reflection. It was because mirrors created an empty feeling inside her when she saw what everyone else did. By avoiding them, she could pretend she was normal.

But tonight was an exception.

Instead of throwing on a pair of joggers and a baggy t-shirt like she did most days, Ruth spent the morning rigorously working on her outfit, shaving her legs, straightening her hair, plucking her eyebrows and even slapping on make-up for the first time that year. She was so delighted with the results that she didn't register the sniggers greeting her when she entered the hostel lounge to find Nicole.

Eric was the first to notice her. His eyes worked their way up from toes that reminded him of cocktail sausages stuffed into too-small high-heeled shoes, to red tights, an orange pinafore dress and a green shawl. There was a plastic lily tucked behind her ear.

'What the actual fuck?' he mouthed at Nicole, who was equally taken aback but pinched his forearm before he vocalized his thoughts.

'Wow, Ruth, look at you!' began Nicole supportively, and

glared around the room to stop the handful of other hostellers from laughing.

'It's a designer dress,' Ruth said with pride.

'By who – Picasso?' asked Eric.

'No, I got it real cheap in a charity shop,' replied Ruth.

'You look beautiful,' continued Nicole.

'She looks like a traffic light,' whispered Eric. Nicole pinched him harder.

She stood up to give Ruth a hug. 'Go and have a fantastic time. And tell me all about it when you get back.'

Ruth swung an unsuitably large handbag over her shoulder, clipping Tommy's face as he entered the lounge.

'Where's she heading dressed like that?' asked Tommy.

'For disappointment,' replied Eric, and moved his arm swiftly to avoid Nicole's next pinch.

It took forty-five minutes for Ruth to traipse from Venice Beach to the Viceroy Hotel in Santa Monica.

At 1.30 p.m. the sun was at its harshest, and she struggled with the rising heat as she walked along the boardwalk in heels that took twice as much effort as her sneakers. Occasionally she had to stop and rub her ankles where the skin was beginning to chafe. She took a paper tissue from her handbag and mopped her wet brow, but as she put it back, one of the false fingernails she'd attached with Pritt Stick caught the clasp and fell somewhere in the sand. She hoped Zak wouldn't notice its absence.

Ruth made her way up a slope towards Ocean Avenue and spotted the hotel. Inside, the air conditioning was like manna from heaven. Muffled music could be heard from behind the closed doors of the restaurant as a pianist played a classical piece she didn't recognize. She removed an email printout from her handbag and re-read it.

Sender: Zakstanleyfanclub@hotmail.au

Dear Ruth,

Just to confirm, Zak Stanley will meet you for lunch at two p.m. at Sugar Palm Ocean Avenue in the Viceroy Hotel, Santa Monica. A table has been booked in your name and Zak will be there to welcome you. He requests no photographs be taken during your meal. Zak looks forward to meeting you.

Yours,
Paul Mollegh, manager

Ruth clutched the email to her chest and beamed, unaware the sweat from her dress had absorbed the paper's ink and left a light stain. She steeled herself, took deep, nervous breaths and strode towards the dining room's entrance.

The *maître d'*, accustomed to receiving guests of a certain calibre at Santa Monica's most prestigious of eateries, consulted a list of bookings and was surprised to find Ruth's name.

'You appear to be the first of your party to arrive, madam,' he said in a hybrid French/American accent.

'Oh, okay,' Ruth replied, checking her watch and realizing she was a quarter of an hour early. 'I'm having lunch with Zak Stanley.' Her eyes lit up as she showed him the email. 'He's a movie star!'

'How lovely for you,' he replied, wondering if the movie

star he'd seated two nights earlier was now involved in charity work.

He led her to a private dining booth overlooking the ocean, and Ruth took her seat. When she thought nobody was looking, she used an embossed napkin to mop her armpits. Meanwhile, silent, derisive chuckles came from the waiters, tipped off by the *maître d'*, rubbernecking from the kitchen's porthole window.

A hundred times Ruth had attempted to rehearse what she'd say when Zak arrived, but right then, right there, her mind was a blank. She wanted to tell him she'd seen every one of the ten films he'd made since his transition from teen actor to Hollywood star. She wanted to explain how she'd used his picture from *About the Two of Us* as her iPad screen-saver before she damaged it. She wanted him to know that she loved him for who he was and not because of his fame or his money. And that, if given a chance, she wanted them to be friends. In reality, of course, she wanted far more; but that would happen in due time, she told herself.

Ruth practised her smile over and over again, readjusted her dress, ordered a Diet Coke, and waited.

28

'Hotdog and a lemonade, just one dollar,' began Tommy, talking through a white plastic megaphone.

He stood self-consciously on an upturned plastic box by the boardwalk as passing tourists stared at him and the mobile food trailer behind him. From inside, he could hear faint groaning; José, the heavily tattooed and recently paroled chef, was watching pornographic video clips on his phone.

'Louder, I need you to be louder,' barked Mr Georgiou in his thick Cypriot accent. He waved his short, stubby arms from the side of his circular frame.

'Hotdog and a lemonade, just one dollar,' Tommy repeated, more forcefully. Quietly he cursed Peyk for getting him a trial on a fast-food stand, despite his desperation to find work.

'No, no, no! Project your voice, and do the English accent more. We're not selling fast food; we're selling a lifestyle.'

You're selling offal in a bap, thought Tommy, and wondered what his brothers would have thought if they could have seen how low he'd stooped to make a living.

'Hotdog and a lemonade, just one dollar!' he yelled, creating loud, grating microphone feedback.

'Yes!' said Mr Georgiou triumphantly. 'Your costume is round the back.'

Tommy frowned. 'Costume?'

Any remaining shred of Tommy's dignity evaporated when, a short while later, he mounted his box enclosed in a man-sized hotdog costume complete with mustard-coloured hat and bun-shaped booties.

'Hotdog and a lemonade, just one dollar,' he muttered, defeated so soon.

'Louder!' bellowed Mr Georgiou from behind him.

The only words Tommy heard from Matty and Declan as they passed by were 'fecking' and 'eejit' as they doubled up in laughter.

29

Ruth waited.

And waited.

And then waited some more.

When Zak was twenty minutes late, she assumed traffic was to blame. When her watch read 2.45 p.m. she began nibbling at the skin around her thumbs and told herself Zak was probably struggling to find a parking space.

Even after an hour and a half, Ruth was still convinced Zak wouldn't let her down. But by 4.20 p.m., the once-snooty waiters were beginning to gaze at her sympathetically as she became the last remaining lunchtime customer in the restaurant.

'May I get you anything else, madam?' the *maître d'* asked as Ruth eventually rose to her feet.

'No, thank you,' she replied, her voice trembling. She removed a $20 bill from her purse to pay for her drinks, but the *maître d'* shook his head and gave her her money back, holding her hand for a moment.

Ruth's face began to crumple so she took a deep breath, straightened the hem of her pinafore, and dropped her head to hide the tears pooling in her eyes.

Even as she made her way slowly along the road in the direction of the hostel, she kept turning her head, hoping to spot a limousine dropping Zak off outside the hotel. She imagined him holding a bunch of colourful flowers in his hand, flustered and hugely apologetic for having kept her waiting. But no such moment arrived. And eventually, when she turned a corner and the hotel was no longer in view, she finally accepted he wasn't coming.

30

As night fell, the snoring emanating from the bunk above Tommy's bed went on for what felt like an eternity.

He had no problem falling asleep to the sound of his roommates chatting, opening and closing doors or using the bathroom. But the constant repetition of the same sound, like a ticking clock or a snorer, would be all he could focus on and left him at the end of his tether.

Tommy could have moved into a private room weeks earlier to avoid nights like this. But he chose the company of strangers over complete solitude because silent nights were no friend of his. They allowed him too much time to reflect on his life, and more specifically, the last two years. And he'd had enough silence to last him a lifetime.

Two Years Earlier: Northampton, England

Tommy's parents sat on opposite sides of the room, his mother in an armchair and his father at the dining-room table. Neither of them spoke.

His father scanned the table covered in 'deepest sympathy' cards and vases of flowers. His mother had yet to remove her hat, her greying curls hanging loosely over her ears. She remained transfixed by two Union Jack flags neatly folded on the coffee table, removed earlier that afternoon by crematorium staff after the purple curtains swathed the matching coffins. Her husband hadn't opened a button on his uniform.

Trays of sandwiches, clumps of torn tinfoil and partially empty glasses were scattered across occasional tables, the carpet and the fireplace. In the hallway, Tommy bade farewell to the wake's last few guests and shut the front door behind them. He rubbed at his eyes, still sore after endless days of tears and sleepless nights. He leaned on the wall and readjusted his crutches, took a deep breath and hobbled slowly back into the lounge.

'Everyone's gone,' he began.

Neither parent acknowledged his presence.

'The crematorium was packed, wasn't it?' Tommy continued. 'The vicar said they were lining up outside because there weren't enough seats.'

His mother and father remained mute, so Tommy made his way towards the fireplace, balanced on one crutch, and stretched his arm to pick up plates and a pint glass.

'I'll make a start on clearing some of this away, then.' He grasped his other crutch and began to leave the room.

'Leave them,' said his mother.

A breakthrough, he thought. An acknowledgement of his existence. 'It's okay, I don't mind doing it.'

'You've done enough already,' she replied coldly.

'I want to help.'

'That's not what I meant.'

'Fiona, don't,' his father interrupted.

'He knows what he did,' she muttered. 'He knows.'

Tommy felt the frustration he'd bottled up ever since the car accident slowly begin to release.

'I know what? Come on, Mum, this is the most you've said to me all week. What do I know?'

His mother looked him in the eyes with a resentment he'd never seen in her before.

'It's because of *you* they're dead. Don't ever expect me to forget that.'

'It's not my fault!' Tommy protested. 'It was an accident. That car driving into us wasn't my fault.'

'But being careless with your phone *was* your fault! Adam unclipping his seat belt to retrieve it was down to you! It was even your fault they were travelling in that direction in the first place! You are to blame for it all.'

'But they offered to give me a lift—'

'No,' she shouted, and pointed a finger at him. 'You took advantage of the fact they'd do anything for you. You might not have been driving that other car, but *you* killed them.'

It was the first time Tommy had heard either parent verbalize what he himself believed. His guilt and shame had been more crippling than his broken ankle and foot. Try as he might to believe otherwise, each time he thought of his brothers, the first picture that sprang to mind was of their bodies entwined in the car's wreckage.

He wanted to reason with his mother, but he had no words. Instead, he continued towards the kitchen with the dirty dishes in hand. But as his crutch caught the table leg, it knocked him off balance and the dishes landed on the Union flags.

'No!' yelled his mother, leaping towards them to wipe off the spilled lager and sandwich crusts.

As he began a stuttered apology, his mother lunged towards him and slapped him across the face and head with a windmill of flailing arms and hands. Tommy fell to the floor, one of his crutches smashing against his lip and cutting it. He tried to shield his face with his hands as she hit him over and over again before his father pulled her away. Eventually his mother collapsed into a sobbing heap on the floor. His father carefully lifted her up, placed a supporting arm around her waist and helped her out of the room and up the stairs, leaving their only remaining child more alone than he'd ever been before.

Today

The corridors were unusually silent as a yawning Tommy abandoned sleep and made his way to the lounge to watch some late-night television. The sudden appearance of Peyk carrying a large, sealed cardboard box startled him.

'Mate, what are you up to at this time of night?'

'Nothing you need to know about, Tommy-boy,' said Peyk as he walked towards room 23, hovering outside until Tommy was out of sight.

Behind the reception desk, Gabby sat drawing a Mexican skull on her forearm with a red felt-tip pen.

'What's in room twenty-three?' Tommy asked. 'There's no key for it.'

'It's a storeroom for Ron's stuff.'

'What kind of stuff? He already has a lock-up out by the pool.'

Gabby started tapping her nose to say it was none of Tommy's business, then turned it around to flip him the finger.

The stale smell of beer on the cushions no longer bothered Tommy as he sprawled across the lounge sofa and half-watched an infomercial for a new juicing machine on the television.

From the corner of his eye he saw a figure he didn't recognize enter and throw himself into an armchair.

'Can't sleep either?' the man began in a British accent.

'Snorer,' replied Tommy.

'You, or someone else?'

'Someone else.'

'Ah, the universal plague of hostels worldwide,' nodded the man, scooping his hair behind his head and tying it into a ponytail.

'Why do they always seem to choose my room?' continued Tommy.

'Have you tried the mattress kick?'

'Yep, didn't work.'

'How about smothering their face with a pillow?'

'I'm sure one of my cellmates on death row would also snore.'

'I'm Jake, by the way,' the man continued, and stretched out a hand. Anyone who first caught sight of Jake, regardless of gender or sexuality, would've been struck by his good looks, and Tommy was no exception. Jake's ponytail hung between his shoulder blades; his dark-chocolate beard matched the colour of his eyes, which were framed by thick eyelashes. His teeth almost shone thanks to a deep tan that dulled monochrome tattoos poking out from under the cuff of his black jumper.

'I'm Tommy – good to meet you,' Tommy replied, trying not to stare too hard. 'Have you just arrived?'

'No, I landed yesterday from New Zealand so my body clock's still on the other side of the world. Is there anywhere round here I can grab a hot chocolate? I've got a craving.'

'There's an all-night cafe further up Winward, about ten minutes from here.'

'Ah, cool. Do you fancy joining me? I mean, if you're not waiting to see a NASA-designed Stairmaster to go with that juicer you seem pretty interested in.'

'Why not? And I'll get the order number for that juicer tomorrow.'

31

Savannah had quickly learned that there are many physical injuries a pole dancer risks on a day-to-day basis that a paying customer would neither consider nor care about.

Friction burns to a performer's inner thighs, the metal pole pinching her skin, calloused hands, bruising from a mistimed mount and cracked and torn fingernails were just a handful of hazards. And there was also the embarrassing risk of accidentally breaking wind when engaging core muscles too vigorously.

After months of dancing for a living, Savannah had experienced all of the above. After each eight-hour shift at the Pink Pussycat Club, she sighed with relief once she'd unzipped her white PVC boots, pulled up her jogging bottoms and spread her toes out comfortably inside a pair of sneakers.

'Savvy, you going to join us for a beer?' asked Mindy, waiting alongside two other dancers who'd also finished their shifts.

'Can I take a rain check? I'm tired, so I'm gonna catch a cab home.'

'Jeez, you're no fun anymore,' replied Mindy. 'It's been weeks since we last hit Sunset.'

'I'm sorry, guys, next week maybe?'

'Okay, we'll hold you to that. Sleep well, baby girl.'

As they made their way out of the changing room and through the club to the entrance, Savannah opted for the rear exit to avoid any overenthusiastic punters making clumsy, last-ditch attempts to woo her.

But as she walked towards the 3rd Street Promenade cab rank, she felt a hand press down heavily on her shoulder. She froze.

'My, my, Savannah. You're a hard girl to track down.'

32

Declan hovered by the side of the bath, listening to the pipes gurgle and splutter before lukewarm water finally dribbled from the shower nozzle.

He climbed under it while Matty stood by the sink, using the last of his cheap disposable razors that should've been thrown away weeks ago. Declan glanced towards his friend and couldn't help but notice how thin Matty was becoming.

Ingrid and Anna, two Belgian women from the floor above them with whom they'd just spent an intimate evening, had just left their room.

'Where are we meeting the girls for breakfast?' asked Declan.

'Starbucks at nine, and they're paying,' Matty replied.

'Bring it on! Croissants, fresh orange juice, blueberry muffins and actual fruit instead of the usual fast-food shite for us, then.'

'Did your girl ask anything about why we're here?'

'Yeah.'

'You didn't tell her, did you?'

Declan glanced at his friend with both eyebrows raised. 'Do you think I'm stupid?'

Thirteen Months Earlier: Navan, Ireland

Since they'd first met at primary school some twenty-five years earlier, Matty and Declan had yet to run out of conversation. They'd repeatedly bicker in the way best friends do about football, women, music and films or anything else that took their fancy. And neither would budge an inch or dare offer a potentially incorrect statistic for fear of giving the other the upper hand.

But as they began wandering through Navan's quiet market square, a nervous silence surrounded them. Both knew what the other was thinking, but neither felt the need to discuss it further than they had already.

It had taken almost an hour and a half to get to the county town on two different buses from their home in Dundalk. But after three reconnaissance trips in the last ten days, they'd grown accustomed to the trek, and they'd often ended the day watching international rugby matches on Sky Sports with the locals in the Central Navan bar. Not today, however. Today it was time to get down to business.

'Ready?' asked Declan, looking Matty firmly in the eye.

'Yep,' nodded Matty. 'Let's do it.'

Together they reached into their jacket pockets, removed black woollen balaclavas and put them on. Then they pulled pistols out from the dark blue duffel bags slung over their shoulders and opened the door to the post office.

33

A shiver ran down Savannah's spine when she felt the hand on her shoulder.

She cursed herself for her stupidity in leaving her revolver at the hostel. It was usually in her handbag at all times when she was out alone, a habit she'd developed soon after the incident on her arrival five months earlier. But she had overslept that morning and left in a hurry without remembering it.

In the two months since her attempted abduction, Savannah had been on constant alert, scouring both the hostel and the Pink Pussycat's clientele for anyone who appeared to be paying her too much attention. She only ever left the club alone to hail a taxi back to the hostel; she no longer walked anywhere alone at night, and she dispensed with headphones when in public to help her remain vigilant.

A dark-coloured SUV with blacked-out windows pulled up in front of her, and by the sound of multiple footsteps she guessed there were at least three people standing behind her. She trembled as the hand on her shoulder guided her towards the vehicle and a man in dark glasses with an earpiece opened the door and ushered her inside.

A husky middle-aged man in a grey tailored suit followed. He removed his horn-rimmed glasses, pinching the bridge of his nose as the door closed.

Savannah hesitated before she spoke. 'How did he find me?'

Silently, she vowed she would scratch, scream, bite and kick until her last breath rather than allow them to drive her away.

Seven Months Earlier: Montgomery, Alabama

She didn't have time to avoid the open hand that slapped her hard across the face.

But its brute force and the element of surprise caused an unguarded Savannah to lose her footing, and she fell against the display cabinet by the porch's entrance. She yelped as someone grabbed the back of her long, mousey brown hair and pulled her to her feet, a handful of extensions falling onto the white-painted floorboards.

Savannah saw the hand rise again and she turned her head to avoid it, but this time her ear received its force. It instantly rang from the pain and muffled the shouting coming from her attacker's mouth.

'You filthy whore!' screamed Reverend Devereaux. 'You goddam filthy whore!'

The last time she had witnessed her father's violence was when one of his cleaners had accidentally dropped a valuable china figurine, shattering it. His immediate reaction was to slap the woman and then fire her, knowing her illegal immigrant status meant she wouldn't dare report him to the police. He then used his influence with the authorities to have her deported anyway.

The Reverend grabbed his eldest daughter and brought her face so close to his that she struggled to focus on him, but she was still aware of a darkness in his eyes she'd never seen before.

'How long has it been going on for?'

Instinctively Savannah knew he was referring to her relationship with Michael. But the attack and the realization that somehow he had discovered her secret prevented her from thinking straight and therefore talking her way out of the situation.

'What? . . . Daddy . . .' she stuttered.

'Don't even try to deny it! Pastor Jackson witnessed that black boy's hands all over you in a coffee shop. Allowing one of *them* to touch you, to be physical with you . . . how could you?'

'But Daddy—'

'Tell me how long.'

'Please . . . let me explain.'

Savannah's heart raced as fast as the thoughts travelling through her head. She desperately attempted to muster up a credible explanation for why she would have kissed a black man at all, let alone in public.

'He's lying,' was all she could think of to say. 'Pastor Jackson is making stuff up.'

'Pastor Jackson does not lie,' her father replied with conviction. 'He showed me the video recording he made on his phone.'

And with that, Savannah knew the game was up. She wasn't sure whom she loathed more, the snitching pastor or the man who called himself her father.

'Have you let him screw you?' he raged. 'Has he been inside you?'

'Daddy—'

'Don't *Daddy* me; you have forfeited the right to call me that. How long has this been going on?'

Savannah didn't reply and sobbed instead. Her ear throbbed, her cheek smarted and she wanted to vomit. She shook her head and refused to reply. She was desperate to jump into her car and call Michael, because when she was in his arms, nothing could hurt her.

'Well, if you're not going to tell me, then let's go see someone who will, shall we?'

34

Today

Ruth was hiding in a bus shelter when she spotted Tommy and Jake leaving the hostel.

While her head was still swimming with the events, or non-events, of the afternoon, she didn't want to even make eye contact with anyone she recognized.

Upon leaving the restaurant, Ruth had spent hour upon hour sat on a bench in a small patch of greenery between the beach and the road, overlooking the bright swirling lights of Santa Monica pier. Her mind lurched from disappointment to anger and embarrassment, but none of it was aimed at Zak; all of it was towards herself for being foolish enough to believe she deserved to be happy.

After the sun set and the night crept in, a homeless man with two bin liners of soda cans slung over his shoulder cursed at her for sitting on his bed. So she left the bench and slowly made her way back to the hostel.

There wasn't enough noise from the passing traffic to muffle her despondent sobs, so she bit hard on her index finger to stem the flow of tears. With each step her shoes dug further into her flesh, so she tore them from her feet and threw them into a trashcan, barely feeling the grit of the sidewalk.

Aware her nose was running, Ruth reached inside her handbag for a tissue. Instead, she unwittingly pulled out the $20 bill the *maître d'* had returned to her. It was folded, but inside appeared to be another piece of paper.

'4765 Sunset Plaza Drive, Hollywood Hills – Zak's address', it read.

It took a few moments before Ruth realized the *maître d'*s action had been the kindest thing anyone had ever done for her.

35

Nicole was perched on the windowsill, willing a waft of cold air to freshen her musty dormitory room, when she saw Tommy leaving the hostel, crossing the road with a man she didn't recognize.

Her brows knitted as she reached for her mobile phone and turned it to camera mode, zooming in to see if she could get a better view of who was accompanying him.

'Who've you got your beady eye on, Sherlock?' began Eric, his head peering over his top bunk.

'No one,' she replied defensively. 'Well, I was just trying to see who Tommy was going out with. It's a bit late.'

'I haven't seen him slobbering over you much today. I presume you've had a little *tête-à-tête*?'

'If you mean have I had a word with him, then yes, I've cooled it,' she lied.

'It's for the best, trust me. Besides, we're leaving in a couple of days; I'm sure that's probably your replacement he has lined up.'

Eric rolled back on his side, satisfied at having Nicole to himself again. 'And is there any chance you can clear your crap up from around the bed before rats start nesting in it?'

Nicole ignored him and returned to her bed, closing her eyes. The sound of the door opening caught her attention. In the gloom, she squinted to catch Ruth quietly entering the room.

'Oh, hey Ruth, have you just got back?' Nicole whispered.

'Yeah, just now.'

'Don't keep me in suspense ... How did it go? How was Zak?'

Ruth paused before offering an answer. 'Really, really great. I'm going back tomorrow. Zak invited me to spend the day hanging out at his house.'

'He did?' replied Nicole, a little louder than she'd intended. 'Oh, wow, well, you must have made an impression on him.'

'I reckon so,' Ruth replied before entering the bathroom with her pyjamas under her arm.

Perhaps appearances could be deceptive, thought Nicole. Maybe she had judged Ruth on face value and once you really got to know her, her personality was more vivacious than on first impression.

Nicole closed her eyes again and shuffled around a little longer before realizing sleep wasn't going to come easy to her tonight. So she leaned over the side of her bed and felt around until she grasped the handle of her suitcase. She partly pulled it out, unzipped it and removed a brown oblong cardboard box.

Eleven Weeks Earlier: London

'I picked up a copy of *Best* and a *Guardian* to read to Mrs Baker during my lunch break,' said Nicole as she rushed past Eric and into the room behind the nurse's station. 'She likes to keep on top of the news, but she's not averse to a bit of celebrity gossip too.'

Eric followed her inside, watched as she unbuttoned her coat and he waited for an opportunity to speak.

'Last night she said her eyes are still causing her problems so I'm going to ask Doctor Zafón if he can take a look at them later.'

'Nic—' began Eric, but Nicole interrupted.

'I know what you're going to say, but the charge nurse can't complain if I'm seeing her in my own time.'

'I'm sorry, Nic . . . Mrs Baker passed away earlier this morning. Zafón thinks it was probably her heart that gave out.'

Nicole's face dropped and she bit her bottom lip as Eric held her and kissed the top of her head.

'I tried to call you but your mobile was turned off.'

'Was she on her own when she . . .'

'I think so.'

Nicole shook her head. 'She'd have hated that.'

Before Eric could reply, the charge nurse appeared.

'Unless I'm mistaken, you haven't transferred to my ward, have you?' she asked Eric.

'No,' he replied.

'Then kindly fraternize with my staff in your own time.'

The charge nurse thrust a small brown Jiffy bag into Nicole's chest. Nicole read her name across the front. Eric eyed the package up suspiciously.

'She left this for you in her drawer,' the charge nurse continued. 'Now spare me the tears, nurse, you've lost patients before.'

'Mrs Baker was special to me,' replied Nicole.

'They all are. Now go and strip her bed, as you have work to do.' The charge nurse grabbed a clipboard and began to walk away, but not before Nicole saw red.

'What is wrong with you?' Nicole asked angrily. 'When did you stop caring for people and become such a bitch?'

'Excuse me?' the surprised charge nurse replied, turning slowly on her heels.

'You heard me. Why do you feel the necessity to be such a cow all the damn time?'

'In my office – now!'

'No,' Nicole replied firmly, and caught sight of Eric's astonished expression. 'Fuck you and fuck your job. I'm done.'

Both the charge nurse and Eric were speechless as Nicole grabbed her coat, stormed out of the room and out of the hospital.

Nicole opened the door of her flat and remained in the doorway, surveying her poky home.

She'd bought most of her furnishings on eBay, at IKEA or in end-of-line sales at Next – her share from the sale of her house hadn't stretched very far. And with just a lounge-diner and galley kitchen leading towards a bedroom and bathroom, she hadn't spent much filling it up. She'd tried hard to make it feel like home but it didn't, and it never would. It was a bridge between her past and an undetermined future. The thought of spending the rest of her life living alone in this box terrified her.

Her charge nurse couldn't understand Nicole's logic, but maintaining the human touch and making time to talk and listen to patients was just as important to her as keeping them clean and medicated. But now she was afraid she'd let her mother's memory down by making such an irrational, life-changing decision and quitting.

On the other hand, Mrs Baker's travel recollections had

planted a seed in Nicole's mind that was quietly germinating. Recently she had begun allowing herself to imagine what it must feel like to live for the moment – to wake up and not have your day mapped out in front of you; to go where you pleased; to meet new people from all walks of life and to absorb sights most people only witness in TV documentaries.

When Nicole thought about it practically, though, she knew she had no savings to do any of that. So she slipped off her coat, closed the door behind her, blew a kiss to a bare-chested calendar photo of Zak Stanley on the wall and poured herself a glass of wine. The next two pre-bedtime hours would be filled, as most evenings were, by a mixture of soap operas and reality TV she'd recorded.

Little did she know that a forgotten Jiffy bag in her coat pocket would soon alter everything.

Today

Quietly, in the darkness of the hostel dormitory, Nicole pulled back the Sellotape that held the lid of the cardboard box in place, and the metallic silver urn slipped out. She ran her fingers down its side and checked to make sure the lid was still secure.

'We'll find a home for you somewhere soon, Mrs Baker,' she whispered.

36

Four empty mugs sat on the counter of the coffee bar as Tommy and Jake spent their second hour flopped in leather armchairs, comparing notes on their travelling experiences.

The walls surrounding them offered a stark warning of what can happen when success and excess collide. They were decorated with framed photographs of iconic actors and singers including River Phoenix, Marilyn Monroe, Janis Joplin, John Bonham, Dee Dee Ramone and John Belushi, who'd all descended on LA to find or revel in their fame and fortune but were taken away at too early an age.

'And you've not heard from your mate Louis since then?' Jake asked.

'Nope. His mum says he's met some French girl and they've gone to Mexico, but I've not heard a thing from him. I keep checking my emails and his Facebook updates but he's gone off radar.'

'Do you miss him?'

Tommy thought carefully about the question before he answered. 'I did at first, but you're never really alone when you're travelling, are you? You're always meeting people in the same boat as you.'

'Yeah, you develop these intense relationships, trade life

stories, then within a few days, you've gone off to search for your own beaches,' said Jake.

'Exactly! And then your name joins the list of a hundred others cc'd on a round-robin email, or you're reduced to a photo on Facebook and have to tag your own name because it's already been forgotten . . .' Jake nodded in agreement. 'You sound like you're an old hand at this,' Tommy added.

'Well, I've been backpacking now for two years so far.'

'It's only been a little over seven months for me, but I've been at the hostel a while. I should be thinking about moving on. So what inspired you to start travelling?'

'Oh, you know, the usual,' replied Jake, vaguely. 'A change of scenery. What about you?'

'Pretty much the same,' replied Tommy, unwilling to cast a dampener on what had turned out to be a pleasantly spontaneous middle-of-the-night.

Ten Months Earlier: Northampton, England

'What the hell are you doing here?'

Louis stared wide-eyed at Tommy, who stood on his doorstep, dressed in his army green fatigues and with a large green rucksack attached to his back. As far as Louis was aware, his best friend had another fortnight left of his fourteen-week phase-one army training in Winchester before he was allowed to visit home.

'I've quit,' said Tommy, matter-of-factly.

'But you signed a contract – doesn't that mean you've gone AWOL?'

Tommy brushed off Louis's concerns. 'Can I come in?'

Louis ushered Tommy into the hallway, up the stairs and

into his flat. Tommy unstrapped his backpack and it dropped to the floor with a heavy thump as Louis asked Alexa to turn down the volume of a playlist he was listening to.

'Mate, you're going to be in deep shit if you've run away,' continued Louis, pensively scratching the blonde stubble on his chin.

'I don't care, I had to leave.'

'Why? Were you getting bullied or something?'

'No, they were a really great bunch of lads, surprisingly, and even the officers are pretty cool once they stop shouting at you. But I just woke up this morning knowing I'd made a massive fucking mistake.'

'I told you this would happen.'

'Yeah, well, you were right.'

Louis shook his head. He took no comfort in Tommy's admission and was more concerned by the ramifications of his friend's desertion.

'I'm supposed to give fourteen days' notice if I want to leave before three months, or my commanding officer can give me permission to leave.'

'And which one did you get?'

Tommy hung his head and glanced at his boots, still shining despite the seven-hour National Express bus journey and two-mile hike to Louis's.

'So you are AWOL, you muppet!'

'Well, I'm not going back. One of the last things Adam said to me was to make a decision and stick with it and to stop wasting time. So that's what I did when I left home. And now I've done it again.'

'I told you not to enlist, mate, I *told* you. I've known you since year four and I know how your mind works. I said you needed to go to counselling after the accident and not make any rash decisions. What you went through . . . Jesus . . . I don't even know how I'd begin to learn to live with that. But you are not Daniel and you are not Adam; you're Tommy. You can't continue what they started because that's just not you, and running away and going to a place where they do your thinking for you isn't going to help.'

Tommy shrugged. When they'd had this conversation months earlier, he'd known Louis was right. But his desperation to win his parents' approval had blinded him. However, even when he'd left home for basic training, they'd failed to wave him off or show an ounce of pride like they had for his brothers.

'So what are you going to do now?' asked Louis.

'It's not what am *I* going to do, it's what are *we* going to do,' replied Tommy.

Louis grimaced. 'Am I going to like this?'

'You might. Do you fancy joining me on an adventure? I've been reading this book . . .' He pulled out a copy of Alex Garland's *The Beach* from his backpack. 'Have you read it?'

'No, but I saw the film. Leonardo DiCaprio, yeah? Didn't turn out too great for him, did it?'

'You're missing the point. Whether he found paradise or hell, at least he was out there searching for something. All we're doing is killing time here. So let's go and find our own beach.'

'What, you want to go on a road trip to find a beach?'

'Well no, I don't mean an actual beach, but a metaphorical one. Let's just pack up our stuff and travel the world. I've got some savings, so what could go wrong?'

Plenty, thought Louis. And eventually, he was proved right.

37

Savannah dug her fingernails into the palm of her hand and felt them bend as she waited for the man to reply to her question.

'Is he in LA?' she asked, her voice beginning to crack.

'Who?' replied the man.

'My father. He knows I'm in LA and that's why you're here.'

'I have no idea who your father is or if he knows where you are.'

'Then who sent you?'

'I'm not the kind of man who can be *sent* anywhere, Savannah,' laughed the man. 'My name is Nicholas Van Lien. You may have heard some of your work colleagues mention me.'

Savannah nodded and unclenched her balled fists. Now she recognized his face; she had seen him at the club a couple of times over the previous few weeks. Mr Van Lien owned two of the largest gentlemen's clubs in Los Angeles, where only the most sought-after dancers were invited to work.

'I'm opening a new club at the end of the year, in that building just there,' he continued, pointing towards an empty unit across the road. 'And I'd like you to be one of my hosts.

I have seen how you work, how you interact with your customers, and you're the kind of pretty young thing who could do well in my employment. Plus there are . . . extra-curricular benefits of working for me, as you may also have heard.'

Savannah was aware of how many young actresses had earned their first big break under his wing. Or just under him, period. His discreet clubs and parties in the Hollywood Hills were a honeypot for Hollywood executives who offered bit parts to aspiring starlets in exchange for their one-on-one company. #MeToo was not in their vocabulary.

'I'm sorry, but no thank you,' replied Savannah.

'This would be something very different from what your current employer offers. At the moment, you're working for scraps. I can guarantee you a regular salary, plus much, much more.'

'It's not that I don't want to; I just can't.'

'Might I ask why?'

Savannah hesitated and contemplated telling him the truth. Instead, she chose to remain ambiguous. 'I have . . . plans . . . so it's impossible for me to commit. Thank you for the offer though, I appreciate it.'

'Take my card, think about it,' suggested Mr Van Lien. 'Now, may I offer you a ride home?'

'I'm good, thank you,' replied Savannah. She accepted his card as the door opened and she hurried back out onto the sidewalk.

As Mr Van Lien's SUV pulled away, Savannah steadied herself against the wall and waited until her heartbeat slowed down to its regular pace.

*

Two Years Earlier: Montgomery, Alabama

Reverend Devereaux kept his sweating palms on Savannah's shoulders as he frog-marched her through the hallway and into the kitchen, where his astonished staff watched, too afraid to intervene.

Tears burned the raw, slapped skin on Savannah's face as her father pushed her out of the house, across the lawns where the plantations once lay, through the water sprinklers and towards a white-panelled workshop. He yanked open the door and shoved her inside and, as she grew accustomed the gloom, she gasped when she spotted the whites of Michael's terrified eyes. He sat with his feet and arms bound together with plastic fasteners around a wooden garden chair; a cut above his right eye bled down his face and into his torn white t-shirt.

'Michael!' she whispered, before the Reverend cuffed her around the back of the head. Pastor Jackson and two of her father's burly security man flanked her boyfriend.

'You are actually crying for this animal?' Reverend Devereaux asked her, scarcely believing what he was witnessing. 'You are actually shedding *tears* for this *thing*?'

'I love him!' she pleaded.

'He's nothing – look at him! A hundred years ago and he'd be castrated and hanging from a tree for what he has done to you.'

'He loves me and he is a good man. He's in medical school, he's going to be a surgeon.'

'I don't care if he's going to be the first black man on the moon, he is a black man, and black men have no place corrupting white Christian families. So let's see how the good doctor is going to put his hands to use after I perform my own procedure.'

In the blink of Michael's blood-soaked eye, the Reverend grabbed a mallet from a workbench and smashed it against the back of Michael's hand. He screamed as the smiling Reverend repeated the action on his other hand, this time also catching the base of four fingers.

'No!' Savannah pleaded to deaf ears.

'Tell me you will never cross paths with him again and I will let him go while he still has his eyesight.'

Savannah wanted to reply but her throat was too dry to speak. She stared at her terrified boyfriend, who was biting hard into his bottom lip to counteract the pain. Her mind raced. How could she promise never to see Michael again? But what choice did she have?

'I won't,' she whispered.

'You won't what?'

'I won't see him again.'

'Good,' replied the Reverend, then swung the mallet and caught Michael clean in the centre of his forehead. Savannah screamed Michael's name as he stared at her, his eyelids fluttering before snapping shut and his head falling forward.

'Now get him out of here,' he barked. 'And lock her in her room.'

38

Today

'Do you want another hot chocolate?' asked Jake, slipping his hand into his jeans pocket and pulling out a faded canvas wallet.

Tommy took a last gulp of his drink and shook his head.

'No, mate, I've got to be on the reception desk in about . . .' He looked at his watch. 'Two hours. Shit! We've been here all night.'

'I know,' replied Jake, glancing out the window. 'It's getting light out there.'

They stood up and headed for the door, waving the waitress goodbye and leaving a tip on the counter.

'Are you coming back to the hostel?' asked Tommy.

'No, I think I'm going to watch the sun rise from the beach. I've seen it come up from the northern, eastern and southern hemispheres, but never from this far west. There's nothing like a new sun in a new continent to start your day.'

'Next time I'll join you,' replied Tommy.

'I'll hold you to that. And thanks for the company; it was really nice chatting to you.'

Tommy squinted at Jake. 'You kind of remind me of someone, but I can't work out who.'

Jake flinched, but hid it, like he'd done on previous occasions when people had said the same thing, before he trotted out the same rehearsed response. 'Ah, I've got a very generic face,' he said, smiling, and headed towards the beach.

'If that's generic, then I'm a horror story,' Tommy told himself, quietly flattered that someone with such worldly experience would want to hang around with him.

39

Day Four

It took an hour and a half before the Metro bus dropped Ruth off on Sunset Boulevard.

From behind the dusty bus window she noticed road signs for places she'd seen on television, like Beverly Hills and Hollywood, but even though they were within touching distance, Ruth had no interest in seeing any of them first-hand. Instead, the base of the Hollywood Hills was where she wanted to be.

Almost 22,000 people lived in the seven square miles between the boundaries of Crescent Heights and Griffin Park. But there was only one face Ruth was there to see.

With Elastoplasts stuck to the back of her heels where the stilettos had blistered them, she began her steep climb up the sidewalk towards Sunset Plaza Drive. The homes were right out of *Selling Sunset*, a property reality show on Netflix she had binge-watched. And the higher she went, the larger the estates became as they competed for the most expansive city view.

Ruth glanced at her watch; it was eight a.m., and twenty-four hours ago she'd been preparing herself to meet Zak Stanley for lunch. He must have been delayed through no fault of his own, she decided, and most likely with work. It was the only explanation. But it didn't matter now, because this was going to be so much better. She was going to his home. *His actual home.* And that was so much more personal than a meal in a public restaurant could ever be.

Ruth could barely contain her excitement as she ascended the hillside, singing along to the soundtrack on her newly purchased smart phone of Zak's first romcom foray, *Getting the Girl.* She was aware of the early hour, but she reasoned there was no point in hanging around the hostel any longer than necessary. She guessed Hollywood stars probably didn't get out of bed until about midday, which would give her plenty of time to compose herself and think about what she was going to say to Zak when their paths finally crossed in person.

It took another half hour and many gulps from her water bottle before the directions Google Maps suggested came to an end. She was here. Zak lived in a two-storey Spanish-style property partially hidden behind a whitewashed wall and metal gates. She could clearly see blossoming trees and palm leaves clumped together in the landscaped garden. When the wind blew gently, she also caught the faint waft of chlorine from a pool.

Ruth placed her hand over her mouth but it was too late to muffle a feverish squeal.

40

Tommy cursed his phone's alarm when it rang just two hours after his head hit the pillow.

He showered, changed into a clean t-shirt, shorts and his favourite Adidas trainers, left the dormitory and headed to the reception desk for the start of a five-hour shift. But he was already pining for the hour-long break between the hostel and his new job inside a hotdog costume directing hungry tourists towards Mr Georgiou's fast-food trailer.

Tommy stared enviously from the corridor window as the sun's rays shone upon the sidewalk, and wondered if Jake had enjoyed his first LA sunrise. He'd enjoyed Jake's company very much, and since he and Louis had gone their separate ways, he missed having a male confidant. Although he'd made many acquaintances at the hostel, it was rare for him to come across people he could relax around enough to completely bond with. And then two potential friends came along within days of each other: Jake, who, while convivial and talkative about his travels, appeared reluctant to give much of his background away, and Nicole, who was witty and attractive but held her cards just as close to her chest as Jake held his.

Tommy became distracted from his musings when he passed the kitchen and paused to watch Matty and Declan puzzling over what do with a seven-pound bag of pasta and twenty cans of chopped tomatoes.

'Where should I stick this?' Matty asked his friend, pointing to the pasta.

'D'you really want me to answer that?' replied Declan, struggling to hook the can opener over the rim.

'Will you look at her!' whispered Matty, staring at two blonde women with Scandinavian accents rinsing their breakfast dishes in the sink.

'Ladies! Could you spare us a moment of your time?' asked Declan.

'What's up, guys?' asked one of the women. Tommy knew her name was Freja.

'Now what kind of accent is that? Dutch, Norwegian?' asked Matty.

'Swedish,' replied her friend Nina.

'Well, you're a beautiful sight for tired Irish eyes. I'm Matty, and this is Declan.'

Tommy shook his head from outside as they took turns kissing the girls' hands as if they were royalty.

'Are you the new cooks?' asked Freja.

'Officially, yes, but unofficially, and don't tell anyone, we're pretty feckin' useless,' said Declan. 'Do you by any chance know what to do with these?'

'You can't make spaghetti?' asked Nina, looking at Freja in mock disbelief.

'It's a Roman Catholic thing, we're not actually allowed under papal law.'

'But dinner isn't until tonight, so why are you starting it now?'

'We thought it might need to, I dunno, simmer or something?' said Matty.

'For ten hours?'

'I told you we could've stayed in bed,' moaned Declan.

Nina whispered into Freja's ear. 'Okay, if we help you, what will you do for us in return?'

Matty and Declan looked at each other, then the girls, shrugged their shoulders and grinned. 'Anything you like.'

Tommy had only been at the reception desk for ten minutes when he learned what the girls had received for their kitchen assistance. Wearing just their trainers and aprons, bare-arsed Matty and Declan boisterously charged through reception whooping and hollering before running across the road and doing star jumps.

As the girls' laughter echoed through the open kitchen window above, Tommy scowled and turned up today's televised lecture from Reverend Devereaux. He considered calling to make a cash pledge if Rev Dev would ask The Man Above to rid the hostel of the current Irish plague.

41

Jake grunted as he completed his fourth set of chin-ups on the free-to-use exercise equipment by the beach, then felt the tape attaching his recent tattoo covering begin to tear.

He hitched up his vest and secured it back in place before crossing his legs, hoisting himself up on metal parallel bars, and beginning a set of bicep dips.

A film of early morning smog had ruined his first West Coast sunrise, turning the sun's golden rays into a grey and purplish fog. But the pollution meant it wasn't too stifling for him as he worked up an early morning sweat.

He lowered himself back to the ground, tensed his arms and watched as the tattooed images from shoulders to wrists came to life. More than sixty hours in artists' chairs around the world had been worth it, he thought. His long hair, beard, muscular frame and the gradual but deliberate loss of his northern accent had all helped to transform him into someone unrecognizable from his former self.

Not even his most devoted fans would recognize who he once was.

Three and a Half Years Earlier: Shepperton Studios, London

Stuart Reynolds stared into the mirror framed by white light bulbs as a stylist placed short strands of his hair in straightening tongs.

His first coat of make-up had been applied after breakfast, then re-applied for dress rehearsals, followed by three more late-afternoon touch-ups and a final dusting an hour before the live shows were to be televised. Familiarity with the process meant he knew that by the end of the broadcast he would remain perspiration-free, but his face would feel heavy, like it had been glued to a brick.

The make-up gave him sharper cheekbones and deeper dimples and his bleached-blonde hair was ruffled to make him look like he'd just got out of bed. The light bulbs reflected in his winter-blue contact lenses and enhanced their sparkle. Although they looked prettier than the brown irises he'd been born with, he felt they were another part of him to add to the ever-growing list of fakery.

For ten consecutive Friday and Saturday nights, he, Gabriel, Josh, Dylan and Ethan had been performing established musicians' hits with their own R&B twist in front of eight million voting viewers at home. Separately, they were five attractive but unexceptional young men in their early to mid-twenties; together, they were a boyband created by TV show *Star People* and its architect, Geri Garland.

Their song choices, outfits, choreography, hairstyling, rehearsal times, accommodation, fitness regimes, diets, interview techniques and social media accounts were all managed for them by a panel of production company executives and a PR team, all hand-picked by Geri. Even their name, Lightning Strikes, had been chosen for them.

The other band members were scattered around their cramped dressing room, hunched over tablets and mobile phones, scrutinizing what social media users were saying about their chances of winning that night's finale. From what Stuart had read on Twitter earlier that day, the consensus was that girl-next-door Olivia Hawkins might just pip them to the post.

'Right, you're done,' said Megan, interrupting his thoughts as she doused his poker-straight hair with a final coat of lacquer. 'Your turn, Josh.'

Stuart vacated his seat just as the door flew open and Geri marched in.

'Christ, it's a right bloody sausage-fest in here,' she yelled in her South London accent as all eyes focused on her. She was wearing her dyed, flame-red, shoulder-length hair in a side parting, and her plump, cosmetically enhanced breasts spilled from the top of her silver sequined dress. Geri was firmly into her mid-forties, but the best surgery money could buy had shaved off at least a decade from her appearance.

She revelled in her role as an intimidating presence. Her young male assistant dutifully followed her with a tablet under his arm and an AirPod plugged into an ear. A different young man flanked Geri every time she appeared, noted Stuart, and he wondered if there was a pile of blood-drained bodies stacked up in her cellar.

'Are you boys ready to go out there and win this thing for Mama G?' she continued.

'Yes,' all five replied, too muted for Geri's liking.

'Well, I hope you've got more in you than that when you get out on that stage, or you're fucked. Stuart, can I have a word?' It was a rhetorical question, so Stuart followed her into the corridor. She flicked her eyes at her assistant, who scampered away like a scolded puppy.

'How are you doing then, handsome?' she asked softly, straightening the lapels of his jacket.

'If I'm honest, I'm shitting bricks, Geri,' Stuart replied.

'Well, as long as you don't shit them on stage, you lot have got this wrapped up.'

'I hope so, but what if the other judges prefer Olivia? Won't it look a bit dodgy when you're the only one there bigging us up? And even Twitter says—'

'Oh Twitter, shitter,' Geri interrupted. 'The public don't know what they want till I tell them. And they don't give a damn what the other two judges think – I pay them to be there and to make me look good. We've got through every week without a problem or a technical fault. Just one more night and we're home free.'

She planted a lingering peck on Stuart's lips and then wiped off the lipstick she'd left with her thumb. With the amount of fillers she'd had injected into her face, Stuart found it hard to tell whether she was being flirtatious or suffering a mild stroke.

'Now get out there and make me proud,' she continued, then patted his left buttock and pushed him towards the dressing room. Stuart took a deep breath and rejoined his bandmates. He glanced around the room, hating that his future lay in the hands of a pantomime villainess and four virtual strangers.

Through the open door, he spotted one of the show's young

technicians walking past with arms full of microphones. Already fed up of his squeaky-clean look, Stuart wondered what it would be like to ditch the contacts, go back to his natural dark brown, wavy hair, grow a beard and get tattoos like the man in front of him had.

'Hold up a minute, Jake,' came a voice from behind the technician.

'I like that name,' thought Stuart idly.

42

Today

Ruth removed her phone from her pocket, switched it to video mode, and started to closely examine the home of Zak Stanley through a two-inch-by-two-inch screen.

At the far end of the house, on the second floor, she could just see wide-open doors with wrought-iron railings surrounding a tiled balcony. She wondered if that was Zak's bedroom. And if his doors were open, he was probably awake already, she figured.

Her eyes were drawn to an intercom with just one button. She took a deep breath and lifted a trembling hand before pushing it. It didn't make a sound, so she pushed it again until a whirring noise above her caught her attention. It was a video camera attached to a tree trunk and pointed at her. She looked up at it and her eyebrows rose, before a woman's voice from the intercom startled her.

'Yes?'

Ruth steadied herself before speaking. 'Hi, I've come to see Zak Stanley.'

The pause felt like a lifetime before the voice spoke again. 'And you are . . . ?'

'Um, I won a competition to meet him . . . but I think there must have been a mix-up with timings . . .' Ruth turned her head and beamed at the camera.

'Mr Stanley doesn't see visitors without an appointment or an invitation.'

'Oh, but I had one yesterday. Can I make another one?'

'You will have to go through his publicist. Thank you.'

'Do you have a number?' Ruth asked, scrambling inside her bag for a pen and paper. 'Hello? Hello?'

The voice did not reply, and the camera continued to target her until she shuffled away.

43

'If looks could kill . . .' said Nicole.

As the second of the week's hostel parties was in full flow, she'd noticed Tommy casting bitter glances towards Matty and Declan from the doorway.

'What do you mean?' Tommy asked sluggishly.

'Those Irish lads with the gift of the gab.'

Matty and Declan sat with their arms around Freja and Nina on a sofa. Every so often, the girls threw their heads back and laughed at something amusing the boys whispered into their ears.

'And love them or loathe them, you've got to admit their spag Bol is pretty moreish,' added Nicole.

'I wouldn't know, I haven't tried it,' Tommy lied, having eaten his helping in his room so as not to give his nemeses any satisfaction. He took another swig from his plastic beer cup.

'Are you a bit drunk, Thomas?'

Tommy ignored the question, but it was obvious from his squinting eyes and slightly slurred speech that he'd gone over his self-imposed three-pint limit. Every person he'd spoken to at the party had thrust a fresh drink into his hand and it seemed rude to refuse them.

'Perhaps.'

'So what is it about them you don't like?'

'They're players. Am I the only one who can see that?'

'I spoke to them earlier in the kitchen and they seem fun.'

'Oh, not you as well. They've been here all of two days and they think they're the dog's bollocks.'

'Aw, are they pushing your nose out of joint?' Nicole teased.

Nicole wasn't far off the mark; and if he was being honest with himself, Tommy missed Louis and the camaraderie a best friend brought. But he wasn't willing to reveal his weakness to someone he wanted to impress. 'I just don't like their attitude,' he replied instead.

'Oh, be quiet, grandad. They're having fun – do you remember how to do that?'

Tommy tried to focus on Nicole. 'Yes, I remember how to have fun . . . and I remember how to do this as well,' he said, then closed his eyes and leaned in to kiss her. But Nicole swiftly moved her head, so that the only thing his lips met with was the wall. From behind the pool table in the corner of the room, Jake winced.

'I think you've had a few too many,' said Nicole. 'Why don't you go and have a lie down?'

A muddled Tommy nodded and shuffled away, red-faced. As he left the room, he couldn't help but notice Matty and Declan laughing at what they'd just seen.

44

Savannah focused on her reflection in the bathroom mirror, adjusting her wig so her fringe sat straight.

A figure was sitting silently on a stool behind the two-way mirror that looked into her hostel bedroom. He edged his face towards Savannah's when she moved closer to apply colour to her lips. Then, inches apart, he mimicked her movements; blinking when Savannah blinked, pouting when she pouted and ruffling his hair when she ruffled hers. It was only when she threw her handbag over her shoulder and walked towards her bedroom door that he pulled his trousers up.

But as Savannah turned the handle, she felt the locking mechanism snap and watched the knob fall to the floor. She tried to re-insert it but to no avail, and then jabbed her fingers into the hole to see if that might unlock the door.

When that attempt also failed, panic set in. Her legs buckled beneath her and she fell to the floor.

Six and a Half Months Earlier:
Montgomery, Alabama

The weeks Savannah spent locked in her bedroom felt endless.

The only contact she was allowed with another person was when one of the kitchen staff passed her a food tray with an apologetic glance and then closed the door again. Three times a day this happened, and not a word was spoken by the inmate or the prison cook. For the first few days Savannah refused to touch her meals, hoping that by starving herself she could force her father to release her. But when it became clear that each rejected tray made no difference she succumbed to hunger pangs, hating herself with each mouthful she took.

With no cell phone or internet to contact the outside world for help, Savannah passed her days flicking through television channels, watching endless *Kardashians* and *Real Housewives* re-runs, home renovation shows and music videos.

She'd peer through the locked glass balcony doors and down the half-mile driveway that led to a world away from the one she detested. Her sister Roseanna had tried to visit but was ushered out of the corridor by their father's staff. Occasionally Savannah spotted her in the garden, playing Frisbee with the dogs and chasing them through the lawn sprinklers. She'd look up at Savannah's room with a shared sadness.

Sometimes Savannah glanced into her en-suite bathroom mirror to reassess the swelling and bruising to her face. At night, when she was enveloped in complete silence, she hoped the ringing in her ear from her father's fist might eventually subside.

The toughest aspect of Savannah's incarceration was the time she'd been given to worry about Michael. She was frightened about what had become of him and the hands he was relying on to make him a surgeon. The most positive aftermath was that following his attack, he'd been dumped with a threat to keep quiet about his injuries or face further consequences. Few would believe his version of events over those of a respected television evangelist, and the only witness was locked away in her bedroom like a character from a fairy tale.

The worst-case scenario . . . well, she didn't want to think about that. The hammer blow he had taken to his head had knocked him out cold, and Savannah feared the lasting damage it might have caused.

Either way, she had ruined his life simply by loving him.

By the tenth day of her incarceration, Savannah briefly contemplated suicide as her only means of escape. But the moment she accepted she had nothing to lose by dying was also the moment she decided she had nothing to lose by doing her damndest to escape.

And by day fifteen, she knew exactly how she was going to do it.

Today

'Pull yourself together, girl,' Savannah said aloud, and tried to steady her trembling hands. She deliberately replaced her short, shallow gasps with deep, drawn-out breaths. Eventually she clambered to her feet and made her way to the bathroom to search for a nail file she kept in her make-up bag. She hoped to unpick the lock with it like she had seen people do on TV.

Suddenly she heard a click at the door, and when she returned to it, it was slightly ajar. She opened it and scanned the corridor up and down, but it was empty. How had someone known she was trapped? And why wouldn't they hang around for her to thank them?

While grateful to be free, it also left her feeling unsafe in the building for the first time since she'd been taken there.

45

Day Five

Tommy scrolled through his text messages regularly, but four days had passed since he'd last checked his emails. Again, there was nothing from Louis in his inbox.

He sat back in his chair with his arms folded, hoping the painkiller he'd taken earlier would soon rid him of his hangover. He remembered bits and pieces from the night before – in particular, crashing and burning in his second stab at kissing Nicole. And he vowed not to make a fool of himself again with a woman who was out of his league and clearly didn't take him seriously.

Suddenly, a small brown paper bag fell into his lap.

'That's just to say thanks for the company the other night; I really appreciated it,' Jake said from the doorway. Tommy opened the bag and found a box of brightly coloured foam ear-plugs. 'They should put an end to sleepless nights with snorers and hot chocolates with jet-lagged strangers,' Jake continued.

'Thanks, mate, but you didn't need to,' Tommy replied, appreciative of the gesture.

'You got much on today?'

'Nope, I have a day off from both the hostel and the hotdog stand. Why, have you got something in mind?'

Thirty minutes later and the bridge of Tommy's nose throbbed where Jake head-butted him. But neither could stop themselves from laughing after crashing onto the concrete boardwalk by the beach. They'd hired their inline skates from a store and clumsily rolled their way only a couple of hundred metres from Venice Beach to Santa Monica before colliding and crumpling into a heap.

'I thought you said you could skate?' began Tommy, rubbing his nose and struggling to get back on his feet without something solid to hold on to.

'Does the blood pouring down my leg look like it belongs to someone who can skate?' replied Jake. 'Shall we ditch these things?'

Jake and Tommy yanked the Velcro straps from their skates, slung them over their shoulders and walked barefoot on the beach by the side of the boardwalk.

'I didn't see you at the party last night,' Tommy said. 'Didn't you fancy it?'

'I was there, but I didn't want to interrupt you while you were making your moves on that girl.'

'Ah, so you saw me get blown out then,' replied Tommy, a little surprised that he didn't feel that embarrassed in front of someone who probably had girls falling at his feet.

'It happens to the best of us,' Jake replied, and patted his new friend on the shoulder. 'Onwards and upwards, right?'

'If you tell me there's plenty more fish in the sea, I'm going to kill you.'

'That depends on how big your bait is and where you dangle it.'

46

'What do you think of this?' asked Eric, and carefully placed a Panama hat on his head, making sure not to displace his fussily waxed hair.

Nicole wasn't listening. Instead her eyes were focused on Tommy and a person she vaguely recognized from the hostel, as they fell into each other and then to the ground. It was only when she spotted the ponytail that she realized it was probably the same guy Tommy had left the hostel with so late two nights earlier.

'Has your toyboy found a new friend to play with already?' Eric teased, following her line of sight. Nicole elbowed him in the ribs.

'He's prettier than you, I'll give him that,' Eric continued, 'but his beard isn't as long as yours.'

'One hair!' Nicole replied defensively. 'You found one hair on my chin a year ago and you're still taking the piss about it.'

'Ah, but that's how it starts; first it's one innocuous little strand poking out of your chinny chin chin, and the next thing you know, you're Dumbledore's double.'

'You're such an arse.'

'And you love me for it.'

Nicole couldn't argue with that. While he was sometimes overly possessive of her and quick to criticize, nobody ever made her laugh as much as her best friend. Neither of them had any relatives they were in contact with, so they had become each other's family. And most people never got to witness how sweet he could be.

Eric removed the hat and placed it back on the head of the dummy, satisfied that Tommy had found someone else to sniff around. Because he needed Nicole's undivided attention.

Eleven Weeks Earlier: Belgravia, London

'What do you think's inside it?' Nicole wondered.

Her voice echoed around an airy room housing hundreds of stainless-steel safety deposit boxes of varying sizes, all stored on shiny metal shelves. Security cameras covered every square inch of the room. Eric glanced at the key in her hand and shrugged.

'I have no idea,' he said. 'So we might as well open it.'

The Jiffy bag Mrs Baker had left for her had completely slipped Nicole's mind in the wake of her dramatic quitting of her job. She'd been slumped on her sofa streaming classic Brit-flick romcoms on Netflix and dreaming of her own Mark Darcy appearing on her doorstep to solve all her problems. Instead, Eric had turned up with a shoulder to cry on, a bottle of prosecco and a slab of something delicious from Hotel Chocolat.

Later that night, he'd reminded her of Mrs Baker's Jiffy bag, and together they had torn it open, puzzled by the contents: an address in Belgravia and a key with an engraved number. The following morning, the hungover pair took the tube into central London, found the door for Safe Securities and pressed the buzzer. After proving her identity with a driver's licence and credit card, Nicole was surprised to learn that a safety deposit box had been registered in her name. A staff member in a smart suit and gloves ushered her towards box number 23 and pulled out a key of his own. Together they inserted them in two locks, turning them in unison before the man removed a foot-long container, placed it on a table, and left Eric and Nicole to open it alone.

'Something tells me Mrs Baker's death could mean a new beginning,' murmured Nicole optimistically.

'Not for her it isn't.'

'I meant for me, idiot. I have a gut feeling there's something in this box that's going to change everything.'

She lifted the lid and, as they saw what was inside, they both frowned in puzzlement.

47

Today

Once the early morning smog lifted, the horizontal wooden floor planks of Santa Monica Pier became red-hot to the touch under the midday sun.

So with their skates still hanging from their shoulders, Tommy and Jake tiptoed barefoot down the concrete road ramp and towards the shadows cast by the shops and railings. Tommy had never ventured onto the pier before, for the same reason he'd yet to catch a bus up to Malibu or hike to the Hollywood sign; there was a fine line between being a traveller and being on vacation.

They glanced up at the arc-shaped entrance sign and wandered slowly past the amusement arcades, aquarium, pub, restaurants and trapeze school. Tommy raised his digital camcorder to record familiar landmarks he'd seen in films and TV shows like *Hancock, Iron Man, American Horror Story* and, embarrassingly, *Hannah Montana: The Movie.*

He pointed it upwards to capture the red and yellow cars moving clockwise on the Ferris wheel as he and Jake continued to absorb the odours of fish and candyfloss until they reached the end of the pier. They found space between a dozen or so fishermen whose rods, perched against the rusty blue railings, dangled into the ocean below. Together they stood in a comfortable silence, staring across the ocean and towards the horizon, each enjoying their day.

Tommy closed his eyes and inhaled the salty scent in the air, while Jake contemplated how many more oceans he might need to cross until he finally found himself at home and complete anonymity.

Two Years Earlier: London

The frenzied cheering started before Lightning Strikes reached the climax of Adele's 'Hello'.

Geri Garland was the only judge to join the audience on their feet, and she applauded wildly with her arms stretched high above her head. Clearly proud of their performance, Stuart and his bandmates hugged and bounced up and down before being joined by *Star People*'s affable presenter, Tracy Fenton.

'Well done, guys,' she enthused. 'That was amazing. Let's go to Rocky Rhodes first – your verdict, please.'

Behind a brightly illuminated TV studio desk, ageing record label boss Rocky's body language announced his opinion before he spoke. 'Gentlemen, I'll be honest with you,' he began with folded arms, 'I hope to God Adele isn't watching this, because it really was a weak performance and nowhere near good enough for you to win.'

However, the jeering audience drowned out any of his scripted follow-up comments, good or bad. Geri stood up again and, ensuring the camera was focused on her, gave him two thumbs down.

'And James Nicholson, you've had number ones around the

world with your band Driver,' continued Tracy. 'Do Lightning Strikes have what it takes to do the same?'

James shook his head and ran his fingers through his hair. 'Sorry, guys, but I agree with Rocky. I thought it was very average. For the final song of this competition, I expected more. I think Olivia might have nailed it.'

'Finally – Geri Garland.'

'Well,' began Geri, looking from side to side at her fellow panellists. 'I think you two need your ears testing, because that was brilliant!' She waited for the audience's roar of approval to die down. 'Boys, that's a modern-day classic, but you brought passion to the song, you made it your own and there will be an injustice tonight if you don't win.'

Behind his back, Stuart crossed his fingers as a floor manager ushered Olivia, their fellow finalist and hot favourite to win, into position next to the band.

Then Stuart held his breath. And it felt like he didn't exhale for the next eighteen months.

48

Today

Nicole and Eric tucked into the takeaway boxes of burritos and salad that they'd carried back to the sunbeds scattered around the hostel swimming pool. It was rarely used thanks to a glorious beach a two-minute walk away and the presence of a towering building behind the hostel that blocked out the sun for much of the day.

They ate in silence. The more Nicole considered it, the more she realized that she was unhappy Tommy had found someone new to spend time with. It wasn't that she hadn't wanted to kiss him the previous evening, when he'd made that failed pass at her, but she was too old for a first kiss fuelled by alcohol and in such deeply unromantic circumstances. Besides, she didn't want any animosity between herself and Eric.

'Hi, Ruth,' she called as she saw the hostel's quietest resident pass by. 'How was your day at Zak's?'

'It was fantastic,' replied Ruth without hesitation. 'He has this great big house and a great big garden and we ate caviar and we drank wine – the posh red stuff that costs tons – and we sat by his pool all day.'

Nicole didn't need to see Eric's expression to know that he didn't believe a word of it either. But as Ruth's fantasy caused no harm, Nicole played along with it. Eric had other ideas.

'What did you talk about?' he asked.

'All kinds of things, really. You know.'

'Like?'

'His films,' stuttered Ruth, 'His life. And . . . um . . . stuff.'

'Oh wow, now I'm really jealous!' interrupted Nicole, aware Eric was trying to catch her out.

'I'm going back tomorrow,' continued Ruth. 'Zak said we could watch some of his films and then I could go see him make a movie. Zak said he might even get me a part.'

Ruth grinned and then headed back to her room, and Eric stifled a chuckle.

'Go on, get it off your chest. I can almost smell the evil about to come out of your mouth.'

'Exactly what part is Zak Stanley going to get her in a film?' laughed Eric. '*Australian Werewolf in Hollywood*? She's clearly living in a fantasy world!'

'I really don't know why I'm friends with you.'

'Come on, Nic, look at her. One of the most famous guys in the world decides he wants her as his best mate? I don't believe a word of it.'

'She won a competition, so he has to be nice to her. And maybe Zak's fed up of Hollywood bimbos and wants to hang out with normal people.'

'I bet you anything she's spent the day sitting in a park talking to herself.'

Nicole shook her head, reluctant to concede that Eric was

probably right. 'I bet you twenty dollars that she's at his house tomorrow like she says she is.'

'Deal,' replied Eric, and shook Nicole's outstretched hand. 'How are you going to prove it?'

49

Although he'd been in the bathroom for just ten minutes, Declan had left the door slightly ajar so as to keep an eye on Matty in the bedroom. His friend lay on his side on the bed reading a dog-eared European copy of *GQ* that he'd picked up in the dining room, completely aware of Declan's beady eyes. The furthest they were ever apart was a partially open door – one of several unspoken rules between them.

'Did you call your mammy?' asked Declan, drying his hands on his t-shirt.

'Yeah, she sends her love.'

'Is she okay?'

'The usual, a bit tearful . . . you know what she's like.'

'And you?' Declan replied hesitantly. 'How are you feeling?'

'I'm good.'

'You know we can go back if you change your mind, don't you? I'll go with you, you won't be on your own.'

'Yeah, I know, but I also know what'll happen if we do.'

Thirteen Months Earlier: Navan, Ireland

Eddy Maguire was proud to have held the title of Navan's postmaster for the last thirty-six years. To take the pressure off his arthritic ankle, he leaned against the counter as he weighed Mrs Norton's parcel. He approved of her traditional use of brown wrapping paper and string to hold it together firmly, rather than cramming it into a padded envelope and reinforcing it with sticky tape.

It was the sudden hollering that startled him more than the sight of two figures wearing balaclavas, brandishing handguns and standing by his open door. Mr Maguire had survived six post office robberies to date unscathed, and he was confident number seven wouldn't be any different. He'd learned from experience that the *modus operandi* rarely varied: remove all the notes from the safe and the till, place them inside the bags the raiders always brought with them as quickly as possible, and once they left, phone the Gardaí. Four weeks later he'd be reimbursed by the powers that be.

'This is a stick-up,' shouted Matty, failing to control his quivering voice. 'Do what we say and nobody gets hurt.'

Mr Maguire chuckled to himself, wondering if all armed robbers read from the same handbook.

'This is a stick-up?' Declan asked his friend quietly. 'Who the feck says that these days?'

'Well, in case you've forgotten, this is our first robbery – have you got something better?' whispered Matty through gritted teeth.

Declan shrugged, so Matty continued, 'Any of you fucking pricks move, and I'll execute every motherfucking last one of you.'

'Really? You're going to start quoting *Pulp Fiction* now?'

Matty's empty threat was greeted by collective disapproval from the handful of elderly customers waiting in line to be served. Matty and Declan glanced at each other, puzzled; they'd expected to be feared, not groaned at.

'Is there any need for that kind of language in front of ladies?' asked Mr Maguire, evidently offended.

'Sorry,' replied Matty, before Declan landed a sharp elbow in his ribs. 'What was that for?'

'Why are you apologizing?'

'Cos I upset the old fella.'

'Less of the old,' interrupted Mr Maguire.

'Little gobshites,' added Mrs Norton, grasping her walking frame and shopping bag. 'It's bad enough you have to rob a post office, but to come in and call us . . . what was it again?'

'Fucking pricks,' replied the woman behind her in the queue, shaking her head.

'Fucking pricks? The mouthy bastards! Shame on you both.'

'Ladies and gentlemen, you're missing the point,' said Declan, exasperated. 'We're here to rob the place, not to make friends.'

'Well, that's a blessing, because with that language, you're not going to make any fecking friends in here.'

'Give me your money, everything you've got,' continued Declan, reasserting his authority, until it was Matty's turn to elbow Declan. 'Please,' he added reluctantly.

To a chorus of further disapproval, Declan used his gun to usher the customers towards the wall while Matty headed for Mr Maguire. Matty hurled their two duffel bags over the thick Perspex counter screens and Mr Maguire complied, stuffing them with euros before throwing the first bag back. Matty wondered why the postmaster didn't look more concerned.

'Will you be wanting the coins too?' Mr Maguire asked.

'No, just the notes, thank you.'

As Mr Maguire lobbed the second bag over his booth, he couldn't help but notice the barrel of Matty's gun was solid.

He'd been eye-to-eye with enough barrels to spot the difference between a real gun and a fake.

'Well, it was nice to meet you all,' added Matty, as he and Declan slung the bags over their shoulders. 'And sorry about all of this.'

'Ah, don't you worry yourselves, lads,' said Mr Maguire, realizing he was now the holder of the divisional record of most robbed post office in the Republic. His wife was always proud when his picture made the local newspaper.

As Declan opened the post office door, Matty grabbed a handful of euros and dropped them into Mrs Norton's shopping bag, offering her an apologetic shrug.

'Sorry for the bad language,' he added, before he and Declan bolted out of the door and through the town.

'Ah, what nice lads,' said Mrs Norton, swiftly changing her tune once she calculated how many Lotto scratch cards she could buy with her illegal windfall.

Suddenly her attention was drawn to Mr Maguire's peculiar gasping sounds, and she turned her head to watch him fall to the floor, clutching his chest.

50

Today

'Where's this?' asked Tommy, as he swiped his way from right to left on Jake's mobile phone.

'This is a wind farm I worked on in New Zealand, set in twenty-four square kilometres of land at the bottom of a hill.'

Tommy and Jake sat under the shade of a lifeguard's tower, drinking bottles of beer – strictly prohibited on the beach – disguised by brown paper bags.

'And this?' Tommy continued.

'That's the Lumbini Buddhist pilgrimage on the India–Nepal border.'

'How did you end up there?'

'I was in New Delhi having a coffee enema . . .'

'. . . as you do . . .'

'. . . as you do, and I got talking to the woman who was shoving the pipe up my backside. When you're naked, flat on your back, with a stranger holding your legs in the air, polite chit-chat's a good way of stopping yourself from farting five litres of Nescafe in her face. Anyway, she told me about this town supposedly being the birthplace of Buddha, so I ended up there teaching English to the local kids.'

'It looks beautiful.'

'Yeah, it is. But the enema was a waste of time, cos I got chronic dysentery and left after a month. Then it was over to Thailand, Vietnam, Singapore, Australia and New Zealand.'

'How long do you stay in each place?'

'It depends. I travel by three rules – never outstay your welcome; always leave them wanting more; disappear when no one's looking.'

'So I should expect you to vanish when I'm not looking?'

'It depends on whether there's something worth staying here for.'

Tommy glanced up and down Jake's two tattoo sleeves, which appeared to be inspired by religious iconography. The lines of numbers running from just below his armpit and down the side of his ribs caught his attention.

'What are they all about?'

'They're the map of my journey from the start to here,' Jake replied. 'Every time a place makes an impact on me, I get a tattoo of the coordinates.'

'So you're like a six-foot-tall, walking, talking Ordnance Survey map.'

'I guess you could say that,' Jake chuckled.

Suddenly a charismatic brunette wearing cut-off shorts and a jumper, surrounded by a group of twenty-something friends, appeared from nowhere and caught their eye.

'Is that Ariana Grande?' asked Tommy, as they watched her make her way towards the beach.

'Looks like it.'

'Wow, she's tiny.'

'I met her backstage once,' began Jake without thinking, and then immediately shut his eyes and cursed his careless tongue.

'You did what? No way! Did you speak to her?'

'For a bit.'

'And?'

'And what?'

'And what was she like?'

'Yeah, she was . . . nice.'

'Backstage where?'

'A show that an old friend was working on.'

Tommy waited for Jake to expand on his answer, or at least offer an anecdote, but neither was forthcoming.

'Don't give much away, do you?' Tommy continued, growing ever more curious and fascinated by his new pal. 'I thought us travellers were supposed to share our life stories?'

'Rule number two: Always leave them wanting more, Tommy. Always leave them wanting more.'

51

Day Six

Eric prayed their pick-up truck hadn't been towed away or ticketed by a meter maid as he and Nicole returned to the street where they'd parked.

Earlier that morning they'd decided to delay planning the next stage of their road trip, which had so far resulted in frustrating dead end after dead end. Instead, they took their minds off their failed journey with a competition to see whether Ruth had been telling the truth about her friendship with Zak Stanley. They'd followed a bus from Santa Monica for over an hour and watched from a safe distance as it dropped Ruth off in Melrose, where she then waited for another ride. They followed that bus for a further thirty minutes before she alighted at the foot of the Hollywood Hills. Nicole jumped out of the truck and made a beeline towards the convenience store Ruth entered, crouching out of sight behind a postal van while Eric parked and ran to join her. They couldn't help but laugh at the absurdity of their behaviour.

When the convenience store door buzzed, Ruth appeared with a bulging plastic bag and began her familiar traipse up the Hollywood Hills. Eric and Nicole waited at a safe distance before they followed. However, twenty minutes into what felt like a vertical walk, they were breathless and their target was nowhere to be seen.

'Bollocks, we've lost her,' said Eric, craning his neck to look around the intersection for signs of Ruth.

'Shhh,' whispered Nicole, 'she can't be that far ahead, and I don't want her to hear us.'

'She'll be too busy listening to the voices in her head to know we're here.'

'Let's just keep going upwards. I read somewhere the higher you go in the hills, the bigger the houses are. And she seemed to know where she was going, so she's clearly been here before.'

Eric felt a line of sweat beginning to trickle from his neck down his back and under the waistband of his boxer shorts. What had seemed like a fun wager was fast becoming a chore, and he was prepared to hand over his twenty-dollar bet to Nicole even though he knew Ruth stood more of a chance of joining the royal family than becoming Zak Stanley's BFF.

They turned their heads when they heard a vehicle behind them and saw a minibus crammed with tourists driving at a snail's pace up the hill. Through the windows, they could hear a tour guide over a Tannoy.

'And further up this avenue is where we find the three Zees,' came a chirpy female voice. 'We call it that because this is where Zac Efron, Zachary Quinto and Zak Stanley live.'

'Bingo,' said Nicole, beginning to jog to keep up with the bus. 'We're making a habit of turning up at people's houses unannounced, aren't we?'

Eleven Weeks Earlier: Holly Cottage, Great Houghton, Northampton, England

The ancient white-painted walls and thatched roof resembled someone's idea of what a cottage should look like and not something that actually existed, thought Nicole as she and Eric opened the wooden gate. They made their way up a crazy-paving pathway towards the front door.

As their taxi pulled away, Nicole recalled it had been a long time since she had taken a day trip out of London. She'd forgotten not everywhere smelled of exhaust fumes and ambition.

Mrs Baker's garden was colourful, pretty and very neatly kept. The flowers and shrubs in the borders were spaced symmetrically, the expansive lawns were the greenest things Nicole had ever seen, and the only remotely twenty-first-century touch was a set of cubed rattan furniture arranged beneath a large cream parasol.

Nicole examined the key in her hand and the address attached to the fob. It hadn't been what either of them had expected to find when they'd lifted the lid off the safety deposit box.

'Do you think your fairy godmother has left you the keys to her castle?' asked Eric.

Nicole shook her head. 'I doubt it . . . but someone's been here recently, because the lawn's been cut.' She looked at Eric pensively and then knocked on the door.

'What are you going to say if someone answers?' he asked. '"A dead woman left me a key and your address – do you mind if we have a nose around?"'

When there was no answer, Nicole inserted the key into the door's lock, but before she could turn it, a surly woman with short, curly hair and a face like thunder swung open the door and looked them up and down.

'Oh, sorry, we didn't think anyone was in,' Nicole began. The woman didn't reply. 'My name is Nicole Grainger and this is my friend—'

'I know why you're here,' the woman interrupted, and stepped back into the house, leaving the door open.

Nicole and Eric glanced at each other, unsure of how to respond. Nicole pulled the key out of the lock and followed her into an immaculately furnished lounge.

'And you are?' asked Nicole.

'Maria. I'm the housekeeper. Wait here,' she ordered, and left the room.

'I think I saw her visiting Mrs Baker a couple of times,' whispered Nicole.

'That scowl is enough to put anyone in an early grave.'

They scoured the room. Photographs in ornate frames covered a piano and two occasional tables, and above a large open fire was a shelf tightly packed with books. Nicole noted most were either travel guides or collections of images from around the world. She moved on to the photographs, some black and white, some colour, of Mrs Baker and her husband, and her son and daughter as very young children.

'Where do you think she's gone?' Nicole asked.

'Probably to put the family skeletons back in their closets,' added Eric, before a cough interrupted them.

'You'll find what you're looking for in there,' Maria instructed, pointing to an open door leading off the kitchen.

Nicole and Eric tentatively walked towards it. The room

was pitch black and colder than the rest of the house, and Nicole groped around the wall for a light switch. She felt a string and pulled it, and as the fluorescent strip light flickered on, Nicole smiled at what she saw. The key Mrs Baker had left in the safety deposit box hadn't been for the house, but for this. And it was a far more exciting prospect than bricks and mortar.

52

Today

'Savannah . . . could I, like, bum, a few bucks off you?' Joe asked when their paths crossed in the hostel corridor.

Savannah knew exactly what Joe planned to spend the cash on, but it didn't dissuade her, so she reached into her purse and removed a $20 bill. 'Promise me you'll use at least some of it for food?' she asked hopefully.

'Yeah, sure,' Joe replied with apparent gratitude. But the years spent watching her father at work in front of a congregation meant Savannah could spot the lie.

She reached her room, then paused when she found the door unlocked. Ron had been quick to replace the broken handle when she'd asked him, and her safety obsession meant that each time she left for work, she'd take a photo of the key in the lock before removing it. So later, when she'd question whether she'd locked the door, she had photographic proof it was secure.

'Hello, roommate, I'm Jane,' came a loud, cheery English accent from behind her.

Savannah jumped as a woman with cropped grey hair made her way into the centre of the room with her hands on her hips and a broad smile emblazoned across a make-up-free face. The woman's body shape reminded Savannah of an egg. She put her in her mid to late fifties, and judging by her cargo pants, checked shirt and walking shoes, she wasn't in Venice for the beach life.

'Is it just us girls?' Jane beamed.

'It *was* just me,' came Savannah's unwelcoming response. She frowned at Jane's open suitcase lying on the spare bed, with rolled-up clothes scattered across the floor.

'I'm sorry I'm a bit messy,' said Jane, 'but don't worry, I'll have this place spick and span in a few minutes. What's your name?'

'I prefer to keep the door locked when there's nobody here.'

'Well, we're both here now, aren't we?' Jane grinned as she continued to unpack.

Savannah sulkily threw her work clothes and make-up box into her handbag, checked the combination padlock was still attached to her locker, and went to leave.

'See you later then, roomie!' continued Jane, undeterred by Savannah's hostility.

'Yeah, bye,' muttered Savannah, deliberately slamming the door behind her.

53

Nicole sighed when she spotted Ruth squatting on the kerb outside what she presumed must be Zak Stanley's home.

Ruth's handbag lay by her side and she seemed engrossed in her scrapbook of stories about Zak. Nicole was now 100 per cent certain that Ruth hadn't spent the previous day with the film star, and wasn't completely convinced she'd even met him for lunch. She preferred to find the good in people, and had hoped that by some strange fluke, Ruth had been telling the truth. But the sight of her, so hopeful and yet so doomed to fail, broke Nicole's heart.

'Should I go over and say something?' Nicole asked Eric. 'I don't want to embarrass her, but she's going to get arrested for loitering or stalking or something.'

'She's not doing any harm,' replied Eric, momentarily sympathetic towards Ruth's pathetic figure. 'I think we should leave her be. It's none of our business what she's doing or why she's doing it.'

'If this is some sort of delusional disorder or if she's having a breakdown, don't we owe it to her to help?'

'You're not on duty, Nic. You need to let this go. You can't save everybody.'

The friends remained in silence for another couple of minutes, neither knowing what they were expecting to happen.

'Come on, let's go,' said Nicole eventually, and reluctantly began the journey back down the hill.

'You owe me twenty dollars, by the way,' added Eric.

'Why?'

'You lost your bet.'

'Technically, I didn't. I bet you she'd be *at* his house. You didn't specify she had to be *in* it.'

'Sneaky bitch.'

'Present and correct.'

Unaware she'd been followed, Ruth carefully placed her scrapbook back inside her handbag and turned around to look at Zak Stanley's home again.

She tried to imagine what it was going to be like when Zak finally left his house and saw her for the first time. She'd walk up to him and when she explained how much he meant to her, Zak would be so appreciative that she might receive a hug or a peck on the cheek. And if she made a really good impression, he might even invite her inside and away from the heat for a cool drink.

So until that happened, Ruth vowed to remain where she was, and removed a club sandwich and a bottle of Sprite she'd bought in the convenience store. After many failed attempts to diet, she no longer cared about what she ate. Zak would love her no matter what size she was.

Ruth had piled on a stone in weight for every year her father had been absent from his family, and there had been seven to date. Many of their family friends thought of Phil as a cliché for leaving his wife for an office intern less than half his age. Denise was humiliated and hadn't seen it coming, and dutifully, their friends took her side and shunned him.

She had only discovered her husband's double life when, by chance, she stumbled on Ling's Twitter feed. She and Phil were supposed to be on a business trip to Italy, not lying on a beach and holding hands in Thailand.

Once Phil moved out of the family home and into an apartment in the city, Denise banned her ex from ever coming back to the house again. Even years later, Kevin still remembered being coached by Denise to tell the police that his father had placed his hand in places no adult should ever touch a child. Kevin tried to go along with the lie but he wasn't clever enough to remain consistent and, after gentle interrogation from a sensitive officer, the investigation was dropped without a charge.

Meanwhile Ruth had tried to maintain contact with her dad, but as the years progressed, he made it increasingly difficult. She missed his hugs and his calling her sunbeam, and sometimes she only remembered how his voice sounded from the recorded voicemail messages she'd hear when she called him. She wouldn't have recognized his handwriting now even if he ever remembered to send her a birthday card.

She took another bite of her sandwich and recalled how Denise had gone on to blame Ruth for his departure, claiming that because she was a plus-size girl, he was ashamed to be seen with her. Ruth refused to believe her. Then, as the contact between father and daughter shrank to virtually nothing, Ruth came around to thinking her mother must be right; why else would a father wilfully ignore his children?

She suddenly snapped out of her thoughts, removed her phone from her handbag, and took a grinning selfie with

Zak's home behind her. She was about to email it to her dad, to give him good reason to be proud of her.

Then she remembered why she could never contact him, or anyone else back home, again.

54

Tommy was returning from a bathroom break when he came across Joe lying face down, sprawled across the landing floor. There was a damp patch covering the seat of his jeans where he'd wet himself before he had managed to reach the bathroom.

Just as Tommy had done on similar occasions before, he checked that Joe was breathing before dragging him into his room and leaving him by his bed so, when he awoke, Joe wouldn't have far to go to sleep it off.

Outside, the large buildings that overlooked the hostel pool offered a welcoming cool respite from the searing heat of the day. Tommy joined Jake where he'd left him, sitting on a cushion placed upon an upturned, rusted empty beer keg and hunched over a table by a chessboard. It was frayed but the squares were still visible, and missing pieces had been replaced with random objects like bottle tops, pen lids and coins.

'I've not really met anyone like you before,' said Tommy, moving his rook horizontally.

'Is that a good or a bad thing?'

'It's all good, don't worry. It's just that you've seen it all, you've done it all . . . you seem, you know, pretty sorted. I wish I was like that.'

'Oh, it's all just an act. I'm just as screwed up as everyone else in this building.'

Jake was far from being screwed up, thought Tommy. In fact, he was probably the most level-headed, laid-back and engaging person he'd ever met. Their day together had flown by, peppered by laughter, shared anecdotes and Jake's traveller's tales. And Jake was pleasantly surprised by just how much he enjoyed being revered by his spirited younger sidekick.

'Are you in touch with your family and friends often?' Tommy asked.

'No, not really.'

'Don't you get homesick?'

'Again, no – it's the sacrifice you make for a fresh start. What's that saying? *In change we find purpose.*'

Tommy nodded. He didn't feel homesick either. Instead, he felt nostalgic for everything he'd lost on the day of the car accident.

'Can I ask you a question?' he asked suddenly.

'Sure.'

'I don't mean to get all heavy and stuff, but . . . do you ever think you might have had the time of your life already, but were too busy to notice?'

'If you think like that, the next forty or fifty years are going to be very dull.'

'I dunno. I can't shake the feeling that travelling might be as good as my life gets. This could be my "moment".'

'There might be hundreds more moments, or there might be just one. Or the "moment" might be a person. I see it like this – people are like the tide. Some come into your life and bring things you'll only need for a short time, and others will bring things you'll carry forever. But some are just destined to disappear beneath the waves.'

Tommy wondered which category Louis had fallen into.

Seven Months Earlier:
Grand Central Station, New York

'We're here, mate, we're actually here. Can you believe it?'

Neither Tommy nor Louis appeared happy as they nervously glanced around the main concourse of Grand Central Station. They craned their necks towards the enormous stars and stripes flag hanging above them and puzzled over the zodiac constellations painted on the terminal ceiling. As they turned, their faces were bathed in the yellow light that poured through six high arched windows.

'Take a picture of me up there.' Louis pointed towards one of the pristine marble staircases and Tommy waited for the rush-hour commuters to thin out so he could take his shot. When they just came thicker and faster, Tommy gave up waiting, meaning Louis ended up resembling a 'Where's Wally' drawing.

In the eight hours since their plane had left Heathrow and landed at JFK, they'd negotiated their way to the terminal via AirTrain and then an alien subway system that used colours, letters and numbers and made little sense. Their back muscles already ached under the weight of their overpacked rucksacks, so they found a quiet spot and began unpacking under the four-faced golden clock atop the information booth.

'We need to streamline,' began Tommy, removing a travel hairdryer, electric razor and smart dress shoes. 'There is so much crap here we don't need. We're going to have to bin it or my spine's going to start falling out of my arse before the end of the day.'

'I don't think we'll be needing these,' answered Louis, removing three cans of Heinz beans, a jar of Marmite and hair straighteners, and dumping them all in a trash can. Then they rolled up their sleeping bags, secured them under the backpack straps and hung their spare trainers by their laces from side pocket zippers.

'Right, where are we going first?' asked Tommy.

As they moved towards the departure boards, their bulky presence became unwelcome with the locals when their rucksacks clipped several shoulders.

'Careful, man!' barked one. 'Asshole, are you blind?' yelled another. Louis tried to apologize but nobody listened. Never cross a New Yorker walking with purpose, he noted.

'This is too intense,' said Tommy. 'I think we should get out of New York, start off slowly to get acclimatized to America and then come back when we're a bit savvy.'

Louis nodded his agreement and studied the departure boards. 'We need a plan. There's a train leaving for Stamford in ten minutes, and another one going to Newark in fifteen.'

'No plans needed; I've got a better idea. We've got no timetable to stick to; we can go anywhere we want, whenever we want. Follow me.'

They walked towards the platforms, searching for a rare ticket booth without a closed shutter. Eventually they settled on a machine and Tommy closed his eyes, pushed a random destination button and inserted a $50 bill.

'Let's see where we end up, shall we?'

Louis grinned and gave Tommy a high five.

*

Louis shielded his sombre face from the lashing rain with the hood of his cagoule.

'We should've checked where the train was going before we caught the first one out,' he began. Tommy glanced around the near-empty station platform as Louis's finger traced a train line in a map book. A vending machine lay on its side, its glass door smashed and emptied of its confectioneries. Both signs informing them of where they'd reached were heavily covered in graffiti, rendering them illegible.

'So where are we?' asked Tommy.

'I wasn't really listening to the conductor when he said where the final stop was,' admitted Louis. 'But we're about an hour out of New York, so we could be north or south. Or west. Or maybe east.'

'Big help, mate.'

'We could be in Rensselaer. No, it's Denville. Or maybe Fairfield. Like I said before, we need a plan.'

'Well, at least we're on the move.'

'I think moving again very soon could be a good idea.'

Tommy looked puzzled until he saw what Louis was staring at. Ahead of them, a bearded man in a tatty army uniform and dirty trainers was pushing a baby buggy loaded with empty soda cans. He shuffled towards them. It was the bread knife in his hand that caught their attention next. They quickly rose to their feet, threw on their backpacks and frantically searched for an exit sign.

'You lookin' at my blade, muthafucker?' yelled the man, wide-eyed. 'Cos it's lookin' at you.'

With perfect timing, a train appeared from around the corner and stopped at the platform. As soon as the doors opened, they darted inside, scurried through the carriages and threw themselves onto seats. They breathed more easily as they slowly pulled away while the man with the bread knife walked alongside the moving train, banging on the windows. Louis leaned towards a woman sitting opposite him.

'Excuse me, where's this train heading, please?'

Tommy and Louis walked towards the departure board at Grand Central Station, no longer caring who they bumped into or what insults were hurled in their direction.

'Let me spell this out for you. We. Are. Making. A. Fucking. Plan,' growled Louis, and Tommy nodded obediently.

55

Today

Nicole never commented on it so as not to inflate Eric's ego any further, but she was always impressed by the way he seemed to know every lyric to every song he heard on the radio. And he didn't have a bad singing voice either.

As they drove back to the hostel from their reconnaissance mission to learn what Ruth was really up to, Eric sang along to both parts of Beyoncé and Shakira's 'Beautiful Liar' playing on a pop radio station. Nicole struggled to keep a signal on her phone long enough to open up Google and seek inspiration on where to travel to once they left Los Angeles.

'Found anything yet?' Eric asked, flicking on the dipped headlights as dusk fell.

'No.' Frustrated, Nicole threw her phone into the glove box. 'I remember Mrs Baker saying something about her and her husband sleeping in the back of the car one night by a lake. If I could get a bloody signal I'd look up lakes near Route 66.'

'That sounds pretty vague, hun.'

'No more or less so than your suggestion of going to Bakersfield just because it sounds like her surname.'

Eric fiddled with the dial on the radio and picked up a classic Seventies music station as the opening bars of a familiar song played. A small part of him still quietly harboured a desire to sing professionally, but – as Geri Garland had harshly pointed out when he'd auditioned to be part of the group Lightning Strikes three and half years earlier – he was more 'old boy' than 'boyband.' He remained grateful that humiliating audition clip had never aired. But now he happily sang along.

'What's this song?' Nicole asked, noting its familiarity.

'How on earth could you not know? It's Don McLean's "American Pie", but I bet you only remember the Madonna version,' Eric sniffed. 'His was a classic and it breaks my heart to admit it but the Queen ruined—'

'Shut up!' Nicole interrupted, and turned the volume up as Don sang about driving his Chevy to the levee. Six verses and eight minutes later, she slammed her hand down on the dashboard triumphantly.

'It's in the song!' she yelled. 'Where Mrs Baker wants us to go! It's in the bloody song!'

Eleven Weeks Earlier: Holly Cottage, Great Houghton, Northampton, England

'We trekked halfway across London, then into the middle of nowhere, for this?' asked Eric in disbelief.

Before them was an old, left-hand-drive white pick-up truck. It was caked in a film of dust and had two flat right tyres, giving it an awkward stoop.

'We could have cut out the middleman and bought a car from *Exchange & Mart*,' Eric continued.

'It's more than that,' said Nicole. 'It's the truck Mr and Mrs

Baker travelled America in on their honeymoon. She didn't mention they'd brought it home with them.'

She peered through the passenger window and spotted an A3-sized wooden box on the tan leather seat. She unlocked the door with the key from the safety deposit box and the hinges of the box squeaked as she lifted its lid. Inside was a handwritten letter.

'What does it say?' asked Eric, still disappointed that their quest had resulted in such a rusty old treasure. Nicole began to read out loud.

My dear Nicole,

Since my beloved husband died, I have spent years searching for a like-minded soul to appreciate what Joseph and I worked so hard to achieve. Reluctantly, I ruled out my family as they were not there when their father took ill or to support me afterwards when I struggled to pick up the pieces. But you offered me the hand of friendship, and I would like to reciprocate. Like me, you long for adventure. My body will not allow me to travel any further in this lifetime, but yours will. And only when you allow the warmth of new experiences to fill your heart will you truly realize how precious a gem your life is.

With everlasting gratitude,
Grace Baker

'I assume she was off her tits on morphine when she wrote this?' Eric asked.

Nicole ignored him, re-reading the letter to herself. Looking into the box, Eric saw rolls of banknotes – ten in total. He reached in to pick one of them up, slid the elastic band off and counted the £50 notes.

'Jesus, Nic – there's ten thousand pounds in here! So she has left you money after all.'

'I think there's more to it than that,' Nicole said thoughtfully. 'Is there anything else in there?'

Eric dug out a business card with a British address that appeared to be a company exporting vehicles to the US, along with car registration documents.

'There must be a clue in the letter,' said Nicole. Spotting an atlas lying under the box, she picked it up and opened it.

'Thanks, Velma. I'll fire up the Mystery Machine – you go grab Scooby.'

'Look . . . she's left a bookmark on the page for Chicago and another one for Santa Monica in Los Angeles. It looks like they're the start and end points of Route 66.'

'It's a bloody long road; where will you begin?'

'Where will *I* begin?' asked Nicole, surprised. 'It's not just *me*, it's *us*. We're in this together, my friend.'

Neither of them noticed Mrs Baker's housekeeper standing behind them, her hands clasped and fingers tightly entwined, silently praying that her panicked decision had been the correct one.

56

Today

Tommy carried the chessboard towards the cupboard where board games were stored. He became distracted by shrieking sounds behind Matty and Declan's closed bedroom door.

He couldn't resist placing an ear to it to hear what was causing the ruckus. But without warning, the door suddenly opened, causing Tommy to lose his balance and fall into a heap on the floor inside, chess pieces scattering across the threadbare carpet.

'We have a guest, ladies,' began Declan as Tommy looked up to find two girls he didn't recognize lying on beds and Matty and Declan wrapped only in towels. Tommy felt himself blush and his hands sprang into action, scrambling around to grab the pieces to put back in the box.

'Next time you can watch if you like!' added Matty, as Tommy took the board and hurried out of the room.

With another successful humiliation under their belts, Tommy vowed it would be the last time he was a butt of their jokes. He would make it a priority to toss the two cuckoos out of his nest as soon as the opportunity arose.

57

Eric leaned back on his plastic chair beside the hostel's two coloured iMacs, blowing cinnamon gum bubbles while Nicole scanned the computer screen.

Her eyes moved from the web pages to the notes she was frantically jotting in a book. Eric was bored – he cracked his knuckles, picked at a scab on his ankle, felt for protruding nostril hairs and glanced at Jake sitting on a sofa reading a book about holistic health and yoga. There was something familiar about Jake, but he couldn't quite put his finger on it. He couldn't think where their paths might have crossed.

Suddenly Nicole slammed her pen down and threw herself back against the chair triumphantly.

'Buffalo Springs Lake, Texas. That's where we're going,' she exclaimed.

'And how did you come to that conclusion, Miss Marple?' yawned Eric.

'I'll explain, but you need to concentrate. The clues are all in that song, "American Pie". Mrs Baker said it was their song – her and her husband. She talked about sleeping in the back of the truck by a lake. She was telling me about their trip around America in 1971 on Route 66 – well, that was the year the song was released. According to Wikipedia the song is about, well at least in part, the singer Buddy Holly dying in a plane crash. That's why Don Henley sings about "the day the music died".'

'Henley? You mean McLean. And everyone knows that.'

'Whatever.'

'But didn't Buddy Holly die in the 1950s or something?'

'Yes, but he was born in Lubbock, Texas. And which road goes through Lubbock, Texas? Route 66.'

'That road goes through a lot of states, Nic, as you well know, because I drove through most of them to get to LA and I swear Lubbock was one of towns we passed.'

'Will you just let me finish?' Nicole replied. 'Read the lyrics. He talks about a pick-up truck and driving a Chevy to the levee – what are we driving?'

'A Chevy pick-up truck. But what's a levee?'

'It's an embankment or flood bank that regulates water levels. And where would you find one of those?'

'At a lake.'

'Exactly, and where did I tell you Mrs Baker and her husband slept one night?'

'At a lake?'

'And near Lubbock, Texas, you'll find Buffalo Springs Lake. There are so many more references in the song to things in the town, like churches and school gyms, dance studios, broken church bells, football teams and even a marching band parade. It all fits.'

Eric knew Nicole was desperately attempting to find clues, but he couldn't help thinking there were probably hundreds of other lakes in the US that would also fit the bill. In the absence of any better suggestions, though, he nodded. And the more time he gave himself to consider it, the more he came around to thinking Nicole might be on to something after all.

'It's roughly twelve hundred miles from here,' she continued. 'If we set off in the morning, we can be there in a couple of days.'

'And what are we going to find when we get there?'

'Let's cross that bridge when we come to it. But I have a gut feeling this is going to change everything for us.'

Nicole had no idea how right she was – but not in the way she hoped.

58

Day Seven

Ruth was unaware of the poppy seeds accumulating between her teeth as she tucked into her third cream cheese bagel of the day.

She sat on a fold-up chair purchased from an outward bound store in Santa Monica, finished her breakfast and reached inside her bag for her knitting. No one had bothered to answer Zak's intercom that morning, but Ruth was positive someone was inside the house as the patio doors were now closed and the CCTV camera quietly changed direction soon after she pressed the button. But a single-minded Ruth wasn't easily dissuaded when she was so close to her goal, so she sat contentedly and continued to knit Zak's jumper.

Nobody seemed to walk in the Hollywood Hills, she observed, as no matter where she wandered – and it was never far from Zak's house – she had yet to talk to another person. Even the uniformed staff entering and leaving Zak's neighbours' homes used cars or vans. Occasionally a jogger would eye her up with suspicion, but that was about it.

Every couple of hours Ruth made her way around the corner, squatted in a patch of bushes and relieved herself. And when the sun began to heat up the sidewalk, she pulled out a stripy parasol that had come with the seat and stuck it into the grass verge.

As the hours of her lonely public vigil ticked past, Ruth's determination to meet Zak grew ever stronger.

Three Weeks Earlier: Victoria, Australia

Ruth nervously played with her hair as the glass elevator rose to the twenty-second floor of the plush apartment block.

The doors silently opened and she scanned the corridor for number 223. She was skittish yet excited and knocked on the solid wooden door a little more loudly than she'd intended, so that the sound echoed through the corridor. Inside, she heard footsteps on the floor before it unlocked and her father answered. He was casually dressed in sweatpants and a t-shirt that was too tight for a man of his age and size.

'Hi Dad,' began Ruth eagerly. Phil looked at his daughter for the first time in almost three years. She was much heavier than he recalled, and it had aged her. She didn't resemble either him or his bitter ex-wife.

'I didn't know you were coming over,' he replied, flustered. He pulled the door partially closed behind him but didn't move towards her.

'I haven't heard from you for ages and I wanted to say hi,' continued Ruth, hopefully.

'You really should've called first.'

'I did. I left messages on your machine, and at work, and on your mobile phone.'

'Oh, right. Okay, well, I've been busy – you know how it is.'

Ruth nodded. 'Can I come in, please?'

'Um, it's not really convenient right now, Ruth. Another time, maybe.'

'Well, I came to say goodbye. I'm going to America to—'

'Okay, well, enjoy yourself,' her father interrupted, smiling vacantly, and began to turn his back on her.

Ruth's heart sank as she realized that her father, who had always seemed to sweep in and out of her life on his own terms, was already terminating their all-too-brief reconciliation. She'd imagined they might spend the afternoon together, catching up on each other's news like old friends. He would ask questions about her job and she would tell him all about Zak and the competition she'd won. Then anger suddenly displaced the disappointment she felt, so she pushed open the door he was trying to shut.

'Aren't you going to ask why I'm going to America?' asked Ruth forcefully.

'Ruth, I don't have time for this. I'll see you soon, I promise.'

'Why don't you want anything to do with me, Dad? What have I done wrong? I'm a good person, I really am.'

Phil took a bulging leather wallet from his pocket, removed a handful of dollars and handed them to her. 'There – you don't need anything from me now, right?'

Ruth couldn't disguise how let down she felt and willed the tears forming in her eyes to evaporate.

Suddenly a little Southeast Asian girl, no more than four years of age, appeared by Phil's waist.

'Daddy, who's this lady?' asked the girl, pressing her hand into his palm. Ruth's mouth slowly fell open as her father struggled to find words.

'She's a friend of mine, sunbeam,' he replied.

'Sunbeam,' repeated Ruth, realizing she'd been replaced.

'Mei, can you leave Daddy alone, please?' said a female voice from behind the door as it opened further. 'Who are you talking to . . . ? Oh, Ruth, this is a surprise.'

Phil's girlfriend Ling made no attempt to invite her in and Ruth had no idea how to respond to the sight of her father's replacement family, or the new 'sunbeam' in his life. She stepped backwards towards the lift.

'Ruth—' began her father, but the lift door closed with her inside before she heard anything else.

59

Today

Eric parked the truck at the hostel kerb, and Nicole and Tommy lifted the suitcases into the flatbed and secured them with ropes.

Eric ignored both Tommy's presence and assistance and remained in the truck fiddling with the radio, leaving Nicole to say goodbye.

'Well,' said Tommy.

'Well,' she replied.

'Good luck with the rest of your vacation.'

'Thanks.'

Nicole wanted to tell Tommy that in different circumstances, she would have returned his kiss – but that the burden of a secret she couldn't reveal would always come between them. But both were aware their moment had passed.

'I've sent you a friend request on Facebook,' she continued, 'so we can stay in touch, if you like?'

'That'd be good.'

He stretched his hand out awkwardly to shake hers; instead she hugged him and gave him a peck on the cheek as an impatient Eric honked the horn.

Watching the truck pull away, Tommy felt a little envious

of Nicole's next adventure, even though she'd been cagey about what it involved or where she was going. But while he'd enjoyed her company, he was also looking forward to spending more time with Jake and learning more about the world by living vicariously through his anecdotes.

Jake had also encouraged Tommy to consider whether it was time to throw to one side the security blanket of the Venice Beach International Hostel and experience more of America by himself. However, when he gave it proper thought, he knew he was still too scared – and too broke – to do it without Louis.

It would take the actions of his past and present colliding before he could ever move forward.

60

'Over there,' began Nicole, pointing to a greenish verge with a panoramic view further up the highway.

Eric pulled the indicator lever down and the truck ground to a halt by the side of the Arizona road.

'What do you reckon?' he asked, turning to face Nicole.

She took in her surroundings. There was nothing but blue sky and flat landscape for mile after mile. It was epically spacious and completely apt. 'Yes, this looks like somewhere she'd love.'

They exited the truck and stretched limbs that felt tight after nine hours of continuous driving. Route 66 both ahead and behind them was silent and should've been straight as a die, had the sun's incalescence not made it wobble like jelly. But the mainly barren landscape was pure picture-book America.

Eric lifted himself into the back of the truck to remove the cardboard box where Mrs Baker's urn was stored. Then he followed Nicole as she walked towards a grassy knoll with a canyon-like drop below.

'Hey, it's Eric and Urn,' Eric joked, and looked to Nicole for approval. She ignored him.

'Didn't Bridget ask why you wanted her mum's ashes?' she

asked. 'What kind of woman gives something so precious to a complete stranger?'

'The kind who couldn't care less, I suppose. People can be shits, hun.'

'And you're sure she didn't say where she'd like us to scatter them?' Eric shook his head. 'Okay, well, let's do this.'

Eric passed Nicole the urn, and she tore off the tape that kept the lid firmly in place. Then she took a deep breath and began to shake the ashes into a light breeze. They stood and watched Mrs Baker make her final journey towards the snow-capped Mount Elden, beckoning from the distance.

'Goodbye, Mrs Baker, and thank you for this opportunity,' Nicole said quietly. Eric placed his arm around her shoulder and felt her head tilt towards him. After a few moments of silence, Nicole wiped away the tears pooling in the corners of her eyes, carefully placed the empty urn on the ground and returned to the truck.

Eric waited a moment longer, absorbing the view of the arid landscape surrounding him.

'Goodbye, mother,' he muttered, and spat on the ground where a small pile of ashes rested.

PART TWO: THE DEPARTURES

61

Day Eight

'Come on, man,' snapped an unusually competitive Peyk. 'It's an easy shot.'

'No pressure, then,' Tommy replied. He arched his back over the pool table, stretching his fingers over the black ball to knock the cue ball into the yellow. It glided into the pocket with ease.

'Lucky,' said Peyk dismissively, as the music in the hostel lounge became louder.

A mixed group of young Australians scanned a TV screen, awaiting direction before frantically aping the animated dance steps flashing before them. Tommy resented the popularity of Matty and Declan's stolen Xbox, and the fact that his adversaries had become the centre of attention because of their gift and charm.

When one girl lost her balance and jostled Tommy, he missed his shot.

'Which rules are we playing,' Tommy asked, 'American or European?'

'What's the difference?' asked Peyk.

'Americans don't play a lot of snooker or three-cushion billiards,' interrupted Jake, potting his first, second, then third red with ease. 'Americans mostly play eight-ball and nine-ball, along with one-pocket or 14.1 straight pool.'

Tommy and Peyk responded with raised eyebrows.

'What? I'm more than just a pretty face, boys.'

When Jake missed the fourth red, he passed the only cue over to Gabby the receptionist. Tommy leaned against the wall, his eyes darting between Jake and one of the amateur dancers who was offering him kittenish glances.

'If this was snooker, would you be going for the pink or the brown?' whispered Peyk, clearly amused with his innuendo.

'What?' Tommy replied.

'You know what I mean.'

'If I do, then you are *way* off. Jake's a friend.'

Peyk shrugged and turned to take his shot. Suddenly the booming bass of a familiar pop song blasting from the TV interrupted their game.

'Hey!' yelled Tommy. 'Turn that off.'

'Why should I?' the Australian girl yelled indignantly.

'Because I said so,' replied Tommy angrily. 'Now!'

'Don't speak to her like that,' warned Declan, who stood by the window with Matty.

'Mind your own business.'

'What did you say?' Declan continued, walking towards Tommy with shoulders squared.

'Leave it, Dec,' said Matty.

The girl turned the song off and abandoned the game as the others in the room glared at Tommy, surprised by his uncharacteristic aggression. He looked at the faces staring at him. Then he walked out of the room, unaware that Jake had already slipped out moments earlier.

Three and a Half Years Earlier: London

The cork from the champagne bottle flew through the air like a bullet, rebounding off a polystyrene ceiling panel in the TV studio restaurant.

A DJ in the corner of the room mixed James Brown's 'Get Up (I Feel Like Being A) Sex Machine' into Prince's 'Gett Off' as Stuart left the makeshift dance floor and helped himself to a glass of Dom Pérignon from a waitress's tray. It wasn't an obvious location for *Star People*'s wrap party, but as the floor manager pointed out, the budget had been spent on the series finale's pyrotechnics, choirs, backdrops and staging. And creator Geri Garland held her purse strings tightly.

All eyes were on each member of winners Lightning Strikes. The other boys were well on their way towards intoxication, but Stuart preferred the control that sobriety brought. He watched with a touch of envy as families hugged their winning offspring and clenched their hands with affectionate pride. Competition-winning fans interrupted them for selfies, and celebrity guests vied for their attention. Stuart, however, was alone, as he had been for almost as long as he could remember.

In need of a moment's peace, he slipped away from the rowdy room and aimed for the bathroom, where he planned to lock himself in a cubicle and process the night's events.

He was about to lock the door when a hand yanked it open – Geri. He stepped back as she squeezed herself into the cubicle.

'I told you you'd make me proud,' she began, placing her hands around his waist. Her breath smelled of cigarettes and booze.

'It's incredible,' began Stuart awkwardly. 'I've been meaning to say thank you for—'

'No need to thank me,' she interrupted, closing his lips with her finger. 'Thank those Asian call centres I paid to push your votes up. And this is just as much for me as it is for you.'

She unclasped Stuart's hand and in it placed a black Links of London box with a ribbon around it. Inside was a silver bangle bracelet. Stuart turned it over and read the inscription: *Never Look Back.*

'Those boys need a frontman and you've got the looks to do it,' Geri continued. 'And I have a feeling you're going to make me a very, very satisfied woman.'

She removed her finger from Stuart's lips and gradually moved it down his shirt and towards his belt, before slipping her hand inside the front of his jeans and cupping his balls.

'Geri, I don't think this is a good idea . . .' Stuart mumbled nervously as her fingers worked their way around his crotch. He could feel his penis hardening and he tried to think of anything that might make it shrink again. Instead, his eyes widened and his buttocks pressed backwards against the cubicle wall as Geri gripped him firmly. Then, when he was completely but reluctantly erect, she kissed his cheek and released her hand.

'I always get my way, Stu,' she added. 'Do as you're told and I'll make you a very rich boy.'

Then, to his relief, she let herself out of the cubicle and slipped away. It hadn't been a one-off event, but Stuart knew that if he said no, his career could crash-land before it had the opportunity to skyrocket.

62

Two thumps on the left-hand side of the shower pipe and three to the right was what it took for water to pour from the shower in Tommy's shared bathroom.

Today, however, there was a special surprise about to burst from the end of the pipe where a shower nozzle should've been attached. It came in the form of a deep gurgling and an intrusion of cockroaches surfing a tide of water.

'Jesus,' yelled Tommy, jumping backwards against the cracked wall of tiles. He lifted his foot to squash them before changing his mind.

Tommy was aware of the saying 'you get what you pay for', and he paid for nothing in the hostel. But the right to basic hygiene wasn't too much to expect, so with the roaches negotiating the slippery shower tray and scuttling down the drain, he wrapped his towel around his bare waist, felt his feet squelch on a sopping wet bathroom mat, threw on his clothes and stormed out of the room.

He was still angry at Matty and Declan for interfering when he'd asked – well, ordered – that girl to turn off the computer game. But he was more frustrated at himself, for allowing his temper to get the better of him. He'd made a fool of himself in front of everyone there.

Now he was going to take his anger out on Ron. He'd

already complained numerous times about the weak water pressure and had been fobbed off with useless promises. Today he was in no mood for excuses.

'Is he in?' Tommy growled at Gabby, seated behind the reception desk piercing her eyebrow with a needle and an ice cube. She shrugged, so Tommy knocked on Ron's door and didn't wait to be invited in.

Instead of sitting behind his desk, Ron was standing with a pile of cash, handing Wayne a brick-sized package wrapped in cellophane. Tommy immediately recognized what was inside: dried, compressed cannabis leaves similar to the ones Peyk was so keen on sprinkling into his Rizlas. Ron and Wayne were clearly startled by Tommy's appearance, and while Wayne scurried out past him, Ron opened his desk drawer and swept the cash inside.

'It's not what it looks like,' he muttered.

'It looks like you're selling drugs to Wayne.'

'Then it is what it looks like.'

'How? Why? You told me to keep him out of this place.'

Ron sighed and ran his hand through his comb-over, apparently wrestling with indecision.

'Things change, Timmy,' he said finally. 'You need to come with me.'

63

The first time Zak Stanley's eyes met Ruth's, she was sitting motionless outside his Hollywood Hills home.

By her fifth consecutive day spent perched on a fold-up chair, Ruth had begun to lose all sense of time. An hour could sail by before she'd realize she'd been staring blankly at the rendered wall in front of her. She'd even counted the leaves on the ivy stems growing up it. But the long-awaited sound of footsteps and an automatic gate slowly opening snapped her out of her unfulfilled daydreams.

She turned around like a shot and there he was: Zak Stanley, in the flesh, and in the presence of his biggest fan.

Zak frowned at her, wondering whether the plump, dishevelled shape was male or female and a threat to his safety. Meanwhile the shape's eyes worked their way up from Zak's tanned legs to his Abercrombie & Fitch-emblazoned sweat shorts, then his white sleeveless t-shirt and the MP3 player strapped to his arm, before reaching his face.

Ruth ached to touch the dark chocolate fringe tucked behind his ears, but she felt paralysed.

Deciding the shape appeared harmless, Zak turned his music up with a remote control attached to his headphones and jogged up the hill, out of Ruth's sight.

She didn't move a muscle for another ten minutes.

64

Jane turned the photograph she was holding face-down on the carpet as she heard footsteps approaching the door.

Instinctively she knew something was wrong when Savannah appeared, clutching her cheek and trying to avoid eye contact.

'Oh my God, what happened to you?' began Jane, jumping to her feet.

'I'm fine,' Savannah replied, only then remembering a new roommate had been shoehorned into her life.

'No you're bloody not, let me have a look.' Jane grabbed Savannah's hand and pulled it away, noting her cut lip and a swelling around her eye. 'What happened to you, darling?'

'Nothing.'

'That's not nothing. At least let me stop the bleeding. I've got some antiseptic wipes somewhere—'

'Please,' begged Savannah, now struggling to control her emotions, 'just leave me alone.'

She dashed into the bathroom and closed the door behind her, locking it. She tore off two sheets of toilet paper, looked into the mirror and began dabbing the drops of blood from her split lip.

In the months Savannah had been dancing at the Pink Pussycat Club, she'd never seen a fight amongst customers, let alone been the cause of one. But that changed when she refused a private lap dance to two drunken redneck tourists who were in no mood for rejection. When one grabbed her arm, she'd yelled for the security men's help, and once the fists began to fly, she had been caught in the middle of the fracas.

Now tired, bruised and emotional, Savannah couldn't fight the urge to cry any longer. So she sat on the toilet seat, held her hands over her mouth and silently sobbed.

This is not how my life is supposed to have turned out, she thought. *Working as a pole dancer, living in a hostel and sharing a room with a middle-aged Mary Poppins.*

But that was what it had become . . . for now, at least.

Six and a Half Months Earlier: Montgomery, Alabama

Savannah watched from behind the linen curtains in her bedroom as her father's black Chrysler began its slow approach along the driveway and up towards the mansion.

As he parked, she took a deep breath. Then, partly shielding her eyes, she drew her arm back and threw a fist-sized solid metal paperweight through her window.

The glass shattered instantly and the paperweight continued its trajectory, missing the Reverend's head by no more than a few inches. The car's windscreen cracked as it rebounded onto the bonnet and then to the ground. Reverend Devereaux's alarm rapidly turned to rage when he raised his eyes to discover his daughter standing defiantly in her window.

The front doors of the house smacked against the rubber stoppers, making the wooden shutters vibrate as he ran up the staircase and towards Savannah's room. For two weeks he had kept her locked away in the vain hope she'd understand that breaking his rules had consequences. But she'd inherited his stubbornness and made no attempt to apologize. And if said apology was not forthcoming by the end of the month, he had reserved her a room at a private hospital in Maine which, he'd been advised, offered a regime of 'medication and forced re-education therapy' that would assist Savannah in coming around to his way of thinking. Now, with this further act of blatant rebellion, he decided to ensure she was en route within the hour.

The Reverend hurried along the hall and turned a key, flinging Savannah's bedroom doors open. He expected to see her still by the window; only his daughter wasn't there. His eyes narrowed and he looked back and forth, scanning the room for her.

Then he dropped to the carpet like a bag of rocks, clutching at his neck.

The Reverend's body convulsed as electricity travelled through the lamp base Savannah was holding. It flowed under his skin and through his veins like thick, boiling liquid. He felt his cold heart beating faster than it had ever done before as it, alongside all his other muscles, tightened. Savannah kept the electrical current flowing through him, watching as, frozen and unable to protect himself, Reverend Devereaux was completely at her mercy.

Time spent with only the television for company had educated Savannah. One DIY show in particular had taught her how to strip the wires from an old lamp and upcycle them for an alternative use. It was only when the presenter had advised caution, as it could transform the lamp into something potentially lethal, that Savannah had realized what she must do.

She wore an old pair of galoshes she found in the back of her wardrobe so the rubber would act as insulation and prevent her from being electrocuted. Finally, when she was sure her father would not be rising to his feet for some time, she dropped the lamp. His body looked sluggish, each breath he took was desperate, his pupils were dilated and his body was virtually motionless.

Savannah swiftly yanked off her boots, slipped on her sneakers and rifled through his pockets, knowing he always carried a large number of bills in his wallet. Then she grabbed a pre-packed overnight bag and escaped the confines of her room.

Her hands and legs shook as her 'fight or flight' adrenaline rush took hold, and she threw herself towards the open front doors. Suddenly a voice behind her stopped her in her tracks.

'How on earth . . .' began her mother, brow furrowed, but clearly wary of the determined expression on Savannah's face. Savannah gave her one last 'don't fuck with me' look, and made for her father's car.

'Please, please, please,' she prayed, hoping that in his confusion over narrowly missing the flying paperweight, he had left his keys in the vehicle. And she thanked God when she found them there.

Once the engine turned over and the handbrake was released, she put her foot on the accelerator and sped away, spitting gravel in her wake.

The Greyhound coach slowly pulled away from its bay outside Montgomery's station and began its long haul towards California.

The man sitting behind the ticket counter's reinforced

plastic screen had advised Savannah the journey would take around forty hours, involve three transfers and twenty-eight stops before she reached her Los Angeles destination. But Savannah didn't care, just as long as the bus took her far away from her life. Every minute she spent on the tired old bus with its faded blue-and-grey seats and empty plastic tables was better than being trapped inside a gilded cage.

Once she'd got behind the wheel of her father's car, her first instinct had been to drive to Michael's campus. She was less than a mile away before she had second thoughts. If she loved Michael, she would have to let him go.

So she turned the car around and headed downtown instead. She left it parked two blocks from the Greyhound station with the keys visible on the dashboard in the hope it might be stolen or stripped, rubbing salt into her father's wounds. She charged the bus fare to the Reverend's black Visa card, then left it by the sink in the public bathroom so others could make use of it before it was cancelled.

Savannah's only possessions in the world were the clothes in her holdall and those on her back. She unzipped her hooded top, placed it against the window and leaned her head against it, watching the rain gently trickle down against the backdrop of a blood-red sky.

Intuition warned her that no matter how far forward she went, Savannah would always be looking behind her, just in case.

65

Today

Ron handed Tommy a spare pair of sunglasses from his pocket as they stood in the corridor facing room 23.

'Your storeroom,' said Tommy, suddenly concerned as to why Ron, who behaved oddly at the best of times, was luring him into an unfamiliar room.

'Put them on,' Ron replied, then knocked three times on the door, paused and knocked twice more. They heard two bolts being pulled to the side and then a key turning, before it opened and Peyk's face appeared.

'I see we have company,' he said, and ushered them in, quickly closing and locking the door behind them. They stood in pitch blackness for several seconds until Peyk opened another door leading into a brightly lit room.

Tommy gazed around in astonishment, his eyes opening wide as he turned his head from left to right and then back to Peyk and Ron.

'What the hell have you two done?'

66

No one spotted Jake slip quietly away from the hostile atmosphere of the lounge and up a flight of stairs towards the fire exit.

He hated confrontation, and was a little taken aback by Tommy's ire towards the girls dancing, but he'd had to leave when he heard the opening chords of *that* song.

The bar across the door hung to one side from a broken screw, so he pushed it open and made his way onto the roof. He realized it wasn't the secret hideaway he'd first thought it might be when he spotted two stained mattresses, a long-disused satellite dish half full of cigarette butts, and scores of empty beer bottles with sun-bleached labels.

Jake walked closer to the edge and leaned against the railings, looking down with a new perspective on the cars parked at 45-degree angles in the street below. Sunlight bounced off their windscreens and rear-view mirrors, and on the sidewalk, throngs of people made their way to and from the beach. His eyes followed them into the distance before he scanned the rooftops of neighbouring buildings, beyond the tops of palm trees and finally the ocean.

He tried to locate Hollywood, wondering if he could ever muster the courage to take a trip there and gain the closure he felt he needed two years on.

As much as he enjoyed the company of other people, sometimes he preferred them in small doses, and today was one of those days. He'd had his fill of being the centre of attention for a lifetime.

Twenty-Six Months Earlier: London

Lightning had certainly struck, not once but three times, as Stuart's band topped the singles charts with a trio of releases.

Then, after a headline-making chart battle, their debut album outsold Ed Sheeran's latest effort two to one to reach pole position. With manager Geri Garland's public relations company driving the promotional campaign at full throttle, Stuart, Gabriel, Josh, Dylan and Ethan's faces were impossible to avoid. From being gunged on a kids' TV show to paparazzi photographers clamouring to take their pictures as they entered nightclubs with models, and with managed TikTok, Snapchat and Instagram accounts, there was nothing about their public activities their fans didn't know.

Privately, it was a very different matter.

With no children of her own – by choice rather than by circumstance – *Star People* was Geri's baby.

She'd created it, so she decided who'd make the live shows. But when the audition process began for season two, Geri grew concerned. She'd later informed Stuart that after a month of travelling up and down the country listening to woeful hopefuls caterwauling, she'd chosen four male solo singers picked for their voices rather than their looks. And as the competition lacked tween fodder, Geri had decided the best way forward was to push them together and create a boyband. However, they lacked one vital ingredient – there was no Justin Timberlake and no Harry Styles, and any boy-band worth its salt needed a sexy frontman. So when Geri spotted Stuart, a handsome young porter working at a Holiday Inn in Bolton, her gut instantly told her she'd unearthed the missing ingredient.

Very little took Geri's breath away, except maybe her first cigarette of the morning, but Stuart made her stony heart race as he carried her Louis Vuitton luggage to her room. He felt her eyes bore into him from behind.

It wasn't just his lean physique or his razor-sharp cheek-bones that made her feel like a teenage girl again. She also liked that he was blissfully unaware of his own beauty and had an innocence she rarely came into contact with in her shallow industry. Such innocence was there to be exploited, and Geri was the perfect person for the job.

The next morning, two crisp £50 notes were all it took to get Stuart's home address from one of his colleagues. 'This will be easier than I thought,' she informed her driver as her Jaguar pulled into a shabby council estate full of high-rise tower blocks.

Talking a shocked Stuart into going along with her plan took little effort, as Geri had made persuasiveness an art form and Stuart had nothing to lose. He surprised himself at how readily he opened up to a woman he barely knew as he recounted his childhood and teenage years spent abandoned in foster care, shuttled between temporary parents and social workers, and how it had forced him to learn self-reliance. He revealed how he'd harboured vague ambitions to find a career in the travel industry, but was willing to put that on hold for what Geri was offering.

Stuart was all too aware that there was more to life than minimum-wage employment and renting a room in a tiny council flat with a friendly Russian couple who appeared to have a never-ending supply of British passports in plastic folders on the communal table. Sometimes, when his hotel shift came to an end, he'd study for his Open University travel and tourism course at a table in the corner of the hotel restaurant while furtively watching families dine together.

So when Geri offered to open up a new world to him – one so far removed from his own, it might as well have been located on a different planet – he grabbed the opportunity with both hands. Fame was something he neither craved nor needed, but Geri had the measure of him.

'See this as a means to an end,' she explained. 'It won't last forever; boybands never do. Just ride the wave for long enough and you'll be set for the rest of your life.'

What she didn't inform Stuart was how much she enjoyed having the power to change a person's life on a whim. She cherished it all the more knowing that she could bring it to an end just as sharply.

With Stuart on board, Geri had a complete, marketable boyband ready to roll off the *Star People* conveyor belt and straight into the live television shows. Four reasonably talented lads whose music teenage girls would stream and whose merchandise they'd pay over the odds for, plus a beautiful lead singer with a sob story everyone would lap up.

Geri's puppets did what they were told, obeyed the clauses in their lengthy contract about not bringing their brand into disrepute, and discreetly bed-hopped behind closed doors with members of girl groups and other reality TV stars.

When the cameras were on them, Lightning Strikes were

the best of friends, larking about and referring to each other in interviews as brothers. But when they weren't working, Stuart barely spent any time with them. He was the only one without a family and was quietly envious of their closeness and their freedom to be who they were. Meanwhile they were green-eyed over him being the focus of fans and journalists alike.

As hard as he tried, there was little Stuart could do to fend off Geri's frequent sexual advances. She only ever required one of two things – to either give him oral sex or to masturbate him, and never in the confines of a bedroom. Instead, it would occur when Stuart least expected it, like in the back of a limousine, a TV show dressing room, a hotel restaurant and even once in an empty recording studio sound booth. Stuart rarely climaxed and Geri didn't seem bothered. She never asked for penetrative sex or for Stuart to pleasure her, a small mercy he was grateful for. It was, he decided, just a power trip for her – another way in which Geri let him know who was boss.

'Don't forget, I know your secrets,' she'd warned him when he attempted to refuse her advances one afternoon.

'Not all of them,' he thought.

'So don't look a gift horse in the mouth,' she continued, before placing his penis back inside the gift horse's mouth.

67

Today

By the time a bruised Savannah finished her solo pity party in the bathroom and unlocked the door, the bedroom was empty.

Jane had left a clear plastic bag on her duvet containing cotton-wool buds, a bottle of witch hazel and a packet of antiseptic wipes. Savannah cautiously checked under her pillow to make sure her gun was still in place, then scooped up the medicines and applied them to her grazes.

The stress of the day made her stomach ache, so she lay on her side and faced Jane's bed. Knowing that she was losing money by not working made her even more anxious, and she struggled to relax. Also, being aware that her new roommate might return at any moment wasn't helping. Quite why a middle-aged woman would want to stay in a rundown backpacking hostel was beyond her. Surely at Jane's age, she'd want better for a vacation than to be surrounded by people with whom she had nothing in common?

Curiosity got the better of her and she decided to snoop. Savannah approached Jane's side of the room and sniffed at a bottle of perfume on a bedside table. Then, when she noticed Jane's suitcase was unlocked, after a cautious glance over her shoulder, she casually opened the lid to find Jane's neatly folded clothes and collection of travel books.

The sound of the door's squeaking hinges startled her.

'I was . . . just putting your first aid stuff back,' Savannah blurted out, looking at Jane and realizing she didn't actually have anything in her hands.

'Oh, I don't mind, have a nose around, my dear. I've got nothing to hide,' Jane replied. 'How's the swelling?'

'A little better, thanks. And I'm sorry for jumping down your throat earlier.'

'Don't you worry about it,' assured Jane. 'So what happened to your face?'

'Some assholes were pissed because I don't do "extras".'

'I assume you don't work in an office.'

'I'm an exotic dancer.'

'Well, good on you, but no job is worth being beaten up over.'

'I can look after myself.'

'Okay, darling, but just in case, I'll keep my medicine box in my suitcase under the bed, so just help yourself if you ever need it again.'

Savannah offered a half-hearted thanks as she returned to her bed.

'Have you got anything on tomorrow?' asked Jane. 'I was going to catch the bus up to Santa Monica and have a wander round the farmers' market. I could use some company and you're the only person here I've spoken to so far.'

'I don't think it's really my thing. The farmers' market, I mean, not talking to you.'

'You can't go back to work till that swelling goes down, can you? So shall we say about nine?'

Savannah didn't have the energy to argue, so she nodded her head and quietly wondered what Jane's ulterior motive was.

68

The two decommissioned dormitory rooms in which Tommy was standing, at the rear of the hostel, had been amateurishly knocked into one large, open-plan space. They left jagged plasterboard edges and exposed brickwork.

But it wasn't the rooms, or the portable lighting rigs throwing out immense heat from their bulbs, that grabbed his attention. That honour went to what lay beneath them.

Inside two dozen garden growbags perched on old mattresses were at least 150 cannabis plants of varying heights. The surrounding walls were chock-full of holes with plastic pipes jammed into them for ventilation. Wires and plugs hung from missing ceiling tiles and black bin bags had been taped to some windows, while blackout blinds hung from others to keep out prying eyes. The windowsills beneath them pooled with condensation.

Like the plants, Tommy remained rooted to the spot, unable to formulate a sentence. He could already feel the sweat from under his arms starting to trickle down his sides. He turned his head towards Peyk, who was standing in just his brightly coloured shorts.

'What the hell? You actually have a cannabis farm in the middle of the hostel?'

'Well, it's nice of you to call it a farm, but we're not there just yet,' Peyk replied proudly. 'Give us a couple of months before we reach that goal.'

'It's like *Breaking Bad* in here.'

'Let's not exaggerate, we're not cooking crystal meth. Not yet, anyway. It's just a bit of weed.'

'A bit? It's a shitload! Look at how many plants you've got in here.'

'It's a productive start.'

'You want to grow even more?'

'Of course. There's no point in half measures, is there?'

'But why?'

'To make money and keep a roof over your head,' began Ron as Peyk returned to work, carefully trimming leaves from one of the taller plants with scissors.

'The hostel isn't worth going to prison over,' Tommy felt the need to point out.

'I think it is,' replied Ron. 'When I came to Venice Beach and took on this old place, I didn't appreciate how much it'd cost to maintain or to run. And if I can't find a way of covering the bills, I'll have to close up.'

'But we're never far from being close to capacity, so surely you must make some money?'

'Anything we earn barely covers the overheads. If I charge more, you guys will stay somewhere else. And I have to make regular payments to a city official who turns a blind eye to this place because it's nowhere near to being up to code.'

'And this is why you keep falling through ceilings,' Tommy said, looking towards Peyk.

'Yep. As we started to make money from the pot, I began replacing the old wiring so we could get more lighting rigs in here. It's not just the people staying here who are in transition – it's the building, too.'

'I approached Joe's friend Wayne to test the market and sell some of our product,' continued Ron, scratching his head, 'and so far he's had a positive response. So we need to up our production, but that takes time. These plants need twelve hours of light a day, and that's a whole lot of electricity.'

'If you don't do this, how much longer does the hostel have left?'

'About two months; three if we're lucky. Wayne's a one-man operation, and he can't sell much weed on his own.'

Tommy took a deep breath and another look at his surroundings. He was all too aware of how illegal the activity in that room was, and in ordinary circumstances he'd have run a mile. But this was no ordinary life he was leading, and the thought of the hostel closing panicked him much more than it being raided by the police. He possessed no working visa, so he'd find it hard to pick up cash-in-hand work. Selling hotdogs for a living wouldn't be enough to support him. And where would he stay if the hostel closed its doors?

Tommy felt safe there, which he knew was illogical given the circumstances in which he'd arrived that first night. He'd made friends and created himself a little universe. If the hostel shut, the only viable option would be to arrange a return date for his open plane ticket and head home. And he certainly wasn't ready for that.

Tommy recalled what Richard, the protagonist in *The Beach* – the novel that had inspired his travels – had done in not-too-dissimilar circumstances. It had not been a 'happy ever after' ending for him. But that was just a story, thought Tommy, as he stood facing his crossroads.

There were two directions he could take. The first was to fall back on his default setting and walk away when a situation became awkward. The second was to slip out of character and step up to the mark.

'I can help you,' he said finally, and folded his arms.

69

Twilight had begun to make its presence felt when Zak Stanley's run slowed to a walk as he approached his home.

The first thing he noticed was 'the shape', now standing by his gate. Despite the failing light he could see from a distance that its eyes were wide open, its lips were apart and it was motionless, gawping at him.

Having a stranger so close to his house made Zak uncomfortable. He'd been victim to several stalkers before, but legal action from an army of retained lawyers had been the most successful way of combating even the more resolute ones. However, this one looked harmless – stupid, even.

'Can I help you?' he asked cordially as he reached her and pulled the headphones out of his ears.

Ruth's mouth was dry, but she couldn't swallow. Zak Stanley had just spoken to her. Zak Stanley! If she could have pressed pause on any moment of her life, it would no longer have been when she still had her father at home; it would've been right there and then.

'Well?' Zak asked again, but when Ruth didn't reply, he decided he was wasting his time. He wanted to cool down in his pool before his party began later that night.

Ruth made imperceptible adjustments to her hair as Zak

pushed a button on a thumb-sized remote control for his gates to open. Then she suddenly burst into life.

'I'm a really big fan,' she blurted out loudly, startling him.

'Thank you.'

'I've come from Australia to see you,' she continued.

Zak eyed her up and down again. He quietly loathed fans who believed that paying to see one of his films meant they were entitled to a piece of him. All it usually took was a few polite words to satisfy them and they were rarely seen again. 'That's a long way.'

'I know, but I won a competition to meet you. I went to the restaurant, but you weren't there.'

'Well, someone's messing with you, because I don't do meet and greets.'

'Oh.'

'It's lovely to have met you, but I try and keep my work life and private life separate, so it's probably best if you leave. But thank you for coming. And have a safe flight home.'

Ruth hesitated, unsure of how to continue before a light bulb flashed in her brain. 'I've made you something!'

She dived into her handbag and fumbled around for the jumper she'd spent a week carefully crafting. But by the time she held it up to show Zak, he'd disappeared behind the closing gate.

70

Day Nine

'Hotdogs and a lemonade, just one dollar,' echoed Tommy's voice through the megaphone in his best Queen's English.

An influx of tourists at a music festival further along the promenade made for a busy day on the beach and an improved footfall for Tommy and José's hotdog stand. Word of mouth about Tommy's latest addition to the menu had already begun to spread, and Tommy had socialized with enough people from different walks of life to predict by appearance alone those who might want to sample his smokable wares and those he should hide his product from. He ensured the two middle-aged women behind the shirtless frat boys he was serving weren't watching or listening when he spoke.

'Can I interest you in the chef's special?' he asked in hushed tones after handing them their hotdogs. Then he slipped his hand inside his uniform and removed a small sachet of pot from his pocket to show them.

'Shit yeah!' they replied.

'Go and see my friend behind the stand and he'll sort you out,' Tommy replied, pointing to José in the mobile food trailer behind them. José was grateful for a cut of both the cash and the product in return.

And Tommy couldn't help but grin at the rush of adrenaline his first foray into illegal activity gave him.

71

The sand's uneven surface made it impossible to predict which direction the football might travel after being kicked.

But it didn't prevent the dozen under-ten boys and girls from trying to gain control of it from Matty and Declan, and scoring. Their parents relaxed nearby under sunshades as Matty and Declan entertained the kids, teaching them how to tackle and allowing them the occasional penalty.

Their new beach soccer school wasn't going to make them rich, but it was earning them fifteen dollars per head per half day, and they enjoyed teaching the eager youngsters the skills they'd need to make an impression on the pitch. Occasionally they'd deliver embellished anecdotes about how they'd been trained by David Beckham and had given up promising apprenticeships at Manchester United to go travelling. Today, though, Declan was the more enthusiastic of the two, and he couldn't help but notice Matty flagging.

'Time out, guys,' he called, scooping the ball up into his arms. 'Go and see your folks and rehydrate before we continue.' As the children scampered away, he turned to Matty. 'Are you all right, fella?'

'Yeah, yeah, I'm just sweating cobs though. The sun's got to me a bit today.'

'I'll get you a drink. Replace your electrolytes and all that.'

'Don't fuss, I'm okay.'

'Or I'll get you a Coke if you want?'

'Dec, give me a break!' snapped Matty. 'I said I'm okay, right?'

As Matty trudged across the sand towards the boardwalk in search of shade, Declan followed him anyway, just to be sure.

Thirteen Months Earlier: Dundalk, Ireland

Dogs' eyes on a dozen painted plates hanging from the walls appeared to watch Declan as intently as Matty did, counting the heap of stolen euros on the kitchen table.

'That's €12,276 in total, pretty good for a first try,' announced Declan proudly. He leaned back on his chair and stretched his arms above his head – their haul was greater than either had anticipated.

'First and only try,' added Matty.

'That's what I meant. It's enough to pay for two seats in Upper Economy to Ibiza and two Interrail tickets, plus spending money for everywhere else we want to go.'

'We need to be sensible, though, we don't know how long it has to last.'

They were suddenly interrupted by the creaking hinges of a porch door. Declan darted to the other side of the kitchen, grabbed a handful of tea towels and threw them at Matty, who in turn covered the cash as his mother appeared, weighed down by two bags of food shopping.

'Can I give you a hand, Mrs O'Keefe?' began a flustered Declan.

'No, it's fine, lads,' she replied. 'What's going on in here? Why do you two look so guilty?'

'What are you on about, Mammy, we're just sitting here talking,' replied Matty in a forced, jovial tone. Matty and Declan looked at each other behind Mrs O'Keefe's back while she placed her bags on the kitchen work surface.

'You two, just talking? Now I know you're guilty of something. Are you staying for dinner, Declan?'

'If you don't mind.'

'Sure it's no trouble. Just move that pile of money you're hiding under my tea towels and set the table.'

Matty and Declan glared at each other again, neither knowing how to respond. So they scooped the money back into their duffel bags and Matty hurried upstairs with them. Before Declan could follow, Mrs O'Keefe held his arm and looked him straight in the eye.

'Promise me, Declan, you'll look after my boy. Please promise me that.'

Declan nodded. 'I won't let him out of my sight.'

Mrs O'Keefe appeared convinced of Declan's sincerity and removed her hand. 'Good lad, I just needed to hear you say it,' she added, and patted him on the shoulder.

72

Today

'It's taken us almost two days in that shitty old truck with the air vents throwing out hot air for this? FOR THIS!'

Eric's frustration reached boiling point, which felt like the same temperature as the cracked brown mud surrounding Buffalo Springs Lake. 'The point is that this is just a lake, like any other bloody lake in the world. I was expecting something more definitive. Something that made it obvious that what was written in the letter was not just the ramblings of a daft old cow on her deathbed!'

'Don't call her that!' shouted Nicole. 'You don't know anything about her.'

'And you do? You barely knew her, but you were still willing to go off on a wild fucking goose chase around the world on her say-so. We could have stayed home and spent the money!'

'You didn't have to come with me,' Nicole replied, close to tears.

'No, and I wish I hadn't. I don't know which one of us is the more stupid.'

After almost two days driving 1,223 miles, only interspersed by a broken night's sleep in a cheap chain motel that made Nicole strangely nostalgic for the hostel, they had finally arrived in Lubbock, Texas. And they'd spent their whole day driving around the town and looking at schools, shops and public amenities to see if anything Mrs Baker had written or spoken about jumped off the page.

They'd downloaded 'American Pie' to play on their phones over and over again, trying to find any more clues hidden in the lyrics – but if there were any, they were very well camouflaged. They weren't even sure if Buffalo Springs was their final stop, and they were still looking for answers.

'*It's Cooler at the Lake!*' promised a colourful banner over the car-park entrance. But once they passed under it, the lake turned out to be no more than an indistinct body of water surrounded by campsites, stores, fishermen, a nature trail and a small, sandy beach.

'Shit, shit, shit, shit!' continued Eric, heading towards the passenger side of the truck and throwing himself into the seat. Then he lifted his foot and twice kicked the air vent on the dashboard with all his might. He glared at Nicole, climbed out of the truck again and stormed off up the beach.

It was the angriest Nicole had ever seen him. She accepted his occasional moodiness and ever-present sarcasm, but she'd never witnessed an out-and-out temper tantrum before. At first she saw the humour in it, especially when his arms flailed from side to side, reminding her of how puppeteers made the Muppets run. But as his rant continued and his eyes darkened, she'd felt something new towards Eric: unease.

As his figure grew ever smaller, Nicole took a deep breath, unaware of the favour he'd unwittingly done her.

73

It had been a long, cold night sitting outside Zak's home in the Hollywood Hills.

To fend off the chill, Ruth wore the jumper she'd almost completed for Zak. Expensive-looking cars and yellow cabs had dropped a couple of dozen people off at the gate up until around midnight, and although she'd strained her eyes to get a better view of them it had been too dark to make out their faces. She was envious of the way the new arrivals were granted immediate access to Zak's estate, and could only imagine what celebrities he might be playing host to. They were so close, and yet so far away. Dance music blasted from his garden until the sun began to rise. Ruth felt resentful of the laughter coming from behind the gates that separated her from her soulmate.

Eventually, exhausted, she fell asleep. She slept through the guests' departures, only waking at the sound of a van's exhaust pipe backfiring. She stretched, took off Zak's jumper, wiped her armpits and face with the moist tissue from a KFC box she'd bought earlier that night and felt her stomach rumble. She had long run out of food, but she risked missing another chance to talk to Zak if she left now.

Ruth's eyes were blurry and too sore to finish knitting the last cuff of the sweater and instead she reflected, admitting to herself that her first meeting with Zak hadn't gone according to plan. She'd sounded like an idiot when she'd spoken.

But once Zak got to know her, his opinion of her would surely change. She was excited about their next meeting, and it came much sooner than she'd anticipated. By mid-morning, his gates opened and his SUV began to pull out of the drive. However, the vehicle braked sharply before it reached the road.

'What the hell?' began Zak, opening the driver's door, pulling off his sunglasses as he exited his car. 'Have you been here all night? Are you paparazzi? Because you can't prove shit about anything.'

Ruth was wrongfooted by his shift in tone from when they'd met the previous day. She panicked and thrust the jumper into Zak's chest. He held it out to examine it – one arm was longer than the other, the neck was huge and the colours garish. When he realized the crude effigy on the chest was supposed to be his face, he couldn't contain his amusement.

'Am I on camera somewhere?' Zak continued. 'This has to be a prank, because this is fucking hilarious!'

'No, it's just me,' she replied, her face aching with disappointment. Then she watched Zak throw her jumper onto the grass verge and get back into his car before driving away.

74

A day in the blazing sun wearing a hotdog costume left Tommy red-faced.

He could smell his own body odour seeping into the costume's fabric and he vowed to ask Mr Georgiou to think again about how to promote the business without the need of his outfit. But even though his face and ankles were sore to the touch, he couldn't stop smiling at his productivity.

Tommy headed towards room 23 and knocked three times, then twice. Peyk answered cautiously then ushered him inside, glancing behind Tommy to check for prying eyes. Once inside and with his sunglasses on, Tommy fished out handfuls of notes from his shorts and handed them to Ron.

'Sorry if they smell a bit,' he muttered, embarrassed.

'Tommy-boy!' interrupted Peyk and patted his friend's back, while Ron began to count the cash. 'Who knew?'

'There's $628 here,' said Ron.

'And we only stopped because we ran out of product,' said Tommy proudly.

Peyk nodded his head. 'Our very own Jesse Pinkman.'

The buzz Tommy earned from doing something he shouldn't have been doing satisfied him and he justified his actions by telling himself it was for the future of the hostel. It didn't hurt that he'd also siphoned off a hundred dollars from his earnings as commission, something he wouldn't be mentioning to Peyk or Ron.

'Same again tomorrow?' he asked, and his co-conspirators nodded their heads eagerly.

For the first time in weeks, Tommy hoped he wouldn't be crossing paths with the long-lost Louis soon. His best friend certainly wouldn't have approved of the direction Tommy's journey was taking him.

75

It had been a quiet day for Jake in Venice Beach.

Out of choice, he kept himself to himself, preferring to throw himself into a book in the solitude of the hostel roof. But try as he might to concentrate on *Shantaram*, he couldn't get past the first few chapters of the 900-page tome and regularly became distracted. Several times Tommy appeared in his thoughts, and Jake wondered what he was up to. He decided to try and catch up with him later and suggest they go for dinner together, as he enjoyed Tommy's company.

Jake couldn't put his finger on why, but something had brought certain memories flooding back that he'd spent the last two years trying to bury. Sometimes waves from his past came crashing all around him, threatening to drown him, and the only way he could avoid going under was to take some time out by himself and process where everything had gone wrong, and who had been the architect of his misery.

Two Years Earlier: London

'So next week is your first Brit Awards, and Lightning Strikes have been nominated in four categories. Has your new life sunk in yet?'

Stuart couldn't decide if the blonde presenter was flirting

with him or just doing her job. He struggled to hear her from their position on the red carpet in London's Leicester Square.

'Yeah, it has, but slowly,' he replied into the microphone. He could see her eyes darting around his face, struggling to find a fault.

'But what we all want to know is if there's any truth in the newspaper stories that you and soap star Katie Todd are getting married in the autumn?'

'Oh, you know what the papers are like – let's just say Katie and I are very happy the way we are, and who knows what will happen in the future?'

'Are tabloid rumours the downside of fame?'

'I guess you get used to it, but the secret is to never give away everything about yourself. Always keep them wanting more.'

Stuart gave the presenter a peck on each cheek before wandering up the red carpet and posing for a picture with actor Zak Stanley, whose film premiere Lightning Strikes had been invited to. Within earshot of their PRs and the press, they offered each other mutual congratulations on their respective success before Stuart rejoined the rest of his band in the cinema foyer.

Zak's assistant had already slipped Stuart an electronic key card to Zak's hotel room. And Stuart couldn't wait for the premiere to finish before he and Zak could spend their first night alone together in three weeks.

Today

'Oh, sorry, I didn't realize anyone was up here,' Tommy began as he stepped through the broken fire exit door. Jake was drinking from a bottle of water, his back against the railings and a book and his sunglasses by his side.

'I was just thinking I'd not seen you for a while,' replied Jake. 'How's your day been?'

Tommy considered recounting how many laws he'd been breaking but decided against it; he didn't want to be judged by someone whose opinion he valued.

'I've been working on the beach for most of it,' he said, and surveyed the roof. 'So you've found my secret bolthole, then?'

'Ah, so is that your mattress and empty bottles?'

'No, but it's a handy place to get away from everyone else. I love this hostel, but sometimes I need a bit of me time.'

'Same here,' said Jake. 'Do you—'

But before he could finish his sentence, the railing Jake was leaning against began to creak. He tried to move his body forward, but he couldn't keep his balance. Instead, he felt his back pushing the railings away from the rusty screws that held them in place. Jake's arms shot out in front of him and his eyes opened wide in blind panic. Instinctively, Tommy grabbed Jake's wrist and, with all his strength, yanked him forward as the railing fell three storeys to the sidewalk below.

Both their hearts pounding, they stared into each other's eyes as their terror gave way to relief. But Tommy's reactions weren't as fast when Jake pulled him forward and kissed him. Instead, Tommy remained frozen for the three seconds it took for Jake to realize Tommy wasn't kissing him back. Jake stared at his friend, immediately regretting his spontaneity.

'I'm sorry,' he muttered, and quickly walked away, back down the stairs and towards his room.

He left Tommy wondering if and how his day could become any more peculiar.

76

'Your trotters are disgusting,' began Eric as an opening remark when he finally came back to the truck.

Nicole kept her bare feet on the dashboard regardless. Her red toenail varnish was chipped, and walking around in bare feet had left her soles dry and in desperate need of a pedicure.

'And while you're at it, maybe you could reacquaint your legs with a razor.'

'Okay, I'll shave my legs when you remove that stick from your arse. My feet are sweating down there so I'm letting them air.'

'I love you, but you are a vile beast,' Eric replied. Nicole took his smile as an apology for his earlier hissy fit, and decided she'd overreacted by worrying about his sudden mood swing. Her ponytail flicked from left to right as the warm wind blew through the open windows, but Eric's face took the brunt of the sun.

'Sweet Mary mother of Jesus, this heat is turning my skin to leather,' he moaned and pointed to the air vents. 'And these are making it worse, because it's like being blasted by a hairdryer.'

'There's a garage up ahead,' said Nicole. 'I'll fill the truck up with petrol and you stock up on more bottles of water.'

Eric pulled onto the dusty forecourt, grabbed his wallet from the dashboard and headed into the store. Meanwhile

Nicole grasped the nozzle of the petrol pump and began to fill the tank. Her gaze took in a station that could have come straight from a book of 1940s American photography. The pumps were decrepit but working, and a number of tiles were missing from the wooden pitched roof of the store.

She looked around the miles and miles of arid land ahead of them, wondering if she should call time on their adventure. *This* had been Mrs Baker's final gift to her, she reckoned; the financial means and the kick up the backside she'd needed to climb out of her comfort zone and spend six weeks on the road, travelling with her best friend. There was no pot of gold to find at the end of the rainbow because it hadn't existed in the first place. Her actual reward was being free to do what she wanted to do, when she wanted to do it. And when all was said and done, she couldn't put a price on that. Perhaps she would try her hand at nursing again, although in a different hospital. She would still need to reapply for a position at the hospital trust, but hopefully they would accept that her resignation had been made in the heat of the moment and while grieving.

As the bell on the petrol pump chimed to alert her the tank was full, the sun caught something in the car that dazzled her eye. She replaced the nozzle and opened the door to inspect the glimmer further, squinting at the air vent Eric had kicked and cracked. The closer she got, the more it twinkled.

She poked her fingers inside, but the broken diagonal plastic strips were in her way. So, using both hands, she yanked at the air vent until it came away. Again Nicole wiggled her fingers inside, and this time she pulled out a small, partially open velvet pouch with a drawstring. Puzzled, she undid the knot and poured the contents into her palm.

It took a moment for her to understand that it wasn't a pouch full of broken glass, but of diamonds.

'Only when you allow the warmth of new experiences to fill your heart, will you truly realize how precious a gem your life is,' she whispered to herself, recalling the words written in Mrs Baker's note that she'd practically memorized in her search for clues. Then she recalled how Mrs Baker had spoken of the night she and her husband spent by a lake while the stars above them 'shone like diamonds'. She turned her head and saw Eric at the cash register, paying for fuel and water.

'Eric!' Nicole shouted, and waved frantically to get his attention.

She was pouring the diamonds back into the pouch, so that Eric could experience the same surprise she had felt, when she noticed a small piece of torn paper crammed into the vent. Her joy was replaced with confusion, and then with alarm, when she read the words.

'Don't let her son find these – they're not for Eric.'

Twelve Weeks Earlier: Holly Cottage, Great Houghton, Northampton, England

They had never met in person, but Maria, Mrs Baker's housekeeper, recognized Eric from old family photographs that were now locked in a chest in her deceased employer's attic.

Maria had expected Nicole to arrive at the cottage after Mrs Baker passed away. But she hadn't expected her to be in the company of Mrs Baker's estranged son.

'Hello, my name is Nicole Grainger and this is my friend—' the girl began.

She was as pretty as Mrs Baker had described her when

Maria visited her in hospital. But the housekeeper clamped her mouth shut and tried to hide her uneasiness at the sight of Eric. He had not been part of the plan.

'I know why you're here,' Maria interrupted, and went back into the house, leaving the front door open. She guessed Nicole and Eric were probably looking at each other, unsure of what to say, as they followed her into Mrs Baker's lounge.

'Wait here,' she ordered and left the room.

Maria closed the kitchen door behind her and uncharacteristically began to panic. She'd last seen Mrs Baker a few days before her death, when she'd told Maria of her plan to change a young nurse's life. With Maria well provided for and bequeathed the cottage, Mrs Baker desperately wanted Nicole to experience the world. The last thing Mrs Baker would have expected, or wanted, was for her daughter or the boy she'd once described as 'a wolf in wolf's clothing' to benefit from her possessions.

So she dictated a letter, which Maria wrote. Then, when she returned home, Maria placed the diamonds inside the wooden box on the passenger seat, along with maps and enough money to get the truck up and running and exported to America. Nicole was then to pick it up at a dock in Chicago, the city that was the starting point of Route 66.

Only when Nicole appeared at the door with Eric, Maria was forced to improvise. She shoved the bag into the air vent and then dashed around the kitchen, silently opening and closing drawers until she found a notepaper and pen. She hurriedly scribbled the words '*Don't let her son find these – they're not for Eric*' on a scrap of paper and poked it into the air vent too, before regaining her poise and showing her visitors the pick-up truck.

She had no opportunity to get Nicole alone and explain what she'd done or what she knew about Eric. She hoped that Nicole would contact her before she left on her expedition, because she didn't have Nicole's number. Meanwhile, Maria prayed that she had made the right decision – because if she hadn't, it was unlikely the diamonds would ever be found.

The call from Nicole never came. But Maria did receive a visitor to the house. And it was the last person she would ever see.

Today

The note tore Nicole apart like a bird hitting a propeller.

She was familiar with the expression 'blood running cold' but had never experienced it until that moment. It didn't make sense, she thought – how on earth could her best friend of two years be the son of Mrs Baker? Why wouldn't he have mentioned such a crucial piece of information while his mother lay dying in a room in the same hospital as him, or when they'd been to her house, or even when he and Nicole planned their trip? Why had he never visited his mother? Nicole knew that he was estranged from his family, but surely once he knew Mrs Baker was terminally ill he would've gone to see her at least once? Was he using his friendship with Nicole to find the inheritance Mrs Baker had already informed Nicole she was withholding from her children?

Nicole's mind continued to race, still trying to find alternative meanings in the scribbled note, but there were none. It was what it was. Gradually, memories of the last couple of months began to fit together like pieces in a jigsaw: Eric's outburst over a woman he never knew; his eagerness to take a two-month, unpaid sabbatical from work and accompany Nicole; and then his fury when they reached Buffalo Springs Lake.

'Eric, you can't be . . .' she said out loud.

'I can't be what?' came a voice in her ear, making her yelp. He laughed. 'What's with you?'

'Nothing! Nothing,' Nicole replied. The rapid speed of her pulse made her body judder. Her fist clenched the velvet pouch, and its contents dug sharply into her hand.

'What happened to the vent?' he asked, noticing the plastic casing lying in the footwell.

'Erm, I was picking at it,' Nicole stumbled, and slowly slid the pouch from her hand and into her pocket. Then she picked up the casing and jammed it back in place. 'Can we go?'

Eric returned to the driver's seat, put his seat belt on and pulled away, ready to return to Venice Beach. As Nicole tried to regulate her breathing, she was unaware the breeze coming through the windows had blown Maria's note under her seat.

77

Some 3,000 regulars made their way to downtown Santa Monica's farmers' market each and every Sunday.

Unlike other markets throughout the city, Santa Monica's appealed to more than single shoppers or restaurant staff picking up the freshest local produce for their eateries. It targeted young and old with food stalls, arts and crafts stands, face painting and pony rides.

'I don't want to sound rude, but do you mind if I ask why you're staying at the hostel and not a hotel?' Savannah began.

'I don't look like your average backpacker, do I?'

Savannah took in Jane's elasticated cargo pants and hiking boots and shook her head. 'No, you don't.'

'Well, there are a few reasons. But the main one is that I don't want to be on my own and that's precisely what I'd be if I stayed in a Four Seasons or a Radisson. Every holidaymaker in those places keeps themselves to themselves, and unless you're specifically going on a singles holiday or cruise, there aren't many opportunities to talk to other people. I know everyone else at the hostel is a lot younger than me, but I'd rather be fruit shopping and chatting to the first exotic dancer I've ever met than sitting around a Beverly Hills swimming pool all on my own.'

'I guess that makes sense. Aren't we all a bit loud for you?'

'Not at all. It's the rattle and hum that I love.' Jane picked up a grapefruit and squeezed it. 'This looks just about ripe enough. It should have a good week left in it.'

'How do you know this stuff?' asked Savannah, who, back in Alabama, had never had call to set foot inside a supermarket, let alone a street crammed with colourful edibles.

'When you're a mum they give you a manual for this kind of thing.'

When a confused Savannah frowned, Jane added, 'I'm kidding, darling.'

'How many kids do you have?'

'Oh, I have two,' she replied casually. 'Well, I had two, but they passed away. It still never sounds like it's me when I'm saying that.'

'Oh God, I'm sorry,' gasped Savannah.

'That's okay. And speaking of children, when is your baby's due date?'

78

There were almost a hundred people of sixteen different nationalities sleeping under the roof of the Venice Beach International Hostel.

But Tommy still instantly recognized the figure walking along the corridor ahead of him, even with the back of his head obscured. The olive-green frayed backpack was a give-away, decorated with dozens of airport security tags, flight labels, Greyhound and Amtrak tickets and stickers hung from straps and zips; a tapestry of wanderlust that could only belong to Jake.

Tommy felt a sudden sense of dismay when he realized Jake had packed up to leave. He'd already lost one ally in Nicole that week, but that friendship was only ever going to be temporary, and Tommy felt that he and Jake still had some way to go.

Meanwhile, as Jake made his way towards the hostel's front door, he was still embarrassed and angry with himself for letting his guard down and befriending Tommy. Even though he hadn't revealed anything about his past life as Stuart Reynolds, pop star, he'd allowed Tommy to get closer than most. Jake hadn't planned to kiss him and he knew Tommy was straight, but he'd let his emotions get the better of him and acted on impulse, not forethought.

Jake was attracted to Tommy, he could admit that to himself now, and like any gay man who'd ever had a crush on a straight guy, he knew nothing would come of it. So, to stop himself making more of a fool of himself than he already had, he reasoned it was better to take himself out of the situation.

'I thought you only left when people weren't looking?' said Tommy.

'Oh hi, yeah,' Jake replied, turning around and clearly flustered.

'So?'

'So . . . what?'

'So you can't leave because I'm looking.'

'I made a bit of a tit of myself so I thought it best I just . . . go.'

'Ah, you mean after you tried to ram your tongue down my throat?' Tommy teased.

'I was a bit emotional. I was thinking about home and, well, I dealt with it the wrong way. I'm sorry.'

'You said being homesick was the sacrifice you make for a fresh start.'

'Using my own words against me, eh? Maybe I'm not as sorted as you think I am.'

'Maybe you're just more human than you realize.'

'Possibly,' thought Jake, 'or maybe I've just made more fucking stupid decisions than you'll ever know.'

Two Years Earlier: London

The tinted windows of the limousine couldn't completely hide the camera flashes as Stuart Reynolds and soap actress Katie Todd pulled away from the red-carpet film premiere and drove towards London's Embankment.

Even though the clock was approaching midnight, the roads were overcrowded and they moved slowly as the audience dispersed towards their vehicles and public transport.

A familiar, frosty silence between Katie and Stuart filled the limo, as it often did when they were left alone. Theirs was a relationship of convenience, dreamed up by their managers and PR experts eager to promote both their brands and rake in the lucrative earnings they generated. In front of the cameras, they were love's young dream, but away from the flashing lights of the paparazzi, they had little in the way of shared interests and even less of a desire to discover common ground in their manufactured worlds.

Katie tucked her strawberry-blonde hair behind her ear, put her fingers down her blouse and pulled out five finger-sized paper wraps from her bra. She expertly tapped out a powdery substance from one of them onto her clutch bag, placed the wraps on it and carefully shaped four lines with her VIP lanyard.

'Haven't you done enough of that already?' Stuart asked. 'You took enough toilet breaks during the film to snort half of Colombia.'

Katie ignored him. She removed a straw from her purse, placed it at the base of her nostril and snorted two lines in quick succession, finishing with a long, hard blink as the cocaine numbed the back of her throat.

'Do you want some?' she asked Stuart, pointing to the remaining lines.

'No, I'm good,' he replied, eager to leave her side and reach their destination.

Stuart had a complicated relationship with drugs. His social workers had informed him that his parents' substance addiction was the reason he'd been removed from them as a toddler and placed into care. He'd since learned his mother had died of a heroin overdose some years later, and he couldn't bear to read the self-pitying story his father had sold to the *Sunday Mirror* about how much he missed his only son – a son he hadn't bothered to track down, until fame came his way.

Stuart hated drugs and how they had torn his family apart. He was aware that the genetic link he shared with his parents meant he was predisposed to addiction, especially if in an environment where drug use was prevalent. While he had avoided those environments as a teenager and young man, now he was slap bang in the centre of one of the biggest – show business. And to fit in with his new life and bandmates, he had succumbed to temptation and dabbled.

At first he'd used amphetamines and cocaine only recreationally with the rest of Lightning Strikes. But then he began keeping a small stash in his apartment for when Zak was in town. Most of the time Stuart only indulged in stimulants with Zak, and that was only to enhance the sex. 'Fucking on coke is like nothing else,' Zak had told him the first night they spent together, and he wasn't wrong.

Tonight, with Katie, wasn't a night he wanted to get high.

'Suit yourself,' said Katie, wiping her top lip with a tissue. 'Not much fun, are you? I don't know why I keep agreeing to this.'

'Because being seen with me makes you front-page news,' Stuart sniped.

'Well, Geri had better not screw me over.'

'Neither of us is getting screwed, the rate this traffic is moving. Driver, how much longer do you reckon it's going to take?'

As the glass partition descended, Katie passed Stuart her handbag with the two remaining lines of coke scattered across it.

'Hold this for a minute,' she said. Her voice wobbled as she accidentally knocked the other wraps into his lap.

'Be careful!' Stuart snapped, but as he gave Katie an angry stare, her eyes rolled back into her head and her body went into seizure.

'We're just pulling in now, sir,' the driver replied as the car moved towards the hotel entrance.

A panicked Stuart knew by heart the well-rehearsed routine that was to follow, but that night would be different. Because, before he had time to prevent it from happening, one of the hotel staff opened his limo door and half a dozen cameras snapped the star of Britain's biggest boyband with two lines of cocaine balanced on his lap, three wraps of it in his hand and a convulsing young actress by his side.

Today

'I'm not gay, just for the record,' Tommy told Jake firmly. 'I mean, it doesn't bother me that you are, but I'm not. I just wanted to clear that up.'

'I know, I know,' Jake replied, and hitched his rucksack further up towards his shoulders. 'I've booked into a hostel in West Hollywood; maybe we could catch up in a few days?'

'You don't have to go. Nobody needs to know you're gay if you'd prefer to keep it quiet. Not that I think anyone here would give a shit, but you can trust me,' Tommy replied.

'People can't let you down if you don't trust them.'

'Another pearl of wisdom, eh?'

Suddenly Tommy grabbed Jake by the cheeks and kissed him – not just a peck on the lips, but a proper kiss.

'There,' Tommy grinned, a little surprised by his own spontaneity, 'we're equal now, so let's put your rucksack back in your room and go get a Chinese.'

A snickering from behind them caught their attention. They turned to find Matty and Declan watching them.

'Very millennial of you, Tommy, keeping your options open,' said Declan, and the two wandered off before Tommy could explain.

79

'How do you know I'm pregnant?' a startled Savannah asked Jane.

Jane put down the punnet of strawberries she was holding at the market stall and took both of Savannah's hands.

'Sweetheart, you're in a hurry to make money in a job that doesn't seem to suit you. Your arms aren't marked and your pupils aren't dilated so you're not spending any on drugs. I don't see any Jimmy Choos under your bed so you're not wasting your money on fashion. So what are you doing with it? Probably saving it. And what for? An endgame, of sorts. Now, it could be to move out of the hostel and get your own apartment, but something tells me there's more to you than meets the eye and that you're doing this job, working these crazy hours and putting yourself in harm's way, because you know you can't do it for much longer. So why could that be? Because you're expecting a baby.'

Savannah was taken aback. 'You got all that from sharing a room with me for a day?'

Jane grinned. 'No, I got all that from the positive pregnancy testing kit you left in the bathroom bin.'

Savannah laughed for the first time that day. 'I do one every two or three weeks just to make sure,' she admitted. 'I know, I know, it's crazy considering I'm almost five months gone.'

'Well, it's a miracle you're not showing yet. And you're keeping the baby when it arrives?'

'Yes. I'm saving for a deposit on an apartment, and Peyk lets me stay at the hostel for free. I'm sure I'll start getting bigger any day now, and there's not much demand for strippers with baby bumps.'

'I don't know, there seems to be a fetish for just about anything these days.'

Jane picked up her strawberries, handed them to the stallholder and removed her purse from her handbag. 'You need to keep up your vitamin C intake. We'll get you some satsumas and iron supplements before we go home.'

Savannah was puzzled by Jane's interest in her. Peyk and Tommy aside, it felt like a very long time since someone had offered her kindness. But she couldn't help feeling suspicious.

'I was about your age when I got pregnant with my first,' Jane continued, 'I spent nine months peeing every half hour or vomiting.'

'I've only had morning sickness a handful of times.'

'You're lucky. Are your parents supporting you?'

'No,' said Savannah quietly, 'we don't really have a relationship.'

'That's a shame, you could really do with their help at a time like this.'

'Do you mind me asking what happened to your kids?' Savannah continued, changing the subject.

'Not at all, my friends get this . . . *awkward* look when I bring them up so I don't get to talk about them much.'

Jane paused and chose her words carefully before speaking. 'My husband killed our children.'

80

Day Ten

'Can I ask what you're doing here, ma'am?'

Zak aside, the private security staff who pulled up outside his address were the first people to speak to Ruth during her week-long Hollywood Hills sojourn.

'I'm waiting for a friend,' Ruth replied courteously.

'Who exactly is your friend, ma'am?'

'Zak Stanley. He lives here.'

'We are aware of that. And does Mr Stanley know you're camped outside his home?'

'Oh yeah, we've spoken a bunch of times. And sometimes he points his camera at me so that we can wave at each other.'

The guards looked at each other, thinking the same thing – she was a nutjob, but a harmless one.

'Well, ma'am, although this isn't a private road, we do have the authority to ask you to move on if Mr Stanley makes another complaint.'

'Oh he won't, don't worry,' said Ruth, trying to convince herself that despite their last fractious meeting, there was still hope for a relationship of sorts. 'We're friends.'

Ruth had already made the decision before the guards' arrival that until Zak returned and they'd had the chance to talk properly, she couldn't risk leaving her seat outside his house to go back to the hostel. So she'd spent a second evening catnapping on the sidewalk, waking each time a car drove past or she heard a voice, and vacating her spot only to traipse down the hill to stock up on sugary snacks at the convenience store or wash in its customer restroom. Food was a necessity, but buying deodorant, a toothbrush or even cheap clothing hadn't crossed Ruth's mind, because the longer she spent away from the house, the more risk there was of missing Zak's return.

And as the security men left and the hours rolled by, Ruth became more and more anxious about why she hadn't seen him in almost twenty-four hours.

81

Nicole took quiet, deep breaths in a desperate attempt to ward off a panic attack.

She'd not suffered one in more than a decade, but she recognized the warning signs of hot flushes, trembling arms and nausea. She knew she must control her body as best she could so as not to give Eric any idea that everything between them had changed.

Eric drove without a break for the first 300-mile leg of their journey on the I-10W passing through New Mexico and Arizona, and then crossing into California. And for most of it, Nicole's head was turned towards the window as she stared at the desert landscape illuminated by an almost-full moon.

Her heart hadn't stopped racing since she had discovered Maria's note, and her hand remained inside her pocket containing Mrs Baker's diamonds. There had been casual and polite chit-chat between her and Eric, but during the many silences, her thoughts were dominated by what to do once they returned to the hostel. She had plenty of time to replay moments and past conversations to try and piece together the Eric Collins-shaped jigsaw.

Time and time again, she asked herself how she'd failed to realize Eric's real identity. The answer was always the same – there had been no reason to doubt him. *Collins*, she thought suddenly, and recalled how Mrs Baker had mentioned Collins was her maiden name when she first told Nicole about her travelling days. But it was such a common surname, why would she link the two?

Nicole also remembered that Eric had once revealed his father had died when he was a child and that his mother had struggled to cope, so she'd packed him off to boarding school. The years had estranged them further.

Several times during Mrs Baker's six-week stay in hospital, Nicole had asked Eric if he would like to meet her, and now she knew why he had made an excuse each time. She hadn't questioned why he declined.

One of the things that disturbed her the most was that days earlier, Eric had even helped to scatter Mrs Baker's ashes without so much as shedding a tear or showing a hint of emotion. Their two-year friendship, during which Nicole had bared her soul to him, had become rotten.

What scared her now was where to go from here. Her pocket was stuffed with a potential fortune, and sitting next to her was a man who'd lied through his teeth to be with her as she tried to find it. What else might he be capable of? Nicole desperately needed to talk her options through with someone, and an ocean away from home, there was only one person she trusted enough to turn to for advice: Tommy.

After their latest failed mission in Lubbock, it didn't take much for Nicole to persuade Eric that returning to Venice Beach would be a positive decision for both of them. They could relax somewhere familiar and plan for their return to London.

'Shall we put some music on?' asked Eric suddenly,

stretching out his hand to turn the radio on. He flicked around the dial until he found a station and chirped along to the chorus of an old Fleetwood Mac song.

And as Eric sang about sweet little lies, both of them were acutely aware of the irony of the lyrics.

82

'You'd like me to tell you what happened to my kids, wouldn't you?'

Jane guessed that after dropping the bombshell the previous day about the death of her children at their father's hands, Savannah might be curious as to the circumstances but might not know how to ask.

After their shopping expedition to the farmers' market, they had discussed many topics, but nothing about the events that had altered Jane's life for good. And, as Savannah had revealed very little about her father or why she'd escaped his grip, she knew that as disclosure was a two-way street, she had no right to bring it up. But if Jane wanted to offer a further explanation, Savannah would be more than happy to listen.

They were at the kitchen sink rinsing punnets of fruit under a tap when Jane stopped and rummaged around in her handbag, removing a plastic wallet. She opened it to reveal a portable photo frame with space for two pictures. A pair of smiling young faces with brightly coloured ice cream covering their lips beamed from behind a protective film, frozen in time.

'That's Gregory,' Jane began, pointing to a boy of no more than five, with bright red hair and freckles. 'And that's Ruby. She's seven . . . she was seven . . .' Her voice trailed off.

Ruby shared her brother's features, and her auburn curls cascaded across her shoulders. 'They're beautiful,' Savannah replied, saddened that the two innocent souls she was staring at were no more.

'Peter, my husband, was a very controlling, very violent man,' Jane explained. 'And I reached the point where I couldn't take any more. I realized far too late that our relationship, if you could call it that, was no place to raise a family. But when I tried to reason with him about it and told him I was planning to leave with the children, it was like I'd pushed a detonator and he exploded. He beat me unconscious and I don't remember much else, only waking up on the lounge floor to find the house on fire. I tried to get upstairs to the kids' bedrooms but the heat was too intense, so I ran to a neighbour's house for help and they called 999. We returned with a ladder, but by then, well, it was too late. All three of them were gone.'

Savannah understood all too well the damage a domineering patriarch could cause. 'Oh Jane, that's awful.'

'The man I married wasn't always bad. I thought there was some good left in him, somewhere. That's why I stayed for so long, because I wanted him to go back to being the man I fell in love with. At least that's what I tell myself, because I don't think I can bear the alternative . . . that I could have prevented this from happening by leaving years earlier and keeping my babies safe.'

'You can't blame yourself,' said Savannah, and placed her arm around Jane's shoulder. 'Is that why you came to America? To get away from what happened?'

'Yes, and because my life had no purpose any more. Every time I think about my children, it keeps them alive inside of me. And it makes me want to do the things they'll never have the chance to do. So I decided to leave my old life and see the world for them. I suppose it sounds a bit silly, doesn't it?'

'No, it's not. Sometimes we have no choice but to leave everything behind just to keep going.'

'What about you? You haven't mentioned anything about your baby's father. Is he still around?'

Savannah took a deep breath. 'I was raped,' she said matter-of-factly.

A look of sympathy spread quickly across Jane's face. 'Oh, darling.'

'It's okay – well, it's not okay obviously, but it could have been worse because I don't remember anything about it. Someone slipped a roofy in my drink and then five weeks and one missed period later, I discover I'm pregnant.'

Jane shook her head. 'The bastard.'

'I know a lot of women might not have been able to keep it, and believe me, I'm pro-choice so I gave it a hell of a lot of thought. And in the end, I decided it wasn't my baby's fault how she was created. It's where we go from here that counts. I won't lie, sometimes I find myself walking down the boardwalk and I see a cute guy who smiles at me and I wonder, 'Was that you? Were you the one who did that to me?' But instead of beating myself up about it, I focus on trying to make the best life possible for the two of us.'

From the corridor, Peyk quietly listened to Jane and Savannah's heart-to-heart and watched as Jane put her arm around Savannah, tilting her head towards her shoulder. And he realized that the night he'd first met Savannah, he'd made a serious error of judgement.

83

The room Jake had vacated less than an hour earlier was still empty and smelled of his aftershave when he returned.

He began removing everything he had rolled up and packed neatly in his rucksack, placing it back into the chest of drawers. And while he knew why Tommy had kissed him and that there had been nothing more in it than to prove a point, he couldn't stop thinking about how good it had felt.

Jake tried to find a reason he was replaying it over and over again, and the only one he could muster was that it had been many months since he had last been intimate with anyone. It was probably just sexual frustration, nothing more. Yet if the explanation was that simple, why couldn't he stop smiling?

He didn't want to admit it to himself, but the last time he had felt like this about someone was a lifetime ago.

Two Years Earlier: London

Stuart paced around his apartment for much of the night, running through his options and devising explanations and excuses for being caught with a convulsing teen soap star and lines of cocaine on his lap.

As soon as the limousine's door had opened and the cameras started snapping, in a blind panic, he'd pushed Katie's clutch bag down into the footwell, showering them both in a cloud of white powder.

Stuart had left an unconscious Katie to face the consequences of her actions alone while he fought his way through more paparazzi than he'd expected would be there, elbowing one of them in the nose and knocking another to the pavement as he darted towards the Cardinian Hotel lobby. Inside the elegant building, guests and staff turned their heads to stare at the commotion outside and all eyes followed a clearly agitated Stuart as he hurried towards the elevators. He pressed the button for the twenty-third floor, where Zak always stayed when in town, and glanced at his reflection in the copper-coloured metal doors. He could feel himself sweating as he tried not to dwell on how social media and the press were about to have a field day with what their lenses had just captured.

Stuart was desperate to see Zak because Zak would know what to do. As a child star, he'd grown up in the public eye and could count on the best Hollywood PR machine money could buy to cover any indiscretions.

He and Zak had first met a year earlier in the green room of a Dutch TV chat show, Zak promoting his latest movie and Stuart and the band performing their new single in an attempt to crack the European music market. They'd chatted politely, but the unspoken spark between them had been impossible to ignore. And when they met up again later that night in the bar of their shared hotel, their dangerous liaison had begun.

Of course, no one was meant to care these days about anyone's sexuality, but the showbiz world still did when it came to selling boybands to teenage girls and movie heartthrobs to the masses. Geri had insisted – even making it part of his contract – that Stuart remain in the closet throughout his time in the band and not embark on any relationships at all. Meanwhile, Zak had grown up in the limelight and never had the opportunity to be anything other than Hollywood's favourite leading man with an eye for his leading ladies.

Geography and gruelling work schedules meant their time together was often brief and always kept under the radar, away from prying eyes. And the covert nature of their relationship suited them just fine because, since their working lives were spent as public property, both appreciated having something that was theirs alone.

As the lift approached the ground floor, a thought suddenly struck Stuart: would it be such a wise move for him to see Zak that night? He'd abandoned Katie in the car, having convinced himself her seizure had been a brief but minor incident, and that if she had any sense – which was debatable – she'd have come round and told the driver to get the hell out of there. If reporters did a little digging, it would only take a small amount of financial encouragement for an indiscreet member of staff to reveal that Zak Stanley was also a hotel guest. It was a long shot, but was them potentially putting two and two together a risk worth taking? So Stuart made a snap decision to get off at the next floor and call Zak to meet elsewhere instead. He hurried towards a rear fire exit he'd used to sneak away after a previous tryst with Zak, and left the hotel.

With his phone battery completely flat, he was forced to wait until the taxi dropped him off at his apartment block a few miles away before he could call Zak from his landline; but it went straight to voicemail. Stuart paced around his flat, took a deep breath and logged on to the *Daily Mail*'s website from his iPad. Though it was only ninety minutes since he'd been papped, there at the top of the page – and also in the infamous sidebar of shame – was his photograph in all its glory: a wide-eyed Stuart Reynolds with two lines of cocaine on his teenage actress girlfriend's handbag. There was also a link to a video of the incident, but as soon as Stuart saw the headline, he knew things were worse than he'd feared. It read: '*Soap actress critically ill after drugs binge with pop star boyfriend: she has seizure while he runs*'.

'Shit,' thought Stuart, realizing that in a no-win situation, he'd made matters even worse by leaving a poorly Katie alone. The media and fans wouldn't care that the drugs were hers, or that she'd done it to herself. He would be the scapegoat. Then it struck him that in his panicked concern for his own well-being, he hadn't spared a single thought for Katie's welfare. They might not be friends, but she was still a person.

Stuart knew he shouldn't, but he switched to the Twitter app and keyed in his name. But he couldn't keep up with the number of threads that mentioned him, many reposting the *Mail*'s pictures. The UK was alight with a new celebrity scandal, and Stuart was in the eye of the storm. Stuart's charging phone suddenly burst to life, vibrating the first of dozens of missed call alerts. They were mainly from numbers he didn't recognize, but he speculated they belonged to reporters looking for exclusives. He'd also received voicemail and text messages from other members of the band. Tentatively he listened to them and grimaced as the words '*fucking idiot*' and '*ruined it for us all*' were thrown about.

With Zak still on his mind, Stuart called him again, but this time a woman answered.

'I'm sorry, but he's still at the premiere after party,' began

Mimi, Zak's sister and personal assistant. But Stuart knew she was lying, because Zak loathed those events and only ever stayed briefly to network with the big players in the industry before slipping out. 'I'll tell him you called,' she added, and hung up. Something about her clipped tone told him what he feared. Zak had already been told what happened. And if that was the case, he knew exactly what was happening in Zak's camp.

There was only one person who could sort this mess out – Stuart's manager, Geri Garland. So he braced himself, flicked through his contacts and dialled.

'Ahh, if it isn't the Wolf of Wall Street,' she began.

'Geri, please let me explain.'

'No need, sweetheart, let Mama G get you out of this one. It looks bad at the moment but I promise you I'll have it sorted by the morning. We'll talk tomorrow.'

'Really?' asked Stuart, surprised by her relaxed response.

'Really. Trust me. Now go and get some sleep.'

Stuart hung up, turned his phone off and slumped into a large leather armchair.

While grateful to her for whatever she had planned, Stuart wondered what Geri would expect as payback for digging him out of his hole.

84

Day Eleven

Nicole had, at best, just a thirty-minute window of opportunity to find Tommy.

Hours earlier, while Eric was filling the truck with petrol, she'd called ahead to the Venice Beach International Hostel and booked two beds in a dormitory room, as she didn't want to be alone with him in a private room.

On their return to Venice, she and a reluctant Eric checked in, and on seeing Gabby covering the reception desk, Nicole momentarily feared that during her four-day absence Tommy too had finally ventured forth on the next leg of his travels.

More than seven continuous weeks together meant Nicole knew Eric's habits and routines, and she counted on him taking his regimented thirty minutes to shower, groom and freshen up. Once he'd announced he was getting out of his sweaty clothes and the water began running, Nicole flew out of the starting blocks.

She sprinted to Tommy's room and found it empty, but was relieved when she saw his sleeping bag and backpack were still by his bed. She considered writing him a note, then decided it'd be easier explaining to him in person what she'd learned about Eric.

She checked her watch, then ran to the lounge and scanned the room for Tommy. The kitchen and courtyard were also Tommy-less, and, out of frustration, she smacked the wall with the palm of her hand. Now she had ten minutes to run to the hotdog stand, inform Tommy she urgently needed to speak to him, and get back to her room before Eric was any the wiser.

En route, she asked herself again if telling Tommy about Maria's note was a wise thing to do. Eric had been correct when he'd suggested she wasn't the best judge of character, and it annoyed her now to think he'd probably been laughing at her expense when he'd said it. But she was honest enough to admit to herself that her track record was poor. So could she really trust a boy she'd known for a handful of days? Or was she setting herself up for more trouble? Unfortunately, she was running out of options.

Nicole's run slowed to a walk when she arrived at the hotdog stand to find the help she urgently needed wasn't working there that day. Where the hell are you, Tommy? she thought, and reluctantly retraced her steps back to the hostel and back to her room.

'Why are you panting?' asked Eric when he stepped out of the bathroom moments after Nicole returned.

'I was exercising,' she lied, flashing him graphics from a fitness app on her phone.

'Too little, too late,' he replied, rolling his eyes. 'I think the horse has well and truly bolted through that stable door.'

85

For three days, Ruth survived on chocolate bars, potato chips, 7-Up and very little sleep.

But it was hope and conviction that spurred her on in her vigil outside Zak Stanley's home – even if, to date, it had only resulted in two meetings with him, and neither of those had gone as she'd envisaged.

Ruth anxiously looked at her watch. By her count, it had been thirty-seven hours and twenty minutes since Zak left his home, and she was desperate to know where he was. Her phone was out of battery, so she was unable to go online and see if his whereabouts had been reported on social media. She'd bought a *USA Today* on her last journey to the store at the foot of the hills, but there was no mention of Zak.

She paced in a circular motion like a caged bear in a zoo. She nibbled the skin around her dirty fingernails and fretted about his safety. What if he'd been involved in a car accident, or if he'd taken ill and was in hospital? How would his friends and family know how to get in touch with her, his biggest fan, to tell her what had happened? Every now and again she pressed the intercom buzzer or waved her arms at the security camera to get attention from Zak's staff, but no one responded.

The more Ruth tried to reassure herself that Zak was okay,

the more irrational she became, convincing herself something terrible must have happened to him. And as sleep deprivation and hunger took its toll, Ruth's emotions switched from anger to frustration, concern and then distress. She promised herself that she would remain exactly where she was, no matter how long it took.

86

As Tommy vacuumed up the remnants of the previous night's party, he wondered if the stains on the threadbare lounge carpet were holding it together.

The vacuum cleaner dated back at least two decades. It was so noisy and vibrated so intensely that he wished he was wearing ear protection, like a pneumatic drill operator.

Sprawled across a sofa, Jake kept him company, skimming through a book on Eastern philosophy he'd plucked from the hostel's library shelf. But he was finding it hard to focus on its teachings in the presence of his friend.

Jake already knew how Tommy's mouth tasted, but now he wondered what his body would feel like wrapped against his own, or how his warm breath might feel on his neck . . .

'*Stop it!*' he told himself and shook his head as if to dislodge the inappropriate thoughts. Again, he tried to remind himself he was only thinking about Tommy in that way because, by choice, he hadn't been intimate with anyone in a long time. 'It's lust you're feeling – nothing more, nothing less,' he muttered under the sound of the vacuum, and placed the book on his lap to disguise his growing arousal.

He was quick to spot Tommy scowl as Matty and Declan walked past the lounge carrying footballs under their arms.

'Boys,' nodded Declan, slowing his pace. 'Our room's free, if you need a little alone time.'

'Oh, fuck off,' snapped Tommy.

Matty turned to Declan. 'I think there might be trouble in paradise.'

'Already?' Declan replied. 'I had such high hopes for them. You know, we're good listeners if you boys ever want to open up, so to speak.'

'Ignore them,' said Jake. 'They're just trying to wind you up.'

Matty winked at Jake as they left and Jake couldn't help but be amused by them. Like everyone else under that roof – with the exception of Tommy – he had a soft spot for their cheeky antics and was more than happy to laugh at himself.

Tommy was still muttering obscenities under his breath as he took a dustpan and brush and began working his way through the first of six sofas, removing the cushion seats and scooping out stray nickels and dimes that had fallen from pockets into the creases. He was stretching deeper to pull out discarded confectionery wrappers when his fingertips touched something leathery. He removed a battered brown wallet and looked inside: it held only a few dollar bills, McDonald's vouchers, an old credit card with the name 'Matthew O'Keefe' embossed on the front, and a driver's licence.

He briefly considered doing the right thing, but his dislike for Matty and Declan was so intense that he changed his mind and, without Jake noticing, approached a plastic bag of rubbish Peyk had cleared earlier. He was ready to toss the wallet away when he noticed a newspaper cutting protruding from the bills. Curious, he took it out and began to read it.

'Yes!' he said, punching the air with his fist.

'Found a winning Lotto ticket?' asked Jake.

'No, but it's close. Nail, meet coffin.'

87

'Jim Morrison was my first crush when I was a girl,' explained Jane, pointing towards artist Rip Cronk's twenty-foot-high mural of the shirtless Doors frontman emblazoned upon a wall.

'I must only have been six or seven when I saw him in one of my sister's music magazines, and he made me weak at the knees,' she continued.

Savannah lifted her head to look at the painting. Although she couldn't name even one of The Doors' songs, she recognized the band's name from what her father called the Forbidden List: a four-page document detailing musicians that, if listened to, would be tantamount to allowing Satan directly into your heart.

'One of the reasons I came to Venice Beach was to see this mural and where Jim moved to when he and Ray finished university and formed the group.'

Savannah nodded along as if she knew to whom Jane was referring. She didn't share Jane's enthusiasm for the subject, but she was growing to enjoy the company of her new roommate. Jane took a photograph of the mural on an archaic pre-internet mobile phone before they made their way a couple of blocks back towards the boardwalk. Savannah linked arms with Jane; it had been a long time since she'd felt so comfortable with a virtual stranger. And the more time they spent together, the more her guard slipped.

Frequently they paused to watch the street performers, dropping loose change into the collection boxes of those they enjoyed.

'You mentioned your sister last night – Roseanna, was it?' Jane asked.

Savannah nodded. 'I miss her; we were pretty close. It's funny you bring her up, because she turns sixteen today.'

'When did you last speak?'

'Months ago.'

'You could always call her, you know. Just to wish her a happy birthday and let her know you're okay.'

'I've thought about it, but I'm scared of what my dad would do to her if he found out.'

'He can't be that bad, can he?'

'You have no idea what he's capable of, Jane,' Savannah replied, and a flashback of the mallet striking Michael's hands and forehead brought goosebumps to the surface of her arms and shoulders.

'The situation at home might've changed since you left.'

Savannah was convinced it hadn't, but the tremendous guilt she'd felt about leaving her sister behind to fend for herself suddenly returned.

88

'I can't find it,' said Matty anxiously, the contents of his backpack strewn across the floor of their room.

'It's got to be somewhere,' replied Declan, stripping both beds of sheets and pillowcases and looking under mattresses.

'Yeah, big help, everything is somewhere.'

'Calm your jets, it's only got the money we made from pawning your necklace.'

'You don't understand.'

'Don't understand what?'

'Please don't be mad at me.'

'What have you done, Matty?'

'My wallet has got the newspaper story inside as well.'

Declan stopped what he was doing and turned to face his friend. 'What?' he said slowly.

'I'm sorry.'

'You fecking idiot!'

'I know, I know, you don't have to say it.'

'But I'm going to, because I told you to get rid of it! If anyone here reads that, we're shafted!'

One Year Earlier: Dublin Airport

Matty and Declan's box-fresh rucksacks disappeared along the conveyor belt as they left the Lufthansa check-in desk and walked back towards Matty's parents.

'You've got everything: your passports, boarding cards, wallets?' fussed Matty's mother. 'You have that bag, don't you? Make sure you have that bag.'

'Yes, I have it. Now don't worry, I've been abroad before,' Matty reassured his mother. But it failed to placate her, and she promptly burst into tears. Matty's father offered her a hug.

'Don't worry, Mammy, you've known all along I have to leave on my own terms.'

'I know,' said Mrs O'Keefe, 'but you're still our little boy and we're going to miss you so much.'

'Let him be, Deirdre,' interrupted her husband. 'He knows what he's doing. Take care of yourself, son.'

Then, as he held Matty's hand, he put in it a silver necklace with a St Christopher pendant attached. 'Thank you,' Matty whispered and then placed it around his neck.

His teary-eyed parents hugged Matty, then Declan, and the boys began to walk towards the departure lounge. Suddenly Matty turned towards them.

'You did a good job, you know. With me. You did a good job. Thank you.'

Matty didn't wait for their reaction or a reply as his own tears began to roll down his cheeks and land on his hoodie. Instead he turned around and continued to walk as Declan placed a supporting arm around his friend's shoulders.

'It's not too late to change your mind,' he said.

Matty shook his head.

'Not a chance.'

The air conditioning blew cold and noisily above the drone of the engines as the plane taxied down the runway towards its take-off slot.

Declan stared through his window at the life he was consigning to his past, at least for the foreseeable future. There was little about it he would miss; certainly not the parents who'd brought him into that world. His mother had prioritized alcohol over her family one too many times before their father asked her to move out. Declan hadn't seen her since.

In the aftermath, the two men had navigated their home in different directions and at different times. Days could pass without their paths ever crossing. And the only reaction Declan received when he told his father he was leaving to travel the world was disinterest.

Now, as the world below him became smaller and smaller, he thought of the future and not of the past. By the end of that day, he and Matty would have sand between their toes as they watched the sun set at Ibiza's legendary Cafe Del Mar before hitting the clubs. Then Spain, Italy, France, Germany, Sweden, Thailand, South America and North America would follow, God willing. After that . . . well, who knew, as they would most likely be living on borrowed time.

Yes, Declan thought, there was much to be excited about, but there was an equal amount to feel apprehensive over too. Sometimes he wondered if he would ever shake off his unease.

'Oh, fuck.' Matty interrupted Declan's thoughts. 'Oh, fuck,' he repeated.

'What's wrong?'

'Look.'

Matty passed him a copy of the *Irish Times* he'd picked up at W.H. Smith's in the airport.

Declan recognized a familiar face in a picture the size of a postage stamp.

'*Postmaster Dies after Armed Robbery*', read the headline.

'What the . . .' gasped Declan, and continued to read. '*A man died yesterday following an armed robbery at his post office a week ago. Eddy Maguire, sixty-eight, who ran Navan's only post office for thirty-six years, collapsed with a suspected heart attack as two robbers attacked his premises. A Garda spokesman said: "We believe they might have been captured on CCTV elsewhere in the town. If that is the case, we hope to quickly identify them before they strike again."*'

'Dec, we killed him,' said Matty quietly, and Declan closed the newspaper. 'We killed someone.'

Declan remained silent, stared at the seat in front of him and gripped the armrest. After a minute or so, he spoke. 'It was an accident, Matty. He must have had a weak ticker; it could have happened at any time to anyone. We have to forget about him.'

Matty stared at Declan and didn't reply.

'Matty, I said we need to forget about him, okay?'

His friend nodded reluctantly and Declan slipped his headphones on, chose a playlist of thumping dance tracks and pumped up the volume to drown out his own uneasiness.

He didn't hear Matty tear the story out of the paper, fold it neatly and place it in his wallet.

Today

By the time their room had been searched from top to bottom, it resembled a midwestern state trailer park after a tornado.

Declan stood in the centre of the room, rubbing his eyes and pinching the bridge of his nose in disbelief.

'I cannot believe you'd be that stupid. Think carefully. When did you have your wallet last?'

Matty closed his eyes and retraced his steps from the night before. 'The lounge!' he suddenly blurted out. 'When we got back from the beach, I stopped off to buy some gum and came straight back in here for the party.'

'Then let's go find it.'

But as they opened their bedroom door, Tommy was standing on the other side with the missing article in his hand.

'Looking for this?' he smiled.

89

Despite Ruth's promise to herself that she wouldn't fall asleep again until she was sure Zak was safe and sound, it took his car horn to wake her up from an unplanned siesta.

Zak glared at her from behind the wheel of his vehicle as the gates to his property opened and he screeched to a halt. Ruth's initial relief that he was still alive gave way to fear when Zak leapt from the vehicle and charged towards her, chest puffed out.

'Why are you still here, you crazy bitch?' he yelled, not giving her a chance to respond. She noticed his dilated pupils and flared nostrils, and took a step back. 'This is your last chance to get the fuck off my street!'

Terrified of Zak's aggression, Ruth was too scared and confused to reply. He pulled out his phone and began to dial a number before walking back towards his house. Suddenly she burst into life.

'No, please don't go, Zak, I just want to talk to you,' Ruth pleaded. 'I've seen all your films and interviews and you seem like such a good guy.'

'I'm an actor; I get paid to be nice, and you ain't paid me shit . . . Hi, I'd like to report an intruder who's harassing me . . . yeah, it's Zak Stanley and I'm on Sunset Plaza Drive . . . yeah, as soon as possible, thank you.'

'We could be friends, I know it,' Ruth added desperately.

'Us? You and me? Ha! You turn up at my house uninvited, and you think we're gonna be buddies? The world doesn't work like that.'

'But it can! Look, that film you were in, *Baby Baby*, the bit where you say, *I know this is the first time we've met, but I don't ever want to lose sight of you again* . . . that's how I feel about you.'

'Jesus! It's just a fucking film! And that's the trouble with people like you – you can't see the difference between what's on a screen and what's real life. So you come to my home and harass me and think we'll be friends? Fool!'

'Please, Zak, please. I know you'll like me if you give me a chance. I'm a good person, I really am.'

'Look at you – you're . . . shit, I don't even know what you are. What's with your clothes? You stink of sweat, I can smell your breath from here. And that hair! Have you ever washed it? Tell me, how would I explain you to any of my friends?'

'We don't have to tell anyone! We could be secret friends.'

Zak paused to take stock of the latest in a long line of obsessive fans. None had been as pitiable as Ruth. In his mind, he'd tried diplomacy, he'd attempted to be polite, and he'd used the cruel-to-be kind approach, but nothing had worked. So when Ruth grabbed his arm, there was only one option left open to him. He swung around sharply and grabbed her by the throat, pushing his face into hers.

'Let me make this clear for the last time – I ain't interested in you or being your pal,' he hissed. 'Now get your stupid ass out of here before I do something you're gonna regret.'

Then he shoved Ruth to the pavement and removed his wallet from his pocket. 'If I was poor you wouldn't want me, would you? For people like you it's all about getting a piece of my fame and my money.'

He threw a handful of $50 and $100 bills at Ruth and she wept as the money and her dreams landed in the gutter.

'There – you don't need anything from me now, right?'

The last time Ruth had heard those words, they had come from her father. She'd promised herself she would never hear them again from someone she loved, and that included Zak.

Zak turned his head when he noticed Ruth's shadow against his gatepost, but before he could react, she had plunged her knitting needles deep into his throat.

90

'It's not what you think,' began Matty, and he and Declan froze, staring wide-eyed at Tommy and the wallet.

'What I think,' said Tommy, 'is that you two robbed a post office, literally scared an elderly man to death and now you're on the run.'

'Prove it,' Declan said.

'I don't have to,' continued Tommy. 'The story might not name you, but I bet the police back home would be interested in knowing your whereabouts.'

Matty and Declan looked at each other, then at Tommy, but said nothing.

'Lost for words, boys? You usually have so much to say.'

Declan cleared his throat. 'Cut to the chase, what are you gonna do?'

Tommy grinned. 'What am I going to do, or what have I already done?'

'Tell me you haven't,' said Matty.

'Hmm, I could, but I wouldn't want to lie to you.'

Tommy instinctively turned his head and lifted his arm up to protect his face when Declan lurched towards him, pinning his arm under Tommy's neck.

'You bastard, you've got no idea what you've done, have you?'

'I know that you think you can get away with anything if you turn on the Irish charm,' said Tommy, his windpipe throbbing under Declan's chunky forearm. 'Well, let's see how far that gets you once you're under the care of the California Department of Corrections.'

'Leave him, Dec, it's not worth it,' interrupted Matty. 'Let's just get our stuff and go, eh?'

'I'd hurry if I were you,' added Tommy. 'It won't take long for that nice officer I spoke to at Dundalk Garda station to call his colleagues in the LAPD.'

Declan punched Tommy in the stomach, causing him to fold in half and gasp for air. Then he grabbed Tommy's t-shirt and reached his arm back, ready to whack him again, before Matty yanked him backwards to stop him.

'Dec, please, don't.'

Declan hesitated and dropped Tommy back on the floor.

'You might not like the way we carry ourselves, but let me tell you this. We'd rather be who *we* are than who *you* are – a petty, spiteful little gobshite who's terrified of losing his place as King Dick in a poorhouse.'

'You have no clue who I am or what I went through before I made this trip,' gasped Tommy. 'And do you think I like dressing up as a fucking hotdog just so I can afford to stay here? I didn't just take a shortcut and rob people to change my life.'

'Don't you wonder *why* we did it?' spat Declan.

'No. Please, tell me – I can't wait to hear your excuse for this one.'

'Because Matty's . . . Matty's . . .' Declan's voice trailed off into silence before Matty finished the sentence for him.

'Because I'm dying, Tommy.'

Tommy hesitated and glared at them both. His first thought was to assume they were lying, until Declan punched a hole in the plasterboard wall.

91

Savannah made the most of the quietness of the near-empty beach.

Instead of sprawling across the sand, today's tourists were distracted by the sights and sounds of an Indian music and food festival spread across the boardwalk. Savannah had already been caught up amongst the throng of performers dressed in their brightly coloured saris and dark hats decorated with white flowers. She'd gratefully accepted a paper plate crammed with food samples that she ate as she walked across the beach towards the shore. Even from a distance she could still hear the singing of traditional Indian folk tunes.

Savannah sat on a blanket with her arms wrapped around her legs and her chin resting on her knees, watching as the tide brought the same piece of sea kelp in and out, over and over again.

Having been raised so far away from the coast, only now could she appreciate how freeing it was to be near to what felt like an infinite body of water that could sweep a person in any direction for as long as it desired. For months, Savannah had lived from day to day, keeping one eye on the present and one eye over her shoulder, waiting for the past to catch up with her. But that afternoon, she allowed herself to consider a future that didn't involve raising a child on a bedrock of fear.

It had been more than two months since someone had tried to bundle her into a van and since she'd fired a gun and accidentally shot Tommy. And club owner Mr Van Lien and his clumsy approach aside, there had been no further threatening incidents.

So beginning there and then, she pledged to make a conscious effort to change. While caution would always prevail, she knew she must learn how to trust people again and not assume any new faces automatically had a hidden agenda.

From behind, she felt the vibrations of feet softly plodding through the sand towards her. Instead of scrambling to her feet defensively, she remained in place.

'I hope you don't mind, but when I saw this little Babygro in K-Mart I had to buy it,' came Jane's enthusiastic voice. She sat beside Savannah and removed a handful of clothes from a bag. 'Well, maybe that was a white lie,' she continued. 'I might've accidentally bought all these things as well.'

'Thanks, Jane, but you shouldn't have,' said Savannah.

'Well, you don't have anyone else to spoil you.'

'Why are you so nice? You hardly know me.'

Jane paused and gazed out towards the horizon. 'For selfish reasons, I suppose. I spent seven years as a mum and now nobody needs me. I feel kind of, well, surplus to requirements, I suppose. I'm sorry if you think I'm interfering.'

'No, you're not. It's . . . nice that somebody cares.'

Savannah closed her eyes, tilted her head towards the sun, and took a deep breath.

'What's wrong, love? Are you feeling a little lost today?'

Savannah paused and put her hand on Jane's. 'You know what? I don't think I am any more.'

Neither Savannah nor Jane was aware of the figure standing some distance behind them, under the shadow of the lifeguard station. Nor did they know they'd been followed for much of the last two days.

92

'Sit down,' said Matty, pointing to a chair in the corner of the room. 'Please.'

Tommy obliged, but kept his hand pressed on his stomach, still unable to breathe normally and fighting the urge to vomit following Declan's blow. He watched cautiously as Matty removed a washbag from under his bed, unzipped it, and poured out a dozen blister packs of tablets. Then he took a second and did the same.

Matty sat down and leaned his back against the wall. 'I've got problems with my ticker,' he began quietly. 'I was born with a congenital heart defect, or to give it its proper name, "a complete atrioventricular canal defect". I had a transplant three years back, but this replacement doesn't like its new home.'

He lifted his shirt to reveal a long, raised vertical scar on his chest.

'They put him back on the donor list before we left Ireland,' muttered Declan.

'But the chances of getting a second match are pretty slim,' Matty continued. 'I've been in and out of hospital my whole life, and I've had enough. I told Dec that I wanted to see the world before it was time to leave it, but the only way I could afford it was if we robbed a bank. It was supposed to be a joke until, well, we robbed the next best thing.'

'No one was going to get hurt, that wasn't the intention,' added Declan. 'Even our weapons were fake. We only found out about yer man's death when we read it in the paper. And we only stole what we needed, we didn't take the piss.'

'We were pretty mortified,' continued Matty. The Gardaí haven't identified us yet from the CCTV pictures, so for the time being we're safe. But all it would take is a tip-off, and who knows what might happen.'

'Wouldn't another transplant work?' asked Tommy, eyeing Matty as he placed his tablets back inside the washbags.

'I'm sick of waiting and I'm sick of these drugs, Tommy. They stop me dying, but they also stop me living. So when my body gives up on me, I want to go out with a smile on my face and my best mate close by. Then I'll know I lived a life.'

The room fell silent for a moment before Tommy spoke again.

'I didn't call them . . . the police. I mean, I wanted to, and I even Googled their number in Dundalk and I was *this* close to doing it, but I bottled it at the last minute. I just wanted to scare you into leaving.'

Matty and Declan let out long, relieved breaths.

'Why do you want us out of here so badly?' asked Matty.

'Why do you reckon?'

'Because we tease you?'

'You do more than that and you know it.'

'But only because you treated us like scum the day we arrived.'

'Yeah, but you were trying your luck to stay here for free. But yes, I know, I was patronizing and I'm sorry for that.

People like you just . . . fit in without having to do anything. It took me weeks to get to know everyone, and that's only because I work here so they're forced to get on with me. And I got . . . well, jealous.'

'Tommy, everyone here loves you, man,' Declan replied. 'You just need to lighten up a bit.' Tommy felt a flush creep across his cheeks.

'So what do you say, shall we call a truce?' Declan continued. 'I mean, I can't guarantee we're not going to rib you now and again, but just give as good as you get, man.'

Tommy nodded and shook hands with Matty and Declan, then passed Matty's wallet back to its rightful owner.

Matty took the newspaper cutting out and ripped it to shreds, letting the pieces float into the bin. And he hoped now that someone else was in on their secret, Declan would have someone to talk to when the inevitable happened.

Because Matty's body was quietly telling him the inevitable wasn't far away.

93

Zak Stanley knew something out of the ordinary had just happened to him, but he couldn't process what it was.

He turned around slowly to face Ruth and felt a foreign object protruding from his neck. As his fingers fumbled around for the source of his discomfort, he felt little pain until he made contact with her knitting needles. Then he understood what the crazy bitch who was gawping at him in terror had just done and his eyes opened wider than they ever had before.

Instinctively Zak panicked and yanked the needles out, but that caused air to rush in and blood to pour violently from the small but deep puncture wounds. His legs began to buckle beneath him as he placed the palm of his hand on his neck to stem the flow. But it was coming too thick and fast from his jugular, pouring down his t-shirt and soaking his chest and underwear.

Zak turned his head quickly, desperately looking for help. He tried to scream but no sound came. He stared at Ruth, his eyes frantically searching hers for mercy. But Ruth remained transfixed by Zak and his urgent need for her; she was the only person Zak Stanley was turning to in his moment of need. Her eyes began to pool with tears as she grinned.

Zak became rapidly weaker and struggled for breath until

his legs finally gave way and he hit the sidewalk, knees first. Ruth knelt down by his side and stroked his hair.

'I told you we could be friends,' she said gently, pulling away the hand he held to his wound. Fearing she might hurt him again, Zak made an attempt to crawl away from her, until she overpowered him by pushing him onto his back then straddling him, holding his arms by his sides. Zak was too sluggish to fight her off.

'It's okay, you'll be okay,' Ruth continued, then she lay by his side, placing her head on his damp chest. She could hear his heartbeat growing fainter and fainter until, after a couple of minutes, it finally rested in silence.

She lifted her head and then slowly placed her lips upon his; Zak's final, bloody kiss would be Ruth's first.

'I'm a good person, Zak, I really am,' she whispered, and hoped Zak understood that now.

Three Weeks Earlier: Victoria, Australia

Ruth picked out a pair of snow-wash jeans, folded them neatly and placed them inside her half-full suitcase.

Next came her supermarket-brand underwear, which she rolled up and placed inside the inner lining of the case, followed by two pairs of sneakers and some high heels. Finally, when everything was inside, she took the washbag from her chest of drawers and unzipped it.

'Make-up!' she said out loud, realizing that if she wanted Zak Stanley to see her at her best at their first lunch together, she'd need to add some colour to her face. But with only a paltry selection of her own, she decided to borrow from her mother's drawer of lipsticks and blushers.

She grabbed a handful of brightly coloured cosmetics and glanced at her mother's body lying under a duvet on her bed. The blood that had flowed from the gash in her head had pooled on the pillow, and over the last half-day had gradually turned brown. She presumed her brother Kevin's pillow would look the same. Ruth tilted her head to one side and reminded herself it was their own fault it had come to this.

The previous night's taunting from Kevin had felt relentless, mocking her decision to travel to LA, laughing about how Zak would react if he ever met her and how she would be scampering back home with her tail between her legs by the end of the week.

'What do you mean *if* Zak ever met me?' Ruth asked Kevin, suddenly. 'I told you I won a competition. I'm having dinner with him. I *am* meeting him.'

'Yeah, about that,' Kevin giggled. 'You didn't win shit. I was messing around with you – didn't you notice the name I gave his manager? Paul Mollegh? Say it out loud, Ruthy, and it sounds like "pull my leg". I told you to leave my iPad and you didn't so you needed to be taught a lesson.'

Ruth refused to believe him. 'No,' she said firmly. 'I spent every dollar I have on a flight and accommodation. You wouldn't do that to me.'

'Would and did,' Kevin replied and looked at her with such pride that she knew he was telling the truth.

Without thinking, Ruth lifted the dog-shaped stone doorstop and crashed it against Kevin's head with such force that he was dead before he even hit the floor. When their mother appeared from the bathroom to see what the loud thud was, it took three blows before her face finally stopped twitching. Then she dragged both of them to their beds, not forgetting to take Kevin's iPad from his desk.

That night, Ruth enjoyed the best sleep of her life.

Two days later, she padlocked her suitcase, put her plane ticket and passport in her jacket pocket and locked the front door, making her way to the waiting taxi and imagining her new life with Zak Stanley all the way to Los Angeles.

94

Today

Some of the guests at the hostel had wandered en masse up to Santa Monica to spend an early evening at Ye Olde King's Head.

The British-themed pub, with its two bars and attached shop, was a favourite of expats and tourists. They would make the pilgrimage to drink or stock up on British biscuits and sweets, surrounded by photographs of celebrity patrons like David Beckham, Sienna Miller and Liam Gallagher. Tables contained pitchers of Magners cider along with pencils and notepaper to nominate potential singers and their chosen tracks for today's karaoke.

Tommy thought Matty and Declan's tuneless rendition of U2's 'Where the Streets Have No Name' was a clichéd choice, but in the spirit of their truce he kept his opinion to himself.

'Go on there, Tommy,' yelled a sweating Declan as he left the stage. 'Get your arse up and give us a song.'

Tommy shook his head. 'I can't sing to save my life.'

'Who cares, we're more Shane McGowan than Bono.'

'Ah come on, you big bollocks,' chipped in Matty, and pointed to Jake. 'Drag yer man up there with you.'

Tommy paused for a moment and turned to his friend. 'Do you fancy it? I will if you will.'

'No mate, my singing days are long gone.'

'You used to sing? Full of surprises, aren't you?'

Jake's heart began to beat a little faster at his error. 'No, no, I meant I'm terrible.'

'Then you'll make me look good!' Tommy replied, and grabbed Jake's arm to lead him to the song choice book. But Jake yanked it back.

'I said no, all right?' he snarled.

He slammed his half-empty glass onto the table, threw open the door and stormed out, leaving behind a confused Matty, Declan and Tommy. Jake barged past Nicole coming in through the door and she made immediate eye contact with a surprised Tommy, who could tell by her anxious glance that something was wrong.

'What are you doing back here?' he asked.

'I need your help,' Nicole replied. 'I'm desperate.'

95

Even as the red mist was descending upon him, Jake was aware he was overreacting, but he couldn't cool his temper in time.

Anger gave way to panic, and the need to leave the pub became urgent. He walked briskly back to the hostel. Everyone he knew was in the bar he'd left behind, so maybe he could gain some peace in the silence under that roof, and hopefully some perspective.

Two Years Earlier: London

Stuart awoke, slumped in the armchair in his apartment where he'd fallen asleep.

The previous night had been the worst of his life, and his brain had reacted to such high levels of stress by shutting itself down. He'd fallen asleep in his clothes and hadn't woken once in almost nine hours. It was now 10.30 a.m.

Zak was the first person who crossed his mind as he wiped his eyes. Over the next few minutes, Stuart called him several times to no avail, eventually remembering that Zak was probably airborne and en route to his next European premiere. In his heart of hearts, he'd resigned himself to their covert relationship having ended: the team Zak employed to advise and protect their Hollywood golden goose would've seen to that.

Stuart picked up the television remote control and hesitantly turned on Sky News. The news ticker scrolling across the bottom of the screen contained nothing about him being caught with drugs, and for a moment he wondered if manager Geri Garland had unleashed her infamous damage-control flying monkeys and they'd worked through the night to quash the story.

He popped an extra-strong coffee capsule into the machine and made himself a drink. But as the noise of the machine faded, the newscaster's words chilled him.

'Now, following the death of actress Katie Todd earlier this morning after an apparent accidental drugs overdose, we head over to a live press conference which is just about to begin in north London with TV's Geri Garland.'

Stuart barely had time to process the news of Katie's death when Geri stepped towards a podium in what looked like her record company headquarters. His eyes widened further when he saw the rest of Lightning Strikes accompanying her.

'I have a statement to make on behalf of Lightning Strikes, *Star People* and IMG Records,' Geri began gravely. 'Firstly, we would like to extend our deepest sympathies to Katie's family and friends . . . we're all thinking of you. Now, I was as shocked as anyone last night by the photographs and video footage of Stuart Reynolds, apparently caught with drugs and leaving a clearly poorly Katie when she needed him most. I have since discovered from Stuart's bandmates that his drug use was not a one-off incident, but an ongoing problem he has had for some months.'

Stuart's coffee mug fell to the floor and shattered.

'Despite many attempts and several interventions from his friends in the band, Stuart has refused to face his demons, which culminated in last night's events,' Geri continued. 'I would also like to take this opportunity to point out that I personally was unaware of Stuart's substance abuse. Lightning Strikes are a band with many, many, young fans. And while we all love Stuart dearly, this is something we all feel is unforgivable. So it is with regret that Stuart's position in Lightning Strikes has been terminated with immediate effect. We wish him all the best in recovering from his addiction and we will provide him with the help he needs if he asks for it. That's all we have to say.'

Geri nodded her appreciation to the scrum of reporters who attempted to ask extra questions as she left the stage.

Stuart remained rooted to his kitchen floor, unsure of where to turn. Katie was dead and the world thought he was to blame. He needed to get out of London as quickly as possible. But where?

Lightning Strikes had been famous in the UK and Europe and now he was equally infamous. But he realized there were places in the world he could go where no one had ever heard of the band. America, for example. The group had yet to conquer the Billboard charts, so he could remain relatively anonymous there. And perhaps if he could track down Zak and get him on his own, he could convince him not to throw away their relationship.

However, before he began making plans, there was someone he needed to confront.

96

Today

The beach was quiet, with the exception of construction workers in the distance building temporary bleachers for a volleyball tournament the following day.

The lifeguard had long since boarded up the windows to his station and headed home, so Nicole and Tommy sat on the wooden ramp, their legs dangling below them, casting shadows onto the sand. Three crushed Nytol mixed with a strong parmesan cheese and sprinkled on Eric's pasta had given Nicole at least a few hours of respite from his all-seeing eyes before they opened again.

'I knew there was more to your trip than you were letting on,' said Tommy when Nicole had finished filling him in on the events of the last few days.

'I'm sorry,' replied Nicole, shaking her head. 'Eric didn't want me to tell anyone . . . and now I know why, considering what was at stake.'

'Why did he never let on Mrs Baker was his mother?'

'She mentioned they'd had some falling out over money and she'd cut her son out of her life, but she didn't really go into detail and it didn't feel right to ask. Now I wish I had – maybe I could've put a few pieces together sooner.'

'Didn't she recognize him at the hospital?'

'He worked in a different ward at the other side of the building, so their paths never crossed.' Nicole rooted around her jeans pocket and passed Tommy the small velvet pouch of diamonds.

'Shit!' he blurted out when he looked inside.

'I know. I've been carrying them around all day; I don't know what to do with them. Eric's dad was a jeweller, so I assume they're real.'

'You need to get them valued.'

'How? I can't keep drugging him and disappearing, can I? The money Mrs Baker left me in the truck isn't going to last forever, so we'll have to go home soon, and how am I going to get these things through customs without shipping the truck back? I can hardly keep them on me, or post them. And I'm scared to death to be alone with him.'

'Why? Has he threatened you?'

'No . . . not yet. But I've seen his temper when he can't get what he wants, and there's a dark side to him I don't want to see again. And if he can keep all this from me, what else is he capable of?'

'I think we need to tackle this one problem at a time. Do you trust me?'

Nicole paused, wondering if she could ever trust anyone again. Then she nodded. She had no choice, she thought.

Tommy placed his hand on the back of hers. 'Then let me help you.'

97

Hollywood Hills

'The home to your right used to belong to Gwyneth Paltrow and Chris Martin back in the mid-2000s,' continued Jenny. 'Despite their conscious uncoupling, Gwyneth remained here until quite recently.'

She switched the microphone to silent mode and yawned, willing her last tour of the day to finish. She drank from a bottle of carbonated water as the primarily European sightseers sitting inside the air-conditioned minibus took photographs of the Spanish-style villa roof behind tall red-brick walls.

It was Jenny's fourth guided tour of the day, and her voice was gradually turning into a rasp. Just one more trip and I can get some rest, she thought to herself as the bus slowly wound its way up the road. She turned the microphone back on and prepared to feign more enthusiasm.

'And this is for the ladies, because just around the corner is the home of actor Zak Stanley!' she continued, as the female tourists and two men chatted excitedly and got their cameras ready. 'Zak has lived here for a year,' Jenny continued, 'And oh, look, his gates are open . . . and that looks like his car . . .'

Her voice trailed off as the minibus driver suddenly hit the brakes, trying to make sense of what he saw. The excited chatter died away as all eyes fell on Zak, lying face up on the sidewalk by his open car door, covered in blood and with a woman pressing her head against his chest.

'Holy shit,' gasped Jenny, as the first of the tourists screamed. Suddenly mobile phones were set to video mode and cameras flashed at the dead celebrity and his companion.

'Call 911,' she whispered to the driver.

98

Day Twelve

With her facial swelling and bruising from the fracas at the club beginning to fade, Savannah disguised her injuries with make-up and returned to work for a six-hour afternoon shift at the Pink Pussycat.

It was an unusually quiet day and Savannah's takings were meagre, but she spent much of her time distracted by a conversation she'd had with Jane. In their six days together as roommates, she'd found herself growing closer to her new friend; and because Jane had experienced so much tragedy in her life, Savannah appreciated her counsel.

The second payphone booth Savannah tried on Fourth Street had a working receiver, so she removed sex workers' flyers from the dial and typed in an out-of-state number she knew by heart. She clenched her fist in her hoodie pocket until the number rang and was answered.

'Hey,' a female voice answered in a sing-song tone.

Suddenly doubting her decision, Savannah pulled the phone from her ear and was about to hang up, then paused and changed her mind.

'Hello?' the voice said again. 'Who's this?'

'Hey Roseanna, it's your sister.'

99

Ron didn't dwell on it when Tommy quizzed him about whether he knew of a jeweller who could offer an honest price for something without asking any awkward questions.

Instead, he flipped through his Rolodex and pulled out a card with an embossed name and telephone number printed on it. 'Tell him you work for me,' muttered Ron, then ushered Tommy out of his office. One phone call and ninety minutes later, Tommy was standing in a brightly lit office above a dry-cleaner in Marina Del Ray.

The deeply wrinkled man with the waxy pallor sitting behind the large desk had yet to identify himself, either on the phone or in person. Meanwhile, two stocky Southeast Asian men stood guard at either side of the steel door Tommy had just entered. If the diamonds were real, there was little he could do if anyone in that room decided he wasn't going to leave with the merchandise he'd arrived with. They could make him disappear and no one would be any the wiser.

The man squinted at Tommy through his thick-framed glasses and rubbed his tongue across his dentures before he asked to see the jewels. He poured them from the pouch into a gloved hand, counted them out with tweezers and carefully examined them one by one through his loupe. Then he weighed them on digital scales and measured them with the tiniest of steel rulers.

Tommy was glancing nervously around the room when a framed photograph on a filing cabinet caught his attention. 'Is that the Hostel in the Woods?' he asked suddenly.

The man pulled his glasses down to the tip of his nose. 'You know it?' he asked.

'Yes, my mate Louis and I stayed there a few months back.'

The man nodded. 'I paid for the place. My son built it and runs it.'

'Rocco, the manager? He's your son?' asked Tommy, surprised, as there was little family resemblance.

'Yeah, he's a good kid. I never really went in for all that hippy-dippy bullshit, but I gotta say, he's done a beautiful job with it.'

'Small world,' replied Tommy, and for the first time, the man smiled.

Three Months Earlier: Missouri

The left-hand side of Louis's face was planted firmly on a *Travel America* guidebook lying on the seatback table.

He quietly snored as the Greyhound bus left the highway and made its way slowly towards the tiny village of Adrian, Missouri. Tommy slipped his headphones into his ears, pushed a memory card into his digital camcorder and began to watch video footage he'd taken of their first two months in America.

There was a Fourth of July fireworks display at Cape Cod; Louis being engulfed by a huge wave at Daytona Beach; Tommy snorkelling in Key West; drinking warm hot chocolates in

Starbucks as the rain poured down outside in Atlanta; Louis clapping along to a gospel choir in a downtown Chicago church; and the both of them covered in blue waterproofs as the *Maid of the Mist* sailed close to Niagara Falls' cascading wall of water.

In a short space of time, they'd amassed a library of memories, and as Tommy glanced at his sleeping friend, he knew that he wouldn't have had the courage to travel America without him. Only once had Tommy experienced homesickness, but he soon came to his senses when Louis reminded him the home he craved had crumbled the day his brothers died. Tommy felt confident being around Louis. But at the same time, he knew the part of him that remained broken meant he was using Louis as a crutch.

In the two dozen hostels they'd passed through in a few short weeks, they'd been in each other's pockets almost twenty-four hours a day. They'd met people along the way, but neither had committed to building fresh relationships with new faces while they had each other for support. There was going to come a time when they'd want to take separate roads, and Tommy hoped that once that happened, they'd still find their way back to each other.

He removed the memory card from his camcorder, placed it back in its plastic case and then glanced at a second one, paused and shook his head.

For almost a decade, the Hostel in the Woods had led a quiet existence, hidden in a forest about thirty minutes from Missouri's Greyhound terminal.

From the moment the battered orange VW camper van decorated with Grateful Dead stickers picked Tommy and

Louis up from the station, the friends understood it was not the traditional version of a hostel they'd come to expect. The van came to a halt under palms, cedars, myrtles and moss-covered great oaks, and from the vehicle's window they saw dormitories housed in hexagonal, two-tier wooden houses, with some perched high in the treeline above the eighty-acre site.

Louis stepped out of the vehicle and grinned as ahead of them, a man swung from a rope attached to a tree branch and plunged into a pool below, where two friends rested their arms on the wooden edges and cheered him on. Behind them, other hostellers busied themselves picking vegetables from small, irrigated plantation areas and swept wooden verandas. According to Louis's guidebook, which awarded the hostel a rave review, accommodation was inexpensive but guests were expected to help with daily chores.

However, Tommy was too overcome by an instant dislike of their temporary new home to notice Louis nodding his appreciation as he took in nature's sights and smells.

'Back to basics, Tommy. No gas or electricity – you cook your own food over open fires, sleep under the stars and boil your water from a well.'

If he'd been looking at his friend, Louis would have seen that no part of this description appealed to Tommy at all. Instead, he was already pining for the bustle of a big city.

Louis was already awake and outside the next morning, acclimatizing himself to his new surroundings, by the time Tommy woke up and unzipped his sleeping bag.

Tommy's lumbar area ached from the firm mattress he'd slept on, so he stretched and ventured towards the porch, rubbing his pollen-affected eyes. His head itched, and he felt small clusters of raised lumps where mosquitoes had dined on him throughout the night. It didn't help to lighten the dark mood he'd fallen asleep in.

Outside, many of the hostel's guests were already awake and eating a communal breakfast around wooden picnic tables. Tommy was looking at his watch, which read 5.50 a.m., and scowling at the ungodly hour when he felt two sharp jabs to his ankle.

'What the—?' he began and glanced down to find an angry cockerel with a razor-sharp beak pecking him. He tried to kick it away, but the bird stubbornly refused, so he broke into a jog as the flapping creature chased him. He could hear people chuckling at his predicament until the bird finally lost interest and returned to wherever it'd been hiding.

'Always a hit with the birds,' laughed Louis, sitting next to two women in oversized checked sleeping shirts. 'Charlotte and Rochelle, this is my friend Tommy.'

As Tommy went for a handshake and Charlotte opted for a peck on each cheek, he became flustered and his hand bounced off her breast instead.

'We're going for a swim, if you fancy it?' continued Louis. 'There's a pool over there made from a natural spring – how cool is that?'

'I need some breakfast first,' Tommy replied, unable to fake any enthusiasm.

'Oh, breakfast was at five, sorry. But there's a peanut Hershey bar in my bag, if you're hungry?'

Without waiting for a reply, the trio began to peel off their clothes and head for the pool. Although Tommy was used to seeing his best friend without a stitch on, he'd never seen him be so public about it.

'When in Rome!' Louis declared, sensing his friend's surprise.

'Remember what happened to Caesar,' muttered Tommy as he headed towards the toilet block. Behind the cubicle door was a hole in the ground and a bottle of organic disinfectant.

He opened his mouth to vent in frustration, but closed it quickly when the stench made him gag.

100

Today

'Oh my God, Savvy, where are you?'

Savannah's sister Roseanna tried to contain the volume and excitement in her voice when she realized who was on the other end of the telephone line.

'It's best you don't know, honey,' Savannah replied, comforted by her younger sibling's voice, 'but I wanted you to know that I'm safe. How are you doing?'

'It's like living in jail here since you left. I hate it,' Roseanna whispered. 'I can't go anywhere or see anyone without Daddy's men following me.'

Savannah closed her eyes, wracked with guilt. 'I'm so sorry. And I'm sorry that I left you, but please know that I had no choice. When I'm settled I'll call and maybe we can find a way for you to come and join me?'

'I really want that,' Roseanna replied, before the tone in her voice altered. 'You need to listen to me, Savvy. Be careful, because I heard Daddy talking and you can't trust—'

Suddenly the line went quiet.

'Can't trust who, Rosie?' Savannah asked, but there was no reply. 'I can't trust who? Rosie? Hello?'

When Savannah heard a deep, throaty cough coming through the receiver, a chill ran down her spine. She slammed the phone back onto its cradle and ran to hail a cab.

101

Matty lay in his bed until late morning, exhausted after a dreadful night of broken sleep.

His dreams alternated between watching the postmaster of the post office he and Declan had robbed falling to the floor over and over again, and seeing himself struggling to fight off a pack of snarling wolves taking it in turns to rip the flesh from his chest.

The sound of a shrill car alarm below his bedroom window made it hard to get back to sleep, so he opened his eyes and felt his head pulsating. Quietly, he took a couple of painkillers from his bedside table and swallowed them with a mouthful of flat Pepsi.

'You okay there?' muttered Declan from his side of the room, eyes half closed.

'I don't want to be a killjoy, but do you mind if I give the beach a miss later?'

'Of course I mind,' yawned Declan, perching up on his elbows. 'How often do they have *Sports Illustrated* beach volleyball tournaments on your doorstep? Just think about the babes in bikinis.'

'I know, I just don't feel so great.'

'What's wrong? Have you taken your meds?' Declan asked, growing concerned.

'Yeah, I'm just hanging. Too many beers at last night's karaoke. I'll sleep it off and maybe see you there later.'

'Do you need anything? Do you want me to find you a doctor?'

'No, it's cool.'

'Okay, look, I'll stay here with you. We'll have a day of chilling instead.'

'Don't been an eejit, you go and have fun for the both of us.'

'No, it's cool. I'll stay.'

'Dec, get the feck out there and enjoy yourself.'

'Are you sure?'

'Yes!'

Declan rolled onto his side to grab a little more sleep while Matty lay on his back, staring at the ceiling and trying to regulate his shallow breaths in the hope the erratic rhythm of his heart might return to normal.

102

Tommy waited the best part of an hour in the office of an unspecified individual in a dubious line of work before the man sitting before him finally offered a verdict on Nicole's jewels.

'What you have here, kid, are sixty-six emerald-cut diamonds,' he began. 'They're very well cut, actually; the clarity is fucking A-1, although to the naked eye there's a little colour weakness.'

Tommy nodded as if he knew what the man meant, and cleared his throat. 'How much do you reckon they're worth?'

'Hmm . . .' the man replied thoughtfully, tapping his chin with his index finger. 'How did you get them?'

Tommy thought on his feet. 'I inherited them.'

Both the man and his henchmen standing by the door laughed. 'Sure you did,' he said. 'Look, if you're happy to offer proof of origin and some paperwork indicating how they came to be in the hands of a skinny little English kid, then you'll get more for them elsewhere. But as far as I know, they could be blood diamonds and discerning buyers aren't going to touch them. I'll give you eight thousand dollars for each of them. So it depends on how quickly you need the cash.'

It was highly probable Mrs Baker's gifts were legitimate, but he had no way of proving it. And Nicole had said she trusted him to do what he thought best if an offer was forthcoming.

The man removed a calculator from his desk and keyed in some numbers with a stubby finger. 'It's your call. Sell them to another dealer for bigger bucks, or walk out of here with $528,000 in cash.'

103

Eric made his way towards the pick-up truck in the near-empty multi-storey car park, tossed a plastic bin bag into the footwell of the rear passenger seat and began clearing the rubbish Nicole had carelessly thrown around the vehicle throughout their travels.

Amongst the trash were local newspapers, fast food wrappers, empty cans and bottles of soda, and photocopies of maps and highways that marked their journey together. He'd learned on their travels over the weeks that she could still make a mess in a rubbish tip. And it was one of the many things about her that grated on him.

As he cleaned, Eric mulled over how Nicole's behaviour towards him had clearly shifted since his outburst in Lubbock. Maintaining his façade day-in, day-out, had been more exhausting than he'd foreseen, and he had done well to slip up just once. But it was a big misstep because it had made Nicole look at him a little differently.

Many times during their return journey to Santa Monica, he'd tried to lighten the mood by engaging her in conversation or singing along with songs on the radio, but these gestures had been largely ignored. And by the time their truck rolled into the car park opposite the hostel, he was ready to slap the sulking out of her.

And now it felt as if Nicole was keeping her distance from him, and if Eric was being honest with himself, it had come as a welcome relief. Back in the real world, there was no doubt he enjoyed her company, even if she was a little whiney at times. But he could dip in and out of her worries and woes if and when he liked. On the road, there was no escaping them. He was a captive audience of The Nicole Grainger Show. He wouldn't have minded quite as much if there'd been something to indicate they were on the right track to unearth his rightful inheritance. But the clues were vague and their execution of her letter poor.

Eric recalled the day Nicole had mentioned a terminally ill elderly patient she had befriended. He hadn't thought much about it as Nicole was a soft touch and had a habit of picking up waifs and strays on their way out of this world. It was only when she named Grace Baker and he checked his mother's online records on the internal hospital computer system that he realized they were one and the same person.

A decade had passed since he'd last seen his mother. It saddened him that her pain couldn't be prolonged, as it was no less than she deserved. And through Nicole and her online charts, Eric was able to keep a close eye on her decline. Coincidence had reunited them, but he couldn't leave it to fate to decide what happened next. And later, when Mrs Baker had left vague instructions of where to find *his* inheritance to *her*, everything between Eric and Nicole altered. She was no longer a friend – she was a means to an end.

However, all these weeks later and still unsure of what his mother had planned for her fortune, Eric was ready to throw in the towel and head home. Once he'd finished cleaning it out, he would encourage Nicole to sell the truck and they could split whatever pittance they'd made from it and price up flights back to London. Or Nicole could stay, if she wanted. Right now, he couldn't care less. His adventure was over.

Eric worked his way through the driver's-side pockets, throwing away receipts and chewed gum wrapped in tight little paper balls, before digging out rubbish from the passenger's side. When he lost his grip of an empty packet of Tic Tacs, it fell under the seat so he fumbled around trying to find it. Instead, he grasped a small piece of paper. He was ready to chuck it away, but its red handwriting caught his attention.

'*Don't let her son find these – they're not for Eric,*' he read out loud.

It took a moment for the significance of the words to sink in. Then, suddenly, Eric understood that he wasn't the only one who was playing a game. Nicole knew who he was and she hadn't said a word. And what's more, she had found something. Something the note said was not for him. But he knew that it was rightfully his.

If Nicole thought she had seen Eric's fiery temper before, she was mistaken. She hadn't seen anything yet. And she had no idea what she was about to let herself in for.

104

Jake and Nicole acknowledged each other with nods when he entered the hostel lounge and sank onto the sofa opposite her.

Peyk messily slurped miso soup from a bowl balanced on his lap and turned the television on, flicking around the stations for a news channel.

Nicole and Jake had seen each other around the hostel, but had yet to talk. Both were aware Tommy played a part in the other person's life, but not to what extent. Nicole recalled that when she'd rebuffed Tommy's advances, he had appeared to shift his focus towards Jake. Now she couldn't help but feel envy that despite Tommy helping her sell the diamonds, it was Jake who now had his attention.

Meanwhile, Jake recognized Nicole as the girl from the hostel party Tommy had tried – and failed – to kiss, and was slightly resentful of Tommy's attraction to her.

And while Nicole anxiously awaited Tommy's return, Jake was also waiting for his friend to reappear so that he could apologize for storming out of the King's Head pub the previous afternoon. He wanted to offer Tommy an explanation for his childish tantrum, but the jury was still out as to whether he could trust him enough to tell the truth about his past life and his subsequent behaviour.

Because Jake knew what could happen when you mistakenly put your trust in the wrong person.

Two Years Earlier: London

Stuart Reynolds was no stranger to loneliness.

Lasting friendships were hard to make in foster homes, and even once he became a member of Lightning Strikes, his feelings of isolation continued. His part-time, behind-closed-doors relationship with Zak Stanley didn't help him to find the meaning of belonging either.

But as Stuart sat on a wall opposite Geri Garland's four-storey mansion on the affluent side of Notting Hill waiting for her to return, he'd never felt more alone in his life. He pulled his hood over his head to shield himself from the drizzling rain.

Eventually he recognized Geri's Range Rover pulling up outside her town house. Her driver opened her door and she exited, slipping on her sunglasses for the five-metre walk from the vehicle to her front door.

'What have you done to me?' Stuart yelled, running towards her. Geri turned around sharply. Another man appeared from the passenger side of her car and pushed Stuart backwards before he could reach her.

Geri glanced over the top of her sunglasses. 'He's no threat. Come in, Stuart, let's get this over with.'

Today

'Fuck, man!' yelled Peyk suddenly, and spat his soup across his bare legs.

He turned up the volume of the television as a 'breaking

news' graphic filled the television screen, along with a photograph of Zak Stanley and the word 'MURDERED!' emblazoned across it.

'Breaking news,' began the female newscaster. 'Police sources have confirmed that actor Zak Stanley has been found dead outside his Hollywood home after a fatal assault.'

'Oh my God,' began Nicole, watching as cameras broadcast live from the street she and Eric had followed Ruth to days earlier. Black-and-yellow police tape had been attached to trees on opposite sides of the road to cordon off the area, while forensic investigators wrapped in blue plastic suits placed numbered markers on the road.

Neither Jake's body nor his face moved as he processed what he was watching.

'According to sources, it appears Mr Stanley was stabbed to death by a stalker,' continued the newscaster. 'His body was taken to UCLA Medical Center and pronounced dead on arrival.'

A small crowd of hostellers began to gather in the room, all stunned and some crying at what was being shown. Nicole suddenly lifted her hands to cover her mouth at the next image to flash across the screen.

'And we have just received this footage taken by a passenger on a Hollywood Hills tour bus. It has yet to be confirmed, but it appears to be an ailing Mr Stanley with his attacker.'

As the HD footage focused in on a bloody figure with her head on Zak's chest, Nicole instantly recognized Ruth.

'No,' she gasped, 'Oh no, no, no.'

Instinctively she wanted to find Eric to tell him the news – until she remembered why she couldn't.

She turned her head to look at Jake instead, but he had already disappeared.

105

The sweat trickled down Eric's face as he furiously rummaged around the truck, searching every nook and cranny. He didn't know what he was looking for, but he knew from the note it was important enough for Nicole not to be made aware of it.

He hunted under the floor mats, down the back of the seats, inside the boot, under the bonnet and even rattled empty soda cans until he suddenly thought of the one obvious place he'd yet to examine. Remembering the air vent he'd kicked at Buffalo Springs Lake and Nicole had later fiddled with, he yanked out the plastic covering, put his fingers inside and rummaged around until he found what felt like a small, sharp stone.

He pulled it out and dropped it into the palm of his hand. Instantly he knew it was part of his mother's legacy – a modest but perfectly formed diamond.

Eric's sister had told him that when their mother sold the business after their father's death, she had kept back some of the stock rather than sell everything. She had believed the supply of diamonds to be finite and thought they would be unlikely to lose much of their value over the coming years.

So when Nicole was left a safety deposit key, an excited Eric had assumed that if the gems did exist they would find them there. Instead, Nicole had discovered them hidden in the truck.

His heart raced as he sat back in the seat and began to consider where Nicole might have concealed the rest.

And he promised himself only one thing: this would not end well for Nicole.

106

'I'm trying, but I'm just not getting it.'

'No, darling, neither do I. Give me Constable or Renoir over this experimental twaddle any day of the week.'

Jane and Savannah's heads tilted at right angles as they stood staring at a 15-foot by 15-foot painting in a plush art gallery on Abbot Kinney Boulevard. Dubbed the 'coolest block in America' by *GQ* magazine, everywhere – from the boutiques to the salons, restaurants and bars – was beyond Savannah and Jane's budgets, but at least the galleries were free to browse. Although quite what they were peering at, neither could be sure.

'It looks like a dwarf playing tennis with an ostrich wearing a bonnet,' continued Jane.

'The plaque says it's a portrait of a post-apocalyptic snowman.'

'Well, who am I to argue with art? I can barely draw a stick man. What do you say to admitting defeat and grabbing an iced tea in the cafe upstairs?'

Savannah followed Jane up two flights of clear Perspex stairs, where they sat on stools sculpted to resemble open-palmed hands. Only a day earlier, Savannah had vowed to herself to be more trusting. But then came Roseanna's warning about not being able to depend on someone she knew, and it weighed heavily on her mind. Several times she'd caught herself questioning Jane about her life back in England to see if her story altered, but there were no discrepancies. She'd even stalked Jane on Facebook, setting up a fake profile so that she could search Jane's. Most of the woman's profile was set to private, but from what she could see, Jane had been honest about everything. She even found the story of her children's murder in online newspapers. Savannah didn't want to doubt Jane's motives in befriending her and certainly didn't want to push her away, but it would be foolish not to act with caution.

'I might not understand art, or even the people in Venice some of the time, but I am drawn to Los Angeles,' continued Jane. 'Not all that show business gubbins of course, but areas like Venice, Santa Monica and West Hollywood. How about you? Can you see yourself raising your baby here?'

'I guess so. I don't think I really have much of a choice for now. Once I save up some more money, I'll rent a little apartment and, when she's born, I'll get a part-time job that doesn't involve taking my clothes off or sliding down a pole.'

'So you know it's a girl, then?'

'Oh, no, I haven't asked about the sex. I just have a feeling.'

'And what about the hostel? From what I've seen, you've made yourself a nice little life there.'

'I've made some good friends here; one in particular who's been there for me when I needed him the most.'

Five Months Earlier: Sunset Boulevard

A blown socket in the air conditioning unit meant the humidity in the Flesh for Fantasy strip bar in downtown LA was unbearable.

Savannah put the handful of $10 and $20 bills she'd scooped from the stage into her bag, then grabbed a towel from her locker and patted herself dry. She drank two thirds of a bottle of sparkling water she'd left by her mirror and once she'd showered, she finished the rest and slipped on her civilian wardrobe.

On her arrival in LA a month earlier, work had been much harder to find than Savannah expected. The cash she'd taken from her father's wallet and the maximum amount she could withdraw using his ATM card in Alabama would, she calculated, last her ten days at most once she found herself a cheap motel to book into. Then she would need to find a job. But her only experience in the working world had been volunteering at a charity for the elderly with friends from the Zeta Phi Beta Sorority House. And without any experience, restaurants and shops weren't willing to consider an inexperienced girl from the south-west.

'You should use that body to make yourself some money,' one waitress at a diner Savannah frequented had suggested.

'I'm not a hooker,' Savannah replied, indignantly.

'That's not what I meant,' corrected the waitress. 'If you can shake your ass and don't mind being leered at by horny guys, you could make a bunch of cash dancing at one of the clubs on Sunset. Just a thought.'

It was an idea that didn't appeal to Savannah, but beggars couldn't be choosers, and right now she was a beggar. Two days and one audition later, and Savannah had a trial at Flesh for Fantasy – not the classiest of establishments, but by no means the worst of the clubs LA had to offer. And although the cheap motel she had made home was a dive, she couldn't wait to get back there now, as the humidity in the club was making her tired and dizzy. Desperate for cool air, she made it out of the fire escape and into the alley before she collapsed, unconscious.

The driver slammed on his brakes when the girl stumbled across the sidewalk and fell into the road.

He leapt out of his car ready to scold her for being drunk, but once he reached for her limp body, he knew alcohol was not the cause of her intoxication.

'Help me, please,' she mumbled, her eyes darting across his face, looking for kindness. 'Drugged . . . my water . . .' Savannah's head lolled to one side, so the man picked her up and carried her to his car, laying her across the rear seats.

'I'll take you to the hospital,' he said, closing the door.

'No . . .' she continued, 'he'll find me . . .'

'But you need to see a doctor.'

'No, no, no . . .'

Even through her haze, she was adamant. The driver was at a loss as to what to do, so he rummaged through her handbag to find an address or a cell phone with a name he could call. He thought it odd that for a girl her age, she had no mobile phone but around $400 in cash.

Thirty-five minutes after he found a key for the Marigold Motel, Savannah was safely lying on her bed in her room. And as she remained in a deep sleep her rescuer, Peyk, made himself comfortable in an armchair.

107

Today

Eric rushed back to the hostel from the multi-storey car park, slipping past the lounge while Nicole and a group of others were preoccupied by something on the television screen.

He didn't have the time or the inclination to discover what had them so silently engrossed. Instead, he bolted up the stairs and along the corridor into their dormitory, where he began to rummage through Nicole's suitcase. But as each pocket only yielded socks, underwear, fridge magnets and postcards Nicole had purchased on their travels, Eric became more and more frustrated.

'Looking for something?' came Nicole's voice from the doorway.

Eric stopped his search and turned around. 'Oh hey Nicole,' he chirped. 'Where've you hidden the paracetamol?'

'Why?'

'Because I'm planning to take an overdose. Why do you think?'

'Unzip the top of the backpack and you'll find them in the box with the plasters.'

'Thank you.'

By the time Eric had finished fumbling around in the bag and turned around to thank her, Nicole had disappeared as quietly as she'd arrived.

108

Peyk didn't question Tommy when a taxi pulled up outside the hostel and he hurried out, grabbing Peyk's arm and leading him up the stairs and into room 23.

'How safe is it in here?' Tommy asked breathlessly.

'Three deadbolt locks and a reinforced steel door safe. I fitted them myself.'

'You've fallen through two ceilings and electrocuted yourself, so forgive me if your DIY skills don't inspire me with confidence.'

'Do you see anyone else creating a cannabis farm from scratch under the unsuspecting noses of every guest in here?'

Peyk glanced down and noticed two large, bulging holdalls with the name and logo of a dry-cleaner's emblazoned across their sides. 'Don't ask,' Tommy muttered, his eyes darting around the room.

Peyk's ability to keep secrets was something Tommy appreciated, and even though he'd yet to discover what made Peyk tick, his gut instinct was that despite his clownish façade, there was a more serious side to him and he could be trusted.

'The room at the back, under the ceiling tiles – store them there,' Peyk replied.

Tommy made his way towards the storeroom and used a stool to reach and remove one of the polystyrene squares.

Through the hole, he placed the bags containing Nicole's cash until they were out of view. As he stepped down, his eyes were drawn to a bathroom beyond the storeroom, separated only by a pane of clear glass. He walked towards it, then took a startled step backwards when he saw Savannah enter. She pulled down her shorts and underwear and sat on the toilet. Tommy remained perfectly still so he wouldn't be noticed, before realizing he was on the other side of a two-way mirror.

'You okay in there, Tommy-boy?' yelled Peyk, and Tommy joined him back inside the room.

'I'll keep your business private if you do the same with mine,' Peyk added. Tommy nodded his agreement.

109

'He called me *Nicole.* In all the time I've known him, he's never used my full name. It's either Nic or hun, but never Nicole. So don't ask me how, but I'm sure Eric's found out I know who he really is.'

Nicole waited nervously for Tommy to finish serving a customer at the hotdog stand.

'You could always admit to what Mrs Baker left you?' Tommy asked. 'You'd get him off your back by splitting the cash.' Nicole pondered his suggestion for a moment before dismissing it.

'I'm not being greedy, but clearly his mum didn't want him to have it. And if he's gone to all this trouble to hide who he is, what else is he capable of doing?'

'Well, that might be a good enough reason to pay him off, if he frightens you. Protect yourself.'

Nicole had left Eric in their dormitory searching for headache tablets and gone straight to meet Tommy at their prearranged destination. He'd explained that while he could have likely got more money if he'd sold the diamonds legitimately, he'd done what she'd asked and made a decision he thought was right. She hadn't disagreed with him.

'This has been a messed-up few days,' Nicole continued. 'First I discover my best friend has been lying to me about who he is, then I find his secret mum has left me half a million dollars' worth of diamonds and, to top it all, the naive girl we were sharing a room with goes and murders Hollywood's biggest star.'

'You haven't heard the update, then?' asked Tommy tentatively, unsure whether Nicole was ready to hear more bad news. 'According to the radio in the taxi, the Australian police reckon she killed her mum and brother before she flew over here.'

'You're not serious! Am I just the worst judge of character in the world?'

Nicole let out a long breath and brushed her fingers through her hair. 'What the hell am I supposed to do, Tommy? This trip was supposed to be a brand-new start for me, but it's turning out to be the worst decision I've ever made.'

Tommy was unsure how to respond, so he placed his hand on Nicole's to support her as two middle-aged women approached them. 'I'll be back in a moment,' he told Nicole.

'Three hotdogs, no mustard, just salad,' asked one of the women and winked. Nicole was too preoccupied to notice Tommy twice flash three fingers to José behind him in the trailer or see him place two sausages in two buns, and then three small bags of pot in a third. The women handed Tommy seventy dollars in return. Moments later, two police officers cycled past and waved at Tommy, who immediately reciprocated.

'So how far are you willing to go to take Eric out of the picture?' he asked as he returned his attention to Nicole.

'What do you mean?'

'I mean, you can't spend much longer living under the same roof as him and avoid being alone with each other. You need to make a pre-emptive strike, because if he's cottoned on that you've found what Mrs Baker's left you and haven't told him, he's going to be mightily pissed off.'

'I'm actually terrified to be around him. But the more I think about his lies, the angrier I get. So over my dead body is he getting any of that money.'

'If you need a head start to get away from here, there is a way,' Tommy replied, his brain slowly formulating a plan. 'But it's pretty hard-core. And it'll cost you about twenty thousand dollars.'

110

'How about you?' Savannah asked Jane as they placed their bags of shopping on their beds. 'Do you like being in Los Angeles?'

'I'm falling in love with it, actually,' Jane replied. 'I've often toyed with the idea of trying my hand at writing . . . I even took a creative writing course a couple of years ago, and I think I have a few stories inside me. Not *about* me, of course, there's enough of those "woe is me, isn't life crap?" memoirs without me adding to the list. But this city inspires me.'

'Don't you need a green card or something?'

'I was born in Chicago, so technically, I am just as American as you. My father moved our family to Cambridge for work when I was a few months old.'

'So what's stopping you from putting pen to paper?'

'Well, nothing really. Ideally, I'd like a permanent base and to set down some roots before I try and discover my inner Anne Tyler. And I can't really do that in a hostel, there's too much hustle and bustle. It's just a thought, and promise me you'll tell me if I'm overstepping the mark here, but what would you think about us finding a place to share together?'

'Oh I don't know,' Savannah replied, feeling herself flinch.

She wasn't at ease being put on the spot, even by a friend, and it instantly made her doubt Jane's intentions. Was this part of some plan to get her away from the hostel and on her own, where no one would have her back? Why would Jane offer a home to a pregnant pole dancer unless she had an ulterior motive? But Savannah couldn't deny the offer was tempting. And despite her doubts, she couldn't refuse it outright.

'My baby will be here in a few months,' she continued carefully. 'Do you really want to live with me and a screaming kid?'

'You have no idea how much I'd like to hear that sound again,' Jane replied wistfully.

She looked away and absent-mindedly fumbled with a gold crucifix she wore on a chain around her wrist.

'Sorry, I shouldn't have said that,' replied Savannah.

'No, no, you didn't say anything wrong. And you're right, darling, it's a daft idea. A young girl like you wouldn't want to live with an old codger like me.'

'Oh no, that's not what I meant. It's just that I can only afford somewhere low-budget, like above a store or something.'

'Well, if money is the only thing holding you back, my husband's life insurance means we could afford a little place in West Hollywood. I had a walk around there a few days ago and it's lovely. Nothing big, mind, but I can cover the rent for at least up until next summer. Maybe he can finally do some good in death that he couldn't do while he was alive.'

Savannah was unsure of what to say to Jane. If genuine, the offer was undoubtedly kind – even though relying on someone else for help had never been part of her plan. And she was desperate for her friend to be for real.

'If you're sure, we could give it a go, I guess?' Savannah replied, and Jane held her hand out to shake Savannah's.

'It's a deal, then,' beamed Jane, and Savannah began to believe that the bad luck which had plagued her for months might be about to change.

111

'Hey, lazy bollocks, you missed a hell of a day,' Declan began as he burst into the room. 'Wall-to-wall *Sports Illustrated Swimsuit Edition* honeys bouncing up and down in the sand in a volleyball tournament . . . it couldn't have been better if I'd dreamed it.'

Matty didn't respond. He lay on his side facing the wall while Declan covered his burned red face and shoulders with after-sun and continued to boast.

'And – get this – we're meeting up with a couple of them for drinks in Marina del Rey tonight. You've got to see them – they're beautiful, Matty, and so fecking clever too. I mean, they'll see right through us eejits but not before we've charmed the arses off them. You up for it? Matty?'

Declan trailed off as he realized Matty was completely motionless. He had spent many, many hours watching his best friend sleeping and studying his breathing patterns, and this wasn't normal. Slowly, Declan moved towards him and felt his own body begin to grow rigid. His arm trembled as he placed a hand on Matty's shoulder and pulled him over onto his back, where Matty remained inert, his eyes firmly closed.

'No, Matty, no . . .' whispered Declan, placing his panicked fingers on Matty's neck, desperately searching for a pulse. He moved them from area to area until finally he found what he was looking for.

Suddenly Matty's eyes opened and he roared with laughter, as Declan stumbled backwards in confusion.

'You fecking idiot!' yelled Declan. 'What did you do that for? I thought you were . . . you were—'

'Dead? You can say the word, you know!' laughed Matty. 'Just think of this as a dry run.'

'Go fuck yourself,' Declan growled, and stormed out of their room.

112

The news of Zak Stanley's death hit Jake with the force of a juggernaut.

Feeling suffocated in a lounge crammed full of strangers mourning the image of a man they'd never known, he made his way towards the open space of Venice Beach and the calming ebb and flow of the waves washing in and out against the sand. He slipped out of his flip-flops and waded into the water until he was waist-deep, allowing his breathing pattern to mimic that of the tide. In and out, in and out, slowly in time with the water's rhythm, until Jake began to feel his calmness return.

Zak had been the person who'd known Stuart best, and even though they'd not seen each other since before the night cameras had caught him with cocaine on his lap and a convulsing girl by his side, Zak's death made Jake feel even more alone in an already isolated life. He'd held on to the hope that one day their paths might cross again. Many times he had imagined engineering a reunion by discovering where Zak lived in Los Angeles and turning up on his doorstep in the hope of closing the chapter they'd left unfinished.

But it had only ever been a daydream, and now Jake would never really know if Zak had ever regretted his decision to ghost him. Three days after making headline news, Stuart's phone and wallet had been discovered lying on the grass by the 500-foot East Sussex cliffs. As far as the world was aware, somewhere in the depths of the English Channel, currents were carrying Stuart's body away, never to be found.

Meanwhile a newly born Jake was on the deck of a ferry sailing from Hull to Zeebrugge, Belgium, using a forged passport purchased from his Russian former housemates in Bolton.

Two Years Earlier: Notting Hill, London

Geri Garland held a key card to a metal panel on her glossy black front door, which opened automatically.

She slipped off her cropped leather bomber jacket and tossed it across a chesterfield sofa in a large, airy hallway. Stuart and her bodyguards followed her into a drawing room and watched as she poured herself a Scotch from a decanter into a chunky glass tumbler, then dismissed them.

'Mmm, that's good,' she purred, taking a long sip. 'It's been a hell of a morning, hasn't it, Stu? They say alcohol tastes better in a heavier glass because the weight of the tumbler can trick the brain in the way it processes taste. But you'd know a lot about tricking people, wouldn't you?'

'Why did you sell me out?' Stuart blurted out.

'Why not?' Geri replied, matter-of-factly. 'Why should I sacrifice a whole herd of cash cows when I only need to send the runt to be slaughtered?'

'But it wasn't my cocaine! You could have helped me convince the papers of that, or come up with an explanation.'

'An explanation? Like what? That you'd had an accident with a bag of flour? If it had just been photos then maybe there'd have been a way out, but you were stupid enough to be recorded with it on your lap. On your bloody lap! They had you bang to rights.'

'But you're not listening to me – it was Katie's coke, not mine.'

'It doesn't matter if it was the Queen of fucking England's coke, it was all over you and a young soap star. As far as everyone's concerned you're the one who killed her.'

'You didn't have to sack me, you could have said you were sending me to rehab. Loads of stars end up in treatment, and I'd have been out after a couple of months and everyone would've forgiven me.'

'Not Katie's parents. Because for the rest of your public life they'd have hounded you in the press. You'd never be allowed to forget running away when that poor girl was dying next to you.'

'I'm the frontman of that group, you told me that yourself. That's why you put me in it. The band can't survive without me.'

'Band? You mean brand, because that's all you are. And don't fool yourself into thinking they're going to split up just because of your stupidity. You gave those boys some competition, something to aim for, someone to beat. They've all developed a bit of charisma now, and without you I'm confident they'll step up to the mark in your absence.'

Stuart swallowed hard – he would not cry in front of her. 'Bullshit, I've read what the fans say on Twitter and Facebook,' he argued. 'I know it's me they pay money to hear sing.'

Geri gave a deep, throaty laugh and lit up a menthol cigarette. 'Are you now so deluded that you've told yourself you have a voice?' she asked. 'You can barely carry a bloody note!

Thank God for autotune! I'll give you credit, though, you're the best bloody mime act I've ever worked with. But you're just a pretty face with no talent. Face facts, Stu, you were an experiment to see if the public would buy a silk purse made from a sow's ear, and they did. And you knew that from the word go.'

'What about you and me?' he continued, desperately trying a different tack. 'I thought we . . . had something.'

Again Geri laughed. 'Let's not go there, shall we, son?'

'I don't deserve for it to end like this,' Stuart pleaded.

'You didn't deserve a million-pound recording contract either, or a Canary Wharf penthouse. But I didn't hear you complaining when you saw the money stack up.'

Geri took a deep drag from her cigarette and inhaled the smoke coming from her mouth with her nose.

'You're not getting it, are you?' she continued. 'You're a liability. Nobody in this business will touch you with a barge-pole. You had some laughs, you saw the world, you lived like a star; now move on.'

'But—'

'But nothing. Sooner or later you'd have fucked it up for yourself anyway. Katie and I did you a favour.'

Stuart frowned and chewed the inside of his cheek. 'What do you mean?'

113

Day Thirteen

Eric finished flossing his teeth and lifted up his vest, studying his reflection in the bathroom mirror as he rubbed at the hairs on his stomach.

He hadn't found the time to manscape in weeks and was annoyed at himself for allowing things to become so untidy downstairs. Not that he'd given anyone else the opportunity to notice, as he'd been on a self-imposed sex ban since their flight landed in America. He turned to his side and pushed out his stomach as far as it would stretch, then inhaled deeply. A six-pack was buried somewhere deep under a fatty layer of convenience food, sugary soda drinks and a recently acquired penchant for blueberry muffins. He vowed he'd have all the time in the world to get back into shape once his mission was complete, and he predicted this would be very soon once he worked out to beat Nicole at her own game.

Now she was aware of who he was and had unearthed his mother's legacy without telling him, the playing field was level and the game could begin in earnest. It was a game he'd win, of that Eric was certain. He did not lose, ever.

For someone who had only a casual regard for the well-being of people in general, even Eric was aware of the irony of choosing a nursing career. After a handful of expulsions from the country's top boarding schools, he'd scraped his way through five GCSEs and scratched a living from part-time jobs as a casino croupier and call-centre worker before joining the health care industry.

It was a career he planned would take him around the world once he branched out into the private sector, as that's where the real money lay. Palliative one-to-one care for the wealthy and terminally ill meant he could earn more in the space of a month than in a year within the NHS. But with two more years of experience still required and his current earnings basic, Eric had used his charm to gain the help of an unattached and somewhat needy hospital pharmacist who inadvertently helped him with a lucrative sideline.

Soon after their first tryst, he'd had the unsuspecting man's shop keys copied. And twice a week after closing time, Eric had hunted for past-their-sell-by-date drugs before they were denatured and sent to an incinerator. He'd also palmed empty order chits while the man was otherwise engaged.

Frequently, Eric swapped Alzheimer's, dementia and comatose patients' regular medication with placebos, believing it made no difference to their well-being what tablets they swallowed: they were doomed anyway. Those pills also sold well on the black market. But while his extra earnings gave him a higher standard of living, it wasn't enough for Eric and unsustainable in the long term. Now Nicole held the key to how he should be spending the rest of his life.

Eric exhaled and let his belly expand, pulled his vest down, and steeled himself for his next performance with Nicole. As he opened the bathroom door he saw her hovering around her bed looking nervous, before she turned in his direction.

'I'm heading out for a bit,' Nicole said.

'Where?' Eric asked with a painted smile.

'To the chemist's,' Nicole replied. 'You used the last of the paracetamol. I won't be long.'

As she left the room, Eric knew he'd been lied to, as he hadn't taken any medication. He glanced suspiciously at their bunk beds and, at first, couldn't put his finger on why they looked different. Then he noticed Nicole had uncharacteristically tidied up around her bed; her clothes and empty bags were no longer scattered across the floor; her sheets and pillow were in place, but her sleeping bag was nowhere to be seen. Neither was her suitcase, he thought. He checked under her bed to see if she'd stored them there, but the space was empty. He went towards the locker area where Nicole sometimes kept her belongings, but there was no trace of her.

'She's running away,' he realized, feeling his rage rise. Immediately he located his toilet bag and rifled through it, shoving something into the pocket of his jeans. Then he ran down the corridor after her.

114

Tommy anxiously drummed his fingers on the reception desk, turning his head to check the clock above Ron's office door for the second time in a minute.

A full day had passed since he'd last seen or spoken to Jake, and he missed him. He was well aware of the transiency of backpacking, but Jake was the only person he had met on his travels who really 'got' him, and he was reluctant to say goodbye just yet. Something told him their friendship was far from running its course.

However, Nicole's troubles gave him more cause for concern than whatever was on Jake's mind and his unexpected outburst at the karaoke afternoon.

Meanwhile, Savannah perched on a stool behind Tommy and placed spacers between her toes, painting her nails in a deep red. He looked jittery, she thought, but she didn't ask why. Everyone was entitled to keep their own counsel.

Every so often she felt twinges in her belly, so she'd gently pat it as if to reassure her baby all was well in the outside world that awaited her. She hoped it wasn't a surge of hormones heightening her emotions or preventing her from thinking rationally, but she had convinced herself that moving in with Jane was the right thing for all concerned. No matter how much she mulled it over, she just couldn't find fault with her friend. The prospect of living in a proper home with someone experienced in motherhood to help guide her in those first few difficult weeks was too hard to refuse.

'Yes,' she reminded herself, 'I've made the right decision.'

Because sometimes trusting a stranger was the right thing to do.

Four Months Earlier: Marina Peninsula Cafe, Los Angeles

Peyk was making the most of the all-you-can-eat waffle bar. He brought a third full plate back to the table he shared with Savannah.

She wore dark sunglasses to shield her eyes from the bright light that added to the haziness of her memory. She poured several spoonfuls of sugar from the dispenser into her second mug of black coffee and gingerly sipped it.

'Do you know what happened last night?' asked Peyk.

Savannah shook her head. 'I remember feeling dizzy when I was changing. I made it out to the alley before I blacked out, but I don't know how long for. Then I came to and reached the road where you found me. And now something doesn't feel right, you know, down there. What if he did something to me while I was unconscious?'

'I can take you to the police if you want? You know, get you examined.'

'What's the point? I'm not sore or bruised and surely I'd be in a lot of pain if I'd been assaulted? And I've showered, so there wouldn't be any evidence.'

'Are you're positive you're safe in your motel room? What if he knows where you're living?'

'You're not helping me feel any better about this.'

'I'm serious. Look, I know somewhere in Venice you can stay that won't cost you a buck, you'll be surrounded by people day and night so you'll be safe. And I know a guy who works on the door at the Pink Pussycat in Santa Monica who could get you work.'

Savannah looked at Peyk and realized that under the strangest of circumstances, and despite not knowing a thing about him, this was the first friend she'd made since she'd arrived in the city.

Two hours later she found herself standing in the doorway of a room at the Venice Beach International Hostel. Inside were two single beds, two lockers and a bathroom with a sink, toilet, shower and a large mirror on the wall.

'It's the best room we have,' began Peyk apologetically, sensing Savannah's disappointment. 'But you'll have it to yourself most of the time. I'll make sure reception only puts people in here if we're busy.'

'It'll be fine. Thanks again, Peyk.'

'Oh, and take this,' he added, and passed her an object from his jacket pocket.

'A gun?' Savannah replied, taken aback.

'It's for your protection.'

'Well, I didn't think you wanted me to rob a bank with it.'

'Do you know how to use it?'

'Of course. It doesn't mean I'm comfortable with it, though.'

Peyk closed the door behind him and left Savannah to acclimatize to her new surroundings. While her motel room was basic, it was still expensive and Peyk offered this accommodation for free. If she worked hard at the new club that

Peyk suggested, it would enable her to save up and afford something better.

Savannah looked at the gun and went to put it in the locker, but hesitated and placed it inside her handbag instead. She began to unpack her clothes and hang them up on the rails, and placed her many cosmetics on a shelf in the bathroom.

And she was unaware that she was already being watched from a room behind the bathroom mirror.

Today

Tommy and Savannah's silence was broken by Nicole, who rushed past the reception desk and out the front door. She glanced over her shoulder towards Tommy, who responded with a nod.

Thirty seconds later, Eric walked briskly past him in the same direction as Nicole, and Tommy sprang into action.

'Sav, can you hold the fort here for a few minutes? I won't be long.'

'Sure, honey, is everything okay . . .?'

But before she got her answer, Tommy was out of the door and running towards the beach.

115

Nicole picked up her pace as she made her way towards the second floor of the car park where their pick-up truck was.

She promptly became aware that she had company, and it took all her strength not to just turn around, stand her ground and confront the urgent footsteps making their way up the concrete ramp behind her. But that wasn't part of the plan. Not yet, at least.

Finally the Chevy was in view. She reached into her pocket as she walked and removed a bunch of keys, examining them to find the one that opened the passenger door.

As she located it, she reached the car but before she could insert it in the lock, she was pushed hard from the side and nose-dived to the floor. Her cheek and wrist took the brunt of the impact, but she was too distracted by the snarling face looking down at her to feel pain.

'Clumsy,' Eric snarled.

116

Tommy's eyes darted in all directions until he caught sight of the two people he'd left the hostel to search for.

He half-walked, half-jogged until they were a few metres away from him, but just as he prepared to approach them with his rehearsed spiel, Jake blindsided him.

'Hey stranger, where are you heading in such a hurry?'

'Hi,' began Tommy, his eyes flitting between Jake and his targets. He was desperate to catch up with Jake and make things right between them. He had yet to learn what had made Jake lose his temper at the King's Head pub, but now was not the time.

'So what have you been up to?'

'Oh, just been busy in the hostel, you know.'

'Okay,' replied Jake, aware of Tommy's reticence to converse. 'Everything all right? You seem distracted.'

'Look, Jake,' continued Tommy, 'I'm really sorry but I'm kind of in the middle of something right now, can we catch up later?'

'Yeah, sure,' Jake replied.

'I mean it, I promise. But there's something I need to do right now.'

'When are . . .' Jake began, but Tommy had hurried away before he finished his sentence.

117

Nicole lifted her head from the car park's concrete floor and struggled to focus her gaze on Eric.

'You pushed me,' she muttered, taken aback by his violence.

'You've been pushing me for days, Nicole,' Eric replied. His imposing figure stood over her, arms folded in defiance. 'Now let's cut to the chase, shall we? Where are they?'

'Where are what?'

'Don't play stupid. Where are my mother's diamonds?'

'I don't know anything about any diamonds . . .' Nicole replied, and clambered to her feet. But she wasn't fast enough to shield her nose from the brunt of Eric's headbutt and she dropped back to the floor, clutching her bloodied face and howling.

Eric let out an exaggerated sigh, then kicked her in the stomach. Nicole's eyes opened wide as she fought to breathe. She'd expected their confrontation to be verbally unpleasant and threatening, but she had never witnessed this Eric before.

'Nicole, you were stupid enough to leave a diamond in the car, along with Maria's note.'

Now it made sense to her how Eric knew about her discovery. She thought she'd covered her tracks, but she'd been careless. Her mind raced as she tried to settle on a reply, but as she struggled to return to her feet, Eric kicked her again.

'Okay, so we'll do this the hard way,' he continued, and as Nicole fell to her side, he climbed on top of her, rolled her onto her back and pinned her arms and legs down with his own. Then from the back pocket of his jeans, he pulled out a small bottle with a clear liquid inside and a syringe. He jabbed the bottle's membrane and drew the liquid up the barrel.

'What are you doing?' gasped Nicole.

'I'll give her credit, my mother put up a good fight for a weak woman. Are you going to do the same?'

Eleven Weeks Earlier: London

The digital display on the medical monitor next to Mrs Baker's bed read 4.45 a.m. when she woke to find someone replacing a syringe driver into her chest.

'Is that you, Nicole?' she asked groggily, struggling to recognize the figure hovering over her. She felt cold breath against her ear when he spoke.

'Hello, Mum,' whispered Eric, to Mrs Baker's horror. He held his face inches away from hers. 'Let's cut to the chase. What have you done with my inheritance?'

Mrs Baker's heart raced and her eyes began to water, but she would tell her estranged offspring nothing.

'You know my sister doesn't need it,' he continued, his voice growing louder, 'and after what you put me through, they're rightfully mine. So tell me where I'm going to find Dad's diamonds.'

Mrs Baker trembled, but again, refused to talk.

'You didn't think I knew about them, did you?'

Mrs Baker tried to turn her head to look away from him until Eric clamped his hand over her mouth. He felt the loose skin on his mother's arms brushing against his own as she attempted to bat his hand away, but she was too weak to hurt him or to shout for help. Eric shook his head.

'One last chance. Where are they?'

Mrs Baker shut her eyes tightly, knowing it would be the last time she ever did so.

'You've left them to Nicole, haven't you? You are, and always have been, a stupid, stupid woman.'

Eric manoeuvred his other hand towards the syringe driver and plunged the needle into it. In less than a minute, a massive overdose of morphine killed his mother.

He took in a deep breath, exhaled, stretched his arms above his head and yawned. Then he turned to face his sister Bridget, who sat in the corner of the room.

'You didn't give her much of a chance to reply,' she said. 'Trigger-happy, as ever.'

'I didn't see you stepping in to protest,' he said as he removed the syringe and replaced it with the original one. 'She was never going to tell me, so there was no point in dragging out the inevitable.'

Bridget picked up her coat from the arm of her chair and walked towards the door. 'Stay on the right side of that nurse friend of yours. She's your only hope of finding what you're looking for.'

'Don't worry about her, she's easy to manage. And remember. There won't be an autopsy because Mum was already terminally ill. But just to be on the safe side, cremation, not burial.'

Today

It was one thing for Nicole to learn that her best friend was a liar, and then to be a victim of his vicious nature. But to hear Eric admit he had murdered his own mother because she wouldn't tell him what she'd done with her diamonds horrified Nicole. She kept a hold on her nerves to keep him talking and to play for time.

'Why?' asked Nicole. 'She was going to die soon anyway.'

'Then why does it matter?' shrugged Eric. 'I did her a favour.'

'You could have just gone to her house while she was in hospital and searched for the diamonds yourself.'

'I did, a day after you and I visited.'

'Her housekeeper just let you in?'

'Not exactly.'

Eric waited for Nicole to catch up with him. The breath left her lungs when eventually, she did.

'Do you understand the lengths I'll go to, to get what I'm owed?'

'But you aren't owed anything!'

'And Saint Nicole is? Just because you befriended a terminally ill, vulnerable old widow? You're the same manipulative bastard I am.'

'You killed two people for nothing! You're evil.'

'For nothing? Is that what you really think? Let me tell you something about your wonderful friend Grace Baker, Nicole. When you're a nine-year-old boy who's being repeatedly raped by your housemaster at one of the top boarding schools in the country; when you turn to the *one person* for help who should believe you, your mother; when that *one person* says it's in your imagination and you're lying because you're homesick; when you beg and plead and then beg and plead some more and you even try to hang yourself with a bed sheet from the wooden beams of the school refectory because you can't take it anymore; when that *one person's* response is to remove you from that school and shove you into another one without even allowing you a visit home . . . When you kill that person, it is *not* for nothing. It's called karma, and as you're about to discover, what they say is true – karma is, indeed, a bitch.'

The manner in which Eric's story tripped off his tongue without pause or hesitation gave Nicole no doubt he was telling the truth. She didn't want to believe that Mrs Baker could have been so dismissive of her son's plight – and it certainly didn't excuse Eric's subsequent actions – but the part she had played in creating this monster could not be denied.

Eric hadn't planned to tell her anything about his past, but when he witnessed a slight softening in Nicole's eyes, it only angered him more. 'Do *not* feel sorry for me,' he ordered, 'when it's your own safety you need to be worried about.'

He jabbed the needle into Nicole's arm as she twisted her body from side to side in an attempt to throw Eric off her.

'Just a little more pressure, and the morphine will reunite you with both of our mothers very soon. Now, for the last time, where are my diamonds?'

Nicole's breathing became sharp and desperate. She had completely underestimated his determination and how much he hated her, and glanced around the empty car park, willing someone to disturb them.

'In the air vent!' she finally declared, 'I found them in the air vent in the truck.'

'I've already looked in there.'

'I know, that's why I put them back there this morning, I thought it'd be the last place you'd look again.'

Eric stared into her eyes, searching for a tell-tale sign she was lying. 'Huh, clever,' he conceded, then removed the needle, yanked her to her feet and frogmarched her towards the vehicle.

'Open it,' he barked, pointing to the door. 'Try to run and I will kill you.'

Nicole unlocked the truck, opened the passenger door and leaned inside to pull the air vent out, but it was jammed. She jabbed her fingers between the plastic strips and yanked hard, but nothing moved. Impatiently, Eric pushed her to one side and with two big tugs, pulled the unit from its casing. Nicole took a couple of tentative steps backwards, but when Eric spotted her, she stopped.

He shoved his hand inside the vent, felt around with his fingertips and pulled out a small velvet pouch.

He turned to look at Nicole and grinned.

118

'You're a bloody idiot, Stuart,' Jake told himself as he watched Tommy run off up the boardwalk.

He quickly realized his mistake, and couldn't remember the last time he'd referred to himself using his former persona. He wondered if it was spending too much time with Tommy that had caused his slip-up, because there was something infectious about Tommy's wide-eyed vulnerability that reminded him of himself before he'd allowed fame to corrupt him. And Tommy also had a quality about him that made Jake want to be completely honest about who he was and who he used to be.

Up until moments earlier when Tommy had brushed him off, he'd even considered broaching the truth with him. But today's meeting was a reality check, because Jake understood Tommy was never going to want anything but friendship from him, and he hated his clichéd behaviour in falling for a straight man he could never have.

No, he thought, and decided against placing his deepest, darkest secrets on Tommy's shoulders. Tommy was probably moving on from their friendship anyway, because friendships made in hostels were transient. And in his experience, that was the case with all his relationships.

Two Years Earlier: Notting Hill, London

'What do you mean, you and Katie did me a favour?' Stuart repeated slowly.

Geri Garland stared at her fallen protégé, briefly wondering if it would be better to backtrack rather than admit the truth. She decided against it.

'What do you think it means?' she snapped. 'Pretty self-explanatory, sweetheart.'

'You set me up? You got Katie to put those drugs on my lap just as we arrived at the hotel?'

'That's pretty much the bare bones of it. And perhaps tipping off the paps on your arrival. But I didn't expect her to shove so much of that shit up her nose that it'd kill her. Typical of Katie though, wasn't it? She was dying for fame and took it too literally.'

'But why?' a stunned Stuart replied. 'What did I do to you?'

Geri laughed. 'Why? Why not? Because I can! And you're right, you didn't do anything to me – but you were quite happy to do a lot to Zak Stanley, weren't you?'

Stuart glared at Geri, unsure of how to respond. Nobody, bar Zak's sister, was supposed to know about their relationship.

'Don't think there's a single aspect of your life I don't know about, Stu,' Geri continued. 'I know about your liaisons with the Hollywood hunk, I know you're not pure as the driven snow when it comes to using illegal substances of your own in the bedroom; in fact, I even have video footage of you two indulging in your sordid sex and coke romps. Which is why you're going to keep your mouth shut about everything that's been said in this room, because if I hear one word publicly from you, my footage is going to "mysteriously" leak online . . . and how much more humiliation can you take in twenty-four hours?'

'If you . . . if you do that,' Stuart stuttered, 'then I'll tell the press about you letting me mime, your secret tax shelters, how you and Katie set me up, how you're really to blame for her death. You'll be ruined.'

'And I'll vehemently deny it all before suing the arse off you. You signed a non-disclosure agreement when I let you into my band, meaning you can't say shit about anything. And it's valid for ten years after you leave – or are thrown out. I've got you over a barrel, sweetheart; a position, if I recall correctly, Zak is quite fond of.'

Stuart stepped backwards, reeling from the storm of threats and revelations Geri was raining down upon him.

'Did you do all of this because I wasn't interested in you?' he asked hesitantly.

'Ha!' Geri laughed. 'Don't flatter yourself. It was only ever about one thing – you doing anything I wanted you to do, when I wanted you to do it. You only had to follow the rules, and you'd have been fine. Instead you fell in love. And I couldn't let that happen.'

'You fucking bitch.'

'You're perceptive, I'll give you that. Now it's been lovely catching up, but if you don't mind, I have a meeting with a young lad who'll do anything for me – or more precisely, who'll do anything *to* me – to replace you.'

Suddenly anger, frustration and adrenaline got the better of Stuart. Without thinking, he sprinted towards Geri, dragging her to the ground and clasping his hands around her neck. Twice he smacked her head against her parquet flooring before her security staff heard the commotion, dashed in and pulled him off her. One held Stuart's arms behind his back as the other punched him twice in the stomach and once in the face.

A stunned Geri struggled to her feet and steadied herself against the drinks cabinet. She coughed and spluttered and her throat burned, but she was still able to find her voice.

'I rescued you from your shitty little life up North, I made you a star and even after I ruined you, I still own you, you little prick,' she bellowed. 'And I will destroy you unless you get the fuck out of my house!'

Stuart struggled in vain as he was hauled out of Geri's drawing room and into the hallway.

'You can't get away with this,' he hollered.

'Already have, sweetheart, already have,' replied Geri, before pouring herself another glass of Scotch.

Geri's security men were too preoccupied with ejecting him from the hallway to notice what he'd swiped from a sideboard.

119

Today

There were many things that terrified Nicole about Eric in a short space of time, none more so than the look of greed and victory spreading across his face as he held the pouch of diamonds in the palm of his hand.

Eric had killed twice for this haul, and she was convinced he would kill again. Her entire body trembled as she looked around for help or an escape route.

'I presume you've had them valued?' he asked.

'How could I? You never let me out of your sight,' Nicole lied.

'Your boyfriend could have done it for you. Remind me to pay little Tommy a visit before I leave.'

Eric poured the contents of the pouch into his hand, but before he could stop her, Nicole leapt into action. She lurched towards him and slapped the underside of his hand, spraying the gems into the air and across the car park floor. Gambling on Eric choosing greed over revenge, she ran as fast as her legs could carry her towards the exit. Nicole's hunch proved correct, as behind her, Eric hesitated, at first unsure of which way to turn before dropping to his hands and knees, frantically grabbing all the glistening jewels he could see.

He scooped them into his pocket and stood up, but as his right foot moved forward, he felt a crunching under his sole. He looked down to see a tiny fragment of shattered glass and hesitated. Then he removed a second diamond from the pouch, placed it on the floor and trod on it. It too left a powdery residue.

'Costume jewellery,' he snarled, and pulled the syringe out of his pocket. 'You're dead, Nicole!' he yelled at her fading, running footsteps as he turned around to pursue her.

'Put the syringe down, sir,' came a stern female voice from nowhere. Eric quickly turned his head to see two uniformed police officers, their pedal bikes by their side. Eric's mind raced. This had not been part of his plan – albeit a plan that had been altered the moment Nicole cleared out her belongings from their room.

'This isn't anything,' he began, and walked towards them, smiling.

The officers quickly reached for their guns and pointed them at him.

'Put the weapon down, sir!' shouted the officer.

'Guys, guys,' said Eric, panicking. 'This isn't a weapon – I'm diabetic, this is insulin.'

He dropped the needle and while one officer covered her partner, the other pushed Eric against the side of the car, patted him down and handcuffed him.

'It says morphine here,' the first officer began, reading the label on the bottle he plucked from Eric's pocket. 'No mention of insulin.'

'I can explain that,' said Eric.

'I'm going to look in the vehicle,' the second officer added, and radioed for assistance.

'You need a warrant,' said Eric nervously. 'Everything in there is rightfully mine.'

'Are you sure about that?' asked the second officer, removing tarpaulin from the flatbed of the truck and looking underneath.

'Um, yes,' replied Eric.

In the back of the truck was Nicole's suitcase, but as the officer unstrapped the buckles and opened it, its only contents were five brick-sized packages of shrink-wrapped cannabis resin. A patrol car made its way up a ramp and onto their level.

'That's got nothing to do with me,' he protested, but his words fell on deaf ears as he was read his rights. As the handcuffs clamped Eric's wrists, he resisted and tried to wriggle free. And as they became tighter, he saw his future and all his plans slipping through his fingers and it all became too much. In a fit of rage, he lashed out, the back of his hand breaking the nose of one officer as another used her taser to shoot 50,000 volts of electricity through his body until he collapsed to the ground.

120

Nicole sprinted through three fire exits, down two ramps and out of the car park. Then she ran across four lanes of traffic, narrowly avoiding being hit by a refuse collection vehicle, before reaching the safety of a bustling sidewalk.

She wasn't ready to stop yet. She raced past the hostel and towards the beach, passing a parade of shops before finally stopping behind a van parked outside a restaurant. She bent double, struggling to catch her breath. Her head, stomach and nose ached, and her mouth felt dry before she was struck by an overwhelming urge to vomit. Last night's Chinese food splattered across the tarmac before she heard a disgusted muttering and turned around to discover she was being watched by diners eating on a restaurant patio just metres away from her.

However, the disapproving stares from strangers were the least of her worries. Nicole waited nervously until she saw headlights appear from the car park exit and a police vehicle leave.

She stood up and squinted at the rear of the vehicle, briefly making eye contact with Eric before he was driven out of sight.

121

'He could have killed you!' began Tommy, as Savannah wiped away grit and dried blood from Nicole's forehead and nostrils.

Nicole lifted up her t-shirt and tentatively felt her ribs; none were broken, but she was quite sure they were bruised. Her nose was, however, fractured, and she realigned it herself with a crack and a yelp before it had time to heal crookedly. Savannah had been eager to help when Tommy and Nicole turned up at her door looking for somewhere quiet to clean up and regroup, and she used cotton wool buds from Jane's first aid kit to clean a wound on Nicole's chin and cheek.

'Why didn't you let me come with you, if you thought he might be that dangerous?' continued Tommy.

'I didn't think it would get so bad,' she admitted. 'He wouldn't have followed both of us, so I had to go on my own. And if you'd been with me, who'd have approached the police on the beach? What did you tell them?'

'That some guy had been selling drugs to hostellers from a pick-up truck, and that I'd just seen him in the car park. What's Eric been charged with?'

'I didn't understand all the technicalities, but when I called pretending to be his sister Bridget to ask about bail, they said something about an intent to supply drugs and possession of a potentially lethal weapon. The truck's been impounded, and because it was shipped over here and we registered it in his name, there's no link to me. And I can't drive, so I'm not even named on the insurance.'

'Why didn't you tell the police what he did to his mom?' asked Savannah.

'Because it's Eric's word against mine and he might have been lying to scare me. Mrs Baker was cremated, so they can't do any toxicology tests on her body, and there's no way Bridget will ever admit to being party to her mother's murder. I need to try and find out more about her housekeeper and if he was telling the truth before I contact the British police and tell them what he told me.'

Nicole sighed and dabbed at the tears pooling in the corner of her eyes. 'If he was being honest about Mrs Baker ignoring his claims of being abused at boarding school, then I feel awful for him.'

'But that doesn't excuse him killing her,' said Savannah.

'I did the right thing, didn't I?'

'I don't think he gave you much of a choice,' Tommy replied.

A few moments quietly passed as they continued cleaning her up before Tommy spoke again. 'Hey, have you forgotten what a wealthy woman you are now? What are you going do with the money?'

'I've not really had time to think about it. I'll probably stay in LA for a while and get my head together.' Nicole held her hand out and placed it on Tommy's. 'Thank you, by the way. It's good to know who your friends are.'

Only Savannah noticed how tense Tommy's hand became in response, before he removed it and began picking up bloody cotton wool buds from the floor, dropping them into a bin. Just two weeks ago, Tommy could only have hoped for a moment of closeness like that. A lot had happened in that short space of time, yet he wasn't ready to admit to himself that there was someone else he couldn't stop thinking about.

'I'm not sure if I want to know the answer to this,' added Savannah, 'but where did you come up with so much marijuana so quickly?'

Ron admitted he wasn't a man to express his emotions freely.

He couldn't recall the last time he'd cried; he'd fallen in love just once in his sixty-eight years, and the only thing that made him laugh was watching video clips of dogs doing silly things on YouTube. He couldn't remember the last time something, or someone, had left him speechless.

So when Tommy walked into his office and placed $19,000 in $100 bills on his desk, his jaw dropped before he'd even realized.

'Tell Peyk he needs to speed up production,' was all Tommy said before leaving him to count the cash. And as he made his way up the stairs, Tommy decided neither Ron nor Nicole needed to know about the $1,000 he'd anonymously pushed under Matty and Declan's door that afternoon.

122

'Man, I really need this,' said Tommy, taking a long drag from a joint.

'I didn't think you approved of my recreational habits?' asked Peyk.

'People keep telling me I need to lighten up a bit, so that's what I'm doing.'

Peyk was more than a little surprised when Tommy appeared at the door of room 23 asking for something to help him chill out after a stressful day. He rolled him a spliff with more tobacco than cannabis to get him used to the taste, but it wasn't long before Tommy's head started feeling like candy floss. They were sitting on either side of the windowsill, looking out of the only pane of glass not covered by a blind or cardboard, when Joe caught their attention, fast asleep on a discarded sofa in the alleyway.

'Looks like someone's too messed up to even make it inside this afternoon,' said Peyk.

'I wonder how it all went wrong for him,' Tommy asked.

'Have you ever taken the trouble to ask him?'

Tommy shook his head. 'I just wondered why he started making such bad choices.'

'Are any of the choices we make the right ones?'

'Man, can we have just one conversation without this weird, cryptic crap?'

'Nope,' smiled Peyk. 'Cryptic is what I do.'

'So you are never curious how Joe's life became such a waste?'

'Who are you to judge him? Just because he hasn't got what you have doesn't mean he's wasted it.'

'He's got no money, no home, no family . . . Nobody deserves that.'

'But a man can live without all those things. And you have more in common with him than you think.'

'Please enlighten me, oh divine oracle.'

'Neither of you has any freedom.'

'Well, that's not true. I may not have much money but I'm not a slave to my next fix.'

'But you're not free from the limits you set yourself either. You're one of the most uptight, frightened little shits I've ever met. You went travelling to escape something – that's clear – then you separated from your friend and you end up here where you hide in the margins, never in the middle of the page. You're too scared to embrace freedom . . . you're like a fish in a bowl looking out towards the ocean but too gutless to make the jump.'

'Where's all this coming from?' snapped Tommy. 'You don't know the first thing about me.'

'Tommy-boy!' continued Peyk, exasperated. 'I've met you and your type countless times, and you're all the same. You're a tourist, not a traveller. You're on vacation. Be honest with yourself, if not me. You have remained in this hostel because it's the safest, most convenient option. You're scared of going home, scared of what to do with your life, scared of what you're feeling for Jake—'

'Jake's a mate,' interrupted Tommy, sounding less than convincing.

'He means more to you than that and you know it. You think he's found what you've been looking for; you think he's at peace with himself. You think he's everything you want to be but are too afraid to find by yourself, so you live vicariously through his anecdotes, hanging on his every word. But he's not any of those things, Tommy. He's a man, and men are flawed, some more than others. You can't live your life through someone like that. You owe yourself more.'

Tommy folded his arms defiantly, his partially stoned mind trying to justify his choices and devise a counter-argument, all the time quietly aware that Peyk's words were ringing true.

'Right here, right now, you can start your life all over again,' Peyk continued. 'You can do anything you want to . . . if you want to see the whole of the world, not just this little corner, then go see it for yourself; if you want to experience a relationship with someone of the same sex, then just do it. In the great scheme of things, it doesn't matter. In the great scheme of things, nothing matters – but you. And the only people who will judge you are those you shouldn't give two shits about. I know that people think I'm a joke – the stoner who is always falling through ceilings. And you know what? I don't care. I know who I am and I know what makes me *me*. Just don't sit here casting judgement on people like Joe when you are too much of a coward to make something of your own life.'

Peyk passed Tommy his joint. 'Enjoy,' he said, and left Tommy alone, utterly bewildered.

123

No matter how many sunsets he'd seen all over the world, the sixty minutes between the day ending and night beginning offered Jake more clarity than any other moment in the day did.

It was the time when he could reflect on what had passed and contemplate what the evening might bring.

'Oi!' shouted a voice in his ear, and Jake's stomach lurched like he was driving too fast over a humpbacked bridge.

He swiftly turned his head to find Tommy. 'Jesus,' he huffed.

'No, but you're close. I thought I'd find you on the roof. I just wanted to apologize about earlier when you saw me at the beach. I was caught up in the middle of something . . . It's been an . . . eventful day.'

'No, I owe you an apology for the other day in the pub. I wasn't having the best of times—'

'Honestly mate, it doesn't matter. Let's just start again. I've brought you a peace offering.'

From behind his back, he produced a bottle of vodka and a bottle of Coke and placed them on the ground. And from the pockets of his cargo shorts, he withdrew two paper cups, a small bag of pot and some rolling papers.

*

'I can't remember the last time I did this,' said Jake, taking another drag from the joint Tommy had rolled. The filter was moist and tasted like Tommy's kiss.

'I smoked a few joints with Louis at this backpacking place in the woods once, but that's about the extent of my relationship with drugs. What else have you dabbled with, then?'

Jake paused, knowing that with the booze and dope relaxing him, he couldn't allow himself to become too loose of lip. 'Nothing more than anyone else,' he conceded.

They sat with their backs to the low wall from where the railings had fallen days earlier but had yet to be replaced. Darkness was creeping in and the streetlights below reflected off the sidewalk, giving them a blue and grey tint.

'A toast,' Tommy suggested, holding up his glass and spilling some of his drink on his leg. It made him giggle, and he wasn't sure why.

'What are we celebrating?'

'I've freed my inner sausage and given up the job on the hotdog stand,' continued Tommy, but decided against telling Jake about giving up his sideline too, or about the $5,000 Nicole had given him for his help with Eric. 'And you know what? For the first time in ages, I can honestly say I'm a happy man.'

'Why now?'

Tommy hesitated before he spoke. 'I lost people close to me not so long ago. It's taken me a while to get my head around it.'

'Oh, I'm sorry, I didn't know. Did you want to talk about it?'

'Yes, one day, but not right now. There's something else I'd rather do.'

Jake wasn't sure if it was the lighting or the weed that

was making him misjudge the moment. Tommy took another swig from his vodka and Coke for Dutch courage and, with Peyk's words still ringing in his ears, took a deep breath.

'And what's—'

Before Jake could even ask his question, Tommy pressed his lips against Jake's.

124

Day Fourteen

Nicole spent much of the night unable to sleep.

Above her bunk, Eric's bed lay empty, stripped of its sheets. His belongings had been tossed into a garbage can in the alley. Each time she moved she felt her bruised ribs, sore head and broken nose. But they didn't hurt as much as Eric's betrayal. Whenever she closed her eyes she saw his venomous face glaring back at her, ready to end her life – and all for the sake of money.

Nicole was reluctant to leave the building's boundaries or venture into the courtyard to clear her head, even though she knew she was being irrational; Eric was elsewhere in the city and behind bars. He wasn't the only person she knew who'd been arrested recently, of course.

In the rare moments when she wasn't reliving her ordeal in the car park with Eric, Nicole worried about what had become of Ruth. Zak's murder was still all over the television and online, and her best guess was that Ruth had been shipped to a psychiatric unit to assess her mental state. When it transpired that she had also killed her mother and brother back in Australia, Nicole understood that her shy, unassuming former roommate must have problems much more deeply rooted than anyone could have imagined. Perhaps Nicole owed Eric a debt of gratitude for dissuading her from approaching Ruth the day they followed her to Zak Stanley's house.

Nicole gave up on rest long before her fellow hostellers awoke, and quietly slipped out of her room to eat breakfast alone in the kitchen and ponder what to do with her new-found wealth. She was certain Tommy could keep her money safe until she made a carefully considered decision. So far, it had only brought her misery and bruising.

After rinsing her dishes, she made her way to the hotel reception to pay for another week's accommodation and found Peyk taping posters to the wall that read 'Free beach party, tomorrow night, Santa Monica, 8 p.m. till sunrise'.

'You got some time later to help me organize food and stuff?' Peyk asked.

'Sure,' replied Nicole, grateful for the opportunity to think about something other than her own troubles. Then, suddenly overcome by the need for company, she was on her way towards Tommy's dormitory. He had been such a good friend to her – more than that, in fact. He had gone above and beyond what she might expect from a friend, especially one she had only met recently. And she wondered if she had been unfair when rebuffing his advances. After all, age was just a number, right? In the great scheme of things, if they had a connection, that was all that mattered.

Up ahead of her, a door at the far end of the corridor opened.

Tommy didn't spot Nicole, but she was aware of him slipping out of Jake's room in just his underwear.

125

Four French girls Tommy had checked into the hostel days earlier stood in a line, stared at the television in the lounge and waited as a timer counted them down.

As soon as The Weeknd's 'Blinding Lights' began playing, the girls followed the on-screen instructions and copied each of the dance moves they were told to follow by an animated character.

'Where did that come from?' Tommy asked Peyk, pointing to a brand new 72-inch television on the wall.

'Ron bought it earlier and rigged it up.'

'Nice to know he's put my earnings to good use,' Tommy replied curtly. 'Meanwhile the water pressure's still non-existent and there's next to no wifi signal.'

'Yet you're still smiling. What have you been up to, Tommy-boy?'

'Nothing,' he replied, willing his cheeks not to blush. 'Let's just say I followed your advice. I jumped out of the fish bowl and it feels good to be in the ocean.'

Peyk nodded. 'Just be sure not to let the current drag you down.'

Tommy rolled his eyes, preparing himself for more vague life lessons. 'Meaning?'

'Jake is not your brother, or your father, or your friend

Louis, or whoever else you want him to be. Don't mistake love for lust.'

'Yesterday you were telling me to stop being a pussy and step out of the margins – now you're saying I can't trust him?'

'Peyk, you're next!' interrupted Bette, grabbing his arm and pushing him towards the game before he could reply. Clearly drunk, she took Peyk's place next to Tommy.

'For an English guy, you're cute,' she slurred.

'What's wrong with English guys?'

'They're too pale and only want to drink beer all the time. You are different. We go somewhere quiet if you like?'

'Thank you, but I'm good,' he replied and moved his head backwards when her lips began to approach his.

From across the room, Jake watched, amused, as Tommy awkwardly rebuffed the inebriated girl's clumsy advances. What had happened on the roof last night and later in his bedroom had taken Jake by surprise. But he couldn't be sure if Tommy's curiosity was anything more than an experiment.

'Hi,' Nicole began, distracting Jake from his concerns.

'Hello.' He frowned at the bruising and swelling around her eyes.

'Didn't Tommy tell you?' she asked, pre-empting his question. 'I thought you two were close.'

'No, he didn't say anything.'

'It's a long story.' But Nicole was reluctant to go into any further detail with someone she only vaguely knew.

As Bette continued to paw at Tommy, she noticed his attention was directed towards Jake and Nicole.

'I think you like that girl in the corner better than me,' she said. 'You look at each other lots. She can come with us too?'

'Nicole's my friend,' replied Tommy stiffly.

'And the boy?'

'Jake's my friend too.'

'You have a lot of friends. Jake is very sexy. He looks like that singer man. What his name . . . like you, English.'

'I don't know who you mean.'

'He was in that boyband on TV. He crash into people then kill himself.'

'Stuart Reynolds?' replied Tommy slowly, and scowled at Bette.

'Shave beard, cut his brown hair short and make blonder, they could be same man.'

Tommy shook his head, then took a moment to closely examine Jake, who was in conversation with Nicole. He took him in from top to toe, marrying the hundreds and hundreds of images he'd pored over of Stuart Reynolds with his friend Jake.

Bette continued to talk, but now Tommy wasn't listening. Instead, the sound of his racing heart drowned out every other noise in the room.

126

Matty lay on his bed watching Declan tidy their room.

No matter where in the world they travelled, Declan made order from the chaos that surrounded them. Even inside the carriages of freight trains they stowed away in, Declan couldn't rest unless he had rearranged what he could to make them comfortable. Matty wondered if he did it because a semblance of order was one of the only things Declan could control in their chaotic lives.

'Why won't you talk about it?' began Matty, breaking a comfortable silence.

'Talk about what?' replied Declan, sniffing the inside of a pair of trainers then grimacing.

'Me dying. It's like having an elephant in the room and you keep ignoring it.'

'Not now, Matty,' Declan replied, refusing to make eye contact but feeling Matty's gaze upon him.

'Then when?'

'I dunno, just not now.'

'It's going to happen, Dec, and the sooner you face it, the easier it's going to be.'

'What's going to be easy about you not being here, you dope?' Declan snapped.

'Look, Dec, we've been through everything together. If you

could've given me your own heart, I know you would've. But you need to let go of the hope that all this is going to continue indefinitely. I'm like half the food in the hostel kitchen. I'm already past my expiry date.'

'I don't want to think about you . . . you—'

'Dying? It's just a word, you can say it.'

Declan folded a pair of jeans and placed them over the back of a chair.

'That's the problem though, isn't it? It's not just a word,' he said quietly but firmly. 'It's something so fecking monumental that nothing will ever be the same again and you won't be here to help shoulder the burden because you will *be* the burden. It'll be all your fault and I'll hate you for it, and I don't want to do that, so until I'm ready to get my head around it, it's something I don't want to discuss.'

'You have to!' said Matty, pushing himself upright. 'When it happens, I want to be ready for it, but I can't unless I know you're ready too.'

'How? Tell me, how?'

'By acknowledging it. The biggest thing you can do for me is that.'

'I can't.'

'*I* have. There've been plenty of moments when I've hated God for putting me through this and thought, "Why me?" But *why not* me? Why does it have to be someone else, why shouldn't it be me? I've stopped being angry at the world, I've had the time of my life over the last year and I've made my peace with the Man Upstairs. You have to do the same.'

Matty recognized the look Declan gave him – the last time he'd seen it, they were little boys and Declan's mother had walked out on her family and wasn't returning. Back then, Matty had gripped his pal's hand tightly and promised Declan he'd never leave him. It was a promise he was reluctantly going to break.

'I'm sorry,' mumbled Declan, and he left the room.

127

A flustered Tommy took advantage of Jake being engrossed in conversation with Nicole and hurried out of the hostel lounge and towards his dormitory.

He took his iPhone from his locker and cursed the empty battery symbol, before heading towards an internet cafe two blocks away. He didn't want to stay in the hostel and risk running into Jake. As he took long strides up the sidewalk, Tommy kept repeating to himself that it was just coincidence. Jake couldn't possibly be the same man as Stuart Reynolds. Stuart was dead. His belongings had been discovered by an elderly couple walking their dogs by the east Sussex cliffs. Tommy had made a trip there once to see for himself Stuart's final resting place.

Tommy entered the cafe, paid the cashier five dollars for thirty minutes' surfing time and plugged his phone into the wall. He began to scour Google Images of Stuart Reynolds on the computer, blowing them up as large as the screen would allow and closely examining every inch of Stuart's face, comparing them to photos he'd taken of Jake.

The online pictures were at least three years old, and both men had the same shaped eyes, only Stuart's were a sparkling blue and Jake's brown. Stuart's eyebrows had been shaped while Jake's were more untamed. The years Jake had spent travelling had given him faint lines drawn across his forehead, framing the corners of his eyes. Stuart's nose was perfectly straight while Jake's was slightly out of alignment, as if once broken.

Tommy scrolled through a dozen more pictures, and while there were similarities, it wasn't even close to being conclusive. Tommy played YouTube video clips of interviews with Lightning Strikes and tried to compare Jake and Stuart's voices – their tones were similar but their accents completely different. Their bodies were also differently shaped – shirtless pictures of Stuart showed an athletic build, pale colouring and no body hair; however Jake had a moderately hairy chest that was much broader, his biceps and abs were larger and he was decorated with tattoos across both arms and down his side. As far as Tommy could tell, Stuart Reynolds had only had one tattoo: a number 23 between his left thumb and forefinger.

As soon as his phone came back to life, he scrambled to open the photos folder and examine photos he'd taken of Jake. He pinched at them to expand shots of Jake's hand and while there was a tattoo in the same location as Stuart's, it was too blurred to read.

Frustrated, he went back online and searched Wikipedia for the reference to the number 23. He found a page dedicated to the so-called '23 enigma': 'The 23 enigma refers to the belief that most incidents and events are directly connected to the number 23,' it read. 'The number is considered unlucky, sinister, strange or sacred depending on the person drawn to it.'

Tommy pushed back on his chair and let go of a long breath. He wondered whether this need to find the bad in a person who seemed so good was some delayed, irrational reaction to being intimate with another man – as if his subconscious was looking for an excuse to end things despite the fun night they'd shared.

He expanded the picture on his phone's screen but this time, he examined the twenty-three rows of tattoos along Jake's ribcage again. Then, using the computer keyboard, he typed in two rows of numbers he saw etched on Jake's body – 34.0219N and 118.4814W.

'Santa Monica latitude and longitude coordinates' read the Google search page. The numbers 43.71964561 and 170.09146595 threw up White Horse Hill in New Zealand, where Jake had said he'd worked. Tommy continued, working from bottom to top, tracing every step of Jake's journey that had taken in India, Thailand, Japan, Italy, Iceland and a dozen other countries. It seemed Jake had been telling the truth about his travels.

The last numbers he typed in were 52.2189N and 0. 9202W – but before he could learn where Jake's journey had begun, a voice suddenly came from behind Tommy's monitor.

'You know you're not supposed to surf porn in public,' said Jake. Tommy's whole body recoiled, much to Jake's amusement.

'What are you doing here?' asked Tommy briskly, shutting down his search.

'I'm stalking you. Well, I saw you leave and wondered where you were going. Why aren't you using the internet at the hostel?'

'The broadband is down,' lied Tommy. 'I just wanted to see what was going on back home.'

'Come and get a hot chocolate with me,' continued Jake. 'You look like you've seen a ghost.'

128

'I wouldn't have put you down as a basketball fan,' Jane began as she arrived at Venice Beach Recreation Centre's open-air court.

Savannah and Nicole sat on steps close to the bike path and under the shade of a giant palm tree, watching a game in progress. Savannah cheered on the team in yellow vests for no other reason than they reminded her of colours Michael wore when she'd watched him play for his college team.

'I've seen a few games over the years,' she replied, remembering happier times. 'How's your day been?'

Jane grinned and said hello to Nicole, but didn't comment on the bruising on her face. She unclasped her handbag and rummaged around inside, finally pulling out a green folder stuffed with papers.

'I've been to four estate agents, or what do you call them over here? Real estate agents, that's right, and I've been to see five houses already. Do you like the look of this one?' She pulled out a brochure and passed it to Savannah. 'It's in West Hollywood; it has three bedrooms with a nice-sized garden in a quiet street.'

Savannah flicked through the pages of photographs of a modest but pleasant home.

'That's beautiful,' said Nicole.

'You don't waste any time, do you?' added Savannah. 'Can we afford this?'

'Don't worry about that; apparently there's a deal to be had for the first six months and we'll see how we get on from there. That's only if you like it, of course.'

'I do, but I have to pay my way, Jane. I have money saved in my room.'

'And you will, my girl, but not until you've had that baby and you're back on your feet. So what do you think?'

Savannah nodded her head. It might not be as grand as the house she'd grown up in and later escaped from, but it was a million times better than the four walls of the hostel she currently called home.

'Let's do it,' Savannah agreed, and Jane swept down to give her a tight hug.

'That's a relief – I signed the contract an hour ago and we can move in tomorrow! Okay, I'm off to call some furniture rental places – you're not opposed to wicker, are you? I have a thing for wicker.'

'No, you knock yourself out.'

'Marvellous, see you later, roomie!'

As Jane walked away with purpose, Nicole leaned over and patted Savannah's belly. 'Looks like you and your mummy have got yourselves a new grandma and a new home,' she said, her happiness for Savannah a little tainted by envy.

'I'd better tell Peyk when he gets here,' said Savannah. 'I hope he'll be okay.'

'I didn't know you were friends?'

'He's a good guy. I owe him a lot.'

A sudden noise alerted them to Peyk's presence behind

Nicole, listening to their conversation. Neither had any idea he was already there. He offered a half-hearted smile before walking away.

'Damn it,' muttered Savannah, standing up to follow him. 'Peyk! Hey, wait up!'

129

Jake kept his hand in his pocket as they made their way along the road to the nearest Starbucks. As they waited for their order, Tommy hovered from foot to foot, trying to catch a glimpse of it to no avail. Even as they sat at their table, Jake held his hand under it while they talked. The frustration of not knowing if Jake had the number 23 tattoo was driving Tommy to distraction.

'I think that French girl at the hostel fancies you,' began Jake, oblivious to Tommy's turmoil. 'She was all over you earlier.'

'Who, Bette?'

'Uh-huh.'

'She'd had one too many.'

'I think Nicole kind of likes you too.'

Tommy sipped his drink and didn't reply, allowing an awkward silence to grow between them. Jake shifted around in his seat as if he too had something on his mind.

'Okay, I'm putting my cards on the table here, mate. I did get a bit . . . you know . . . green-eyed when I saw you with Bette. And I know it's daft because you're a free agent and we've only spent one night together, and I know I'm being irrational but I feel like we have some sort of . . . connection. Do you know what I mean?'

Tommy glanced towards the table and stirred his drink with a wooden stick, refusing to make eye contact with Jake.

'Or not,' Jake continued, a little crestfallen. 'You're not making this easy for me, are you?'

'When did you say you started travelling?' blurted out Tommy, throwing Jake with the swift change of conversational direction.

'What? Um . . . about two years ago or so.'

'When, exactly?' Tommy persisted.

'October or November, I think – I can't remember. Why?'

And then it happened. As Jake ran his fingers through the long strands of his hair, he then reached out to tear open a packet of sugar. It was there as plain as day, the number 23, etched between his thumb and his forefinger.

There was no longer any doubt in Tommy's mind. Jake was Stuart Reynolds.

'Tommy!' said Jake. 'You zoned out. Have you been at the funny fags again?'

'Sorry.'

'Why do you ask when I started traveling?'

'No reason.' Tommy looked at his watch. 'Look, I've got to go, I have a shift on reception soon. Really sorry. I'll catch you later, okay?'

He dropped a $10 bill on the table and left, his legs shaking beneath him.

130

'I'm really sorry you heard it that way,' began Savannah, catching up with Peyk further down the boardwalk. 'I don't want you to think I'm ungrateful.'

When Peyk's eyes reached Savannah's, she knew she had hurt him.

'No, I don't think that,' he said quietly, stopping to watch boarders soar off jumps and fly through the air above the concrete bowl of the skate park.

'What you did for me . . . that night and ever since . . . it was so sweet and helped me get my head together and save money, but this is such a great opportunity for me and the baby.'

Peyk nodded.

'You know I can't raise a child at the hostel, and Jane – well, she has experience and knows what she's doing with babies. And I trust her like I trust you. In fact I know less about you than I do about her. But the next few months are going to be tough for me, and when the baby arrives I need to be able to rely on someone who has been through it all and come out the other side. Besides, you know that a hostel is no place for a kid. Plus, it's not like you're never going to see me again. We'll still go for coffee every week and my daughter's going to need an uncle. Even if he's a mad Dutch one.'

'I hope so,' Peyk replied.

Savannah rubbed his arm reassuringly and, as she turned around to head back to the hostel, she felt a slight thump in her stomach. 'She just kicked! My baby just kicked!' she giggled and grabbed Peyk's hand to place it on her belly. 'Did you feel it?'

'I did,' he said, grinning.

'She wants to say goodbye to her crazy uncle.'

As she walked away, Peyk thought he caught a glimpse of a man carefully watching Savannah from a distance.

131

By the time the two girls Matty and Declan met over lunch had left their room, Matty's chest felt heavier than ever.

Once the girl whose name he couldn't remember had climaxed, he'd faked his orgasm to bring the lovemaking to a halt and tucked the empty condom under his mattress without her noticing.

Of all the increasing aches and twinges he'd suffered silently from over the last few weeks, these were pains he was unfamiliar with. At first he'd put them down to sexual overexertion, but when they failed to taper off with medication, he gradually accepted it was more serious than that. Matty felt his body was slowing down, the clockwork inside him readying itself to grind to a halt.

'Those girls were fecking incredible!' said a still breathless Declan, opening the window to let the sex out and the fresh air in. 'Did you see where she had her fingers? Dirty birdie.'

Matty faked a laugh and quietly regulated his breathing. He knew telling Declan he was unwell would only worry his friend, and the afternoon they were enjoying would finish with him lying in a bed at the public Los Angeles County and USC Medical Center undergoing more tests that would only tell him what he already knew.

'You know, I hope you find someone,' Matty said eventually.

'What are you on about?'

'I mean I hope you find someone to settle down with – do the whole marriage, house, two-point-four kids, a dog and a Volvo thing. I like to think you'll be happy.'

'Please don't start this again,' replied Declan, knowing full well the conversation was heading down a road he'd no wish to travel.

'I'm not, I'm just thinking out loud.'

'You'll probably do all of that before me.'

Matty gave Declan a knowing smile and then closed his eyes, counting the beats his useless heart was trying to hit.

132

Day Fifteen

Peyk surveyed the crop of plants in his cannabis farm in room 23. They made him proud.

After gathering enough leaves, he placed them in the drying room in the corner of the converted dormitory and hung them upside down. From experience he knew that drying them too quickly meant they'd lose their taste, and if stored somewhere damp, mildew and mould would ruin them. It had to be done just right.

He hadn't questioned Tommy two days ago when he'd taken five bricks' worth and returned with $19,000 in cash, and Tommy had offered no explanation of where the money came from. Peyk assumed that it, like the bag full of cash hidden above the ceiling tiles, had something to do with Nicole. The sale had rapidly depleted Peyk's stock and would take time to replace, and time wasn't on Peyk's side. Like his product, he too had a shelf life.

Peyk would miss this room and the role he'd played in its creation. He had grown accustomed to the room's stifling humidity and lack of ventilation. He was taking a break to rehydrate himself and mop the sweat from his brow when the familiar coded knock came at the door. As he opened it, Tommy pushed his way inside.

'Hey, I told you to come in sideways so you let minimal light out and nobody sees—' Peyk began, but Tommy was in no mood to listen.

'I don't care if the whole of LA knows what you're doing,' replied Tommy. 'Why didn't you tell me that you knew who Jake really was?'

'Ahh,' replied Peyk and nodded, then returned to the plant he was pruning.

'Earlier, when you said, "Don't let the wrong people drag you down," you were warning me to be careful of Jake, weren't you?'

Peyk shrugged and passed Tommy a spare pair of sunglasses to protect his eyes from the powerful glare of the lamps surrounding them. Tommy slapped them out of Peyk's hands.

'I don't get it – we're supposed to be mates, then you find out who he is and you don't tell me?'

'It wasn't my place to, Tommy-boy. You had to find out for yourself. Do you believe in fate?'

'What's that got to do with anything?'

'There's a saying that goes "fate determines who enters your life; your actions decide who stays." So who I am to interfere with yours or anyone else's destiny?'

'But before that you were encouraging me to see if there might be something else between us. You're a walking fucking contradiction.'

'I wasn't encouraging you, I was suggesting you kept an open mind and your wits about you.'

'How did you know about who he was? About our connection?'

'It's not important.'

'It is to me.'

'Maybe it was necessary to get to know Jake before you met Stuart.'

'Who the hell are you to decide that?'

'I didn't. You made the decision yourself.'

Tommy wanted to punch Peyk as hard as he could, but he knew that his anger was misplaced. All he wanted now, above all else, was to return to when it was just Tommy and Louis on their travels and everything else was uncomplicated.

Three Months Earlier: Hostel in the Woods

The night air surrounding the Hostel in the Woods was cool, and the smell from Pauly's joint overpowering.

The young American with the shoulder-length hair and handlebar moustache hadn't stopped talking at Tommy for twenty minutes about why he'd never kill a cockroach. The essence of his theory, as Tommy understood it, was that the cockroaches you could see were the stupid ones who'd taken a foolhardy risk and been caught out in the open. By killing them, you'd be left with a race of covert, intelligent ones. And, according to Pauly, that had the potential to bring catastrophe to the world, although quite how, Tommy didn't have the energy to ask.

He was weary after a day spent chopping firewood and was quietly resentful of Louis for enjoying the fire Tommy had built. Louis was becoming steadily drunker, and he sang along as Stefan played Avicii's travellers' anthem, 'Wake Me Up', on his guitar. Tommy also felt a pang of envy when he saw Louis holding hands with a red-headed Australian woman he'd been chatting to earlier that day.

Tommy was acutely aware of the widening gap between them since they'd arrived in the woods, a location that had brought out a side to Louis Tommy hadn't seen before. Going back to nature appeared to suit him more than the large cities Tommy enjoyed exploring – and that worried him.

'There's nothing here to remind you of the outside world, is there?' said Louis, swiping at the forest undergrowth with a discarded branch as they explored. Tommy couldn't recall the last time he'd seen his friend so relaxed. He, however, was becoming the opposite.

'You're saying that like it's a good thing,' he muttered as he followed a few paces behind on the woodchip path, trying to avoid nettle stings.

'And it's not?'

'Actually no, Louis, it's not.' Tommy stopped. 'I've had enough of hearing people banging on about the beauty of trees, crapping in a hole for a toilet, being bitten by mosquitoes and eating tofu instead of meat with every meal. I want a hot shower, an HD TV screen and a Nando's.'

'Do you want to go home?'

'No, I just want out of here. We've been here a week now and I'm bored off my tits. There's nothing to do. We need to leave.'

'When?'

'Now? Well, not right now, but tonight when the minibus goes to the station?'

'Okay,' Louis replied quietly, and continued to walk.

*

The rest of their day was spent in silence as an awkward atmosphere hung over them.

Tommy packed his rucksack and planned their route to Memphis while Louis did his own thing. And as evening approached and the minibus spluttered to life, Tommy strapped his rucksack to the roof rack while Louis took a lingering look around him.

'Pass me your bag,' Tommy asked, but Louis didn't move.

'I don't want to go,' he replied.

'What? We said—'

'No, *you* said. This is my beach, Tommy.'

'What?'

'That book you brought with you and keep talking about . . . the reason we both came travelling was to find our beach, right? Well, I've found mine and I really like it here, and I'm not ready to leave. You and I want to see different things, so I'm going to stay for a while.'

'But I thought we were going to do this trip together?' Tommy tried to suppress the fear bubbling in his gut.

'We are and we have, but it shouldn't stop us doing stuff on our own, should it? We don't need to be with each other all the time. We've spent two months tanking around at a million miles an hour, never stopping anywhere or getting to know a place for more than a few days at a time. I want to be a part of somewhere for a change, and this is a good place to begin.'

'Okay, we'll stay here then if that's what you want.'

'No, mate, *I* want to stay here but I don't want *you* to because it's going to make you miserable, and I know better than most people how much sadness you've already had in your life. This trip is the chance of a lifetime, and I'm not going to be responsible for you not grabbing every opportunity you can. You can do the next bit on your own, trust me.'

Tommy looked down at his feet and said nothing, because he knew Louis was right.

'Let's meet up two months from now in that Los Angeles hostel you liked the sound of,' continued Louis. 'The one in Venice Beach?'

'Okay, if that's what you want.'

'Yes, mate, it is what I want, and it's what you need. And Tommy – I hope you find your beach there.'

Tommy nodded, hoping for the same thing.

133

Today

Like an army of worker ants, a dozen hostellers carried kegs of beer and trays of food in plastic wrappers from the kitchen, down the corridor and to the hired van Peyk had left parked outside.

Eager to take her mind off reflecting on her ghastly last few days, Nicole appointed herself as coordinator and rallied the troops to help prepare the food for the beach party in Santa Monica later that night. Jake was last in line and picked up a 24-pack of Budweiser.

'Thanks,' said Nicole, casually giving his muscular arms the once-over and hoping she hadn't been spotted. If there was something going on between Jake and Tommy, then Tommy had impeccable taste in men.

Neither was completely relaxed around the other. Both were certain they had feelings for Tommy, and both suspected Jake had won in a battle that had never been declared. But as he hadn't seen Tommy since their awkward Starbucks visit together a day earlier, Jake was no longer so confident of his victory.

The speed at which Tommy had abandoned Jake and rushed away both disappointed and saddened him. His only explanation for it was that Tommy regretted what had happened between them, regarded it as a one-off and was now too embarrassed to admit it.

Already that morning, Jake had paid a visit to Tommy's dormitory and found his bed unmade and empty, before glimpsing the edge of a photograph peeking out from under Tommy's pillow. Curious, he edged it out and saw two almost identical faces – young men who must be twins, he assumed, and who bore a strong resemblance to Tommy himself.

'You haven't seen Tommy around, have you?' Jake asked Nicole.

'No, not in the last couple of days. I assumed he was with you.'

'He's probably got a hangover,' Jake lied. 'He'll be keeping a low profile until it wears off.'

Nicole paused, and chose her words carefully before speaking. 'Jake, will you promise me you'll look out for him? I know it's not my place to say, but he's had a lot to deal with in the last few years, so please don't let him down, okay?'

'I won't,' Jake replied, curious as to what Tommy had confided in Nicole and not him. 'You can trust me. You can both trust me.'

And for the briefest of moments, even Jake believed the words coming from his mouth.

'Penny for them?' asked Savannah when she wandered into the kitchen to find Nicole sitting alone in silence and staring blankly at the wall. Empty food wrappers surrounded her.

'Oh, you don't want to know,' Nicole replied. 'How was your last night at work? Jane said it was your final shift.'

'Yeah, my baby bump feels like it expanded overnight so I can't hide it anymore.'

'When are you moving out to suburbia?'

'As soon as I pack my stuff I'll catch a cab to West Hollywood with Jane.'

'Do you need help packing? I haven't got much else on until tonight.'

'Sure, that'd be great.'

As they walked arm in arm towards her room, Savannah caught Nicole glancing at her stomach but apparently thinking twice about asking a question. However, Savannah guessed what was on her mind.

'Kind of messed up, isn't it? Not knowing who the father of your baby is, even if he walked past you in the street,' she began, and then explained the circumstances surrounding the night she became pregnant.

'I don't know what to say,' said Nicole. 'I can't even begin to imagine what you've been through.'

'That's why this new start is so important to me,' Savannah replied firmly. 'I'm done with being a victim. And I'm sure as hell not going to raise my child to think I'm one either.'

The first thing Savannah noticed when she unlocked the door to her room was Jane's empty bed, stripped of its sheets and pillowcases. Her suitcase was no longer under her bed and the bathroom was cleared of her toiletries.

'Wow, she's so organized,' said Savannah. 'She must have got the keys early and moved her stuff already.'

'Didn't she tell you she was going?'

'No, we arranged to meet here later and then head up to the new place. She'll have left me a message at reception.'

The last two days had been a steep learning curve for

Nicole, and her natural instinct to trust people had crumbled. Something told her all was not right with this set-up. An object in the dustbin caught her eye.

'Whose are these kids?' she asked, picking out a photo frame with two smiling faces inside.

'They're Jane's,' replied Savannah, puzzled.

'Why's she thrown them away?'

'I don't know.'

'Savannah, I don't want to worry you, but I don't have a good feeling about this.'

Neither did Savannah, and she marched over to where her locker was, moving it to one side to reveal the space behind the wall where she hid her earnings. It was empty.

'What's wrong?' asked Nicole.

'All the money I've saved, I keep it here. It's gone.'

134

Matty glanced around the walls of the pawn shop while an assistant found the corresponding pink ticket to the one Matty presented him with.

All around him, acoustic and electric guitars sat on plinths. Three separate drum kits were arranged to fill corners and a variety of brass instruments balanced on shelves. The place was a graveyard of abandoned ambitions. He wondered how many dreams had died in this one shop.

'This the one?' the shopkeeper asked briskly, and passed Matty a silver chain and Saint Christopher pendant.

The necklace was the last gift Matty's parents had given to him before they waved their emotional goodbyes at Dublin airport a year earlier. He hadn't told Declan he'd pawned it the previous week so they could afford to eat, even though it had upset Matty greatly. But thanks to the ten $100 bills someone had anonymously shoved under their door, he could now buy it back. Both suspected Tommy had something to do with their cash donation, as he was the only one aware of their situation, but they respected his desire to keep it quiet so they held back from mentioning it.

Matty paid the shopkeeper and gripped the necklace tightly in the palm of his hand, confident its next owner would treasure it as much as he had.

135

Nicole and Savannah hurried to the hostel reception desk where Gabby sat with her feet up, engrossed in her Kindle.

'Gabby, is Jane still checked in?' Nicole asked, her bruised ribs aching from moving so quickly.

'Surname?' she replied, irritated by the disturbance. Nicole looked towards Savannah.

'Doherty.'

'There's a Jane Doherty who checked out at nine forty-five this morning,' continued Gabby, scanning the guest register.

'Did she leave a forwarding address?'

'No. Why would she?'

'Tell me this isn't happening,' Savannah said, her voice beginning to crack. 'That was all the money I had in the world.'

'Have you got an address for the new place?'

'The brochure's in my bag upstairs.'

'Good, you go and get it and I'll hail us a taxi.'

Nicole dashed outside and scanned the passing traffic. She had no reason to notice the brown station wagon parked on the opposite side of the road or the driver sitting behind the wheel.

*

Nicole and Savannah didn't say a word to each other as their cab drove along Wilshire Boulevard in the direction of West Hollywood.

Nicole was accustomed to consoling hospital patients when they'd received bad news, but today she had nothing up her sleeve to ease Savannah's concerns. Meanwhile Savannah, spine rigid and fists clenched tightly into balls, remained silent. She was desperate to be wrong about Jane, hoping against all hope that there'd been some mix-up, and the woman who was about to help turn her life around was not actually a scam artist who had been running a long game to get her hands on Savannah's cash. Why on earth had she told Jane that she kept her savings in that room?

After a frustratingly long forty-five-minute journey in heavy traffic, the taxi reached its destination in a leafy West Hollywood suburb. Nicole paid the driver, slipping him extra to remain by the kerb until they knew one way or another whether this was a terrible misunderstanding or deliberate deceit.

Savannah's legs felt heavy and clumsy as she stepped out, steadying herself against the car's door frame.

'Deep breaths,' advised Nicole, taking Savannah's arm as the brown station wagon drove slowly past them and parked further up the street.

Slowly, they walked up the crazy paving that separated the lawn, towards the house Savannah had only seen in a brochure. The upstairs curtains were closed and the blinds in the downstairs windows pulled shut.

'Good luck,' added Nicole, as they reached the porch.

Savannah rang the doorbell, but was greeted by silence. She pressed the button again, but still there was no response.

Finally she knocked, and then again, more loudly. And when she pulled the door handle and discovered it was locked, she couldn't hold back her emotions any longer.

Nicole made her way towards the window and peered inside, but it was too dark to make out anything but an empty, furniture-less room. She turned to Savannah and shook her head.

Savannah had already accepted the inevitable. Once again, she was a victim.

136

With no credit left on his mobile phone, Declan used the pay-phone in reception to call home to Ireland and check up on his younger brother.

Meanwhile, Matty made the most of his time alone to take a look at photographs of their travels he'd had printed on his way back from the pawn shop. He temporarily forgot the aches in his chest and focused on a picture of himself wrapped in warm winter ski wear in Grenoble, France, drinking a yard of ale at a bar, and laughed at a passed-out Declan lying on a Moroccan street. He removed a selfie of the two of them inside Rome's Coliseum, folded it in half and placed it in his shirt pocket. Then he put the envelope of photographs under Declan's pillow, along with their *Travel America* guide with his crucifix placed inside.

All at once, Matty felt light-headed and sensed his pulse racing, so he sat on his mattress, closed his eyes, placed his head in his hands and composed himself. Although they had stayed at more desirable places, this was the only hostel where Matty had felt truly comfortable and he was sure that when the time came to leave Declan alone, he would get the support he needed from the people around him.

Matty reflected on his time in Los Angeles and was confident he and Declan had gone out of their way to endear themselves to their fellow hostellers. They'd never lied about their intentions in their pursuit of the opposite sex, and as both had been upfront about what they were looking for, their consciences were clear. The only thing troubling Matty about his forthcoming journey into the great unknown was the death of the postmaster and the role he and Declan had unwittingly played in it. He hoped that with just one transgression to his name – albeit a large one – he'd be allowed through the pearly gates.

'You ready for some scran before the party?' said Declan, bursting into the room. 'Cos if I don't eat soon, someone's gonna have to organize a feckin' benefit concert for me.'

'Only if you're buying,' Matty replied, trying his best to put a brave face on the chest pains that refused to go away.

137

'How could I have been so dumb?' sobbed Savannah, 'I thought Jane was my friend.'

'Sweetheart, I'm so sorry,' replied Nicole, trying to console her. She knew all too well how easy it was to be duped by someone you trusted.

'It's not your fault, honestly. Sometimes we put our faith in people and they end up hurting us more than we ever thought possible. We'll find a way of sorting this out, I promise you.'

'How? She has all my money. If I can't trust Jane, I have no one.'

Nicole pulled a packet of paper tissues from her pocket and handed one to Savannah as they began to make their way back towards the waiting taxi. She hadn't known Savannah long, but she wanted to help and she had the financial means at her disposal to do so.

'You're here already!' a voice behind them suddenly chirped. Both Savannah and Nicole turned their heads quickly to find the front door open and Jane standing there, a bin bag in one hand and an empty cardboard box in the other.

Jane was suddenly aware of Savannah's tears. 'What's wrong? Is it the baby?' she asked, panicked.

'You're here! But we knocked on the door . . .' cried Savannah.

'Sorry, I was out the back scrubbing the bins. The last tenants left the place like a pigsty. What's happened?'

'I thought you'd left me.'

'Don't be silly! Why would I do that? I wanted to make the place shipshape before you and the furniture arrived. Oh, and I brought that money you hide. Honestly, you need to get that in a bank. It's not safe to just leave it lying around.'

'But your kids' pictures were in the trash?'

'They've been in my luggage so long they've become dog-eared, so I got some reprints done and bought a nicer frame. Have I done something to upset you?'

'Sorry, Jane, we were worried – you disappeared so quickly,' replied Nicole. 'And Savannah's money had gone.'

Jane clasped her hand to her throat as if only now understanding how her actions had been misinterpreted. 'Oh Savannah, how could I have been so stupid? I am so, so sorry, I just got ahead of myself without thinking. I'm your friend and I'm not going anywhere. I hope you can believe me?'

When Savannah nodded, the two of them embraced.

'Now get your bum inside and I'll put a brew on. Will you be joining us, Nicole?'

'Thanks, but I'm going to head back to Venice and help with tonight's party. Do you want me to pack your things up for you, Savannah?'

'Do you mind?'

'Not at all. Come by and pick them up when you're ready.'

When Jane put her arm around Savannah's shoulder and the two headed into their new home and new life, for

Nicole it restored a tiny shred of faith in people, something Eric had taken away from her.

But as her taxi pulled away, the brown station wagon parked further up the street remained.

138

Nicole borrowed a key from an uninterested Gabby and let herself into Savannah and Jane's room.

Her ribs still hurt so she moved at half her normal speed as she folded up t-shirts and towels and packed them into Savannah's suitcase. With Tommy flying below the radar and Eric out of her life and awaiting a court hearing, she had never felt so lonely in a building full of people. Once she finished doing this for Savannah, she'd change into a more suitable outfit and catch a lift with some of the others up to the party in Santa Monica. Hopefully a night of music and beer might take her mind off her woes.

Recent events had exhausted Nicole physically and emotionally, and she had no energy or desire to keep travelling alone. But she also had little reason to return to England. However, she did have two holdalls hidden in the hostel containing more money than she knew what to do with. She had yet to decide how to use it.

Nicole scooped up half a dozen bottles of shampoo, conditioners, fake tan and body glitter, then tested out Savannah's perfumes by spraying them on her wrists. But as she went to place one inside a bag, she tripped over the bathroom mat. She tried to keep hold of it but yelped in pain when she twisted her torso awkwardly and the bottle flew through the air before colliding with the full-length wall mirror. She watched in horror as it shattered into pieces across the bathroom floor. Then she screamed for a second time when she saw the face of a terrified man in a room behind where the mirror had been.

'Ron!'

139

The photographs in the brochure Jane had shown Savannah didn't do their new home justice.

Savannah entered under the tiled pitched porch roof and into a light and airy reception room. Through the kitchen window ahead, she saw into the colourful planted garden where a sprinkler threw water into an arc above the lawn. Inside and to the left, behind glass doors, was an empty dining room, and, to the right, a lounge also lacking furniture.

'The beds are already here, but the rest of the furniture won't arrive until tomorrow,' advised Jane.

Savannah didn't care; she was already in love with her new house.

'You don't know where to look first, do you?' asked Jane. 'I was the same.'

'It's beautiful; thank you so much for organizing all this,' Savannah replied, and embraced her friend.

'Oh, while I remember, your money.' Jane opened the drawer of a cabinet and handed Savannah a bag with her savings inside. She slipped it into her handbag, promising Jane she would bank it in the morning.

Jane led Savannah into the kitchen and poured hot water from the kettle to make two mugs of herbal tea. 'Go and have a look around while I pop to the loo.'

Savannah picked up her mug and wandered from room to room, wondering if Jane had been economical with the truth about the rental price. But she wasn't going to question either her friend's generosity or, in fact, anything else about her. Each time she had done, Jane had proved true to her word.

'We're home,' she whispered to her stomach and smiled. 'We're home.'

'She's here,' Jane said curtly.

Inside the locked bathroom she spoke quietly into a mobile phone. 'I'll give her a stronger sedative before she goes to bed, but wait until I call you before you send the car.'

'Don't give her anything that will hurt the baby or you'll have me to answer to,' came the sharp response.

Back in Montgomery, Alabama, Reverend Devereaux hung up the phone and took a long, deep breath. His plan had been elaborate and expensive, but then, his daughter was a lot like him – intelligent, cunning and resilient. He could not make the same mistake as before, thinking he could simply hire people to bundle her into a vehicle and drive her home. When he had attempted that, she had shot two of her abductors.

No, he had to be patient. Plan B was always going to be a long game, and 'Jane' had been worth every penny of his investment.

140

Ron and Nicole stared at each other, both equally frightened and uneasy.

Nicole took a step backwards, having learned from her showdown with Eric that when backed into a corner, human behaviour could return to its most basic, animalistic form at the drop of a hat. And she was in no condition to fight back. But the anger she felt towards Ron was stronger than her fear of how he might retaliate.

Confrontation did not sit well with Ron but, try as he might, he couldn't find a way out of this situation. And in his sixty-two years on the planet, he had placed himself in many an unusual situation.

Ronald Arthur Hancock had never met anyone he could call a friend.

Home-schooled on a remote corn farm in Oklahoma and with no brothers, sisters or neighbourhood kids to play with, Ron was accustomed to his own company.

He was a shy, scrawny seventeen-year-old on a drive into town for farm supplies when the tornado struck. Ron and the general store's customers took cover in the storm shelter until the violent, rotating column of air passed. By the time Ron returned to his home later that afternoon, it was scattered in pieces across the great plains, along with his parents' bodies. He was left with nothing but a generous insurance payout.

Being alone was made harder because Ron lacked the social skills that most other people appeared to take for granted – the ability to empathize, relate to or identify with others. He'd been told by his father these were necessary smarts to get by in life, but the developmental disability in his brain caused him to freeze when anyone, even a familiar face, tried to engage him in polite conversation. As a result, much of his time was spent alone in his trailer, passing the time practising communication skills with his reflection in the bathroom mirror.

Ron made a rare excursion one Presidents' Day when Uncle Sam's Great American Circus rolled into town. As the townsfolk enjoyed the rides, stalls, animals and performers, it was the hall of mirrors that transfixed him. He was fascinated by how flexible glass contorted his face and body into mutated shapes. By simply standing and doing nothing, he could become something or someone unrecognizable from himself. It was, ironically, a moment of clarity.

His first job came weeks afterwards, working for a mirror manufacturer in Tulsa. Despite his lack of experience, he was employed as an apprentice and learned how to mix the reflective coating, apply it to suitable substrates and construct frames from various woods, metals and plastics. He was in his element, and each time he completed a commission he saw something different about himself in his reflection.

A decade had passed when Ron was tasked with manufacturing a five-foot-square two-way mirror for the Texas State Penitentiary at Huntsville. As he hung it in the warehouse for a final check and polish before transportation, he quietly enjoyed being able to observe his workmates from one side while not being seen from the other. A two-way mirror allowed him to be a part of the world without ever having to interact with it.

Ron joined his foreman Hank on the truck ride to Huntsville to fit the mirror in a small, green-bricked, brightly lit room. On one side where the mirror was to be installed sat a row of wooden chairs, and on the other, a stainless-steel table with five leather straps and two wrist restraints.

'It's where the death row boys get the needle,' Hank explained. 'The witnesses can watch him die, but he ain't gonna see them. All he can see is his own reflection and the light going out of his own eyes.'

Butterflies circled Ron's stomach, and for the next fortnight all he could think about was the mirror he'd fashioned and the stories it would be able to tell. When child-murderer Bobby Miller's execution date was set for a month's time, Ron contacted the prison and made up a story, suggesting the mirror might have a near-invisible hairline crack in need of urgent repair.

After giving it a detailed once-over in a convincing performance, Ron asked if he could remain there to witness the execution. The suspicious chief eyed him up and down – it wasn't a request he received often – but concluding Ron was innocuous, consent forms were signed and countersigned, and Miller's execution was the first of almost sixty Ron observed over the next two and a half decades. He gained no pleasure or thrill from watching a state-sanctioned murder; it was the ability to covertly watch someone at their most vulnerable that enticed him.

Executions weren't a weekly or even monthly occurrence

in Texas, meaning Ron travelled the country seeking them out. Sometimes he'd pose as a long-lost member of the victim's or perpetrator's family needing closure or to offer support; on other occasions, he pretended to be working as a reporter for an obscure small-town publication with a make-believe vested interest in the execution.

Not every appointment went the way Ron intended. When in Alabama he discovered the observation room contained a window and not a mirror, he walked out. In Arizona, he felt short-changed when a curtain was drawn as soon as the lethal injection was administered. But over time, the criteria for witnessing an execution became tougher and the identity checks more rigorous, and Ron was refused entry more quickly.

When his employers shut up shop in the recession, Ron's savings and farm insurance payout funded his travels across America, and eventually he found himself as the oldest guest at a decrepit backpacking hostel in Los Angeles. The owner had made it known she'd happily sell for a bargain price, so Ron ploughed all his money into purchasing it.

It wasn't a decision his physician recommended. Over the last five years, Ron had suffered what he described as 'little episodes' but which a specialist informed him were mini strokes. 'They're warning signs,' he was informed. 'So try to avoid stress. It makes the heart work harder, which makes your blood pressure rise and can cause clots travelling to your brain.' Stress soon became an everyday occurrence in his managerial role.

The only time he could truly relax was when he was surrounded by the opposite sex. He had yet to meet a woman who would make any impact on his life, but his body had urges that needed satisfying. And it was during one of his frequent visits to a private peep show booth in a local strip club that he instantly fell for a beautiful young dancer. Her name was Savannah, he learned, and it was as if he was the only person she had ever danced for behind that two-way mirror.

'You watched Savannah while she was in her bathroom?' Nicole cried. 'That's disgusting! Jesus, Ron, she trusted you. How many other women have you been spying on?'

'I wasn't spying – someone had to look out for her,' Ron replied, his voice trembling. 'She was vulnerable and she needed me.'

'She was only vulnerable because of people like you taking advantage of her.'

'I didn't take advantage, I just needed to be close to her.'

'Yeah, I can see how close you've come,' Nicole replied, with a disgusted glance at the discarded tissues lying scattered across the floor. 'You're sick.'

'I'm sorry, please don't tell her,' replied Ron, and Nicole recognized angst in his eyes. He moved towards her and a wary Nicole winced as she reached to grab a piece of the broken mirror, holding it in front of her like a weapon.

'Why shouldn't I tell her? Because she'd see you for what you are? This isn't normal behaviour, Ron, surely you can see that? And Savannah needs to know.'

'But if you tell her she'll never come back, and I'll never see my . . .' Ron's brow wrinkled and he clasped his hand over his mouth.

'See your what?' asked Nicole.

When Ron didn't reply, the penny dropped for Nicole.

141

The thumping beat of electronic dance music was blasting from six large speakers surrounding a DJ's booth as around 600 hostellers danced and drank across the floodlit Santa Monica beach.

Partygoers had walked or been bussed in from Los Angeles's six hostels in Venice, Santa Monica, Hollywood and Hermosa Beach to mark the end of the summer with an all-night celebration. As a rule LA's vast beaches were legally out of bounds by ten p.m., but tonight was an exception, courtesy of a tourism initiative to promote the city's hostels as places to stay rather than to use as a stopovers between more traveller-friendly regions like San Francisco or San Diego.

The LA Tourism Board and hostel managers collaborated to fund two photographers and a film crew to take pictures and video footage for a print and online viral video promotional campaign. Posters of suggested hashtags including #LoveLA and #THEVacation were everywhere in the hope that partygoers would want to show off to their friends at home and the night would trend. Marshals handed guests wristbands, coloured to match their respective hostels and keep unwelcome gatecrashers out.

On Matty's insistence, he and Declan kept a little distance between them and the throngs of people. They were sitting in a quieter section of the beach, Declan tucking into a second cheeseburger while Matty lay on the sand, propped up by his elbows, staring out into the horizon. He kept his exhaustion to himself.

'D'you reckon we should start thinking about moving on soon?' asked Declan, oblivious to his friend's condition.

'Finish your food first.'

'I don't mean leaving the beach, I mean leaving LA.'

'Why? You love it here, we've made friends here.'

'I know, it's been a blast. I just thought you might want to try somewhere else.'

'Nah,' said Matty, shaking his head. 'If you're happy, I'm happy, and this is a good place to be.'

Declan grabbed a plastic cup of beer and a bottle of water for Matty from an ice bucket behind him.

'Water, great, thanks,' sniffed Matty, although even the thought of alcohol passing his lips made him nauseous.

'It's good for you – it flushes out your bad toxins.'

'It hasn't flushed you away.'

They paused to stare at two girls dancing nearby.

'You're losing your touch,' said Matty. 'Look at the blonde one; she's been giving you the eye all night. Go over and talk to her.'

'Well, I guess it would be the polite thing to do. Are you coming?'

'No, I'll be all right. I have my Evian to keep me company.'

'Stay out of trouble,' replied Declan, and wandered over towards the girls as Matty watched.

'I'll be with you in spirit,' he smiled.

142

'Oh my God, please tell me Savannah's baby isn't yours?'

Nicole glared at Ron in their standoff amongst the shards of broken mirror and glass in Savannah's bathroom. The piece she'd use to fight off any potential attack remained firmly in her grasp.

She genuinely hoped to hear a firm 'no', but Ron's shamed silence gave Nicole her answer.

'You drugged and raped her and got her pregnant, didn't you?'

'I didn't drug her, I found her when she needed help,' replied Ron. 'And don't use that word – I didn't rape anyone. I love her.'

Four Months Earlier: Savannah's Motel

Ron sat in an armchair in the corner of Savannah's motel room, drumming his fingers across the arm, watching her as she slept under a quilt.

Whatever drug had been slipped inside her water bottle in the strip club had had the desired effect, but not for the perpetrator.

Weeks earlier, watching her from his usual seat in the shadows at the back of the club, Ron had been able to tell

Savannah wasn't like the other girls she shared a stage with. From the moment she'd strutted past him in her underwear and caught his eye, he knew they'd just shared something special. However, his frustrating inability to engage with strangers meant he didn't capitalize on their connection. Instead, he pulled his baseball cap down towards his thick eyebrows and sank ever deeper into his chair.

During a fortnight of frequent return visits, Ron watched as Savannah contorted her limbs around a pole either on stage or in a back room, surrounded by peep show customers who could sit in private booths pleasuring themselves behind two-way mirrors. He'd spent close to $1,000 getting to know her body better than she knew it herself.

That night, four months ago, the stars had aligned and their worlds collided without him having to say a word. Ron could barely believe his eyes when a distressed Savannah stumbled in front of the car as Peyk picked him up from the club. Together, they lifted her into the vehicle and laid her out across the back seat, and when Peyk found her motel key inside her handbag they drove her back to her room and put her to bed. Ron deliberately failed to mention he knew who the girl was, but offered to stay with her while Peyk got some supplies.

Savannah had been unconscious for around thirty minutes before Ron hesitantly plucked up the courage to approach her side of the room. He knelt by the bed and tentatively ran his rough fingertips through her soft hair. Gradually he moved his mouth closer to hers and gently kissed her lips. Then he slowly slipped into her bed, unbuckled his belt, slid down her shorts and guided himself inside her. In less than a minute, it was over.

By the time Savannah awoke in the morning, Ron had left and Peyk had taken his place, fast asleep in the armchair. And in the back of the cab returning back to the hostel, Ron believed he was in love for the first time in his life.

Today

Nicole shuffled uncomfortably from foot to foot, finding it difficult to comprehend that Ron couldn't see his actions had been despicable towards the woman he claimed to love.

'If you didn't rape her, then what do you call it when a woman is unconscious and can't say no to sex?' she continued. 'Reluctance?'

'It wasn't like that. Savannah is so beautiful, and I'd sit at the back of the club watching her dance and she had this look in her eyes, like she was alone, like me. We understand each other.'

'Ron, this is all in your head, can't you see that? I knew you were a bit different, but this . . . Christ.'

'I told you, I love her.'

'"Love" doesn't give you the right to do that to someone! Can't you see that?'

'She's been let down so many times before – if you tell her, you'll destroy her. Please let her keep thinking I'm her friend. For Savannah's sake.'

'That is the last thing you are.'

'Then what do you want me to do?' asked Ron out of desperation.

Nicole closed her eyes and shook her head. She wanted to call the police, but she knew that would be Savannah's decision to make and not hers. She also knew the right thing to do would be to tell Savannah everything she'd learned at the earliest opportunity. It must have been hard enough for Savannah to come to terms with her unborn child being the product of rape, but if she then discovered the rapist was a man she'd lived under the same roof with, how much tougher would that be to digest? She'd appeared so pragmatic over impending motherhood and her new life with Jane that Nicole didn't want to be the one to ruin any of that. So she made a snap decision.

'I know what you can do,' she eventually replied. 'And you need to do it tonight.'

143

'Guys, that's a dumb idea. Guys! Guys!'

A marshal was shouting through a megaphone as a handful of young people ran towards the ocean at Santa Monica to go skinny-dipping.

Peyk watched as two lifeguards approached the water's edge and shone powerful torches on the naked figures larking around in the waves. He didn't bother to check if they were watching when he sparked up a joint with his cigarette lighter.

'Got one spare?' asked Nicole.

'Sure,' replied Peyk, and handed Nicole a ready-rolled joint from his back pocket.

'It's a good turnout,' she continued, lighting it and taking a long drag.

'Sure is.'

'Want to join me in a toast?' she continued, and held up her beer cup to Peyk's. Peyk nodded. 'Aren't you going to ask me what we're toasting?'

'Let me see,' he replied, pretending to think. 'Ahh . . . you buying the hostel from Ron.'

Nicole's eyes opened wide. 'How could you possibly know that?'

Just an hour earlier, she had taken Ron's bank details and

promised to wire him a fair price for the hostel in due course on the proviso he left there and then. With his options limited, he had little choice but to agree. As Ron crammed his belongings into the back of his car, Nicole hailed a taxi and headed towards the beach party with a renewed sense of purpose.

'I may walk around stoned most of the time, but nothing escapes me,' Peyk replied.

'Apparently not.'

'I think it's a good idea. Ron will never accept what he's done.'

Nicole hesitated as she tried to make sure Peyk had just said what she thought he'd said.

'What? You know what he did to Savannah and you didn't tell her?'

'Ron will suffer with or without my interference. He will never get to meet his child, watch her grow up, see his own eyes reflected in another's or be able to love or be loved unconditionally. And that's worth toasting.'

Peyk clipped Nicole's cup with his own and wandered away, leaving a coil of smoke unspooling behind him.

144

Ron didn't hear the cars behind his vehicle blasting their horns at him.

The traffic lights he'd come to a halt at on Santa Monica Boulevard had long turned green, but he remained stationary and motionless, much to the frustration of those behind him. Some reversed and overtook him in the other lane, cursing him with words and hand gestures as they passed. But Ron wasn't listening.

It was only the third vehicle he had ever owned and he had travelled much of America in it, flitting from city to city on his quest to participate in viewing as many death row executions as possible. And now it was taking him away from everything and everyone he had grown to appreciate.

In the space of a day, Ron had lost everything. His beautiful Savannah, any chance he might have had of seeing his child, the building he called home. And now his life.

His physician had been right to warn him about avoiding stressful situations. And moments earlier, as the traffic lights turned to orange and he began to slow his car, the anxiety of his confrontation with Nicole had caused a weakened blood vessel in Ron's skull to burst and bleed into his brain. The haemorrhagic stroke killed him within less than a minute.

145

Matty had never felt a tiredness like the one he felt that night.

He glanced wistfully across a beach illuminated by bonfires, lanterns, coloured lights, glow sticks and the red tips of cigarettes. Every so often, Declan turned away from the girl he was flirting with to check on his friend, and Matty would force his eyelids to remain open and offer a reassuring wave. But as soon as Declan's attention was diverted, they fluttered to a close. All he wanted was to fall asleep and wake up in the body of someone else.

'Everything all right, my friend?' asked Peyk, throwing himself onto the sand, cross-legged.

'Yeah, just watching my boy in action,' Matty whispered.

'So you've said your goodbyes, then?'

Matty looked quizzically at Peyk before realizing that Peyk understood. 'Yeah, I have,' he eventually replied.

Peyk nodded and continued to stare ahead of them both. 'Does he know?'

'No . . . he's having a laugh and it might be the last time he gets to do that for a while. I don't want to take that away from him.'

'Would you like some company?'

Matty considered it for a moment, but decided he was

happy being on his own. There was something quite empowering about dying on your own terms.

'I appreciate the offer, but I'm good.'

'It's been a pleasure,' said Peyk, rising to his feet and shaking Matty's limp hand.

'Likewise. Explain to Declan for me, tell him . . . tell him—'

'He already knows, Matthew. Don't worry about that.'

Before Peyk was even out of sight, Matty's eyes were already closed.

146

As pop music made way for classic R&B, Nicole left the group of French students she'd been dancing with and was making her way towards the shore when she spotted Tommy, alone.

She'd only had three cups of beer, but combined with her first joint since her college student nursing days, they'd made her giddy. It was medicinal, she told herself, and it had certainly eased the pain of her bruised ribs when she moved. But the expression on Tommy's face soon sobered her up.

'You look like you're carrying the weight of the world on your shoulders,' she began. Tommy didn't reply.

'Savannah's moved out of the hostel,' Nicole persevered. 'I think she's going to be really happy at Jane's place.'

Tommy nodded but again, said nothing.

'Have I upset you?'

'No,' he replied. 'Not everything is about you.'

'Oh, okay,' Nicole replied, surprised by his offhand attitude. 'Is it Jake? I know you two are—'

'Jake and I are nothing.'

'I saw him heading towards the beer tent a few minutes ago.'

'And?'

'And I thought you might want to know. Sorry.'

Nicole decided it was not the moment to bring up her hostel acquisition and began to walk away, before stopping.

'Tommy, please talk to me, you're worrying me.'

'If you see Jake again, tell him to meet me on the pier. He'll know where.'

But before Nicole could respond, Tommy had the bright lights of the fairground in his sights.

147

The Ferris wheel offered panoramic views across Santa Monica's coastline, way beyond the commercial shopping area and up and along Route 66.

Mechanical failure had temporarily shut the rollercoaster, so all four corners of the nine-acre pier were eerily quiet long before its midnight curfew. From its furthest end, Tommy heard the grinding mechanism slowly moving the giant wheel as the tide below crashed against the pier's wooden stilts. He stood with his back to the rides, staring at the blinking orange lights on buoys bobbing against the ocean's current.

'You're a hard man to find,' said Jake, approaching Tommy from behind. He placed his hand on Tommy's shoulder, then let it fall towards the arch of his back and held it there. 'Why are you up here on your own when the party's down there?'

'I used to love fairgrounds,' Tommy said, staring straight ahead of him. 'My parents would take me and my brothers to the fair when it came to Abington Park every summer. My brother Adam won me a goldfish at one of those hoop stalls; eight years later and it's still alive. Unbelievable, isn't it? For eight years it's been swimming around in circles, day in, day out, all on its own.'

'I didn't think goldfish lived that long.'

'It's outlived Adam. And Dan.'

Jake paused. 'Are they the people you mentioned you'd lost?'

Tommy fell silent.

'Do you want to talk about it? It might help.'

'I think you've done enough already.'

'I don't follow,' said Jake, but he wasn't offered any further explanation. They remained in a stilted silence, before frustration got the better of him.

'Why are you pushing me away, Tommy?' he snapped. 'I'm old enough to accept rejection, so be honest with me.'

'Be honest? Okay, how's this for honesty. Do you remember when you said there was a connection between us? Well, you're right, there is.'

'Okay, but that doesn't explain why you're—'

'Not a connection in the way you think,' Tommy interrupted.

'I don't understand.'

'You talk about honesty, Jake, but just how honest are we with each other? The night you arrived and we went out for drinks, we agreed one of the best things about travelling is that you get to hear a complete stranger's life story. Well, we're long past being strangers but we don't know the first thing about each other, do we? So do you want me to start?'

Jake nodded, puzzled by the ire slowly warping Tommy's face.

'I came travelling when my family fell apart after my brothers were killed in a car accident.'

Jake paused and squinted at Tommy, unsure how his story related to him. Suddenly Tommy turned and looked him straight in the eye.

'Are you sure you don't know where this is going, *Stuart*?'

When the blood drained from Jake's face, both men knew exactly where this was going.

Two Years Earlier: London

As Stuart Reynolds left Geri Garland's house, the only thing he had any control over was her car.

He'd swiped her driver's keys from the sideboard while her security team were more interested in bundling him out of the house than frisking him. Stealing her Range Rover was a tiny victory against the woman who'd systematically built him up only to tear him down.

He fought his way through the congested London traffic towards the M1, replaying the events of the last eighteen hours but struggling to come to terms with them. Zak was refusing to answer his phone calls; Katie was dead; his Lightning Strikes bandmates had turned their backs on him and the woman he loathed had hung him out to dry.

As much as he hated it, there was only one place where he could retreat and regroup: his former flat in Bolton. While he hadn't lived a great life before fame and fortune came knocking, it had been more authentic than the one he was living now.

When the overhead gantry signs warned the motorway ahead was closed at junction 15, to Stuart's frustration, he was forced to follow the diversion signs and drive towards a signposted estate called Hunsbury.

It was then, without warning, that it happened. It began with feeling his heart beating faster and faster, as if it wanted to burst out of his ribcage. Then he began to struggle for breath, and the more anxious he felt, the more his temperature soared. He frantically searched for a button to lower the window and feel cool air against his hot face, to try and regain control of his body.

Stuart failed to notice the first red light he passed through. By the time he'd driven through the second, it was too late to hit the brakes.

After being pushed fifty metres along the road, the vehicle Stuart ploughed into finally came to a rest on its side, almost broken in half by a broken man.

A shooting pain tore up his nostrils and spread across his face when the airbag deployed, fracturing his nose. But Geri's bulky vehicle offered him much more protection than the people in the car he'd collided with. He blindly fumbled around to unclip his seat belt, and once he'd opened the door he staggered outside, his legs almost buckling beneath him.

He stood motionless as he stared in horror at the carnage before him. Surely nobody could have survived this? he thought. It was impossible. But he was too inert and blinded by fear to look inside and see for himself. It was only when he heard voices behind him, turned his head and spotted figures hurrying towards the scene that he came back to life.

He pulled his hood up over his head and limped past what had once been a Mini, trying and failing not to look through the broken windscreen. He clamped his hand over his mouth when he saw two mangled bodies lying in the front seats, and he could just about make out a third figure in the back of the car, motionless but for his blinking eyes.

Stuart dry heaved as the voices behind him became louder; then, with all the strength he could muster, he ran. And he didn't stop running for another two years.

148

Today

What had begun as Declan striving to chat up a girl he didn't know had turned into something quite unexpected, and with someone familiar.

He was taking a break from flirting with the girl Matty had pointed out earlier and began to trudge across the sand to check on his friend. But before he reached him, he bumped into a fellow hosteller. They'd seen each other around the building many times and had spoken briefly, but the beach party was the first place either of them had ever exchanged more than pleasantries.

The conversation flowed naturally without Declan relying on his tried and tested lines, jokes and flattery, and he gradually became aware that he was winning her over by being himself. For the first time in a long time, if ever, Declan found himself making plans to meet a girl the next morning for breakfast, rather than waking up with her.

'Lazy bollocks, you'll never guess who I've been gassing with,' he began, as he reached Matty and sat down beside him. Declan couldn't take his eyes off Nicole as she chatted to another hosteller. She occasionally turned her head to glance at him. 'That Nicole girl, Tommy's lass. She's a bit special, that one, do you hear me?'

When Matty didn't acknowledge him, Declan turned to see him lying on his back, his head resting on a folded blanket and his eyes shut. Declan turned his head again to stare at the party in front of them. As much as Declan would have liked to talk to Nicole for longer, he always had breakfast to look forward to. He looked back to Matty.

'Hey, sleepyhead, let's get you home.'

But even as the words tripped from his mouth, Declan knew that Matty had left him. For a full minute, he remained as lifeless as his friend, his brain processing what it meant now the inevitable had arrived.

Then, gently, he placed Matty's hand into the palm of his own and he lay down by his friend's side, staring up into the night sky as fireworks illuminated it in whites, greens and oranges.

'I'm not ready,' Declan said quietly. 'I'm still not ready.'

149

'*Stuart*.'

Tommy pronounced such a small word with such venomous precision, there was no doubt in Jake's mind his cover was blown.

He took two steps back and with narrowed eyes he glared at Tommy, hoping to find something in his friend's expression that revealed this was some kind of sick prank. But there was nothing but disgust written across Tommy's face.

One Day Earlier: Venice Beach

The key to the hotdog stand remained in Tommy's possession even after he quit his job.

In desperate need of solitude in a city of noise, he waited until his replacement had changed out of his costume and José had locked up for the night before he let himself in.

The 10-foot by 10-foot room was windowless and reeked of manufactured meat, but it was air-conditioned and, most importantly, quiet. He knew who Jake really was; there were two pieces of the puzzle left that he had to put together before the full picture was complete.

Tommy threw his bag to the floor and removed his mobile phone, waiting for a signal to appear. Then he skipped through his photos until he found the one with Jake's torso tattoos on display. Jake had told them they were of every significant place he had visited, the ones that had made the most impact on him. Then, making a mental note of the first set of coordinates, he typed 52.2189N and 0.9202W into the search engine. Within a split second it revealed a map of Hunsbury, Northampton, the place where lives had ended, altered and begun again.

A strangely calm Tommy took a memory card from his pocket, the one he had always refused to view. Now was the time to face his fear. He placed it inside the camcorder he'd also brought with him. His finger hovered above a button, then he braced himself before he pressed play.

First came what he'd recorded as their car drove through the streets of Northampton – his arms and chest prickled upon hearing the voices of his brothers teasing him about porn websites. Then came their words of encouragement about finding a job, and Tommy knew what was coming next.

The footage became a blur when the camera slipped out of Daniel's hand and into the footwell. Then as the other car hit his, the camera was hurled elsewhere until it came to settle close to Daniel's body, the now cracked autofocus lens fixated on the broken windscreen.

Tommy could still recall every second he had spent conscious in the rear of that car. The odour of broken fluid pipes, the sharpness of glass crunching beneath his legs as he tried to move and the voices of panicked onlookers outside.

Then, as the camera continued recording, he watched as a figure – a face mainly shadowed by a hoodie – slowly limped past the car, pausing to look through the windscreen and clasp his hand to his mouth.

Tommy rewound that moment of footage and watched it again, then pressed pause. When he zoomed in, Stuart Reynolds's bloody face filled the screen.

Today

'We looked at each other, do you remember?' continued Tommy. 'You were trying to get away when just for a couple of seconds, we made eye contact. Then puff, you disappeared, just like that.'

'Tommy . . .' Jake began, his eyes having conceded defeat. But Tommy wasn't prepared to listen.

'It was the police who told us they were searching for you in connection with the crash. I knew who you and your shitty band were anyway, but I'd never really taken much notice of you. I did remember seeing you on TV the morning of the crash – something to do with the death of a soap star?'

Jake opened his mouth but closed it again. Tommy wasn't ready to be interrupted.

'Your fingerprints were all over that car, so it should have been a no-brainer that you were to blame. Then the police said there was no evidence you were behind the wheel that day. Your manager refused to confirm you'd stolen it, she said she often let you borrow it. There was also no footage of you on CCTV or police cameras, no blood or DNA on the airbag, and no you. Even the footage of your face on my camera wasn't enough – they said it was too blurry. And I wasn't reliable enough as a witness because I'd been through "a significant trauma that could affect my memory". Then the next thing we know, you've apparently killed yourself. All the papers started feeling sorry for you, saying you couldn't live with the guilt and how that's girl's death destroyed your mental health. But we knew the truth, and once we set them straight, they crucified you like you deserved.'

Jake brushed his hand through his hair and rubbed his cheeks. He'd spent the last few years exploring a multitude of religions and belief systems. He'd studied with teachers and seers and he'd immersed himself in books and websites, all to help him atone for his past and understand how to move forward and turn his back on Stuart. His ribs were inked with the coordinates of every location he'd seen, to remind him of how far he had travelled both physically and spiritually. But in this moment, it all counted for nothing.

'I was obsessed with you at first,' Tommy continued. 'I hated you . . . in fact *hated* is probably an understatement. But your suicide, well, that made the pain ease a little – not much, mind – but eventually it was just about enough to help me crawl out of my hole and start trying to live some kind of life again. Only now I know you're not just alive, but that you and I have . . . that we've . . . shit, I can't even say it . . . now you've made me hate both of us, not just you.'

Jake swallowed hard as he willed his arms and legs to stop trembling with Tommy's every word. Eventually, when he thought Tommy was ready to listen, he spoke.

'I'm sorry, Tommy, I'm so, so sorry,' he began. 'I need you to understand, I was a different person then; I was so fucked up – I'd lost everything I'd ever worked for. I was at such a low point and I wasn't thinking straight, and when that accident happened, I panicked and I didn't know what to do.'

'What you chose to do was run away. You killed my brothers, you left me for dead, and then you ran away.'

'People on the street were coming to help you. I saw them, that's why I went. There was nothing I could do.'

'But you didn't know that for certain, did you, Stuart?'

Jake reluctantly shook his head.

'That's what I thought,' continued Tommy, before raising his fist and catching Jake clean on the jaw.

150

Savannah dreamed she was floating somewhere between the bed in her new home and the ceiling above her.

She felt her body drift through the door, turn mid-air above the landing and gradually descend the stairs. But when she felt two arms supporting her back and legs, she understood she wasn't floating. She was being carried.

She opened her eyes but the walls surrounding her swirled like water flowing into a plughole. Her lips and throat were dry, and when she tried to speak, she could only hear herself mumble. Instantly she likened the feeling to when she'd stumbled out of the club and into the path of Peyk's car, and a new terror began to rip through her. But her body was under too much sedation to spring back into life.

Savannah was lugged across the hallway, but there was a pause when she reached the lounge. Through her misty eyes, she thought she saw Jane, sitting on a chair with something covering her mouth. Why was she letting this happen? Then she realized Jane was unable to budge because her arms and feet were bound to the chair legs and her mouth gagged. A trickle of blood began inside her ear and ran down her cheek. Her eyes were wide and as desperate as Savannah's.

Scared, Savannah desperately wanted to kick and punch the person carrying her, but her limbs barely twitched.

However, it was enough to make the person whose arms held her notice the dead weight he was lifting was reviving.

'It's okay, Savvy, I'm gonna get you out of here,' a male voice whispered. Savannah's tired eyes slowly widened. She looked down at his strong, bare brown arms and then up towards his face.

'Michael?' she mouthed, and felt the familiar warmth of her former boyfriend's breath as he carried her out of the front door, down the path and towards his brown station wagon, which had been parked out of view for much of the day.

151

Jake staggered backwards and clutched his jaw where Tommy had just whacked him.

Tommy clasped his fist with his other hand, trying to disguise his obvious pain. Jake began to pace up and down, hoping the movement might jolt his thoughts back into a normal running order.

'What happened happened, and there hasn't been a day that's gone by where I haven't prayed to God it hadn't,' he offered, his palm still clenched to his face. 'You don't know how bad I feel.'

Tommy narrowed his eyes and laughed. 'How bad *you* feel, Stuart? Really? So this is about how *you* feel, is it?'

'No, no, that's not what I meant,' continued Jake, closing his eyes, frustrated with himself. 'Tommy, Stuart Reynolds died as well that day. I don't want to be the person I was then, and I'm not, I swear to you, I'm not. You know me, the *real* me.'

'The real you is a coward who thinks a couple of months in a Buddhist temple means he's absolved of all his sins. Well, newsflash, Stuart, you're not. It's nowhere near enough.'

'Tommy, please . . .' he begged and put his hand on Tommy's arm.

'Take that off me or so help me God, I will kill you.'

'I understand why you're upset.'

'You have no idea what I am!'

When he felt Jake's fingers grip him more tightly, Tommy pushed him hard in the shoulder. Desperate to prove to Tommy his sincerity, Jake tried to hold Tommy's arm again, but Tommy punched him hard on the side of his face. Jake lost his balance and fell to the ground as Tommy shouted to quell the discomfort in his knuckles.

'Why did you run away?' yelled Tommy. 'Why did you just leave us?'

'I wasn't thinking straight,' continued Jake, pulling himself up to his feet. 'I didn't think there was anything I could do to help.'

'Stop saying that! You didn't stay to find out.'

'I know! I know! But Tommy, we can work our way through this . . . it won't be easy, but I really believe we can if you just try. You have to give me a chance.'

'You know what the most pathetic thing about all of this is?' Tommy wiped his eyes and sniffed up the snot dripping from his nostrils. 'Me. I'm the most pathetic thing, because when we were together I thought if I couldn't be like you then maybe I could be with you. How ridiculous is that? That I could learn from you. And it turns out the one person I looked up to the most was the one who took so much away from me.'

Tommy shook his head and glared at Jake. He had got so much off his chest but he felt no better. He knew he must walk away now or risk his anger getting the better of him.

As Tommy turned his back on him, Jake grabbed hold of his arm one last time. Without thinking, Tommy punched Jake again, missing his face and catching his throat. Jake staggered backwards, struggling to breathe, and failed to prevent another blow from catching the bridge of his nose. Both of them heard the bone pop. Now, like a man possessed, Tommy rained more blows on Jake as his adversary attempted to shield himself with his forearms. But not once did Jake retaliate. He was taller, broader and more muscular than Tommy, and he knew it wouldn't take much to overpower him. But it wasn't what he wanted. Tommy needed to cause pain and Jake needed to feel it.

Jake staggered backwards into the railings while Tommy continued on autopilot, unleashing every drop of wrath and ferocity his body possessed until he was close to exhaustion.

Then they remained there, rooted to the floorboards of the pier, shattered, battered, bruised and fighting for breath.

'I love you, Tommy,' Jake gasped. 'And nothing you can do to me will stop how I feel.'

He dropped both arms so he was completely unguarded and the most vulnerable he had been in as long as he could remember. Without thinking, Tommy lurched towards him and punched him in the side of the head with every last ounce of strength left in him.

And it was enough for Jake to lose his balance and topple backwards off the pier into the dark, choppy waters below.

152

Savannah slept across the rear seats of Michael's car for most of the first few hours following their escape from Los Angeles.

He used the handbag he'd taken from her room as a pillow for her head. And as he drove, every so often he'd reach behind him and place two fingers on her wrist to check her pulse or turn the radio off to hear her breathe. It was a sound he wasn't sure he'd ever be familiar with again after she had so suddenly vanished from his life.

When he'd bundled Savannah into his car from Jane's house, he'd briefly but gently informed her that Jane was a private investigator employed by Savannah's father to locate, befriend and then return her home by any means necessary. Savannah wasn't sure if it was this news or the sedatives still circulating around her bloodstream that made her feel so queasy. Either way, she did not feel well. Most people have never been drugged once in their lifetime, she thought, and here she was with two incidents under her belt, each with differing end results. She quickly fell back to sleep.

A purple and orange patchwork of light made way for night as Michael stretched out his fingers as straight as he could manage above the steering wheel. They were healing nicely, he thought, although his orthopaedic hand specialist had warned him they might never function as fully as they once had. Michael was grateful his university tutors had shown understanding about the 'car accident' that had rendered him useless as a potential surgeon, permitting him to change courses when the following semester began.

It was a rush of fresh air coming in through Michael's window that finally woke Savannah. She sat herself up and took deep breaths as she stared at him, still in disbelief that they had been reunited.

'It's really you,' she croaked. 'I thought I was dreaming.'

'Drink some water,' he urged, and passed her a bottle from the passenger seat.

'Where are we going?'

'Well, I figured we could head to Arizona and we can decide from there.'

Savannah nodded. She had so many questions, she wasn't sure where to begin. But for now, they could wait. Because all she wanted to do was take in the only man she had ever loved.

153

'He's dead,' came a voice in a measured tone.

Tommy stopped in his tracks on the way back to his dormitory. He turned around slowly to find Declan sitting on the floor, staring at the '*Welcome to Wherever You Are*' poster on the reception area wall. Tommy's mind raced twenty to the dozen, trying to figure out how Declan could possibly know what he had done to Jake on the pier.

'He's dead,' repeated Declan.

'It wasn't what it looked like,' Tommy replied carefully. 'It was an accident.'

'He was my best mate.'

Tommy hesitated. 'I don't understand.'

'Matty's . . . gone. He's . . . dead.'

'Oh, Christ, I'm sorry.' Tommy's fear made way for relief and then concern. 'What happened?'

The diversity of Venice Beach's residents and visitors made the unusual usual. So nobody who passed Declan carrying Matty's body over his shoulder in a firefighter's lift along the boardwalk had even given him a second glance. It had been the longest journey of Declan's life.

Once he had returned Matty to the security of the hostel and carefully laid him on his bed, he'd been at a loss as to what he should do next, so he ventured through the silent corridors and back towards reception. There he slumped to the floor and leaned against a wall, entwining the fingers of both his hands together as if in prayer. He fixated on the poster's words and knew that without Matty by his side, Declan had no idea where he was.

Meanwhile Tommy was short of breath, having run the mile and a half from Santa Monica back to Venice, only stopping midway to prop himself up against a parking meter and vomit into the road. His clothes were soaking wet and his fist so painful that his knuckles were folding in on themselves.

Repeatedly, he replayed the two seconds it had taken for Jake to disappear over the pier's railings and the heavy sound the water had made when his body slapped against its surface. Tommy had squinted into the dark waves below him, horrified by what he'd done, calling Jake's name – not Stuart's – but receiving no response. He'd then sprinted the length of the pier and then back on himself across the beach, rushing waist-deep into the water, shouting for Jake over and over again. In desperation he'd used the flashlight app on his phone, but it wasn't powerful enough to illuminate more than a couple of metres ahead. And after a frantic fifteen minutes or so, he knew it was too late.

Tommy had hurried back towards the beach party, hoping against all hope to catch sight of Jake amongst the revellers, but he wasn't anywhere to be seen. Suddenly feeling exposed and vulnerable, he'd made the decision to return to the hostel. And now he had to clean up the mess he'd made.

'Where is Matty now?' Tommy asked Declan.

'He's in our room.'

'Okay, why don't you come with me to the lounge? I need

to go to my dorm and get changed, then I'll come back and we'll decide what to do next. Okay?'

After leading Declan to the sofa, Tommy made his way up the corridor to remove any trace of Jake from the hostel. He opened a cupboard door and grabbed a roll of plastic bin liners, planning to hide Jake's belongings in the alley dumpster for the following day's collection. Then he would change the booking register so it looked as if Jake had checked out earlier that day and continued with his travels.

But as he approached Jake's room, the normally locked door was ajar. He held his breath as he slowly pushed it open, his hope rising that Jake was there, bruised and battered but safe and well.

The room was empty of all Jake's belongings. Even the bed had been stripped of its sheets.

You're alive, thought Tommy, and let out a long sigh of relief. Jake must have survived his fall, returned to the hostel before him and cleared out. He scanned the room for any trace of the man and focused on an open locker. From inside, he removed a scrap of paper.

'*What we are never changes, Tommy,*' it read, '*but who we are never stops changing. Remember me better than I am. Jake.*'

As much as he hated Stuart Reynolds, a significant part of Tommy was already missing Jake. Now he understood that Jake's purpose in Tommy's life had been to help free him from that goldfish bowl.

But in doing so, it meant Jake had chosen to keep running. Where to, Tommy had no idea.

*

Twenty minutes after Tommy dialled 911, an ambulance arrived outside the hostel's entrance to take Matty's body away to Santa Monica's UCLA Medical Center.

Declan followed the stretcher on which his friend lay as it was carried from their room, along the corridor, down the stairs and into the back of the vehicle.

Many of the other guests who'd returned from the beach party quickly sobered up at the sight and stood in a silent line of respect as one of their own embarked on his final journey.

154

Savannah couldn't take her eyes off Michael as he drove.

She had moved from the rear of the car to the front passenger seat to be next to him. There were some scars on his hands from her father's assault, and a small, concave wound in the centre of his forehead. She shivered when she recalled the sound her father's mallet had made when it collided with Michael's skull.

Savannah slipped her hand under her jumper and held her stomach. She hadn't had the opportunity to tell him that she was pregnant and that he wasn't the father, but she would need to bring it up soon. He deserved to know the truth.

She listened intently as Michael explained how he'd searched for her everywhere he could think of back in Alabama, but to no avail. Then, just when he was about to reluctantly give up, he'd received an unexpected email from Savannah's sister Roseanna.

He agreed to meet the desperate-sounding girl in a busy shopping centre where she tearfully revealed everything she knew about the whereabouts of her sister in Los Angeles, gleaned from flirting with one of her father's young assistants. The boy had told her that Reverend Devereaux had put up a $250,000 reward to find his daughter, and several private detective agencies were fighting to be the first to bring her home. They'd all begun at the Montgomery Greyhound station where she'd purchased a bus ticket to LA using his credit card.

But trying to locate one person in a city of almost four million was like looking for a needle in a haystack. There were more than a thousand hotels and motels in LA – although they knew the money she'd withdrawn from her father's account wouldn't last for long, so she'd likely pick affordable accommodation. That narrowed the field down to around three hundred motels.

One agency's team was deployed to the city to visit all the cheap dives and boltholes armed with photographs of the missing Savannah, but with no success. Another hired a personality profiler to build up a picture of her likely pattern of behaviour. Based on her hobbies, talents, skills and qualifications and a need to keep a low profile, they narrowed her potential line of work down to cash-in-hand jobs where few questions would be asked – cleaner, waitress, sex worker or stripper. And at the Flesh for Fantasy strip club, they eventually found their target.

The Reverend showed no loyalty to any of those hunting his daughter, and was happy to pass on updates and information from one detective agency to another. One paid one of Savannah's colleagues a $1,000-dollar tip to drug her water bottle with Rohypnol. But they lost track of her, and by the next morning Savannah had disappeared, quitting her job.

Weeks passed before another detective located her, dancing at the Pink Pussycat Club and residing in a backpacking hostel. Savannah constantly surrounded herself with people either at work or in the hostel, making her a hard target to pick off. But Reverend Devereaux was an impatient man and sent his own team, all guns blazing, to swipe his daughter from the street. No one involved anticipated that Savannah might be armed and ready to retaliate.

Meanwhile, a persuasive British private detective heard on the grapevine about the bounty and asked the Reverend to give her the opportunity to find Savannah. And when he agreed, Janet Davies became Jane Doherty. She took a softly softly approach, winning Savannah's trust with a sympathetic backstory belonging to somebody else.

'Your father got wind that Roseanna was seeing his employee and fired him,' continued Michael. 'The last piece of information your sister could get was that one of his people had moved into a room with you at a hostel in Venice. But I never heard from Roseanna again.'

Savannah shook her head and willed herself not cry for her sister. If it was the last thing she did, she would find a way to get Roseanna to safety.

'It's okay,' Michael reassured her, sensing Savannah's frustration. 'You weren't to know.'

Michael explained he'd arrived in Los Angeles six days earlier and begun following Savannah and Jane from a safe distance, waiting for the moment when he could approach his girlfriend on her own and lead her to safety. On several occasions he'd considered just bursting his way into the hostel and finding Savannah, but he couldn't be sure Jane was working alone.

When Michael followed Jane to the house in West Hollywood, he contacted the real estate agent from the number on the board outside and was told the property was being rented for a week to use as the backdrop for a series of photoshoots. So Michael knew he must act quickly. And although he abhorred violence towards women, Jane would be the exception to the rule. The moment she'd opened the front door thinking it was the Reverend's team, he'd knocked her out cold.

Savannah was scared that if she took her eyes off Michael even for a moment, he might disappear and she'd wake up to find herself caught in another of the series of nightmares that had plagued her life. He kept glancing to his side to return her gaze.

'It's all going to be okay, you know,' he said. 'You, me and the baby, we're going to be just fine.'

'The baby?' she replied. 'You know about the baby?'

'Yes,' he said. 'Roseanna told me.'

'Oh, okay.'

Savannah reached into the footwell and placed her handbag on her lap. Then she slowly slipped her hand inside it and fumbled around until she found what she was looking for under the envelope containing her savings.

Before Michael knew what was happening, there was a gun pointed at his temple.

155

It had been a long night for Jane, gagged and tied to the chair in her lounge.

She ran through the range of escape methods that her military training had taught her, but the stranger who'd burst through her front door that night and taken her by surprise with a right hook had made an impressive job of securing her. She cursed herself for resting on her laurels once she'd had Savannah sedated.

The cuckoo clock above the fireplace revealed it had been almost six hours since she'd watched helplessly as a man she'd seen once leaving the Reverend's house carried Savannah out of the front door. The two dozen times she'd heard her mobile phone ring also told her that her client would be furious at not receiving his promised update. She didn't know how she was going to tell him that Savannah had been taken from right under her nose.

Suddenly the front door handle turned and Jane watched as three men entered, each as broad-shouldered and burly as the next. They glanced around the hallway and up the staircase before they spotted Jane. The tallest of the trio approached her and ripped the gag from her mouth. She drew in a long, deep breath.

'Where is she?' he asked gruffly.

'Someone came and took her. Untie me – we need to move fast.'

Instead, the man cocked his head and stared at Jane, then took a mobile phone from his pocket and dialled.

Jane couldn't hear what he said to the person on the other end of the line, but she guessed who he was reporting to. And when he drew a gun from the back of his trousers and screwed a silencer to the end of the barrel, she immediately knew what he'd been ordered to do.

156

Declan stood with his back to the window, staring at Matty's empty bed.

Matty's zipped-up sleeping bag still bore the impression of his lifeless frame, and he could smell his friend's knock-off Tommy Hilfiger aftershave lingering in the bathroom. Declan turned around, lowered himself onto his bed and lay back. His pillow felt lumpy, but as he moved to fluff it up he found the well-thumbed *Travel America* guidebook, which had inspired many of their excursions. As he opened it to a bookmarked page, out fell Matty's silver St Christopher necklace. Declan placed it around his neck and tucked it inside his t-shirt. He also noticed a packet of photographs but couldn't bring himself to open them just yet.

'Declan, are you in there?' came Tommy's voice from the other side of the door.

Tommy tentatively entered and saw a Declan he hadn't met before: a man divided between the selfishness of grief and relief that his friend was no longer suffering.

'I think this is for you to watch,' Tommy said, and handed Declan his digital camcorder before giving him privacy. 'He asked if he could borrow it yesterday.'

Declan pressed play and Matty's face appeared across the tiny screen.

'Hey, eejit. Well, if you're watching this then you know where I am. I'm sorry I didn't say goodbye. I tried, but as you said, you weren't ready to hear it. You know, I don't think I've ever thanked you for being my best friend. I wouldn't have lasted as long as I did if you weren't there to kick me up the arse and force me to live whatever time I had left. So, thank you. Be happy, Declan, enjoy your life, and don't waste time thinking about me, okay? I've had the best time I could have possibly had, and that's down to you. You're my man.'

With a grin and a final wink, the screen turned to black.

For the first time since he'd discovered Matty's body, Declan curled himself up into a tight ball and allowed himself to cry like he'd never cried before.

157

'Oh my God,' said Nicole, gobsmacked by the events of the night that Tommy had just relayed. 'I actually don't know what else to say.' She kept her grip on the ice cubes inside a tea towel which she'd wrapped around his knuckles to reduce the swelling.

They sat on two chairs by the side of the hostel swimming pool. Nicole had listened intently while Tommy spoke from the heart for over an hour. He left nothing out, from the aftermath of the accident that killed his brothers, his family's treatment and blame of him, his brief stint in the armed forces and his separation from Louis, to how he developed feelings for Jake before realizing who Jake really was, and their final confrontation.

Nicole understood why Tommy hadn't raised the alarm when Jake toppled over the railings at Santa Monica pier. She tried to imagine what she might have done had it been Eric who'd fallen, and she knew that she would not have tried to find him in the water afterwards.

'Just how bad are we at judging character?' she asked. 'Me with Eric, you with Jake.'

'We make quite a pair.'

'So what are you going to do now?'

'Well, I've put it off for long enough, so I'm going to start making plans to continue my travels. I've been here for too long; it's time to stand on my own two feet and really see the world before I go home. For the first time in my life, I'm a free man.'

Nicole nodded. She understood the desire to travel, but now wasn't the right time for her. Instead, she wanted to plant some roots, and Mrs Baker's money would allow her to do just that with the hostel.

'When do you plan to leave?'

'In a week or so?'

'Do you mind if I tag along?' a voice behind Tommy said. He frowned, then turned his head. His face lit up when he saw who was speaking.

'Alright mate,' said Louis, as Tommy leapt to his feet, and the two friends jumped up and down as they embraced. 'Mum said you called, and I was just up the coast so I thought I'd drop in and say hello.'

'Where the hell have you been?'

'Had my phone nicked in Baja, didn't I, and lost all my contacts and passwords.'

'Well, you couldn't have picked a better time to get here.'

Louis unstrapped his backpack so it dropped to the floor as Tommy introduced him to Nicole.

'*The* Louis?' she asked. 'I've heard so much about you.'

His friend looked around the pool, the building and over the wall to the floodlit beachside promenade. 'So have you found your "beach" then?'

'No, I found something much better than that.'

Tommy glanced at Nicole and the two began to laugh at the absurdity of the last couple of weeks.

'I've been stuck on a Greyhound for the last nine hours. Tell me all about it over a cold beer or ten.'

'Absolutely. Nic, you up for it?'

'No, you boys have got some catching up to do. I'll see you later.'

'So what's been going on with you, then?' Louis asked as the two made their way back into the hostel. 'What have I missed? And what have you done to your hand?'

'Where do I start?' replied Tommy.

158

'What the hell, Savvy?' began a panicked Michael. 'Why are you pointing a gun at me?'

'Pull over,' Savannah replied coldly.

'What are you doing?'

Savannah cocked the trigger. 'I'm not going to ask you again.'

Michael did as he was ordered and directed the car towards a dirt verge.

'Now give me the keys and get out, slowly,' Savannah demanded. Michael obeyed, and she followed him out of the car. She stood two metres opposite him with the gun pointed directly at his head.

'Savvy, what's going on?' Michael pleaded.

'Tell me again how you knew I was pregnant?' Savannah asked slowly.

Michael hesitated. 'Your sister said you told her.'

'No, she didn't. Try again.'

'Roseanna told me the last time we spoke – really, she did,' continued Michael, swallowing hard.

'When I called Rosie, I didn't say anything about the baby. You said the last she heard about me was just as Jane moved into my room. At that point Jane didn't know about the baby either. So if you haven't spoken to Rosie since, then the only way you could know is either through Jane or my father. So which one are you working for?'

Michael's mouth moved but his throat suddenly felt dry.

'Which one?' Savannah repeated, more firmly.

'Your father,' Michael eventually replied.

'Why would you do that to me?'

Michael looked at his feet, unable to meet her gaze. 'The $250,000 reward . . . that's a hell of a lot of money, Savannah. I told him I could bring you home, so he told me everything Jane and the other PIs had found out.'

'And did Jane know my father was pitting you all against each other?'

'I don't think so. He doesn't care how you come back, whether it's with me or her – it doesn't matter, just as long as one of us did it—'

'So you sold me out.'

'Yeah, I did,' Michael replied, his tone becoming angrier. 'But then you were the one who ran away and didn't tell me where you were going. All I knew was that my fingers were busted, I have a dent in my head and my girlfriend didn't want anything to do with me.'

'You didn't even give me the benefit of the doubt! I kept away from you to protect you. My father said he'd kill you if I saw you again.'

'That money was going to pay for the rest of my education and my rent. When you left, I had nothing. Loving you robbed me of my career, so what else was I supposed to do?'

Savannah shook her head, disgusted by his excuses. Yet she wasn't entirely surprised to learn Michael had switched allegiances; she was learning quickly that she couldn't trust anyone but herself.

'Look,' Michael continued, regaining his composure. 'It's not too late for us; we can just drive away and start again, forget about the money. A clean slate, just you and me and the baby.'

'You think I'd want you anywhere near my child? You're a fool, Michael. And I'm a fool for trusting you. Now start walking before I start shooting.'

'What?'

'Start walking, over there,' Savannah replied, pointing her gun towards a fence and a field full of corn, 'and don't stop until I'm gone.'

'Savvy,' pleaded Michael, 'let's talk about—'

The sound of the gunshot rang out, and the bullet landing inches away from Michael's feet made him quickly realize there was no talking her round. He looked at her one last time, turned his back and began to walk.

Wiping a tear from her cheek, Savannah climbed into the driver's side of the car, started the engine, locked the doors and slowly pulled away.

She didn't look back at Michael in the rear-view mirror; instead, she rubbed her stomach and understood she didn't need anyone to rescue her from her old life.

EPILOGUE

One Year Later: Venice Beach International Hostel

Nicole sat behind the hostel's smart new reception desk, closed the spreadsheet of finances on her laptop screen and then scrolled through her bookmarked websites until she found the right one.

She had revisited the *Mail Online* page so many times in the last few weeks that she almost knew the article off by heart.

'*British Drugs Dealer Killed During Prison Riot*,' read the headline, followed by a mugshot of Eric taken a year ago in his orange, jail-issue uniform. The story reported that while awaiting trial for the cannabis discovered in the boot of their pick-up truck, he had become embroiled in a behind-bars fracas in which a solitary stab wound pierced his heart. He had died instantly. Nicole felt nothing but relief. Soon after his arrest, she had sent an anonymous email tip-off to British police investigating the murder of Mrs Baker's housekeeper, suggesting Eric was responsible and where to find him now. But she had no way of discovering if it had been taken seriously. However, it no longer mattered; Eric had got his just deserts, one way or another.

Nicole shut the lid of her computer and turned her thoughts

to more positive things. She looked around the recently redecorated hostel reception with pride. Half of the rooms had been furnished with new bunk beds, the plumbing was in full working order, new carpets had replaced the threadbare ones and there was wifi throughout.

She estimated she had spent around a quarter of the money from Mrs Baker's gift on getting the building up to code, but there was much more work to be done. Other money had been swallowed up by lawyers to ensure the property was legally in her name, along with a work permit and a visa to stay in the country. As the hostel's standards improved she could afford to charge higher rates, and a viral marketing campaign across social media assisted in its promotion and popularity.

Eric wasn't the only person who crossed her mind today. She wondered how Savannah was and estimated her baby must be at least seven or eight months old by now. Nicole was also puzzled as to why Savannah had not returned to the hostel for the rest of her belongings or stayed in touch. Perhaps she had realized she needed to close the book on her past completely before she could start afresh with Jane. It was understandable, if a little disappointing.

Tommy, however, had remained in touch by email as he and Louis made their way around much of the rest of America, alternating between big cities and the wilderness, and taking cash-in-hand work to fund the extension of their trip. A few months after leaving, he had emailed Nicole a photograph of him with his parents, who'd flown out to meet them in Seattle. Their reconciliation brought a warm glow to her heart, but at the same time, it saddened her that there was no one from her own past waiting to reconnect with her.

Ruth was also playing on Nicole's mind. Months earlier,

news reports had revealed she had been sent to the Twin Towers Correctional Facility, Los Angeles's largest mental health unit. After being declared unfit to stand trial or be repatriated back to Australia, there was little choice but for her to remain there. There had been no updates since, and Nicole worried whether Ruth had been swallowed up in the system or was actually getting the help she so desperately needed.

The subject of Ruth was also one of the last conversations she'd ever had with Peyk, because the day after she'd sent Ron packing, he too had disappeared from the hostel. Nobody witnessed him leave, and when Nicole checked the register of visitors back three years, she found that he had never actually officially been a guest or assigned a room. Even his cannabis farm that Tommy warned her about the day he left had returned to its original purpose of two empty dormitories. He left as he had lived, an enigma.

'Fancy coming to the beach for a bit?' asked Declan, appearing from upstairs with white paint flecks stuck to his face and dungarees. In Peyk's absence, he had become the hostel's handyman.

'Sure,' Nicole replied, and Declan planted a kiss on her lips. She rubbed his arm affectionately.

'Good, because baby Matty says he needs his mammy to relax more.' Declan pointed to her swollen belly. 'We've only got six weeks before he arrives and we don't need you stressing about this place.'

'Okay, okay,' Nicole chuckled. 'There's just one thing I want to do first.'

She took the paintbrush and pot from Declan's hand and approached the poster on the wall that read '*Welcome to*

Wherever You Are', one of the only items of decoration to remain from Ron's days.

Then, with several simple brush strokes, she painted across four of the words so that it simply read '*Welcome*'.

ACKNOWLEDGEMENTS

Revisiting and rewriting this book has been a wonderful experience. When I've finished a novel, I'm always ready to move on to the next project and so I don't have time to dwell on its predecessor. But updating this book has encouraged me to take a time-out from the hustle and bustle of my usual edits and realize how much my life has changed since it was first self-published. It's reminded me of how fortunate I've been to have had such amazing support from my readers. So thank you to everyone who has been with me for almost a decade now.

It has also brought back a whole bunch of memories from my own backpacking days around America in my early twenties. The hostel I write about is a fictionalized version of an actual hostel in Venice Beach where I spent one of the most exciting summers of my life. And while some of the characters are very loosely based on the travellers I shared my time and dormitories with, none have suffered or created the trauma I've put my characters through! Some twenty-six years after staying there, I was fortunate to revisit that hostel and some of the locations in this book during a 2018 California road trip. Hostellers and backpackers really are some of the most wonderful, diverse and crazy people you could ever hope to meet.

The thank-yous I offered in the original version of this novel remain.

To my mum, Pamela Marrs, for encouraging me as a child to embrace books. And to John Russell for your faith, your optimism and your confidence – and for helping to make poor Ruth appear just that little bit darker. You also have my gratitude for putting up with me constantly hunched over my phone tracking download data and mumbling random figures at you. There's been a new addition to our family since I first wrote this, so thank you to our son Elliot for distracting me from rewrites with imaginary cups of tea, by rearranging my bookshelf and demanding trips to the playpark.

A huge thank you to my Facebook Fairy Godmother, Tracy Fenton, for your continued, unwavering support and friendship along with the rest of THE Book Club. I'm now fortunate to have added other online book clubs to my list of ways to distract myself during the day, including The Fiction Book Cafe and Lost In A Good Book. Rest In Peace, Bee Jones. I'll see you in the big library in the sky.

To my old *Herald & Post* colleague – and former LA Woman – Nicola Pittam, thanks for your help with Los Angeles's geographical locations. Likewise, to John Wallace for help with Ireland's locations and language. I'm also grateful to Kath Middleton, Samantha Clarke, Anne Lynes and Katie Elizabeth for your invaluable proofreading skills, and to early reader Stuart Goodman.

My admiration goes to the writer Alex Garland, someone who in all likelihood has no clue who I am, but to whom I am indebted. *The Beach* is one of my all-time favourite novels and should come with every backpack sold.

A whopper of a thank-you goes to my editor, Gillian Green,

for your faith in this book. This is our third project together and I look forward to many, many more – even if you don't believe men wear bracelets.

And finally, my appreciation goes to Sean Mabbutt, my longest-serving friend and former backpacking buddy: 1992 was a heck of a year, one that neither of us will ever forget. I couldn't have done it without you. Up for a thirtieth anniversary Greyhound trip for old times' sake?